**"You said we were to be the children
the true Kahless deserved."**

"Only *after* we have succeeded—then will I decree who the
'true Kahless' really was. Some wisdom ascribed to him
is useful. Some has been twisted and must be discarded.
Put your faith in me to decide." His eyes narrowed as they
focused on her. "Or do you think you can decide better for
yourself?"

"No. It's just that our tactics—"

"Are my tactics. I think you have been deciding things.
Is that how the Starfleet commander eluded you?"

"No, my lord!"

"Worf escaped to warn *Enterprise*—and saved the lives
of people who intended us harm. People who had staged an
event honoring the *petaQpu'* who stole my house. Allies of
the Council, who would put you all in chains for another
seven generations. Did you free him?"

Valandris stiffened. After a moment, she responded. "I
answered my conscience."

"You will answer *me*."

STAR TREK®

PREY

BOOK 2
THE JACKAL'S TRICK

JOHN JACKSON MILLER

Based on *Star Trek* and
Star Trek: The Next Generation®
created by Gene Roddenberry

POCKET BOOKS
New York   London   Toronto   Sydney   New Delhi

Pocket Books
An Imprint of Simon & Schuster, Inc.
1230 Avenue of the Americas
New York, NY 10020

This book is a work of fiction. Any references to historical events, real people, or real places are used fictitiously. Other names, characters, places, and events are productsof the author's imagination, and any resemblance to actual events or places or persons, living or dead, is entirely coincidental.

First Pocket Books paperback edition November 2016

POCKET and colophon are registered trademarks of Simon & Schuster, Inc.

For information about special discounts for bulk purchases, please contact Simon & Schuster Special Sales at 1-866-506-1949 or business@simonandschuster.com.

The Simon & Schuster Speakers Bureau can bring authors to your live event. For more information or to book an event, contact the Simon & Schuster Speakers Bureau at 1-866-248-3049 or visit our website at www.simonspeakers.com.

Manufactured in the United States of America

10 9 8 7 6 5 4 3 2 1

ISBN 978-1-5011-1580-6
ISBN 978-1-5011-1605-6 (ebook)

To Ken Barnes,
who introduced me to Trek fandom:
peace and long life

Historian's Note

After Commander Kruge died on the Genesis Planet (*Star Trek III: The Search for Spock*), control of his house wasn't settled until his loyal officers were put down. Discommendated, the Kruge loyalists settled in the Briar Patch. Their descendants grew into skilled hunters who hated the Klingon Empire.

A hundred years later, in 2385, Korgh—Kruge's protégé—dispatched Cross, a Betazoid illusionist, to pose as Kruge, back from the dead. The discommendated were armed with a bird-of-prey squadron, the Phantom Wing, and became the Unsung.

The Unsung massacred the nobles of the House of Kruge. They kidnapped the clone of Kahless. They then declared their intent to cleanse the Empire; their first act was the execution of the clone.

Taking control of the House of Kruge, Korgh blamed his trumped-up crisis on the Federation, embodied by Picard and the *Enterprise*. An upcoming summit planned by Admiral William Riker was imperiled. Unbeknownst to Korgh, Cross kept Kahless alive for reasons known only to him (*Star Trek: Prey—Book 1: Hell's Heart*).

The main events of this book begin in March 2386, several years after the *U.S.S. Enterprise*-E's 2379 confrontation with the Romulan praetor Shinzon (*Star Trek Nemesis*). The prologue takes place in 2367, after Ardra was caught duping the people of Ventax II ("Devil's Due" TNG). The interlude takes place in 2293, shortly before the explosion of the Klingon moon, Praxis (*Star Trek VI: The Undiscovered Country*).

"I bide my time."

—*inscription on Kaiser Wilhelm II photos
distributed in England thirty years
before the start of World War I*

OVERTURE

2367

One

"**B**uxtus Cross . . . you are charged . . . with premeditated murder . . ."

The voice of the paunchy human in the doorway was gravelly and halting as he read the charges from the padd in his hand. Balding and not hiding it very well, he wore one of the lavender coats lately popular with the Federation's bureaucrats. The heavy satchel in his other hand caused his whole body to sag. He recited the words as casually as if he were reading from a lunch menu.

". . . impersonation of a Starfleet officer, fraud, use of holographic equipment with intent to deceive, and forgery . . ."

Buxtus Cross gathered up the playing cards from the little table in the legal conference room of the prison transport *Clarence Darrow* and rolled his eyes at the new arrival. *What a production.* The chamber Cross had been arraigned in back at the Federation spaceport had teemed with identical specimens, all harried creatures dashing about playing their legal games. That was the place where the twenty-year-old Betazoid had first heard the charges spoken aloud, delivered from the bench before a roomful of waiting defendants.

It had been the biggest room Cross had ever played—and absolutely not the show he'd had in mind.

The speaker finished reading the charges aloud and fully entered the consultation chamber. The force field barring the doorway reactivated an instant later. "Emil Yorta," the human said, his nose crinkling as he approached the table. "I'm, ah, the permanent advocate appointed to defend you." He offered his hand to Cross, who shook it indifferently and returned his attention to the playing cards.

"I'm sorry we were so late in getting under way," Yorta said, plopping his overstuffed satchel onto the table before wandering the brig's spacious client conference room in search of the other chair. "Ever since the Borg attacked Wolf 359 earlier this year, a lot of the Federation's support craft have been retasked. We, ah, lowly civil servants don't have an easy time getting around."

"My trip to prison has been delayed—and you think I'm disappointed?" Cross harrumphed. "Okay." He cast his eyes again on Yorta and really focused this time. The guy was a disorganized mess. "Wait. *You're* my defender? I thought you'd be an officer."

"No—and that's a bit of luck," Yorta said, dragging the seat to the table. Standing by it, he fished inside his bag. "As it turns out, your dishonorable discharge from Starfleet was officially issued the morning of the, er, crime. So while you still fall under the Federation Judicial Code, you'll be prosecuted as a civilian." Finding a combadge in his bag, Yorta looked up from under bushy eyebrows. "Of course, that's the same dishonorable discharge that the other side will be claiming is your motive."

"Easy come, easy go."

Yorta sniffed. "That's not how I would look at it, but let's move on. Hold on a moment." He pinned the combadge to his lapel and tapped it. "Brig monitor?"

A gruff voice responded. *"Yes?"*

"This is Defender Yorta in consultation cell—ah, cell eight, I guess. I'm starting my conference with my client. Deactivate surveillance sensors until further notice."

"Sensors off. Advise your client no funny business."

Cross looked up. "Funny business?"

"He's telling you not to mutilate your lawyer," Yorta responded, taking his seat. "And I make a lousy hostage. No one's traded anything for me yet."

"That's reassuring." Outside, Cross could see the guard saunter to a desk just out of earshot. The woman had little to do; the Betazoid was short and slight, no threat to anyone—at least not in that way. And a localized transporter inhibitor protected the entire brig.

Yorta's eyes scanned his padd. "Here it is. Ah—you're to be tried sixteen days from now at Starbase 11."

"That soon?"

"The murder of an officer is as serious as it gets. Even civilian justice speeds up for that—but not as much as Starfleet's does. Either way, a conviction could result in a detention center like Thionoga—no fun at all. That's why I'm here. We, ah, can use the transit time in preparing your defense."

"I didn't think you were here for the food." Cross shrugged and stretched back in his chair, propping his feet on the table. "Speaking of, when do we eat?"

"I don't know how you can be so cavalier. You're accused of a murder."

"Yeah, but just one." *The one you know about.*

In fact, Buxtus Cross had killed three people. His first murder had been a desperate act, but he had gotten away with it so cleanly that he had been tempted to kill again, just to see if he could replicate the feat. By the third death, he was past personal amusement and into new territory: playing to the crowd.

The defender studied his padd. "Says here your parents were both civil engineers—they died in an accident a few years ago." He looked up. "I'm sorry."

"I'm not. They dragged me to every colony world in the quadrant, from one construction job to the next. If I wanted time with them, I'd need to schedule a groundbreaking."

"Ah, yes," Yorta said, reading further. "I see it here—'sullen and withdrawn as a youth.' We can use that. But it looks like they tried to take assignments where there were sizable Betazoid communities."

Not that I ever had time to fit in, Cross thought. The closest he'd come was at fifteen, when he'd finally stayed in one place long enough to form friendships. On a colony world replete with warm springs and roiling geysers, he'd grown close to Gregor, a human who had taught him close-up magic, and to Cenise, a vivacious Betazoid who'd invited him into her extracurricular stage productions. Together, they brought him out of his shell; together, they had broken his heart. Gregor *knew* how Cross felt about Cenise—and yet he had taken her away nonetheless.

So it was in a fit of jealous despair one day that Cross acted—and indeed, it was *acting* that did Gregor in. While they were scouting locations for a vid project in a remote area, Cross told Gregor that their beloved Cenise had gone wading in a lake known for a dangerous geyser—and that she had disappeared. Convinced of Cross's word and far from help, Gregor had wasted no time in bravely dashing into the body of water. He paid the ultimate price when the geyser erupted.

Young Cross was gripped with terror over what he had done, but that was soon replaced by something else. On telling Cenise of Gregor's fate, his telepathic senses were overpowered by the girl's genuine shock and sadness. Unaware he was doing it, Cross perfectly replicated and reflected those emotions, seeming as devastated over Gregor's death as she was.

And not the least bit guilty.

Having gotten away with murder once, and after becoming a ward of the state following his parents' deaths, Cross approached his next homeworld almost looking for a chance to try it again. The person he eliminated there, a drama department rival, had never been a friend, and that made the murder much easier. He had successfully impersonated his victim over a communicator, insulting the parentage of a local Gorn criminal known for his temper. Cross hadn't delivered the fatal blow, but in a way it was just as satisfying. His performance killed.

Which brought him to Lieutenant Fenno, a boob of a Bolian and the reason Cross was aboard the *Clarence Darrow*. No one had pretended Cross would last ten minutes as a Starfleet counselor; he studied others not to help them, but to do better impressions of them in the Academy residence hall. In Fenno's situation, he had gotten the hardcase officer's mannerisms down precisely. It had come in handy.

"It says here," Yorta said, "that Fenno had filed a report that would have drummed you out of Starfleet. But then you filed another report using his image—generated on a holodeck?"

"Just his image," Cross said, suddenly proud. "The dialogue and movements were based on my performance. No one could tell the difference."

"Ah, yes—I read that. But the holodeck computer alerted Fenno he had been impersonated."

"Stupid thing." Cross had never been good with technology. How was *he* to have known about the safeguards?

"It's alleged that Fenno told you he'd found out, and that he summoned you to his office to wait until he could call security." Yorta's eyes narrowed as he read the rest. "But soon after you arrived, they say you replaced his favorite raktajino mug with one that released a chemical fatal to Bolians."

The enchanted goblet trick. It had been easy. Cross had pretended to stumble over a chair, replacing the mug with a bit of sleight of hand before delivering it to its destination. The prisoner smirked. "You should have seen it. Fenno took a huge gulp, staggered out of his office into the common area, and collapsed. And there I was, with no medical training, desperately trying to revive him—and shedding tears when I failed. I got rave reviews."

"Until the autopsy discovered the poison, which had to come from somewhere. The replicator you used to create the trick mug kept a record of it."

"I thought I had deleted that. I always trip over the technical stuff."

Yorta cocked an eyebrow. "You're admitting to the crime."

"Of course."

"Then I don't understand why we're doing this." Yorta sat back and placed the padd in his large coat pocket. "Why am I here? You could just plead guilty."

"And go straight to Thionoga? No, no. I want the trial. Days with a captive audience? It might be my last performance."

Yorta stared. "Performance?"

"Oh, yeah," Cross said, picking the deck up from the table. "I've been working on some things." He fanned the cards. "Pick one."

Yorta scratched his head and rose. "Young man, I think you're in for a—"

"All hands, red alert! This is the captain. Battle stations!" The overhead light in the room took on a crimson tint, and an alarm blared. Over Yorta's shoulder, Cross could see the guard outside leave her desk and dash madly up the hallway.

Yorta tapped his combadge. "Bridge, what's going on?"

"We've been boarded—by the Borg!"

Two

The five minutes that had followed were the most peculiar of Cross's young life.

After the initial announcement, they'd heard a running commentary over *Clarence Darrow*'s comm system. Because *Darrow* was a hybrid administrative vessel and minimum-security prison transport, its guards were trained for keeping people in, not others out. The reported sighting of several Borg drones suddenly materializing amidships, so soon after Wolf 359, sent the crew into audible apoplexy. No one could tell where the invaders had come from; no Borg cube could be seen on any sensor.

Every fourth word Cross heard the crew saying was *retreat*. Every fifth word was an expletive.

Yorta had supplied some swear words of his own after realizing that no one was going to answer his pleas. With the guard absent, he and Cross were equally trapped. Yorta displayed energy heretofore unseen, rushing around the conference cell looking for any way out. Bewildered, Cross had simply sat and watched in curiosity, nervously shuffling his cards. What could *he* do?

By the time Cross heard a commotion outside, Yorta had already overturned the conference table and was in the middle of shoving it toward the doorway. When a Borg drone appeared beyond the force field, advancing robotically toward them, Yorta shrieked like a startled chimpanzee. He spun in panic—only to put his right foot directly into the opening of his fallen satchel. He sailed forward, smacking his head against the back of his chair. Then Yorta fell to the deck, senseless.

Cross dropped his cards in his lap and grabbed his armrests as the drone deactivated the force field. He had seen images of the Borg before, but the real thing was far more fearsome. Elongated mechanical arms bore frightening cutting implements, while wires jutted grotesquely from the skin of the one-time person underneath. A laser attached to the drone's eyepiece swept the room. Cross stared at the intruder, hypnotized.

Then he looked more closely. The laser was fainter than he'd expected, and broken, as if it were projecting through nonexistent smoke. And the drone seemed rough around the edges—literally. The sharp angles of the Borg's implants seemed soft, fuzzy.

The Borg drone entered the consultation chamber and looked directly at him. That jolted Cross out of his seat, but with nowhere to go in the small room, he simply put the chair in between himself and the drone. It spoke in a monotone. "Identify yourself."

"Cross. A prisoner. I'm nobody."

"Do not interfere, or you will be assimilated."

He chuckled anxiously. "You don't want to assimilate me. I'd mess up your whole civilization."

Clanking as it went, the Borg walked past the overturned table and beheld the fallen Yorta. Its attention turned to the satchel on the deck. As the Borg knelt to rifle through the bag, Cross gawked at the creature's head.

The drone looked up at him. "What?"

"The side of your head." Cross pointed. "There's something growing out of it. Er—besides all the wires and metal, I mean."

A wave of electrical interference coursed across the creature's massive frame. There was something protruding from the Borg's head, for sure: big and fleshy. The drone ignored him, continuing to search the satchel. Unable to find what it was searching for, the drone cast the bag to the deck and stood.

It turned to Cross. "Have you seen a female?"

Cross was first startled to have been asked anything, and then by the question itself. "Any particular one?"

"She was going by the name Ardra."

Cross thought for a moment—and then snapped his fingers. "Just a second." He slipped out from behind the chair and scrambled to beside Yorta's unconscious form. Rolling him over with difficulty, he located the pocket that held the padd. "I think he had the prisoner manifest here."

"Give me that," the Borg said, reaching for it with its one clawed hand. Cross scuttled away back to his chair.

For several seconds, the drone stood and read. With a mechanical sound that somewhat resembled an aggravated grunt, the drone pitched the padd away. Touching one of the controls at its wrist, the Borg spoke. "It's a bust. Ardra's trial was moved up. She was sent ahead on another transport."

"Damn," came an answer from somewhere in the drone's equipment. And then: *"Understood. We're beaming the team out now."*

Several seconds passed, during which Cross watched to see if the drone would go anywhere. Nothing happened. It spoke again. "I'm still here, *Blackstone.* Beam me out."

"We can't."

The drone froze, clearly concerned. "What do you mean, you can't?"

"I mean we can't get a lock. Something's wrong."

Cross raised his hand tentatively. "Transporter inhibitor. It's shielding the entire brig."

Seemingly confused, the drone stared at him—and this time, its whole body flickered. *"Blackstone,* do you read an inhibitor field? There wasn't supposed to be one."

"It's new," Cross volunteered. "I heard the guards talking about it."

The Borg drone responded with what seemed like genuine alarm. It moved jerkily around the chamber just as Yorta had. "This is serious, *Blackstone*. Where's the nearest beam-out point?

"In places you don't want to go. The guards are regrouping. Hang on, Gaw, we're going to try some things."

The drone just stood there, shifting uncomfortably. Now that he wasn't terrified, Cross paid attention to what his empathic talents were detecting. He hadn't expected to pick up much emotion from the Borg drone, but this felt different—as if the drone belonged to a species that Betazoids had trouble reading. He realized why when a flash of light transformed the drone into . . . *a Ferengi.*

"Oh, great," the pudgy figure said, disgusted. "Illusion compromised, *Blackstone*."

"We thought killing the projection might help us beat the inhibitor."

"And?"

"It didn't. And the field's stopping us from reestablishing the illusion. Oops."

"And conveniently, I'm already in a prison cell," the Ferengi said. "If I don't talk to you again, you're all fired." He found the chair Yorta had struck and took a seat.

Cross stared at him, more mesmerized now than when he'd thought he was dealing with a Borg. "Your name is Gaw?"

"And you're Cross. Glad to meet you, cellmate."

"That illusion—you *faked* a Borg invasion?"

"For a while." Gaw shook his head. Cross figured him for young middle age. "We have a cloaked ship that projects images around individuals. Don't ask me to explain—the tech's secret."

"But it's not enough." Fascinated, Cross, turned his chair around backward and straddled it, facing Gaw. "I mean, I could tell you weren't Borg—and not just from the glitches. You weren't selling it."

Gaw looked at him and shrugged. "I don't usually work in the field. I'm a truthcrafter—one of the engineers. I create the illusions. But we still need people to act out the parts—and our practitioner got pinched a few years back. We were hoping to spring Ardra so she'd take over our crew."

"The person you were looking for."

"I don't know her real name. She tends to stick with the name of the last character she played."

"Method acting," Cross mused. "What was she in for?"

"Impersonating a deity."

"A *deity*?"

"A devil, actually. She'd put one over on the Ventaxians, but good. Then some busybodies ruined it. Damn that *Enterprise*."

It sounded like a good enterprise to Cross. "So you guys are a team of what, *con artists*?"

"These days. But I think the days are numbered."

Cross's mind swam. He'd never heard of anything like it: roving groups of high-tech charlatans, capable of fooling the Federation? It sounded amazing—perfect, in fact. Perfect for him.

For the first time since the intruder had entered, he listened to the announcements over the public address system. The crew was getting its act together, now that the other "drones" had transported off. It wouldn't be long before they'd work their way back through the prison decks. Hopping off the chair, he bounded again toward the stirring Yorta's body.

"What are you doing?" Gaw said, only mildly interested.

"Saving you." He found the combadge pinned to Yorta's lapel. Taking a breath, he tried to remember just what the attorney had sounded like. Then he pressed the control and spoke. "Bridge!"

A moment passed. *"What is it? Who is this?"*

"This is Emil Yorta," Cross said, winking at the Ferengi as he spoke in another man's voice. "There's, ah, one of those Borg things in the hall here. I need you to drop the, ah, whatever it is and beam me out of here!"

Then they both heard the response: *"Stand by, Yorta."*

The Ferengi's eyes widened as, a moment later, the body of the prone defender shimmered and vanished. Gaw quickly touched a control on his wrist bracelet. *"Blackstone,* the field's down!"

"We see it," responded the voice from earlier. *"Just in time—the guards are about to re-enter your deck. One to beam out!"*

Gaw stared at the young Betazoid, grinning as he rose from the floor where Yorta had been. "Hold on, *Blackstone.*" He tilted his head at Cross. "What are you in for, kid?"

This time, he perfectly mimicked the arraignment judge. "Buxtus Cross, you are charged with premeditated murder, impersonation of a Starfleet officer, fraud, use of holographic equipment with intent to deceive, and forgery . . ." He watched as Gaw's eyes lit up. "And that's not all I can do." With a quick sweep past his sleeve, Cross made his deck of cards appear in his hand. "Want to see a trick?"

"Maybe later." Gaw thought for a moment and then announced, "Two to beam out, *Blackstone.* I think I've found something here."

ACT ONE

THE TIGERS' MASTER

2386

"Dictators ride to and fro upon tigers that they dare not dismount. And the tigers are getting hungry."
—*Winston Churchill*

Three

If you're looking for a good time, an old Starfleet saying went, *just follow the floating bottle of champagne*. It was most surely headed for a starship waiting to be launched.

Some of the best parties Admiral William Riker had ever attended were at christenings—or, rather, in the after-hour gatherings once all the speeches had been given. Certainly launches in Starfleet were moments for pomp and ritual, with officers and civilians turned out in their dress uniforms to cheer a massive engineering achievement. Starships either ended their lives violently or in obsolescent obscurity; rarely was anyone invited to see a ship broken down for scrap. The time for partying was up front, while all a vessel's promise still lay ahead.

Riker wasn't surprised that attending the launch of a Klingon ship was a completely different experience. *Jarin*, a modern *B'rel*-class bird-of-prey, had been commissioned a year earlier by the House of Kruge, with the Klingon High Command helping coordinate its construction in the house's shipyards. The christening had been conducted right in the construction hangar with very little ceremony. Riker expected that was normal for Klingons, who on creating a warship would have been eager to send it on its way to battle. There were no speeches, no songs; those were things for after a victory, not before. A few gruff words from a presiding general and it was part of the Klingon Defense Force, ready for departure under her newly minted commander.

It was the christening of this ship, commanded by the somewhat boyish Bredak, son of Lorath, that had brought Admiral Riker to Ketorix. Bredak's grandfather, Lord Korgh—once the *gin'tak*, or manager, of the House of Kruge—had taken charge of the house following the assassination of the family elders at Gamaral. Over a short period, Korgh not only had gained control of one of the Empire's great houses, but he had become an immensely popular—and incendiary—figure on the High Council.

Lord Korgh also had acquired the ability to make Riker, a diplomatic envoy of the Federation, sit on his hands like a supplicant. Klingon Chancellor Martok had given the go-ahead for the diplomatic conference that Riker had been charged with organizing on H'atoria, but that planet was under the administration of Korgh's family. As wily at a hundred twenty years old as dealmakers a third his age, Korgh had wheedled a role in deciding exactly when and where on H'atoria that the conference would be staged.

Then Lord Korgh had proceeded not to return Riker's calls.

The admiral wasn't one to be kept waiting—especially when his assignment was idling the crew of his flag vessel, the *Starship Titan*. When his diplomatic aide, Lieutenant Ssura, discovered that Korgh would be making his first trip home to his house's manufacturing center since ascending to power, Riker had made it his business to be there.

He and Ssura watched from afar as Korgh gave his grandson a hearty embrace. Korgh's entourage had grown in recent days; he had three burly bodyguards, a nod to the ongoing threat to his house. Then Bredak saluted those on the platform and boarded. Moments later, the landing ramp rose and massive engines ignited.

"Is that all?" Ssura asked, the Caitian aide's feline eyes fixed on *Jarin* as it lifted into the air. "That's the whole thing?"

"That's it," Riker said. "Show's over."

Or maybe not, he thought as the lead Defense Force officer present descended from the highest level of the platform toward him. He'd seen General Kersh before; a sturdy Klingon woman just entering middle age, she hadn't yet spoken a word to him. Seeing Riker at the bottom of the steps, the dark-skinned Kersh looked as if she'd smelled a foul stench. She bared her teeth to him. "Still here!"

"Still here," Riker said. "The United Federation of Planets wishes *Jarin* and its crew all success in its future missions, General."

"How could it succeed?" Kersh looked back at the vessel, wobbling in midair as it worked its way out of the crowded hangar. "I have put a child in charge of a warship because he is the grandson of a man who less than a month ago was answering my family's door." She turned back and glared at Riker. "The great 'Lord Korgh' should be thanking you for your incompetence!"

Riker bristled. Kersh had plenty of reasons to despise him. In what had come to be known as the Takedown Incident, troublemakers from an advanced civilization had taken control of Riker and several others, sending them on missions of mischief. It was Riker's bad luck to have been dispatched into Klingon territory, where he'd attempted to disable an outpost Kersh was defending. No one had been injured—Riker had made sure of that—and damage to the outpost was minimal. Kersh's pride, her honor, was another matter.

That, however, was only the beginning. Protecting a ceremony on Gamaral on Riker's orders, the *Enterprise* had failed to stop the massacre of the nobles of the House of Kruge—including Kersh's grandfather, J'borr. Former *gin'tak* Korgh had then stepped up, declaring himself the adopted son of long-dead Commander Kruge. It wasn't clear that Kersh could have inherited the house; Klingon rules about gender and property were sticky. But it was clear that Kersh blamed Riker for Korgh's new status.

He reached for anything innocuous to say. "The Empire stages a fine ceremony."

"Much different from the one you ran, Riker. No unarmed civilians have been murdered." Kersh gestured to the scaffolds all around. "But there is still the chance for you to destroy Klingon property."

Riker and Ssura looked at each other. *What the hell do you say to that?*

The general didn't give them the chance to think of anything. She turned on her heel and made for another set of steps leading downward onto the hangar's factory floor. She had gone scarcely a few meters when she stopped to berate an unfortunate laborer, sloughing off during the ceremony.

"That could have gone better," Riker said, his words easily masked by the sounds of work in the hangar.

"I don't understand," Ssura said. "Commander Worf's file on Kersh says that she is sharp and dependable."

"She can be that and still hate my guts." The admiral turned back to look at the platform behind him, where Korgh was giving an interview to someone. Riker didn't have a firm grasp on how the media worked in the Empire, but Korgh clearly did. The new lord rarely passed up the chance to spread the word about all the ways the Khitomer Accords had failed the Klingons.

Korgh was in middle of a harangue when Riker finally succeeded in catching his eye. He kept on talking to the interviewer, the hint of a smile appearing on his face as he made Riker stand down below. The admiral crossed his arms, willing to wait as long as—

Something changed. Korgh's eyes looked up, above Riker's head—and his expression switched to surprise, alarm.

Riker turned, even as Ssura grasped his arm and pointed upward. *"Sir!"*

They had passed it on the way into the hangar: a disruptor cannon, mostly assembled and intended for eventual placement on the wing of a bird-of-prey. Weighing tons, the drab green mass of metal had been slung over the factory floor by an immense crane system. The chains securing it were on the move, slipping from the pulleys above—and now the gun was in motion, too, falling toward the woman standing beneath.

"Kersh!" Riker took two steps and leaped from the catwalk he was on. Kersh noticed him but not the gun—now turned missile—spearing down toward her. Startled, she put her hands before her in defense, but his momentum was too great. As his tackle sent them both tumbling into a pit for a lift, the cannon struck the spot where she'd stood with a colossal clang.

The depression was only a couple of meters deep, but it was enough to knock the wind out of the two of them. Recovering first, an unknowing Kersh clawed free from beneath Riker and reached for his neck in the shadows, intent on strangling whoever it was that had struck her.

"Stop," he said. "It's me, Riker!"

Lost in rage, Kersh wasn't listening. The admiral had begun to fear that she might accidentally kill him when there came a new interruption: blazing orange disruptor fire, peppering the upper walls of their pit. Kersh's eyes widened, and her grip loosened.

He wrested free from her. "Strangle me later! We're under fire!"

Four

Whatever benefits the large metal-lined pit might have had as a foxhole were seriously undermined by the location of the assailants somewhere in the upper catwalks of the hangar. The snipers were at right angles to each other, giving them shots on all but one corner of the recess. The admiral and general huddled there for long moments—until they heard footsteps and return fire.

When the shots on the pit walls subsided, Kersh drew her sidearm, something Riker hadn't been allowed to bring into the facility. "Now," she said, asking for a boost. He helped her scramble out—and accepted her aid in return. They crouched beside the fallen cannon, which had left a sizable dent in the flooring where Kersh had stood earlier.

One of Korgh's bodyguards, sheltering the old Klingon behind a stack of girders, gestured toward the gantries up ahead. Korgh's other two protectors were scaling the ladders as more guards entered the hangar from the far end.

"Ssura!" Riker called out.

"Here, sir!" The Caitian was off to the side, having used his catlike climbing abilities to partially scale a tower of equipment for a better view. He pointed. "Admiral, I see them!"

The assailants had doubled back and were on the catwalk level directly above. Riker could tell exactly where they were from the clanking footsteps on the gridwork deck over their heads. It was the only alert Kersh needed. She set her disruptor on full power and fired upward at the grating. A male Klingon voice screamed. If the catwalk deflected part of the beam, it wasn't enough to save the person above.

Was it person or persons? Had she struck them both? Riker backed up, trying to get a view of the catwalk from below. Instead, he saw a masked figure plummeting down toward him, disruptor in hand.

Unlike when Riker leaped onto Kersh from above, the admiral was primed to react—and did, shifting to his right foot. With no pit to tumble into this time, when the attacker caught him on the way down, they simply hit the deck and rolled. Wrestling, Riker alternately saw the floor and the face of his attacker, obscured by a protective industrial mask.

His back against the deck, the admiral kicked upward, forcing his opponent off him for a moment. It gave the attacker a chance to bring his disruptor in front of Riker's face. *"We must punish the Empire—and those foolish enough to ally with it!"* Fingering the trigger, he called out, *"We are the children of the true Kahless!"*

A pair of powerful hands grabbed at the shoulders of the attacker and ripped him from his position atop Riker. Kersh hurled the aggressor backward, tumbling him head over heels into the mechanical pit that had recently saved her. Riker heard a howl accompanying the crunch of landing.

A pained moan emanated from below. *"We . . . are the* vor'uv'etlh *. . . who will not fall . . ."*

"You just did," Kersh said, handing her disruptor to Riker. He hustled with it to the side of the pit as Kersh clambered back down into the hole.

The dazed assassin—if that was what he was—struggled to get to his knees. His welder's mask had been knocked askew, and he fumbled about ineffectually for his fallen disruptor. Kersh delivered a jarring kick to the faceplate, causing him to career backward against the wall of the pit. The fight left him, and he sagged.

Riker noticed his dingy uniform was identical to that worn by the other laborers in the hangar. The only difference was the mask. The Unsung, the terrorist Klingon sect that had killed Kersh's relatives and assassinated the clone of Kahless, wore masks, Riker knew—and the attacker had just invoked part of their manifesto.

Seeing Ssura approach, Riker passed him the disruptor and shimmied back down into the pit. Having located and pocketed the injured man's disruptor, Kersh ripped the mask from his head.

Riker wasn't surprised to see a Klingon face behind it, not here. The surprise was all Kersh's. She gasped. "*You!*"

"You know him? Who is he?"

"A coward." Kersh spat, disgusted. "This worthless *targ* served under one of my best sergeants years ago. He wanted a promotion—but instead of issuing a direct challenge, as a warrior should, he and his brother killed their superior in his sleep!" Kersh grabbed the battered assailant's collar and shook him. "Was that your brother up there on the catwalk? Speak!"

"The disruptor blast . . . he died in front of me," the shaken Klingon said. His nose and mouth bled from Kersh's kick.

Kersh ripped an employee badge from his chest. Barely glancing at it, she tossed it to Riker. The admiral read the name on it. "Your name is Har'tok?"

"When he had a name," Kersh said.

Riker blinked. "You mean he's discommendated?"

"Of course." Kersh searched Har'tok's clothes, not bothering to be gentle about it. "How else should we deal with those who would attack the unsuspecting?"

Their methods haven't changed, Riker thought. He compared the face on the badge with the battered visage before him. It was the same person—yet their Klingon prisoner looked a good deal older. Something didn't add up. "This guy didn't just sneak in here. He's been working here for years."

"It happens," the general said, indifferently rising and

stepping away from the attacker. "The dishonored drift around. We don't keep track of them."

"But Ketorix is a strategic supply center." From what Riker had seen, the factory and hangar alone held enough munitions to blow up the whole city. "How could someone like him get clearance to work here?"

"Easy, if he knew how to do something useful in his former life." Kersh wiped her hands on her sleeves. "Straw bosses will use anyone as labor to cut corners. They don't ask questions. They don't care that he's a nobody."

"I could have been somebody, Kersh. My brother too," Har'tok moaned, almost out of his wits with pain. "But you ended all that when you pushed for discommendation. And now you've killed him!"

This was revenge? Riker again considered how long Har'tok and his brother had been working there. "You came to work here hoping for a chance to kill Kersh?"

Har'tok looked away. "No. We were told we could find a way to something better while working here. But no one came for us."

"Something better?" Riker asked. "Who told you that—and what did they mean?"

"Never mind. It doesn't matter." Har'tok glared up at Kersh. "When we saw *her* today, we acted."

Kersh crossed her arms before her. "I don't understand. I've visited this facility many times—you would have had plenty of chances. What's different about today?"

"Because I know now—I *am* someone." Defiance filled Har'tok's eyes, replacing the pain. "The Unsung have risen. A new day has come for generations of discommendated. It has come for all of us!"

"Not for you," came a voice from above. Riker looked up to the edge of the pit where Korgh loomed overhead, flanked by two of his bodyguards. As one, the guards fired their disruptors down into the hollow. Riker instinctively backed away from weapons fire in such a small space—but the shots of Korgh's minions were precise. Har'tok vanished into nothingness with an agonized squeal.

Riker looked at the seared spot on the metal wall where the worker had been—and then back up at Korgh. "You could have questioned him!"

"We do not hear his kind, Admiral." Korgh knelt and offered Riker a helping hand to exit the pit. Kersh followed without aid. The lord faced her once they were topside. "General, you are sure these were the only two?"

"Yes. They were condemned by the High Council after acts of cowardice."

Korgh sighed audibly. "It is what we have all feared, then. This is the fault of the accursed Unsung."

Riker looked again at the badge in his hand. The Unsung had been native to Thane in the Briar Patch before they went on the run—led, according to Worf, by someone posing as Commander Kruge, back from the dead after a hundred-year absence. The Unsung had been formidable and deadly; Har'tok looked nowhere near as professional. "Are you sure it's the Unsung, sir? I don't think these characters are connected with them."

"You are correct, Riker—and that is the problem. The Unsung number only two to three hundred. But there are plenty more discommendated individuals—and their descendants—who might well be inspired to violence by them." Korgh scowled. "*That* is what we have most feared—and your Starfleet's acts have brought it all to pass."

Riker swallowed. He disagreed with Korgh's characterization of what had happened, but he couldn't doubt what he had just witnessed.

"Now, Admiral," Korgh said, straightening his rich robe, "what was it exactly that you wanted to see me about?"

Five

She had killed and killed, but it had given her no enjoyment.

Valandris was Klingon by blood, even if the people of the Empire chose to deny her existence. She and her companions of the Unsung valued hunting over all else—even the so-called honor the hypocrites of Qo'noS gave lip service to. The green-skinned Orions were a new species to hunt, and she had stalked her first ones days earlier on a mission in the Hyralan Sector. They had not impressed her—and to her disappointment, the specimens on this nameless world weren't good sport either.

No—they were worse. *Dinskaar*'s crew had at least put up a defense. This was extermination: going from building to shabby building, wiping out pirates wherever she found them.

Someone lunged from behind one of the racks in the warehouse. Valandris thrust her *d'k tahg* into the neck of a lime-faced boy just barely old enough to constitute a threat. She had never used the Klingon name for the blade before, but her people's new leader had told them it was all right. *Chu'charq*'s stores were full of such weapons.

"Only Klingon society is tainted," Lord Kruge had said, his crackling voice reminding his listeners of the death by fire he escaped long ago. *"There is nothing wrong with their blades. Sanctify them in the blood of the unworthy."*

A disruptor blast fired from the nearby office went wide over her head. She pulled her weapon from the junior pirate's back and flipped it around in her hand. This time she hurled it. The blade sliced the tepid air, sailing from one room into the other—before ending its flight in the face of the husky being who'd fired at her. All flab, he collapsed heavily in the office, surrounded by the worthless trinkets he'd evidently lived for. His countinghouse had become a charnel house.

The place went silent. Valandris sighed. There had not been a single Orion as good at combat as Leotis, the boss she'd fought aboard *Dinskaar*. And he had been terrible. She retrieved her weapon from the fat man's skull.

Her eyes went from the bloody floor to the contents of the building, a temporary structure so old it had become permanent. There was nothing worth having here, no prize to take. Potok, the founder of her colony of discommendated Klingons and their kinfolk, had banned the taking of hunting trophies; they were signs of status, and in his unyielding ideology, those who could never have honor deserved nothing else. Generations of hunters on Thane had nevertheless sneaked teeth, scales, and fangs from their kills as secret remembrances. But this place held mostly shiny baubles and illicit substances, the currency of the Orions' nefarious enterprises. All were worthless to Valandris.

She stepped outside. Colored a soothing cerulean by the nebula above, the night was far from peaceful—but it soon would be. The Orions who used this camp as a hideaway were in their death throes. Half her people hadn't even used their masks for this attack: the pirates knew who and what the Unsung were, and that had provided terror aplenty.

From her crew on *Chu'charq*, she recognized her young cousin Raneer leading raiders on a charge against fleeing pirates. Raneer had improved since her first encounter with the Orions, Valandris thought—though she couldn't be learning a lot here.

There didn't appear to be anyone left to fight—until from behind the door of a dilapidated wooden shack, something exploded. Or, rather, *someone*: a hulking Orion strongman, flying limply through the air before landing with a meaty thud on the ground outside. His attacker lumbered out after him, fist drawn and smiling.

"Come on, get up!" The baldheaded Klingon showed his mouthful of broken teeth. "I've already spotted you an arm. Get up and fight!"

Valandris chuckled. Over fifty, Zokar was one of the older members of the Unsung; the violent wildlife of their planet kept life expectancies short. A *zikka'gleg* had claimed Zokar's arm, just after he arrived as an émigré to the planet of the condemned. Rather than give up, the injury had made the brawny ball of spite meaner.

His opponent, meanwhile, might have given up—or might not have. Valandris could see him stirring. "Forget it," Zokar said after waiting seconds for the giant to recover. He quickly drew his disruptor pistol and vaporized the Orion.

"There," he said, putting the weapon away. He saw Valandris and smiled. "What did you think of that?"

"Not much."

"He was better inside."

"That's not it," she said. "He was going to get up. He should have died fighting."

Zokar sneered. "What, you're Kahless now?"

"The clone?"

"I mean the one from the ancient days. 'Die standing up'—that's one of his lines." Zokar waved to the gutted camp. "If you haven't noticed, these fools don't exactly follow the Klingon ways. And neither do we."

That much was true. Discommendation had taken their heritage away, stolen it from generations of Klingons on Thane whose only crime had been being born to the wrong parents. They owed the Empire and its morals nothing—and their savior, all.

"There he is," Zokar said, pointing. The two birds-of-prey involved in the raid, *Chu'charq* and *Rodak*, sat at the edge of the clearing, their landing ramps down. An entourage exited the former. Four mask-wearing members of the Unsung in black combat gear escorted a slow-walking pair down into the ruined camp. There was the mysterious robed woman N'Keera, high priestess to the Unsung, supporting he who was her constant companion and their infallible leader: the legendary Fallen Lord.

Kruge.

"I am pleased," the old Klingon said, pausing to breathe deeply. They had been cooped up aboard the ships since their fiery escape from Thane; Valandris wasn't surprised to see him taking a constitutional here, as he had done so often at home. Sharp eyes set into a face scarred by ancient flames looked on the camp with satisfaction. "Yes, I am pleased. Well done."

Zokar stepped forward first and bowed. "I told *Rodak*'s people these Orions wouldn't be much—they're rear echelon, total homebodies. Looks about right."

Valandris rolled her eyes. Zokar was a rarity among the Unsung. He had lived more than half of his life in the Klingon Empire, leaving to join the exiles sometime after losing his name. Even then, he had refused to shut up about where he had come from, defying even Potok's commands. Since Kruge arrived a year earlier promising to lead them all on a mission to reshape the galaxy, Zokar had wasted no opportunity to show that he knew more than anyone else about where they were headed.

Valandris and Zokar joined the group, and the escorts fanned out, making sure no one remained alive to harass them. "This camp belonged to a dishonorable wretch named Fortar," Kruge said, walking along.

"Fortar, indeed!" Zokar laughed. "The Klingons have been after his head for twenty years, my lord. They've never found where he holes up."

"They never asked *me*. One has to have a mind for how the enemy thinks." Kruge glanced meaningfully at his aide before looking around. "There will be no room in our new order for such beings. This is a beginning."

N'Keera spoke softly, gesturing to the huts and shanties. "Were they storing riches here?"

"As they would define them," Valandris said. "I have seen them. The spoils of a dead-end culture."

"Spoils," Zokar said. "Should we burn them?"

Valandris saw N'Keera wince at the word *burn*—and Zokar did so, too, once he saw her response.

Kruge stared at Zokar for a long, dangerous moment. Then he laughed. "You can mention fire before me without fear. I left my fear of it on the Genesis Planet before your sires and grandsires were born."

Zokar breathed easier.

"No, once you are certain the Orions are all dead, return your crews to your vessels. Rest, meditate—steel yourselves for our exploits to come. Our other birds-of-prey in orbit will alert us if anyone approaches."

"Absolutely." Zokar, his old bluster returning, gestured toward *Rodak*. "I offer you my team's ship, Lord Kruge. I flew aboard birds-of-prey back in the Defense Force—I have trained my people well." He smiled cheekily. "I know you flew with crack crews before. Let us give you another chance to do so."

Valandris saw N'Keera and Kruge look at each other. Sensing discomfort, Valandris spoke up for her vessel. "*Chu'charq* is our lord's base of operations, Zokar. It will continue to be."

Zokar scowled at her. "There are no titles in this movement, Valandris. You don't deserve special status."

"Really? Unless I miss my guess, I'm the one who killed Fortar."

"Bah! Slaying fat overlords does not impress—"

"Silence." N'Keera raised her hand and spoke sternly. "Lord Kruge will take this up at a different time. For now, return to your vessels as your lord has commanded."

Kruge sniffed at the air. "Perhaps an extra hour of meditation for you both would be in order as well."

Valandris and Zokar nodded, chastened. "Yes, my lord," they said in unison.

Kruge stepped forward, leaving the group. "N'Keera and I will stay on the surface for a time. I would like to walk the camp—to see for myself what you have done."

Valandris's eyes widened. "You shouldn't go without bodyguards, my lord. It might not be safe."

Kruge stopped suddenly and looked back. He raised an eyebrow. "Do you believe me an infant, Valandris, to be kept in a crib?"

She looked down. "Of course not."

"I will have you know, when I was six days old, I killed my wet nurse in mortal combat—after which I was sent to live in the pen with the guard mastiffs. They taught me manners and gave me a taste for meat." Kruge bared his teeth at her—at first menacingly, before it resolved into a canny grin.

Everyone laughed—including Valandris, with relief.

He strode from the group. "To suit my young nanny here, I will not go alone. My dear N'Keera will join me." He offered his hand, and the young Klingon woman slipped from the group and took it. "If there is danger, you will know it. Carry on."

Valandris and Zokar glared at each other, neither wanting to be the one to depart while Kruge and N'Keera were still in sight. Once their master and his aide had gone around a bend, they remained frozen a few seconds longer.

Finally, Valandris threw up her hands in aggravation and started to walk away. "I have people to find."

Zokar chortled. "That's right. Kruge dismissed you first— *Nanny!*"

She turned long enough to return a gesture that he had taught her.

Six

"**W**e're all right," Riker said over Captain Christine Vale's combadge. *"Just a little excitement."*

She stood in the alcove and tried to hear over the music. "Do you need backup, Admiral?"

"If I couldn't bring it with me before, I can't have you send it now."

Vale had never liked how often diplomacy and safety wound up at cross-purposes. After the Kruge family had been attacked on Gamaral, *Titan's* security chief, Lieutenant Commander Ranul Keru, had implored Riker to take a squad with him to Ketorix. He had refused. The invitation was only for him and his aide, and he didn't want to offend Lord Korgh by implying that his security forces weren't up to the job.

Obviously, they hadn't been. "Your message said the attackers were copycats?"

"That's not for dissemination. I'll get into that when I return. We're waiting here in the hangar while Korgh and Kersh order stepped-up screening for the facility's workers." He paused. *"I know you're supposed to be off shift, Chris—sorry if I woke you."*

"Actually, I'm in the officer's club. While you've been down there, I answered a hail for you from the Kinshaya."

"And that explains why you're in the bar. What did the Pontifex Maxima have to say?"

"Actually, it was the—let me see if I've got this right— the second secretary for the Office of Infidel Relations. She said all Kinshaya diplomats are spending the year in prayer, and that they 'would sooner have their wings clipped before attending a conference hosted by the demon Klingons.'" Vale took a deep breath. "I told her that the first secretary had given us the same message but had called the Klingons 'devils,' and that we needed clarification on which they meant."

"Nice." Riker laughed. Yeffir, the current head of the Episcopate, was a reformer and relatively reasonable—but getting to her through the church bureaucracy had become impossible of late. *"I'll send up Ssura to return the hail. Save me a seat at the bar—if I ever get out of here. Riker out."*

Vale edged out of the alcove and back into the moody shadows of the officer's club. *Titan* had two on this deck: a jazz-themed room and, at the far end, Beale Street, named for the Memphis avenue on Earth where W. C. Handy popularized the blues. Both bars suited the tastes of the trombone-playing admiral who, after all, had been *Titan*'s captain for several years—and in recent times the clubs had become a barometer for shipboard morale.

When *Titan* had been out exploring, as a Starfleet vessel was intended to be, the peppier jazz club saw the most use. But whenever Riker's promotion meant he drew diplomatic assignments, more officers could be found listening to the somber piped-in ballads sung by people who had it worse than they did. Counselor Deanna Troi contended that counting the number of people "on Beale" at any given time was as good a diagnostic tool as she'd found.

Troi was waiting for her outside the alcove, anxious to hear about her husband's situation. Returning with Troi to the bar, Vale shared what little she knew and reclaimed her drink. "Do you think it's wrong for a new captain to want to lock up an admiral so nothing else bad happens to him?"

"As long as his daughter and I can visit him in the brig," Troi said, smiling. She put her empty glass on the counter. "Speaking of Natasha, I owe her a story."

"Well, you've heard about Will. What's stopping you?"

Troi nodded in the direction of the other end of the bar, where a young Skagaran officer stood alone. "I think Lieutenant Kyzak is continuing to win friends. I have seen four different people get frustrated talking to him and wander off."

"Where's Melora Pazlar? I thought they were friendly."

"One of them *was* Melora." Troi studied the young man from afar. "I think rustic charm only goes so far in space. I'm sensing he could use a word."

"Go," Vale said, putting down her drink. "I've got this one."

"You're a saint." Troi slipped off her chair and started to walk away. She stopped momentarily to call back. "I like today's hair, by the way."

"Yeah, it's, uh . . . brown," Vale said, eyes rolled. She sighed. "Haven't felt very creative lately."

She shrugged and headed for the end of the bar. Except for a few red facial protrusions, Kyzak could have passed for a human—if that human was a holodeck character in an Old West program. His off-duty ensemble consisted of a replicated-suede vest over a dull burgundy striped shirt, with tan canvas trousers set off by a silver buckle. A red silk kerchief was wrapped around his neck. Odder civvies Vale had not seen—but they were for real, and so was he.

One of the newer members of the crew, the ops officer descended from a sect of Skagarans whose culture long ago had been contaminated with that of the Ancient West of Earth's North American continent. After their discovery by Captain Jonathan Archer and the crew of *Enterprise* NX-01, the Skagarans had slowly integrated into the Federation. Kyzak brought a rustic outlook to Starfleet, as well as a supply of sayings Vale found idiosyncratic at best. His tendency to revert to bromides on days when he felt out of place had annoyed more than a few. He was a decent officer, which was all that mattered—but it was taking him a while to adjust to shipboard life, and his company seemed to be an acquired taste.

Vale sidled up to the bar beside him, aware that in "sidling" she was acting like a character in an Ancient Western. She was likewise surprised by the greeting that somehow came out of her mouth: "How's the roundup going, Lieutenant?" *Damn, he's even got me doing it!*

"Things are all right, ma'am. Belly up to the bar." His lips puckered, and his eyebrows went down. "I guess I shouldn't say *belly* to a captain, should I?"

"I'll have to check the regulations."

He sighed and ordered another bourbon and branch. He turned around and leaned his back against the bar, looking out at the wide array of species represented in the club's patrons. Some were looking back, Vale noticed—though they were trying not to be seen doing it. "Folks still don't know what to make of me, do they?" Kyzak asked.

"*Titan* has more different kinds of people from different places than any ship in the fleet. You're this week's curiosity. It'll pass."

"Except I've been here more than a week. And to be honest, if I was more comfortable talkin' to people, I'd be doing a better job."

"How so?"

"Well, there's some stuff I don't really get—about this mission."

Join the club, Vale wanted to say. "What can I clear up for you?"

"Well, it's Admiral Riker, to start with. When they transferred me here, he was a sector commander for the frontier sectors of the Alpha Quadrant."

"He still is."

He raised his eyebrows. "Ain't this the Beta Quadrant?"

"This is where the Klingons live," Vale said. "Admiral Riker has a lot of experience dealing with them. That's why the Federation asked Starfleet to send him to set up the H'atorian Conference."

"I guess I figured that much. But that's another one. I've been to the briefings, but I'm still not sure what the thing's even about. And I've asked people, but they . . ." Kyzak trailed off before turning back to the bar. "Captain, we didn't do too much with politics where I'm from. Everything past the planet next door is kind of out of the way."

"You went to the Academy. You studied interstellar relations."

"I shouldn't say it to a superior officer, but I just barely passed."

"I know what you mean." Vale attracted the attention of the bartender, who refilled her drink. "It's pretty simple. It has to do with trade routes, and reciprocal access agreements, as well as establishing rules for armed vessels, and how many can travel together at once. Then there's the availability of emergency services, which—"

Vale stopped when she saw his eyes go as cloudy as the absinthe in her glass. He was earnestly trying to follow, but another tack was necessary.

She took a deep breath. "Okay, consider your right hand."

Kyzak held his up, and she started pointing to his digits.

"Your thumb represents the Earth and the bulk of the Federation. Your pinky finger's all the new Beta Quadrant members that have recently joined the Federation. And the three fingers in between are the Klingon Empire."

"I gotcha. This agreement is so we get to travel to our own."

"No, we already have the right to cross Klingon space. That's in the Khitomer Accords." She was glad to see Kyzak nodding along. "No, the problem's your other hand."

He put down his drink and held up his left. "This one."

"That one. Now, the thumb of your left hand represents the Romulan Star Empire—and the fingers include systems belonging to the Kinshaya, as well as some remote outposts maintained by the Breen, and some minor tributary systems."

"The Typhon Pact powers. I'm following."

"Clasp those hands together." She watched as he interlaced his fingers.

"Like this?"

"*That* is what the Beta Quadrant frontier looks like, once you get right out to the edge. A lot of the best routes from the main body of the Federation to the new members—"

"From the thumb to the pinky."

"—from the thumb to the pinky, require crossing not just Klingon space, but the territories of powers that have gone to war with the Klingons in the past. They *despise* each other. What Admiral Riker and the Federation are trying to do is lace a corridor right through the center of all those fingers—a free-flight corridor available to everyone to use."

Kyzak looked at his hands and smiled. "And those House of Kruge people are making things hard on the admiral because one of these fingers belongs to them."

"That's right," she said. *There's a joke I could make about which finger, but I'm not sure you'd understand it.*

Kyzak unclasped his hands and slapped them on the bartop. "I sure appreciate this, Captain. I think I've got it." Grinning in appreciation, he added, "I'm sure Admiral Riker will get 'em all sorted out fast."

"If anyone can do it, he will," Vale said. Then she lowered her voice in mock secrecy. "But between you and me, Lieutenant, I'm not sure the left hand knows what the right hand's doing." She finished her drink and headed for bed.

Seven

Buxtus Cross was thirty-nine, nineteen years removed from his escape from the *Clarence Darrow*. And while he had kept himself in shape, when he looked at his hand he saw the pale, scarred palm of a hundred-forty-year-old Klingon burn victim.

The hand was allegedly that of Commander Kruge, back from the dead and a hundred years older. It was an illusion, projected by his truthcrafters: the engineers aboard his support ship, *Blackstone*, which sat cloaked and parked near the Orion camp. Whenever Cross stood before a mirror, he could see the holographic visual projected around his body; so could the truthcrafters, via the sensors in his contact lenses. Whenever he spoke, *Blackstone*'s remote force-field projections attenuated his vocal sound waves to match that heard in past recordings of Kruge's voice.

The rest—Kruge's mannerisms, dialogue, and intonations—came from Cross and his acting abilities. He had used them all in the past year, transforming three hundred descendants of the real Kruge's discommendated followers into a fighting force now feared across the Empire. His Klingon patron, Korgh, had concocted and financed the scheme; the truthcrafters' tech and Cross's acting had made it all possible.

That, and the help of the woman walking beside him: the Klingon mystic N'Keera, in actuality a supporting character played by his lovely Orion assistant, Shift. "N'Keera" drew closer to him as they walked between the buildings of the camp. "It's good to walk outside," she said, gripping his arm. "We've been cooped up in the ship too long."

"Feels like being born again."

Gaw had already given Cross a new life, springing him from *Clarence Darrow* years earlier. The truthcrafters had needed an actor to serve as their "practitioner," the person who inhabited their projected illusions; Cross had needed roles and freedom. In their years of collaboration, he had learned what it meant to live the life of a true magician. His was the ultimate actor's challenge: creating reality. Together they had fooled sophisticates and primitives alike, always escaping detection.

Their success—*his* success—had become the envy of their rivals in their secret world, in the shadowy places where they congregated to exchange stories. And while the practitioners of the Circle of Jilaan had honored no one with the title Illusionist Magnus since the marvelous Jilaan passed from the scene, Cross was certain he was just one or two daring feats away.

Nothing so far had compared to this: walking onto a planet of Klingon exiles and convincing them he was the famous leader who fell into a sea of lava a century earlier. The inferno had reduced the real Kruge to his component molecules in seconds; as Cross had spun it, he had been transported away in the moments before. After a year of working on the exiles and with the aid of Korgh, Cross had created a cult that threatened order everywhere, so long as he had the Unsung's support.

Cross did have that—and he didn't intend to give it up. Not yet, not when the payoff was near. A small part of it was up ahead. In her guise as N'Keera, Shift read the Orion markings on one of the huts. "This is it," she said, her voice tremulous. "The countinghouse."

"You all right, Shift? I know these were your people."

"They're not my people," she said, striding forward and reaching for the door handle. She looked around to make sure the Klingons were gone. "Let's do this."

The door opened. There was a dead Orion youth on the dirt floor just inside, his blood already dry. The outer storage area was otherwise as Valandris had left it—except for the people rummaging around, inventorying the riches on the shelves. *His* people. According to plan, they had beamed into the building from *Blackstone*, with the Klingons of the Unsung completely unaware of their presence. A Bynar pair, 1110 and 1111, worked with a multispecies group inventorying the warehouse's contents.

Gaw, *Blackstone*'s chief effects specialist, was first to address him. "Is that Kruge I see?" The Ferengi stepped out from the office. "All hail the mighty Klingon king, burned to a crisp but keeps on walking."

"*All hail!*" came responses from the other workers rifling through the countinghouse's goods.

Gaw looked much the same as when Cross had met him years earlier—after the Ferengi had stopped pretending to be a Borg drone, that is. He smiled at "N'Keera," took her hand, and bowed. "Looking good, dearie. Are you ready to shed this guy? Trust me, I have better lobes."

"All right, all right." A chuckling Cross snapped his fingers. The Betazoid's normal appearance returned, as did the lithe form of his emerald-skinned Orion companion, Shift. He much preferred this look to her N'Keera incarnation, although there had been something clouding those beautiful eyes most of the day.

He knew what it was. "This is the place?"

Shift took a deep breath. "This is where Fortar worked . . . the man who *sold* me."

"Aha," Gaw said, stepping out of the doorway he was in and gesturing inside. "I suspect that's the gentleman in question there."

Tentatively at first, Shift took a step forward—and then another, before arriving in the doorway. Cross approached from behind. In the back room, the corpse of a fat Orion lay sprawled out on his belly, having fallen as he went for the door. He had bled out, making the ground by his head mucky and gross. His hand still clutched a disruptor.

Gathering her courage, Shift knelt and turned the immense Orion over—and saw where Valandris had pulled her *d'k tahg* from the dead man's bloody face.

"It's him," she whispered, recognizing something even in that mess.

Cross looked down on the scene with indifference. "Yeah. Revenge served cold, right? It just took some Klingons."

"Right," she said. She stood, took one more look down at Fortar, and gave his body a kick before heading back into the main room. Cross followed and closed the door behind him, hiding the gruesome scene. He was still surprised she'd been willing to touch the body.

He had met Shift in a bar he frequented between schemes. An admirer of her obvious physical charms, he'd since grown impressed with her acting skills. She'd gone from girlfriend to apprentice without sacrificing the former, which made him happy; such situations seldom worked out well. She had even helped them select targets, using her knowledge of the pirates in the region to help Cross choose strikes for the Unsung.

She'd known that Leotis, her most recent owner, trafficked in the sort of information that had helped the Unsung carry out the massacre at Gamaral. And her knowledge of the boltholes used by Fortar's band had given the Unsung a mission while they waited on Korgh's next command—a mission that simultaneously gave Shift her revenge while contributing to the truthcrafters' coffers. *Nothing like a little bonus action.*

Cross loved efficiency. He watched as several of the other *Blackstone* crewmembers used practiced haste, locating and stacking bricks of gold-pressed latinum. Gaw turned to rummage around in a basket of gems, his hands wrist deep in riches. 1110 and 1111 chittered excitedly to each other in their binary language. This would be a decent haul.

Composed again after her earlier moment, Shift looked about in wonder. "Your people sure love their loot, Gaw."

"We've got to have it," the Ferengi said. "An outfit like ours eats, drinks, and breathes money."

She shook her head, puzzled. "I've never understood that part of the operation."

"That's because you're training to be a practitioner, not a truthcrafter," Gaw said. He clicked his tongue. "So much to learn."

"Don't let this guy rib you, Shift. I was new once too." Cross put his arm around Gaw's shoulder. "He was looking for someone else and found me instead. But he was prettier when I met him. He was disguised as a Borg."

Gaw rolled his eyes. "Sometimes I think I should have left him aboard that prison ship. It would work out better for our bottom line."

"Ouch," Cross said, withdrawing his arm. "See if *we* find Orion camps for you to loot again."

The Ferengi evaluated a handful of gems disdainfully. "Half this stuff is junk. I'm more worried about the big score. Are you sure your silent partner's going to come through for us?"

Cross waved off the concern. "With what I know about him? I'm not worried. Besides, he still has no real idea what my powers are, or how we do what we do. He knows

I have a cloaked support ship, but not what it does. As far as he knows I represent a great alien technology far beyond him—and so he knows not to vex me."

"Vex." Gaw looked at Shift. "Who talks like that?"

She laughed.

"Trust me," Cross said, "he's in the dark." Cross had been careful not to reveal to Korgh how they did what they did. The more mysterious they seemed, the greater the price they could ask.

Gaw handed a green gem to Shift. "You were asking about money. The technology the Circle of Jilaan uses is from a unique branch of holography—older than any of us, but different. Better. More versatile. The parts required to generate our illusions can't be successfully replicated, and they can't be bought at a local bazaar. We need hard currency to trade for it."

"I know *that*," Shift said, studying the facets of the rock. "What I meant was I don't understand what Cross gets out of all this." She passed the jewel to her lover. "You live well, but you don't seem to care about the riches."

"The story's my reward," Cross said, discarding the rock. "I've got to take you to a circle convocation one day—you can find out just how many things in history never really happened as you heard, because there was a practitioner and a truthcrafter team at work somewhere." His eyes sparkled. "Like the time Surak appeared to the Vulcans on Garadius IV. That was actually Jilaan, like me playing Kruge. Or our *next* trick."

"Ah, yes," Gaw said, frowning. "I suppose you're referring to your secret guest, back on *Chu'charq*. Kahless the Unforgettable—or is that Kahless the Clone?"

"Kahless the Hungry," Shift said, suddenly reminded. "I'd better get back to him. He gets out of sorts when I miss his feedings."

Cross gave her a squeeze. "I'll be along after I help Gaw go through some of this stuff." He smirked. "And besides, you're both wrong. I call him Kahless the Genie."

Gaw laughed. "Why?"

"Because that ancient spirit bottled up in our ship's hold is going to make all our wildest dreams a reality. Too bad Kahless won't live to see the results."

Eight

If the way Korgh could insult him in one breath and speak kindly the next surprised Riker, something else didn't: the speed with which life could go back to normal in the Ketorix compound after an attempted assassination.

To a degree, the latter was just how Klingons did things. Riker had seen it in action as an exchange officer: someone could die for shipboard "discipline" and everything would go on as usual. He also understood the larger reasons behind Korgh's swiftness in clearing away the evidence of yet another attempt on a member of his house, Kersh, someone he appeared to barely tolerate. Calling attention to the attempted assassination wouldn't shame the memories of the wrongdoers, because they had no honor left as far as other Klingons were concerned. And while making an example of Har'tok's fate might serve as a deterrent, it also might give other discommended Klingons ideas. It was better to keep the matter private in the name of security. The Klingons had taken aside the media representative who'd been interviewing Korgh earlier; Riker imagined the gag order had been given.

The rest went quickly. Workers had already disposed of the fallen cannon by the time Riker and Ssura had left the hangar, and a fresh unit had been hoisted into the assembly line to replace it. Others were working on the damage to the floor. Har'tok and his brother had been invisible in the eyes of the Klingons; soon, no hint would remain they had ever been in the compound.

After Riker sent Ssura to *Titan* to brief Vale, Korgh had finally shown some hospitality, inviting the admiral back to the house's industrial headquarters. Picard had visited the place days earlier, with Lieutenant T'Ryssa Chen, before the massacre at Gamaral. That was a topic, Riker found, that seemed to come up in every conversation with the lord of the house, no matter how ancillary.

"It was important that I attend my beloved grandson's ceremony today," Korgh said as he walked through the building with Riker. "Bredak's father, General Lorath, is out hunting down the assassins that escaped Captain Picard. Not once, but twice."

But who's counting? Riker wanted to say.

Korgh approached a large pair of heavy doors. "I know you are not here to honor my grandson—but to talk of the conference. Are you ready at last for us to hold it?"

"Yes, I have agreements to attend by all the parties involved."

Korgh looked at him skeptically. "Even the Kinshaya?"

"We had a sense they might attend at one point. Now we hear it's a religious holiday for them—"

"When is it not?"

"—but I'm hoping their ecumenical authorities will allow someone from the new civilian government to attend. Even someone representing a trade group."

Korgh gave the doors a mighty shove. Riker beheld the atrium of the family museum beyond—and the massive statue at its center. He tried not to react to it. Chen's report had warned him that the focal point of the atrium was an oversized statue of Commander Kruge slaying one of the griffin-like Kinshaya as it writhed in agony. He had little doubt why Korgh had chosen this point in his tour to finally bring up the conference.

"We should speak frankly, Riker," Korgh said, leading the way into the room.

"Please."

"It was your idea that this conference be set on H'atoria, a holding of my family. And I know why."

"I'm sure you do. It's located along the free-flight corridor we're proposing."

"That's not the only reason." Korgh looked up to the graven Kinshaya and smirked. "You chose H'atoria because you thought it was the only world where both Klingons and Kinshaya would attend a summit. And that is because in the Kinshaya mind—if such a thing exists—H'atoria is *their* planet."

Riker couldn't deny it. The Kinshaya and the Klingons had passed the planet back and forth, most recently in the wake of the Borg Invasion. "They may think that, sir—but the reality will be obvious to all. You've resettled the world. It is Klingon."

"Had they said they owned Qo'noS, would you be wanting to stage your event in the Great Hall?" Korgh laughed and shook his head. Then he looked past Riker and brightened with recognition. "Ah, cousin!"

Past the statue, Riker spied Kersh approaching from a long corridor, lined on one side with doors. Communicator in hand, she looked none too pleased by Korgh's form of address. "I am not your cousin, Korgh. You will call me *General*."

"And I am a lord—*your* lord. And there are so few now left in our family, General, that you should welcome reinforcements to the line, adopted or natural." He glanced at her communicator. "What kept you?"

She gestured behind her in frustration. "I had to find a secure area to contact Qo'noS about the attack. I tried to enter my grandfather's office here, but the door was locked."

"And it will remain so." Korgh stepped past her and pointed down the hall. An ancient Klingon woman stood before one of the doors with a cart; Riker presumed she was a cleaner. "Those offices were for the heads of the family while there was no single ruler of the house," Korgh said. "J'borr is dead, as are all the others; the *may'qochvan* is ended. Only I will have offices in this building. I—and my sons and grandchildren."

"This is something we should discuss," Kersh said, her tone acidic.

"We just did." Korgh averted his gaze to the ceiling of the atrium, lit by braziers. "But I will grant a boon in respect of your lost patriarch. Once the terrorist crisis is over, I will convert J'borr's space to a trophy room. Until I have more grandsons who need accommodations, of course."

Kersh fumed. Wasting no time, she got on with her report. "About your terrorists—"

Korgh's eyebrow went up. "They are not *my* terrorists."

"Yours, ours, the ones delaying your precious trophy room!" She growled in disgust. "The Defense Force told me there have been no further sightings of the Unsung and the Phantom Wing."

Riker nodded. That tracked with what Starfleet had reported.

"But," she continued, "there have been eleven different incidents involving discommendated Klingons since the Unsung broadcast their threat."

Eleven? The news stunned Riker. Chancellor Martok had been keeping lids on lots of things. "Are they all like what just happened in the hangar?"

"No. Four were acts of violence, vandalism, or sabotage in which Unsung sympathizers were implicated. The others are less clear." Kersh looked to Riker. "These are cases where citizens attacked discommendated Klingons, out of fear or a desire for revenge for Kahless's murder."

That's almost as bad, Riker thought. "This is getting out of hand."

"So glad you've noticed, Admiral," Korgh said. "Fires tend to spread." Riker watched as the old Klingon cast his eyes toward one of the tapestries on the wall. Like the others, it depicted Commander Kruge in some twenty-third-century battle, but it had been crafted to look ancient. He stepped toward it and contemplated silently.

Kersh glowered at Riker. "These imitators *are* a danger—as we've just seen—but we cannot get distracted. Destroy the Unsung, and we end the menace they inspire."

"That's the plan," Riker said. "Admiral Akaar has already submitted to the Defense Force a proposal to network Klingon and Starfleet ships together into a tachyon detection grid, similar to what we used during your civil war to thwart Romulan intervention."

A touch startled, Korgh looked over his shoulder. "I thought *Enterprise* could not sense the Phantom Wing vessels?"

"No, but between your engineers and ours—"

Kersh snorted. "This group has ranged from the Klach D'Kel Brakt to Gamaral. That's the width of the Empire. There aren't enough ships in the galaxy to screen that much space."

"The idea would be to select likely targets and then use local ships to interdict," Riker explained.

"Likely targets," Korgh repeated, still facing the tapestry. "Like your conference, perhaps?"

The admiral inhaled. "I wasn't going to suggest that."

"But obviously it could be a target," Kersh said. "Your diplomats and ours together." Her voice quickened. "It could be bait for a trap. The tachyon grid could be positioned there."

Riker's eyes widened. After working so hard to make the conference a reality, it felt wrong to treat it as a trap. "The other guests would not appreciate that amount of firepower in the sector when they can only bring a single vessel. The Kinshaya would surely never fly into a sea of Klingon and Federation ships. Security is important, but we can't let it scuttle the thing it's trying to protect."

"That is not the only problem," Korgh said, turning. "The terrorists could strike anywhere else along the frontier while our vessels are preoccupied at H'atoria. They could even strike here." He shook his head. "No, I won't allow it. Our worlds must remain protected. But you've given me an idea."

Riker watched as Korgh approached them. "The conference will go forward," he said, "and on H'atoria. I know of a site on the surface no enemies could breach; its reputation alone should keep the Unsung away. *Spirits' Forge.*"

The admiral wasn't sure what Korgh was referring to, but Kersh was. "I know those people," she said. "They will never agree."

"They answer to me," Korgh said. Before Riker could inquire, he went on. "As do you, General Kersh—in this matter. You will be the Empire's lead negotiator during the conference."

That flummoxed her. "Me?"

Riker's mouth opened. It took a few moments for him to find the words. "General Kersh is not part of your diplomatic corps."

"But she represents this house and has always defended its territory." Korgh crossed his arms. "You were in the room, Admiral, when Chancellor Martok gave me the sole right to choose the negotiator representing the Empire."

Kersh sputtered. "But I don't even *want* Riker's damn corridor!"

"Lord Korgh . . ." Riker started. Kersh was worse than the worst-case choice he'd envisioned. Korgh was setting the conference up to fail—just as he'd feared. "I'm not sure—"

Korgh cut him off. "The decision is mine. These are our worlds you're looking to send traffic past, Riker. Kersh has a stake. As general she will be able to coordinate offworld security."

Kersh formed her words slowly. "I . . . would have to have orbital surveillance assets in place. If we cannot station ships, then satellites." She glanced away. "We could use Starfleet's help in that."

"Our great alliance at work." Korgh stood between the two and slapped one hand on Riker's shoulder and the other hand on Kersh's. "I'll leave you two to the details. I'll take care of Spirits' Forge." Korgh withdrew his hands, pivoted on one heel, and walked off with the vigor of someone half his age.

Kersh watched him leave before looking back at Riker. Her right upper lip went up in a look of disdain.

Joy, Riker thought. *This keeps getting better and better.*

Nine

Korgh peeked through the double doors back into the atrium in time to see Riker and Kersh transporting out. Once they were gone, he opened the doors and laughed long and hard, his guffaws echoing throughout the chamber.

It had been a day of surprises, but it had worked out for the best. The only surviving adult heir of Commander Kruge's cousins, Kersh had threatened to become a thorn in his side. As she was a high-ranking officer with the Defense Force, he could not count on her loyalty to the family first—especially to a branch whose legitimacy she'd challenged in the Great Hall before Martok and the entire Council. Drafting her into the negotiations ensured she wouldn't have time to cause trouble.

Someone else had nearly eliminated her threat altogether, without Korgh lifting a finger. While the old Klingon delighted in the attack by the nobody Har'tok and his nobody brother, he had not put them up to it. It was happenstance—although perhaps not entirely coincidental.

For years, as *gin'tak*, he had quietly allowed discommendated workers employment in the various Kruge family factories. It was a dishonorable practice, but a rule obeyed by no one was no rule. Critically, it had given him a source of discommendated Klingons with technical skills who could become émigrés to Thane. He never dealt with them directly; Odrok, or one of her minions, would arrange passage on a multileg journey terminating with a transporter ride down to the surface of the planet of exiles. Most invitees went, vanishing in the night, missed by no one. Those who refused to go were soon silenced, killed in industrial "accidents" or their sleep. The practice had kept Thane's talent and gene pool fresh while Korgh waited to unleash the Unsung on the Empire.

Har'tok and his brother had gone to work for his factory independently after somehow hearing of the secret passage. The lord hadn't known they were discommendated; his house's factories employed hundreds of thousands, and he did not keep track of everyone. They had never been approached to emigrate. But while Korgh hadn't put the disruptors in their hands, it was his policy that put them into position—and it was the message his Unsung puppets sent that declared it open season.

Korgh thought the occurrence interesting, underscoring the fire he had lit under the current order. But he loathed random elements. While another strike against the House of Kruge might otherwise fit into his narrative, he didn't want attention drawn to the factory's lax personnel policy. That policy was no more: there was no Thane colony any longer, and Korgh had no need to restock the exiles. He had just summarily ordered all discommendated workers ousted from all factories house-wide.

It would anger them, surely, and their coworkers might figure out there had been dishonored curs in their midst. The result would be more unhappiness and paranoia, and that served him. Lynch mobs were fine as long as they did their business off his property.

His property. It felt good to think it. He had been *gin'tak* for the House of Kruge for so long, kowtowing to nobles whose existence offended him. The atrium he had spent so much time in, with its treasures, was now all his. He walked down the long hallway, seeing the names of the fallen nobles beside their office doors. He would have to have those plates removed once things quieted down. But there was still another act to come, and, hearing movement behind the door to the office belonging to Kersh's late grandfather, J'borr, he determined to get to it. Using his master key, he opened it.

A cleaning cart sat parked inside the door. Beyond, dressed in the rags of a slave laborer, the cart's owner sat at a grand desk surrounded by panels depicting various areas of the Beta Quadrant. She was old—a hundred thirty—yet her eyes were wide and intelligent, and her wrinkled hands worked actively across the interface before her. She was not surprised to see him. "My lord."

"Odrok."

Korgh sealed the door behind him. He had transformed J'borr's office years ago into a secret lair where he and Odrok, his engineering and intelligence expert, could work on their plots without being disturbed. It was as safe a place as any. Incredibly old, J'borr had never set foot in the office that belonged to him—and until Kersh's attempt earlier, no one in his line had even asked about it. No one would have thought anything of the *gin'tak* entering, nor a laborer.

He stepped before one of the star maps and studied it. Decades earlier—after having gone through the pain of losing the Phantom Wing squadron on Gamaral—Korgh had ordered Odrok and her engineers to make modifications to the stealth positioning systems aboard the birds-of-prey. Designed to allow the vessels to inform one another of their positions while cloaked, the systems had been modified so that Odrok could track the Phantom Wing's location from light-years away.

The signals involved were only detectable by those who knew where to look. He did, of course; Korgh vowed he would never lose the squadron again. He knew the technical support vessel of his hireling con artist, Buxtus Cross, was also with them. The support ship had to follow the Phantom Wing in order to project the illusion that Cross was the reborn Commander Kruge. Korgh had no way of tracking the support ship, but it generally stayed close to the squadron; otherwise, Cross would just appear as his simpering Betazoid self. Only "Kruge" could command the Unsung.

Korgh idly studied the star map. He pointed to a blinking location on the screen. "This place—where are they?"

"The Phantom Wing is in the Azure Nebula," Odrok said. "They have been destroying a series of hangouts belonging to Orion pirates."

"I did not approve this." Cross had specific orders: his Kruge character was only to direct them against targets Korgh named. This was new.

"The Unsung are restive. Cross cannot keep them aboard their ships so long without action."

"Birds-of-prey have training rooms!"

Odrok frowned. "They are Klingons who have lived their whole lives outdoors, my lord, free to hunt. Our ally cannot control them indefinitely."

I suppose not. It was good that the charade was not far from its scheduled end. "I imagine Cross heard of these pirate nests from that Orion wench of his. Did they leave survivors?"

"Certainly not."

"Fine. His wait is soon to be done." The Azure Nebula was a good hiding place for them, Korgh thought; comfortably close to his next target. "I have scheduled the H'atorian Conference—and I already have a plan for the Unsung in mind." Quickly, he told her his intentions.

Odrok nodded. "Spirits' Forge. I would not have thought of that." She looked on Korgh with admiration. "I will signal Cross."

The lord turned toward the door. Odrok stood up. He looked back. "Something else?"

Her expression was plaintive. "You mentioned waiting," Odrok said. "I was going to ask about . . . about *me*."

"What now?"

She gestured to her shabby robe, the uniform of a laborer. "Must I continue to dress like this to enter? The House of Kruge is yours. This building is yours—and vast, and empty. No one would know if I lived openly here."

This again? Odrok used to only complain about her lot in life when she was drunk. Yet she seemed sober now. "We cannot compromise the work you have been doing for me."

"I have assumed many new identities before. No one would connect me with my past work for you—and I could continue my monitoring of the Unsung, just as I am doing now. I could pose as an advisor." She looked at the floor. "Or something else."

Korgh laughed. "A kept woman, then."

She looked directly at him. "I was thinking more of your wife."

Korgh stopped laughing, and his eyes narrowed. "My wife is dead."

"So you are free to take another."

Korgh shuddered. He had never considered Odrok in that fashion. When they met she was half again as old as he was—thirty to his twenty—and while a hundred years had brought that ratio down to nearly nothing, he still saw her as something other than an equal.

She stepped out from behind the desk and walked to his side. Korgh looked about. "I do not understand this prattle, Odrok. Were you drinking? Where is the bottle?"

"There is none. I told you back on Qo'noS I wanted to come out of the shadows. I have been your secret agent too long."

"But a wife? You do not care for me, nor I you. Not in that way."

She touched his arm. "I have been with you longer than anyone has—*including* your wife."

"*Stop!*" He did not strike her, but he came close—staying his hand before it reached her face. "You will not speak of Kaas again."

"She was a means to an end, Korgh, like everything else in your life. *Like I am.*" She paused. "You are near victory," Odrok said, her chin high. "I have helped you these hundred years. I have acted without question. I have even gone to prison obtaining things you needed. I deserve more."

She was key to his projects' success; Korgh had to placate her without accommodating her absurd demand. He crossed his arms and spoke more calmly. "You merely grow impatient, Odrok. I know impatience. I have waited for my revenge a hundred years. I have my house—but I have not yet won for Kruge what he always desired: supremacy for the Empire. We cannot have that while we are shackled to the Federation." This time, he took her arm. "We must do this, my most loyal ally—for Kruge."

She closed her eyes and nodded. "For Kruge."

He opened the door and stepped forward. Standing in the aperture, he turned and looked on her, trying to put on his kindest face. "We will . . . talk again, Odrok. Once this project is complete, I will have more time to think on personal matters." He gestured behind him. "You will find bloodwine in the cupboard just beyond the atrium."

Eyes back on the floor, Odrok said nothing as he departed.

Ten

Kahless wept.

It was not a very Klingon thing to do, especially given his species' lack of tear ducts. Yet legend had it that Kahless the Unforgettable had filled an ocean with his tears upon the death of his father—and while Kahless the clone had no father, he had a sea of troubles of his own.

So he sat on his hands and knees and bemoaned his fate—not wailing, as one in an opera, but pounding at the deck in frustration and anger. He could not free himself. He could not fight. He could not kill himself. What else was left?

He had tried it all before, immediately after being imprisoned here on *Chu'charq*, one of the Unsung's birds-of-prey. He was not in a cell, but a storeroom on deck one, protected by a single force field. The pretend-Klingons who held him, Cross and Shift, could not place guards over him; they were hamstrung by their own treacheries. The Unsung had participated in his alleged execution. For Kahless to be seen alive and in their midst would reveal to all that the cultists' master was neither Kruge nor Klingon.

In those early hours, once the sedative they'd given him had worn off, he'd rifled through the storeroom looking for any possible weapon against his captors, any means of escape. But he'd been noticed—and sedated again. That time, when the emperor awoke, he found a leather manacle firmly secured around his leg. If Kahless left the room, Cross had informed him, the embedded sensor would trigger an injection causing instant and prolonged paralysis. Cross had a handheld control unit he could use to do the same, were he provoked; Kahless could feel the injector pressed against his skin. There was no chain, but he was still leashed.

They had stopped sedating him—and that is when the real test began. No, not the incessant conversations the little Betazoid fraud kept trying to engage him in. It was something worse, something that had long since become a secret shame to him: Kahless had not had a drop of blood-wine since just before the massacre at Gamaral. And his thirst was eating him alive.

His hosts aboard *Enterprise* had given him all the drink that he wanted, as their special guest—and even his bunker lounge on Gamaral had been fully stocked. Then his kidnapping changed everything. He had only taken water during his brief servitude on Thane, but he had been too tired then to even think.

Once captive aboard *Chu'charq*, with nowhere to go and nothing to do, he had remembered his needs. He hated to ask his jailers for anything, but he finally swallowed his pride and asked for ale. Even that had proven futile. The cultists running the vessel had no truck with liquor, and none was available. Kahless figured it would be hard for Cross to lead such a bunch as "Kruge" and be seen replicating bloodwine.

So he had been stone sober for the longest amount of time he could remember—and it had sorely tested him. For days in his makeshift cell he had shaken and slept, slept and shaken. The taste of water sent him retching into the portable sanitary unit provided for his relief. One night he had awakened with a pain in his gut and a terror of closing his eyes again, should the heroes of centuries past return from Sto-Vo-Kor to judge a wretch who presumed to succeed a legend.

Was it a fever? Withdrawal? Exhaustion? He could not know which, and it did not matter. The Unsung had nearly broken him on Thane, forcing him to do slave labor in pits filled with excrement. Another week there would have meant his death. What he was experiencing now was partially a consequence of that horrific experience.

And yet, somehow, Kahless missed the vile pit. The Unsung, in their zeal to bring him low, had done him a favor. It was miserable work, but it was work—honest labor of the sort that the lowliest Klingons of the poorest worlds of the Empire did with honor. It was the first time he had ever done anything like that. He had been born in middle age, with memories of another man's life—and yet he had been allowed to want for nothing. He had been created to be a legend, only to be demoted to become a mere figurehead emperor. And then he'd been allowed to retire early, to go off to a quiet world and paint pictures by a stream.

The true Kahless was unforgettable. Kahless, clone of Kahless, was not. A side character in history who in the future might be recalled by someone with a mind for trivia. Or perhaps by a scholar, who would say he had served as living evidence of the lengths to which Klingons in his time would go to manufacture honor.

He was supposed to serve as an example, leading his people to a better life. But even a child understood that one had to see the path to be able to lead. And he had never been a child.

The door beyond the force field opened. Kahless rose from the deck. It was the Orion woman, carrying a tray with food and water. She paused only long enough to pick up the remote control for his manacle. Then she deactivated the force field and placed his food on the deck just inside.

Kahless looked at it. They had done this dance several times; there was no sense rushing her, not with that controller in her hand. Instead, he simply stared at the food while she reactivated the force field again.

"Eat," Shift said.

Kahless eyed the plate. It was that odd wriggly food the Unsung ate on their world. Not horrible, but not Klingon. "You eat it."

"I don't eat that stuff. Believe me, if *Blackstone* hadn't catered our meals on Thane, we'd have starved."

He believed that. Kahless couldn't imagine the squeamish Cross touching a single piece of *gagh*. "Where is the little commander today?"

"Cross?" Shift sat down in the hallway outside the force field, her back against the wall. "He is surveying the battlefield."

"Battlefield." Kahless snorted as he moved over to the tray. "Cross is a ludicrous being, unable to grip a *d'k tahg* without wetting himself." He picked up the metal plate, grasped a handful of food, and began to eat. He studied her. She seemed lost in thought. "So," he said between bites, "the exiles killed Orions this time?"

"Yes."

He smiled. "Such a shame. Did they slay any of *your* relations out there? Tell me they did."

"Okay, I will." She looked directly at him. "They killed my father."

Kahless sat up. "What?"

"Fortar, lord of the camp." She looked at the back of her hand. "He was my father. He was also the one who sold me into slavery as a girl." She paused. "I had Cross direct the Unsung here."

Kahless's eyes bulged. He dropped the plate with a clank, scattering food. "You could do this—to your father?"

"As easily as he ruined my life." She glared at him. "I told you what he did. I was 'too pretty,' he said. Not to sell me would have been wrong."

Wrong? Kahless didn't understand the Orions at all. "To

sell a child? Such a person would be beyond reproach." He was angry for her—but also at her. The whole thing made no sense to him. "*Your father!*"

"I have not considered him my father since then." She braided her dark hair idly. "The act was easily done. A loose strand of my life, which I was finally able to cut off."

"Does your man know who his thralls killed in your name?"

"Cross? No. He believes Fortar was one of my former owners—which was true enough. I may tell him the rest. I may not." She stood and straightened her frock. "He prefers me to remain light and joyous. This would run counter to that."

"No doubt." Kahless's eyes narrowed.

She looked at him, smiled primly, and found a padd to work on.

And for you it is just another day. Kahless looked down into his cup, which held water, and then back at her, going on with her business. "I think," he said slowly, "that Cross does not know what he has in you."

"No one ever does. Now eat. I'm not going back down into that galley today. It stinks."

Eleven

"**B**ux, I'm glad you brought up Kahless," Gaw said as he studied the digital files in Fortar's warehouse office. His favorite golden pince-nez on his nose, he glanced over at Cross. "I didn't want to call you on it in front of your sweetie—"

"But you never . . . tell us . . . anything!" Cross said, lowering his head and baring all his teeth in a perfect impression of Gaw.

Gaw gave a throaty sigh. Cross, lounging in the dead Orion's chair with his feet propped on the desk, shoved his hand back inside his bag of cheesy popcorn and returned to munching. Since impersonating Kruge, Cross had been living off food transported from *Blackstone*; he'd been excited to discover the Orion's warehouse included crates full of rare delicacies from faraway worlds. He'd waited impatiently to eat until the dead body had been transported away.

"I'm serious this time," Gaw said, manipulating the pirates' inventory interface. "We were joking about Kahless earlier, but you really sprang this idea of keeping him alive on us. You can't keep doing this, pal."

"I saw a chance, Gaw. We had to move fast."

Very fast. While Cross was still on Thane, Korgh had ordered Kahless's death. As Kruge, Cross was to have ordered the Unsung to execute the emperor on a vid feed broadcast to the whole Empire; it would give Korgh an incident he could profit from politically.

On an impulse, Cross had made a switch. A truthcrafter facsimile of Kahless had been slain, fooling even the Unsung executioners who killed him. They'd actually killed Potok, the overthrown leader of their colony, instead.

Gaw and his crew knew, of course, but no one had told Korgh back on Qo'noS. Since the "execution," Cross had kept Kahless imprisoned in a small hold away from everyone else on *Chu'charq*. "He's not trying to escape anymore, if you're wondering. The anklet idea worked like a charm. He swears at it a lot."

"I can imagine." Gaw stopped working at the interface and turned toward the Betazoid. "Look, I get that you're planning on doing something with him after this Kruge scheme is over—but we already modeled his body holographically back when we faked his assassination. His "character" is in our systems. Why do you still need him alive?"

"Because I don't *have* him yet." Cross closed his eyes and began reciting a line in Klingon. The phrase was about as flowery as the gruff language got.

Gaw growled in frustration. "Again with the Klingon. What the hell was that?"

"The Fifth Precept. 'We do not fight merely to spill blood, but to enrich the spirit.'" Cross took his hand out of the bag and put his thumb and forefinger together millimeters apart. "You see, I've just about got the pronunciation right. But when the clone says things like that, he hits different words than I do. I always stress the word *enrich*."

"That makes two of us."

"And did you see me inhale deeply when I hit the pause? The clone does that when he takes a breath before following an infinitive with another infinitive."

"You don't say."

Cross wiped his face. "But he *doesn't* do it if the subject of the sentence is someone who offends him. Instead, his nose twitches."

Gaw stared blankly at him. "Fascinating."

"You bet it is—and I can't get that kind of detail from

watching vids. I can't just mimic his sayings; I've got to get the personal interaction part down. So I've been talking to him every day. He tries to ignore me, but I can usually provoke him into responding." Cross crumpled up the bag. "He also chants and sings the saddest songs you've *ever* heard when he thinks we're not watching."

"So all this is why you're keeping him locked up on *Chu'charq* and not in *Blackstone*'s imaging cell?"

"Precisely. I need him where I'm at." Cross gesticulated to the air, growing more excited as he spoke. "Gaw, if I want to replace Kahless, I'll be following another act. Nobody knows what a hundred-forty-year-old Commander Kruge would look or sound like. But the clone's been out there speechifying in front of big crowds. Not much in recent years, but the Klingon media's kept him present. The Klingons all have an idea of what Kahless should look and sound like."

Finally comprehending, Gaw nodded. "Before long you'll know what he breathes like, eats like—and how often he scratches his backside."

"And which hand he uses." Cross tossed the crumpled bag away and put his feet on the floor. He hunched forward in the chair, put his elbows on the desk, and excitedly laid out his plan. "So for our Unsung job, our secret patron is going to pay through the nose, right? We can use that to refit *Blackstone*—"

"I like it so far."

"—and several other craft, and we can also build some stationary truthcrafting equipment. With all that, I can raise the *real* Kahless from the dead, just like the clone was supposed to be—only we'll do it with all the light and fire of Sto-Vo-Kor, so nobody can doubt it."

Cross explained that when the Clerics of Boreth staged Kahless's return using the clone, they had chosen not to stage his big return in a public setting. "Instead, they just had him appear to Worf. But when you're running a con built on mass belief, Gaw, big events matter. You want the audience to feel connected to the story you're spinning from the start. That's why when I appeared as Kruge to the exiles, I didn't show myself to just one person. We arrived on a bird-of-prey to make sure a lot of people were watching. But according to the official story, nobody even recorded the instant of the clone Kahless's appearance."

Gaw thought for a moment. "Maybe they were afraid someone would see through their effects work. It's not their specialty, for sure."

"But it definitely is ours. So we're going to pick a time and place where everyone important will be watching. Maybe in the Great Hall, in front of the High Council. I'll make a big entrance—as *the* Kahless." Cross gestured toward the port, beyond which *Chu'charq* and *Rodak* were just visible, parked decloaked on the far edge of the camp. "We've already practiced our Klingon legends on a bunch of lunatics. For the next show, we open wide. This one's for *all* the Klingons."

"And then their whole empire is ours," Gaw said. He smiled, in spite of his earlier skepticism. "You're really too much, you know that? That sounds amazing. The sort of thing Jilaan talked about our people doing in the old days."

"We are the makers of miracles, my friend. And the Klingons will fight not merely for blood—"

"But to enrich *us*, beyond the dreams of avarice." Gaw smirked. "There's your first new precept." He removed his pince-nez and paused. "But wait. Didn't you say earlier you were going to do away with Kahless when you were done?"

"Of course. I don't need an understudy."

"Right. So when?"

"Soon. Once the Unsung operation's done." Cross bounded

up from the chair. "Speaking of that, I'd better get back into character and back to the loonies aboard *Chu'charq* before they start howling and rending their garments in my absence. I'm expecting our special friend to send us our next mission at any time."

Gaw nodded. Then he snapped his fingers. "Wait. I just saw something on Fortar's manifest for this place. I think I can send you back with a little surprise—something that'll make Kahless's *real* final hours a little better."

"Hey, Kahless, ol' buddy."

Seated at the foot of a stack of boxes in the small port hold on *Chu'charq*'s deck one, Kahless glanced once at Cross and looked away. "I do not answer to costumed clowns."

"Oh." Cross snapped his fingers and dispelled his Old Kruge incarnation. He'd needed to be in character to return to the ship, but he often forgot to signal the truthcrafters aboard *Blackstone* to deactivate the projection when he was in private. "How's this?"

"I do not answer to clowns outside of costume either."

"You'll speak to me when you see what I've brought you." Cross looked back. Shift was in the hallway, dressed as N'Keera and hefting a metal crate with both hands. Remembering, Cross sought for and found the controller for Kahless's anklet. "I don't think you will want to escape anyway when we drop the force field—not when you see what this is."

Kahless simply sat and watched as Cross deactivated the field and Shift brought in the crate. Setting the big box down, she stepped back and the force field reactivated. "Thanks, babe. I couldn't have one of the Unsung bring it up the ladder. They might see him."

"No worries." Shift snapped her fingers and appeared as herself once more.

"Go ahead, Kahless. Open it."

The emperor sat motionless for several seconds. Curiosity outweighing defiance, Kahless finally moved over and unlatched the case. Cross watched the clone's face with expectation as the lid creaked open.

Kahless stared into it. "Bottles."

"Romulan ale. Aged to perfection," Cross said as Kahless lifted out a liquid-filled container. "We found it out in the camp warehouse—whole crates of it. I figured you might like a few bottles."

"Felt like more than a few." Shift looked at him. "You got the Unsung to carry this onto the ship for you?"

Cross grinned. "I told them it held ancient Klingon scrolls that I'd found in the blasphemous Orions' sanctum." He watched as Kahless, seemingly hypnotized, drew forth one bottle after another and placed them on the deck beside him. "I know it's not your bloodwine—but it should do in a pinch."

Kahless's eyes were fixed on the bottles. "This . . . is because I refuse to talk to you—to help you in your damn fool plot to replace me."

"Questioning my motives? I'm hurt." Cross shrugged in innocence. "Just figured you'd like something besides water with that stuff the Unsung call food."

It was true, of course: chats with Kahless were what he needed, and anything to loosen the Klingon's tongue would help.

Especially now. "Our special friend's assistant sent the message while you were out," Shift said, gesturing to the padd in her hand. "We're go for the last phase."

Cross smiled at her and then at Kahless, who continued to sit spellbound. "You hear that, Emperor? You won't be stuck here much longer. So drink up."

Twelve

"**A**s you were," Jean-Luc Picard said as the door sealed shut behind him. "I should hope there is never a need for an *Enterprise*-F. But if there is one, they should put a conference table in stellar cartography. We seem to spend an inordinate amount of time here."

Geordi La Forge looked back at the captain from the railing and smiled weakly. "I'm thinking of having cots brought in."

Picard understood why. Following his receipt of a message from Qo'noS, he had thought to call three of his senior staffers to his ready room. When a quick check with the ship's computer told him everyone he wanted to see was in stellar cartography, Picard had simply headed there himself. Since the *Enterprise* had departed the Briar Patch, the holographic planetarium had become a regular haunt for Worf, La Forge, and the security chief, Lieutenant Commander Aneta Šmrhová. If they weren't due on the bridge or in other departments, the three were nowhere else.

They were hunting. Hunting the Unsung, and the dozen birds-of-prey that had so far eluded both Starfleet and the Klingon Defense Force. Of course, the regular interfaces to *Enterprise*'s computer systems provided every fact that needed retrieval and made all kinds of analyses possible. When it came to an interstellar search mission, however, there was something about standing amid holographic representations of the surrounding stars that helped the conscious mind. Many of the species aboard *Enterprise* were spatial beings; sometimes seeing elements in exact perspective provided insights unavailable from a flat panel.

Picard could see the three had been running another study looking at candidate signals, possibly emanating from a companion vessel that La Forge suspected was either escorting or trailing the twelve Phantom Wing warships. Since discovering the existence of the so-called Object Thirteen, it had gripped La Forge's attention for days.

But finding it again had been difficult. "Any luck?" Picard asked.

"Computer, freeze analysis," La Forge said. "It's slow work—and harder than it has to be."

"How so?"

"Klingon space teems with vessels traveling back and forth under cloak, using devices manufactured in many different periods. Under our agreements with the Klingons, we never look for them." The engineer gestured toward the scatterplot of glowing points hanging in the space above their heads. "But as soon as our bogey left the nebula and started into Klingon space, our problem stopped being the size of the haystack. It's all the other needles."

"I have been consulting with the Defense Force," Worf said, "trying to get a list of what they have where." He took a deep breath and shook his head. "They have not always been helpful."

That surprised Picard. The broadcast execution of Kahless by the Unsung had led Chancellor Martok to pledge the full assets of his Empire to the search—and he had assured Starfleet that any of its vessels searching would have full cooperation. "Is it line officer paranoia—a reluctance to reveal where all their ships are, even to a friend?"

"It's that, but more." Šmrhová looked up from the padd she was studying. "I hate to say it, Captain, but it's *us*."

"They blame the *Enterprise* for what happened on Gamaral and Thane," Picard said.

"It is not a legitimate complaint," Worf said, frustrated. "No one could have done otherwise in this situation. And we could do more now, with their aid."

Picard faced La Forge. "Compile a list of candidate signals that remain unexplained. I will send them directly to Martok. We will allow the Empire to distinguish between what it is legitimate traffic and what is not."

"It would leave us with a smaller set to study," La Forge said, weariness evident in his voice. "I appreciate it."

"Captain, is there news from Ketorix?" Šmrhová asked.

"Chancellor Martok shared his investigators' report," Picard said. "The attempt on the lives of Admiral Riker and General Kersh appears to have been inspired by the Unsung, but shares no direct connection. Martok said he understands why Admiral Riker wanted Starfleet informed, but he wants the incident kept quiet."

"He would," Worf said. "He must keep order."

Picard studied his officers. They were undefeated, but they were definitely beat. La Forge and Šmrhová, having been foiled at Gamaral by the Unsung both on the surface and in space, had been focused on the crisis almost exclusively in the days since. And Worf, having lived as the Unsung's hostage, had been in perpetual motion, barely keeping his rage in check. How long, Picard wondered, could they keep driving themselves like this?

He took a breath, no longer able to delay getting to the main reason for his visit. "I am glad to find you three here. Geordi told me about the plan you were working on."

"Yes, Captain." Worf nodded toward the engineer. "It is connected to the attack the Unsung made on the *Enterprise* while you and I were on the surface of Gamaral."

Surrounded there by the cloaked birds-of-prey of the

Phantom Wing, the *Enterprise* had taken fire from the ships. The ability to attack while cloaked was not the only modification made to the vessels: using technology stolen from the Hunters of the Gamma Quadrant, the Unsung had opened tiny rifts in the *Enterprise*'s shields long enough to beam boarding parties in. After they had disabled several of the ship's transporters, they beamed out in the same manner.

While beaming through shields was *nearly* impossible, it was not beyond some advanced life-forms, and there had been desperate occasions where ways had been found. Those, however, usually required inside information about the shield harmonics of the other vessel. Miles O'Brien had exploited such knowledge in beaming from the *Enterprise*-D to the shielded *Phoenix* years earlier. The Phantom Wing's demonstrated ability was so tactically disruptive that La Forge had put half his engineers on finding a counter.

La Forge had proposed to do something similar. "Your plan as I understand it," Picard said, "involves our beaming someone—or *something*—aboard a Phantom Wing vessel, correct?"

"Presuming we could find one." La Forge sighed

"Transporting onto a cloaked vessel." Picard goggled. "Simply amazing."

"We wouldn't be rewriting the book on starship combat. We suspect this tactic will *only* work on the Phantom Wing vessels."

"Explain."

La Forge launched into a dissertation on how the subspace emitters aboard *B'rel*-class ships projected their signals with no loss, even when the vessels were cloaked. "The emitters create tiny islands of stability in the spatial distortion of the cloaking field, just long enough for a confinement beam to get out. But in order to use the brute-force method the Unsung stole from the Hunters, they would have to keep the emitters in a state of constant charge—which means there's always a rotating series of pinpricks in the cloak, so to speak, making it possible for a transport beam to travel out."

"Or come back in," Picard said. "Can we use this method to discover where an Unsung vessel is?"

"No. The way they've got their cloaking devices set up, the only way to sense the existence of the field is to prod it up close with a transporter beam—using a dynamic fractal equation to search for the holes in the field. As soon as we got a transporter lock, we could beam in."

The captain blanched. "How would you know where you were going, without seeing the bird-of-prey?"

Šmrhová spoke up. "Knowing the shape of the cloaking field even momentarily, Captain, gives us the location of the field's emitter—and we already have the basic schematics for the Phantom Wing vessels, which Lord Korgh provided Chancellor Martok. From that, we would direct our transporters to target a location where our team would both activate a tracking device and disable the cloak."

"And the transporter's safeguards would guarantee you would materialize in a safe location," Picard said. "Have you chosen the target zone?"

"We have," Worf said. "The catwalk over deuterium fuel storage is an isolated space—with easy access to the plasma conduits that supply the cloaking device, far forward. Both the catwalk and the room below are likely to be unattended. I do not expect any trouble."

Picard stared at him. "Number One, you intend to go?"

"Yes, sir."

Picard looked to his security chief and read her expression. "You too, Lieutenant?"

"Yes, Captain."

La Forge raised his hands. "I'm staying aboard. Someone has to make sure this works."

Picard shook his head, amused at his team's innovation and daring. Each of the three had a reason to seek redemption following the events on Gamaral and Thane—and this mission to bell an invisible cat was in line with what he expected from his crew. "As long as you're certain it's safe, I have no objection. Just—"

"Bridge to Captain Picard," called Lieutenant Konya. *"Message for you, sir, from Admiral Riker."*

The captain knew if Will couldn't wait until they could hold a subspace conversation, things were going from bad to worse. "Go ahead."

"'Lord Korgh has given his consent for the H'atorian Conference to be held in a site known as Spirits' Forge,'" Konya said. *"The admiral said that name would mean something to Commander Worf."*

"Spirits' Forge," Worf said solemnly. "It means something to all Klingons. It means Korgh is sticking his finger in the eyes of the Unsung."

Thirteen

"*The lord of the house!*"

Korgh descended the stone staircase from the transport platform and squinted at the route ahead. It was a walk through fire, or so it seemed.

An elongated land bridge connected two promontories to form a dumbbell-shaped island. Every few meters along its black shores, rivulets of lava meandered to a churning sea. Now and again the resulting clouds of steam and gas parted long enough for Korgh to see more of the paved walkway stretching ahead, leading half a kellicam toward the fortress on the northern knob.

There was no chance Korgh would lose his way. Klingons in battle dress stood every so often along the length of the causeway, posted in pairs, with one at either side. Each held a *bat'leth*, the weapon of legend, after the first one forged in a river of lava by a single hair from the immortal Kahless. As Korgh approached the two sentries nearest him, he could only see their eyes, watchful and serious. The nose and mouth of each was covered.

The colossal warrior who had spoken stood before the small guardhouse at the foot of the stairs. Identically garbed, he issued a salute.

Korgh returned it. "*Qapla'*, Ernor, Head of the Watch. I have come to visit, as I said I would."

"It is good to see you, Galdor—or should I say, Lord Korgh." Ernor offered a folded cloth. "The fumes are bad today. You may want to cover your face on the path."

"I fear nothing. But if you insist." Korgh took the gauzy material the sentry offered and wrapped it around his head, covering his nose and mouth. The gases created by the roiling cracks surrounding the one-time isthmus had only been a nuisance in the old days, but the planet had been angered. Now as they walked the sweltering path, a heavy, noxious cloud always hung at their feet.

When Korgh had first visited Spirits' Forge, early in his tenure as *gin'tak* for the House of Kruge, everything about H'atoria had been different. Oceans covered most of the planet, with small, lushly forested continents providing a home to both the Klingon colonists and the amphibious native subject population, the Selseress. There were few resources on H'atoria worth exploiting; its principle value was its location, near several transit routes along the frontier. It thus attracted Klingons who found a certain sort of duty appealing: those who would stand sentinel, at the tip of the spear.

When the Romulans and the Kinshaya had variously attempted to test the Klingon Empire in those days, they had found the guardians of H'atoria maddeningly tough to defeat. One location served as a particular symbol of dogged Klingon defiance: an ancient walled forge on a northern peninsula nearly surrounded by volcanic rifts. Warriors had used the facility as a final redoubt—and from it, had successfully pushed their enemies back. Since then, it had served as a fortress. Over time, the title "Sentry of Spirits' Forge" took on a certain prestige, symbolizing the willingness of a Klingon to trade fame and glory for the anonymous austere honor of defending the Empire.

The legend of the Sentries had grown when, as a group, the defenders stood their ground against the Borg Invasion. The planet had been wracked by the Borg's bombardment; whole landforms plunged beneath the waves, isolating the ground that held Spirits' Forge and creating a new island from the peninsula. Every Klingon on the surface perished, while undersea only a few of the native Selseress survived.

Yet the redoubt, amazingly, still stood. Unoccupied when the Kinshaya briefly invaded H'atoria three months later, the fortress was the first place Klingon forces took back. A powerful midair force field had been added to protect the main structure, while a retinue of Sentries stood, ever watchful, along the peninsular path to the smaller promontory with its shuttlepad and beam-in zone.

The haze clearing as they walked, Korgh saw that the fortress looked as he remembered; dark wafts rose from its stone chimney. The pavement below was in worse shape. "More cracks have developed."

"H'atoria tries to rid itself of us, but we remain," Ernor said. "Between the Borg's handiwork and H'atoria itself, several sections have been undermined."

"I will see that it is reinforced. That is in my power now. You have my word."

"I need no more than that." Ernor nodded. "News of your elevation reached us even here."

"Did my true identity surprise you?"

"No. None of the nobles you served ever visited us. But you came, several times."

"It was my duty."

"Bah. You cared what happened to the holdings of the house—supporting us when they refused to commit to repairs here. It was clear even then you deserved to have the title." Ernor shook his head. "Still, it is bad business, what happened to the others—and to our great emperor Kahless. Has anyone found the scum who killed him?"

"The so-called Unsung? No. But many are looking, including my son." Korgh had told the truth: his firstborn, General Lorath, was leading the search, even though he had no idea that his father knew exactly where the assassins were.

"I hope the assassins come here. Had we been present at Gamaral, we would have shown the Federation how to protect guests."

Korgh regarded the warriors lining the way as he walked. "I'm glad to hear you say that, Ernor. You know of the H'atorian Conference?"

The giant nodded. "Everyone wants the freedom to fly through this system. There's some sort of agreement being talked about."

"Yes. What do you think of that?"

Ernor straightened. "I serve, my lord. It is not my place—"

"Nonsense. You must have an opinion."

The guardian looked down at him keenly. "The treaty would make it easier to get to some of our worlds. But it puts many foreign ships in our space—and H'atoria's never seen the visitor that wasn't bringing a blade or a bomb."

"And so?"

"Bring them on." Ernor pounded the tip of his *bat'leth* on the stone surface. "It will give my Sentries something to do. They don't like it when we go a year without being invaded."

Korgh laughed. "You're about to get visitors sooner than you think. Because I intend to hold the conference right here, in the Spirits' Forge." He pointed to the fortification.

"You've been inside, my lord. We're not set up to entertain."

"Your mess hall will do. The key is protecting the guests—and projecting confidence in our own defense. I can think of nobody better suited to do that than the Sentries of Spirits' Forge."

Korgh explained that the island offered a reasonably small zone to be secured. The shield was already present, and the shoreline's state of volcanic upheaval made an amphibious assault unlikely. Ships in orbit could screen the rest. Transport inhibitors would be positioned along the narrow causeway to the landing area.

"It's our honor to serve," Ernor said. "Doing it here sends the right message. It taunts the Unsung. We represent everything the dishonorable *targs* despise. You show them we do not fear them."

"Precisely."

Ernor chuckled. "Some of your more feeble guests may expire on the walk to the fortress—or die in fright from our food."

"These are diplomats. They'll say they want to experience life here just as we do, but secretly bring along their own supplies. And you may make sport betting on how many breathing masks will be brought out on the walk."

Ernor had led Korgh to the fort, where the lord first paid respect to the forge inside, where warriors tempered new weapons. Afterward, he reviewed the space and personnel in preparation for the upcoming event. The mess hall would indeed suffice; the party would not be large. Neither Kersh nor Riker would doubt the security. The Sentries were ascetics, but definitely not priests: every waking hour not spent guarding the land bridge, they practiced in the petrified forest directly behind the fortress.

After bidding Ernor farewell, he kept on his face-covering as he scaled the staircase to the southern highland. His transport was far overhead, no doubt waiting for his signal.

Instead, he produced from the folds of his cloak a different communicator, the one that Odrok had designed for him. He set the channel and activated encryption. "You know who this is," he said. "Have you arrived?"

Several moments passed before a response came. *"Cross here."* Cross was using a similar encryption-enabled communicator, provided to him by Odrok in one of her many runs to Thane to supply his conspirators. *"Chu'charq is overhead."*

"In orbit?" Korgh looked up suddenly.

"No, directly above you. Careful looking up, or you'll bump your head."

Korgh casually glanced about. He could see H'atoria's native avians circling, but not a bird-of-prey. If the wildlife sensed its presence somehow, Korgh could not. No sound cut the ocean air. "You don't need to be this close."

"Valandris wanted a better look at this place. Don't worry, if any sensors could spot us, they'd be screaming already. My associates in Blackstone *are hovering off to your right."*

Korgh did not look.

"You know, this is as close as we've ever been. Sure you don't want to find a place to talk? We've never met face-to-face."

And we're never going to, Korgh thought. "Just prepare to do the job my assistant informed you of. I have started to put your payment into motion."

"My people will be glad to hear it," the Betazoid said. *"Remember, we don't take Klingon darseks. We need something we can spend easily."*

"You will have it." Korgh looked around before kneeling. Pretending to adjust his boot, he slipped a small device onto the surface. "You see what I am doing?"

A few moments passed. *"Yeah,* Blackstone *sees you. You've put something down by your foot, right?"*

"Take it."

Korgh waited several seconds and watched as the object transported away in a tiny blaze of orange.

"Okay, Blackstone *just beamed it up. They tell me it's some kind of gadget. What is it?"*

"It is the key to your payment. When this task is finished, I will tell you where to find the lock it sits. And then we will both have what we want."

Fourteen

"Commander Tuvok."

"Commander Sarai."

Without another word, Dalit Sarai entered the turbolift that Tuvok had just vacated. Pausing in the hallway for a moment, he looked back at the dark-haired Efrosian woman just as the doors closed in front of her. The Vulcan then spent the entire walk down the hall wondering why he had looked back.

Vulcans did not surrender to emotion. Except, perhaps, during *pon farr*, when logic took a biologically enforced holiday, or when the mind suffered from some illness like Bendii Syndrome. Yet several times in recent weeks, Tuvok had been forced to dismiss thoughts of an indignant nature. After speaking with his spouse, T'Pel, and meditating on why he was experiencing annoyance, he had traced back the first incident to *Titan*'s last visit to Starbase 1 orbiting Earth.

Admiral Riker had returned from a Starfleet briefing with his portfolio as sector commander. He had promoted Sariel Rager and Aili Lavena, two of *Titan*'s ablest officers. Christine Vale was given command of *Titan*. She had been the *de facto* holder of that post since Riker's promotion, and Tuvok felt the move both overdue and deserved.

Approximately forty-eight seconds later, Commander Sarai had stepped forward, introducing herself as *Titan*'s new executive officer.

Tuvok's life had never been ruled by ambition—at least not his own. His parents had pushed him into Starfleet while he was in his twenties; he had found the experience unpleasant enough to be worth abandoning all the work he'd put in. Decades later, when he returned to Starfleet, he chose to set his own course rather than chase promotions; he had always spoken frankly regardless of the consequences to some imagined future. It was more important that he remain true to himself while advancing the mission, be it intelligence work or exploration.

His presence on *Titan* was proof of it. After returning from the Delta Quadrant with *Voyager*, he could have sought and gotten a command of his own. Instead, he taught at the Academy, and later took an intel assignment on Romulus. It was following that mission that he agreed to serve with Riker aboard *Titan* on an interim basis.

The temporary posting had lasted seven years—and counting. He had gone to the Delta Quadrant and back in that amount of time.

Titan had become a home for him and T'Pel. It had been more than an adequate challenge of his training and skills. When Riker's sudden elevation to admiral, months earlier, had created a vacancy at executive officer, Tuvok had assisted not out of ambition, but because of duty. He had done what was expected of him, and more.

But then Commander Sarai had become executive officer when the position was formally filled. He did not know if he had even been considered for the post.

Logically, he had no objection. It was a title he had neither desired nor sought. The Efrosian had the training and skills; she had performed well under duress during *Titan*'s recent encounter with the Solanae. Leonard James Akaar, Tuvok's former colleague aboard *Wyoming* and now commander-in-chief, had personally given her the post. He and the admiral had had their disagreements, but Akaar never would have done so without reason.

And yet Sarai had managed to alienate several of *Titan's* officers in record time. Tuvok she had treated with cool respect. But her unforgiving personality had struck a nerve with others. It was common knowledge that she supported Ishan Anjar, the disgraced politician who had argued for a more aggressive posture for Starfleet.

Was resentment a reasonable response? Had the resentment been earned? Logic told him the answer was no—yet the question had occupied his mind, and that he resented without compunction.

Tuvok's step quickened as he reached the officer's club at the end of the hall. The stage was empty, but a piped-in vocalist was saying something about the thrill being gone. With a shift change approaching, the club was nearly barren at this hour—but he still saw whom he was looking for, drinking alone at the bar. "Good evening, Admiral."

Riker looked up, dark circles under his eyes. "Commander, are you singing the blues?"

"I do not experience color as metaphor."

"Of course not." Riker smiled, set his glass down, and stretched his arms on the railing of the bar. "Were you looking for me?"

"The computer said you were here. I did not know if you were returning to your operations center."

"No, I'm done for the day. Deanna and Natasha are long since asleep, so it was just me and a sandwich." He nodded in the direction of an empty plate. "Now it's just me." He shook his head. "Did I say I was done for the day? You wouldn't believe the mess this conference has become."

Riker described the arduous negotiations he had undertaken since departing Korgh's compound. "We had to promise Tocatra, the Romulan envoy, that Starfleet would only send one vessel—and that the Klingons would send no further forces beyond H'atoria's normal sentry presence.

The Breen would only attend if the Kinshaya did—and the Kinshaya would only disrupt their holy year to send someone if we read their sacred text into the record. All sixty-eight volumes of it."

Tuvok knew the Kinshaya of old. "Predictable."

"And that's just to get them to the table. We haven't talked about the shape of the table yet." Riker sighed. "Sorry. You wanted something?"

Tuvok thought carefully before deciding how to phrase his answer. "Since we entered Klingon space, I have been drilling *Titan*'s crew against attacks by boarding parties as *Enterprise* experienced. This is a necessary task—if repetitive."

"The whole ship's been doing a lot of waiting around. 'They also serve, who only stand and wait.'"

"John Milton. I understand our assignment is important to Starfleet and the Federation. But *Titan* otherwise saw no tactical situations requiring my aid at Qo'noS and Ketorix, and the Klingons will be running security at H'atoria."

Riker nodded. "I started brushing up about Spirits' Forge yesterday. Those Sentries of theirs wrote the book on standing and waiting."

"Precisely. I have come to believe that my skills might be better utilized in this crisis—particularly those involving my first area of expertise, science. Captain Vale made that observation herself—and it is with her permission that I mention it to you."

He peered at Tuvok. "Well, there is something," Riker said. "I could detach you to work with the Unsung task force."

Tuvok's eyebrow arched. "I understood that *Enterprise* and the other vessels involved with the search were here at Chancellor Martok's invitation and coordinating with the Empire."

"They are. But we can multiply our contribution if we're

not limited to searching just where our capital ships are. Smaller ships may be able to chase down additional leads."

"Leads, sir?"

"For you to discover," Riker said, stopping to down the rest of his drink. "You bring us something, and we'll make sure you get all the assets you require."

Tuvok considered for a moment and nodded. It would be a better use of his skills. At H'atoria, the *Titan* and the Klingons would be focused on warding off threats. The same responsibility over Gamaral had made it impossible for the *Enterprise* to pursue the departing attackers. Someone needed to be on offense.

"The idea is sound. I will speak with Captain Vale."

"I was about to say that." Riker pushed his stool back from the bar and stood. "The job's yours, but I'm never going to question her authority again. I've learned my lesson."

Following Riker to the exit, Tuvok understood. Being an admiral was a learned skill, just like being a captain or first officer. It was possible that an independent assignment might give him the challenge he needed.

They turned in different directions in the outer hallway. Tuvok paused and called after Riker. "Admiral, your exertions are worthwhile. The struggle for peace is important."

"If I didn't believe that, I'd be crazy to keep at it. Good night."

Fifteen

Like all those who stood watch at Spirits' Forge, Ernor slept lightly. It was a consequence of having spent years at a time on watch detail. He was always a heartbeat away from acting.

It didn't matter that no one had molested H'atoria or the fortress since his posting here. He had stopped no one but a few soggy Selseress from swimming too close to the island; his Sentries carried disruptors for such purposes. But his duty was to the fortress, to his house, to the Empire—and most importantly, to his honor. Kahless the Unforgettable had made the upholding of personal honor his most important precept. Ernor would stand watch even if no invader ever set foot on H'atoria again.

His state of constant awareness had meant that he never slept deeply enough to dream. He did not miss it. Apart from battle, what could a Klingon long for other than to be stationed at so legendary an outpost?

There was something else, though he had never imagined it would come to him.

Ernor slept, as all Sentries did, sweltering on the naked stone floor in sight of the central furnace. Fueled by a tap into the volcanic rift that now threatened to undermine the island, the kiln cast a glow across the room at night. Still enervated after Lord Korgh's inspection, Ernor rolled over and opened one eye.

The shadows changed. When the room grew inexplicably brighter, his other eye opened. Sensing a presence in the room, Enror bolted upright, *d'k tahg* in hand.

"Who dares?"

"I am Kahless," came a voice, resonating through the room like thunder. *"And I have returned!"*

The other sleepers woke to see what Ernor saw in front of the furnace: the glowing form of a Klingon warrior, his body crackling with eldritch energy. He seemed unaffected by the heat from the kiln behind him—and while he resembled the late and lamented clone of Kahless, the figure's eyes glowed a brilliant white.

"What are you?" Ernor raised his weapon. "How did you come here?" The part of the island that held the fortress was shielded; no one could have transported in. "Are you the clone, who was assassinated?"

The mysterious visitor stepped away from the furnace, extended his hand, and spoke again in that harrowing voice—louder than any Klingon could shout, using words that appealed directly to their souls. *"I am the Unforgettable. It was the fall of my messenger that drew me back."*

"That—that is not possible!" Ernor looked around to see if his companions were seeing the same thing. They, too, were spellbound.

"I came from Sto-Vo-Kor. I came to see you, Ernor, and all the Sentries. The Empire is in crisis. The time is nigh. You are needed."

"Needed!"

"There is a great battle ahead. I have no need of monks or politicians—but rather those warriors who most exemplify the tenets I set forth." Energy coruscating across his body, the apparition stepped toward the listeners. *"You are those warriors."*

"We are ready, Kahless!" shouted one of Ernor's younger companions.

Dazzled, Ernor did not know what to say. He watched as the specter—sometimes there, sometimes not—pointed to a door on the northern side of the room. *"Destiny lies beyond."*

Ernor found his voice again. "That leads to the petrified forest, in which we train."

"No, the Barge of the Dead is beyond—and I will take you there. Muster what troops would join you on the greatest adventure."

The captain of the watch turned. "Many of our number are guarding the pathway on the isthmus. I will call to them—"

"I will appear to them soon. But you must go first."

That made sense to Ernor—as much sense as any of this did. No one outside the room would ever believe what was happening, not without having the same experience. But happening it was, just as the ancient texts that he and his comrades studied had foretold. His faith, his years of diligence were finally being rewarded. He looked to the wall. "I will come. Let me get my *bat'leth*."

"The only weapon you need is your honor. I will arm you."

The Sentries looked at one another in excitement and awe. They were to be an army, following behind Kahless: the answer to the dark times that had befallen the Empire. What more could any Klingon wish?

Ernor knew the answer. *Nothing!*

He ran out into the darkness. And he was not alone.

"I am Ernor, son of Glak. And I die for—"

For nothing, Valandris wanted to say as she cut the Klingon's neck. He had needlessly shouted his presence below her rock perch, giving her the advantage she needed to drop down and surprise him. The son of Glak, whoever that was, collapsed into the darkness and shouted no more.

It had been bloody work, far more difficult than any of their attacks on the Orions. They had the advantage of their black armor and masks, but they'd been forced to do without energy weapons so as not to alert the Sentries watching the land bridge, on the far side of the fortress. And even unarmed and disoriented in the dark, the Sentries had fought wilder than any animal of Thane when the Unsung pounced upon them from their hidden positions among the craggy pillars. She could see Zokar a short distance away, gutting another unfortunate. It was his fourth or fifth kill. She was sure he would tell her the final count soon enough; there was no one left to fall.

The H'atoria mission had come as a surprise to all of the Unsung—and yet it was so wonderfully characteristic of Kruge and his plots that every single warrior in the squadron had desired a role. Back in the Azure Nebula, Kruge had returned from the Orion camp to *Chu'charq* with a metal crate containing what he said were ancient Klingon scrolls. After private meditation up in the deck one sanctum he shared with N'Keera, Kruge had described a vision sparked by the aged texts.

The vision had been of an island rounded at either end with a land bridge at the middle, much of it separated from its ocean by roiling lava trenches. The undead minions of Gre'thor lined the isthmus causeway, but the real power was in the larger landmass to the north. There sat an infernal stronghold, a pleasure pit where the unworthy came to mock honor and the honorable. It was a real place, Kruge had realized—and while its appearance had changed, he knew it was a planet that had belonged to his house.

They had arrived some time earlier, the ships of the Phantom Wing hovering cloaked in air, reconnoitering. The famous Sentries of Spirits' Forge had not detected them. After a time, Kruge had asked to be transported down into the *hensyl*'s den itself, utilizing the same transporter systems that had allowed the Unsung to infiltrate the *Enterprise* at Gamaral. The aerial force field protecting the northern knob of the island had been of no use at all in stopping him—or in preventing her forces from setting up their ambush.

Valandris and her companions had objected to Kruge taking an active role in luring the Sentries outside. But he held firm—and amazingly, he had succeeded. They did not know how he had done it, but it was hard to discount the power of someone who had defeated death long before any of them were born.

The battle ended, she and her companions found Kruge alone in the fortress—the so-called Spirits' Forge—walking around carrying a lantern as one hypnotized. Sensing the arrival of his warriors, he spoke. "I built this fort. More than a hundred years ago, back when I added H'atoria to my holdings. To the holdings of the Empire."

"I had heard of this place before," Zokar said, flicking the blood from his knife. "It was a forge before the Borg struck. Afterward it became a mighty citadel—holding the respect of many."

"Once, perhaps. But you know how my family treated my holdings—just as you know how the Empire failed you. These 'Sentries' were all bluster—minions of the would-be nobles you faced on Gamaral."

"They are dead," Valandris said.

"Cutting the head off the beast was but a start. The serpent still writhes." Kruge turned, his ancient face lit by the lantern. "I no longer fear the fire. We will turn this forge against them—and leave only ashes."

Kruge spoke to a handheld communicator, and an instant later, N'Keera appeared, transported from *Chu'charq*. Valandris stoked the brazier at the center of the common room. Looking about, she saw tapestries on the walls, along with several cabinets holding scrolls and books. N'Keera stepped toward a small desk and located a padd, which she read from.

"My lord, it appears a team from the Empire is arriving tomorrow to install transporter inhibitor towers along the walkway to the landing site."

"Then it begins. She is coming," Kruge said. "We knew she would."

Valandris looked up. "Who is coming?"

"There is someone you did not slay on Gamaral," N'Keera said. "Kersh, granddaughter of J'borr. All that was vile in our lord's family now exists in her person. She has invited our enemies, the Romulans and the Kinshaya, here to H'atoria in order to bargain the world away."

"And brokering the arrangement is none other than our ridiculous excuse for an ally, the Federation." Kruge snorted. "Does anyone here doubt their intent? They mean to carve the limbs from the imperial body before Starfleet deals the death blow."

N'Keera's voice lowered. "We even have reason to believe that Kersh is in the pay of the Romulans."

"That's not right," Zokar said. He gripped his *d'k tahg* tightly. "Let her come. I will cut her in two." Zokar had experience with Romulans, Valandris knew. She suspected it had something to do with how he was discommendated years earlier.

Raneer, crouching beside the main doorway leading south from the fortress, called back. "The Sentries on the path have not moved."

"Their shift ends when the first moon rises," N'Keera said, gesturing toward an alcove where clothing was stored. "Take the Sentries' garb and gear. Mask yourselves against the gases as they do. And when you reach their stations to relieve them, you will slay them and cast their bodies into the purifying flames."

"If they are worthy," Kruge said, "they will emerge from the fire just as I did. And truly this place will be a forge for spirits. But I hold little hope for them. No, the only spirits I hope to hone here are yours."

Valandris watched as Zokar and the others eagerly began stripping off their armor in preparation for their new disguises. Another ambush for the Unsung. Worf, she knew, would certainly not approve.

Nor, she suspected, would the person whose name Ernor had spoken in death.

With N'Keera busy distributing the Sentry's gear, Valandris stepped tentatively toward Kruge. He noticed her. "Yes?"

"Those we attacked," she said. "They called for Kahless."

"As they whimpered and died?"

"No. They were searching for him—expecting to find him."

"Did you smell the breath on the Sentries before you slew them?" Kruge laughed. "The louts were stinking drunk when I found them, Valandris. It is all they do here—I suspected as much. It was a small thing to lure them outside with a ruse. Kahless was the name I chose, but with superstitious fools like these, any would have done."

Valandris nodded. Kruge's explanation made sense.

But as she looked around, she saw only the sacred scrolls and volumes. She wondered where the empty bloodwine bottles were.

ACT TWO

THE WOLF'S DISGUISE

2386

"It is useless for the sheep to pass resolutions in favor of vegetarianism, while the wolf remains of a different opinion."

—William Ralph Inge

Sixteen

" . . . *a Klingon who kills without showing his face is no Klingon at all.*"

Valandris sat with her pack on the floor of the fortress's mess hall and ate as she read from the aged book. After Kruge and N'Keera had beamed back to *Chu'charq* to rest, Valandris had found the tome in a protected place amidst the belongings of the Sentries. Given the book's place of respect, Valandris had been surprised that the volume wasn't in better shape. It had been read nearly to tatters.

The book reprinted the *qeS'a'*, an ancient text supposedly bearing the teachings of Kahless the Unforgettable; the words she had just read constituted the Third Precept of the ancient warrior's code. That such a code even existed was news to her. The elders on Thane had said nothing about it to their offspring. That was their philosophy: since they had been discommendated, with seven future generations of their descendants similarly condemned, there was no need to teach their children and grandchildren a heritage they could never strive for. History and tradition connected an individual to the past, to something greater. Discommendation was all about being cut off.

That was the most generous interpretation for her lack of knowledge. Valandris saw darker motives. General Potok was all about keeping control of his community, and that meant keeping the young in the dark, with no ambition or pride. He had kept them asleep—only to be roused the year before when the Fallen Lord arrived to tell them they deserved better.

Potok had been overthrown, but it had not brought about a reintroduction of Kahless's teachings. The resurrected Kruge styled himself as a new warrior prophet, distinct from and better than the ancient Kahless. He'd actively discouraged them from asking about their past; Kruge told them he had already seen all the strengths and weaknesses of Klingon society, and that he was crafting something different. Kruge's words were the only ones that mattered.

And yet, something made Valandris uneasy.

Killing the captain of the watch and several of his companions had only been the start of her activity at Spirits' Forge. As Kruge and N'Keera commanded, she had dressed in the gear of a Sentry, walked out onto the land bridge in the still-moonless night, and in synchronicity with similarly garbed Unsung had fired her disruptor at the guard she was pretending to relieve. The Sentries' job was to stand watch protecting the fortress. They had never considered danger could come *from* the fortress, dressed in friendly colors.

The tactic was nothing new. She had a lifetime of stalking and pouncing on prey. She had launched surprise attacks on both *Dinskaar* and *Enterprise* in sensor-proofed combat gear. But it wasn't until she talked with Worf, on Thane, that she'd realized that Klingons saw combat differently. Battle, the ancient Kahless had contended, revealed the inner spirit— and in such a hallowed activity deception had no place.

She had read the section of the *qeS'a'* again and again, struggling to understand. Didn't Klingons spend enormous resources developing technologies to cloak their spacecraft? A hundred years' work had been put into the cloaking systems of the Phantom Wing. While cloaked, they could operate their transporters and even fire—and while some of the later émigrés had told her the latter was somehow taboo, she couldn't understand a culture that simultaneously praised forthright activity while making deception easier.

Worse, the rules—*more accursed Klingon rules!*—forgave acts that had harmed her own. She had been thinking about her last moments on Thane for days. Worf had killed her cousin and childhood friend, Tharas, and had defended himself by citing the tenets in the very book she was holding. Worf had announced his presence to Tharas before striking, and that made it all right? Tharas was still dead, his young daughter fatherless. How many of her people's lives on Thane had been made miserable because of the Klingons and their damned honor?

And yet . . .

As she had started killing sentients in Kruge's name, Valandris had found something inside her at odds with the way she was going about it. She had felt the same thing earlier on the causeway, incinerating the guard she had surprised. The kill had been unsatisfying. Looking back, she felt the same about Ernor as well. Would she regret striking at the *Enterprise* next?

And Valandris was still at pains to understand her response to Worf on Thane. Not only had she freed him after Tharas's death, but she had alerted him to Kruge's plan to immolate Worf's would-be rescuers in the Unsung compound. All for the man who murdered her best friend.

If it *was* murder. She didn't know anymore.

What was she becoming?

Booming laughter erupted from the corridor. Several of Zokar's crewmates from *Rodak* entered the mess hall through the door beside her, chatting happily about their exploits. They proceeded toward the pile of backpacks that had been beamed down. Suddenly self-aware, Valandris quickly shoved the book underneath her own pack on the floor.

"What's that?"

"Nothing," Valandris said, before she even saw who had spoken.

Zokar stood over her, smiling. "Dinnertime at last. Let me see what they sent you." He leaned down to grab at the pack with his sole arm—and she yanked it away from him. In the act, the book beneath slid between Zokar's feet.

Her hand shot out for it—but the older Klingon stomped on the book with his boot. "What's this?" Reaching for it, he brought it upward. His eyes widened as he read from the cover. "*Oh*."

Valandris stood. The others were looking at them now, she saw. Neither she nor Zokar had ranks, but everyone saw the unofficial ship leaders as rivals—and under Kruge, that had increasingly become the case.

"Where'd you get this?" he asked.

"Something I found. It's nothing."

"I agree it's nothing. Nothing but trouble." Pivoting, he marched through the doorway into the next room, which held the great glowing furnace open to the infernal underground rift. Valandris followed, as did several onlookers. With a whisk of his hand, Zokar sent the book sailing into the kiln.

"No!" Valandris said, starting for it. A second later, she was on the ledge of the open kiln, trying to find any part of the volume. Burning pages fluttered over the hell pit, and she clutched at them.

Zokar hauled her back from the edge. "Are you mad, woman?"

Not mad, but angry. Valandris wrenched away from Zokar and punched him in the nose. Laughter rose from the other spectators. She spun and gave a withering look that silenced all.

Zokar wiped the blood from his nose with a growl—and then laughed it off.

She gave him her next bad look. "What did you do that for?"

Standing by the fire, his eyes gleamed. "Trash should be burned."

"Have you even read it?"

"Have I *read it*?" Incredulous, Zokar gawked at her. "Val, that claptrap is drilled into our heads in the crèche."

"Is that right?"

"Damn right. I was discommended by the Empire, Valandris. Personally. Not some ancestor of mine, like you people." The bald Klingon pointed to the smoking brazier. "And believe me, this *qeS'a'* business is nothing but guff. Chains made of words, to enslave you to people long dead—people who may never even have existed."

"So Kahless wasn't real?"

"The clone? I cut his jugular. The blood was real enough." Several listeners laughed.

"No, I mean the first Kahless."

Zokar groaned in aggravation. "The scholars go back and forth on that. But that's not important. It's what they do with the things they say he said." He jabbed at his chest with his index finger. "They puff us up with ideas that we can belong in their heroic afterlife—but only if we do everything their way. And if they find you lacking? Forget it. There is no appeal."

That brought a rumble from the others present. Certainly, it took nothing to convince the Unsung of the Empire's corruption.

Zokar continued. "Kruge's different. He's got a plan. You saw the broadcast he sent: he called us 'the children the true Kahless deserved.' That wasn't just a slam at the people who discommended us. He's willing to use Kahless and their other symbols, to hijack them, to transform them—to turn them to our ends. We'll remake society our way. Then *we're* the gods." That elicited whoops.

"Maybe." Valandris turned and found her backpack. She

had lost her appetite. Before she exited, she looked back at Zokar. "How long ago did they discommendate you?"

"Forty years ago, just about. I was even younger then than you are now. And believe me, nothing's changed."

He eyed her, and she stared back. Then, after a moment, she said, "I believe you."

She could do nothing else. Zokar had made perfect sense—and no one in the room had more experience with the Klingon Empire. She knew he was probably right.

But she didn't know if she deserved to be a god.

Seventeen

Since the Unsung had slipped past *Enterprise* in the Briar Patch, Picard felt as if he was chasing shadows. The squadron had the ability to range too far—and too many craft in and around the Klingon Empire had cloaks similar to the Unsung's, except for Object Thirteen. That was why he had been willing to entertain La Forge's wild transporter scheme: there was little chance that it would be used.

Things looked different when standing beside the fresh landing gear imprint left by one of the starships of the Phantom Wing. Heavy rains had washed away many of the traces of footprints, but there was no doubt that a massacre had taken place. *Enterprise* had discovered corpses strewn everywhere in the Orion pirate camp, rotting in the mud.

Gloved and masked, his wife and chief medical officer emerged from the hut nearest the landing zone. Picard stepped away from the rut and tromped over to meet her. Spotting him, Beverly Crusher pulled off her protective mask.

"Status?"

She exhaled a deep breath. "We're transporting bodies directly to the morgue. We count eighty-nine dead Orions, as well as fourteen members of five different species."

Worse than Gamaral, Picard thought. "Other species. Klingons?"

"No. We suspect they were hirelings or slaves. The Unsung killed them all." Crusher predicted his next question. "It happened sometime between three and seven days ago. We'll narrow it down in the autopsies."

"I won't keep you." He gave her a sympathetic look. It was dismal work, but it had to be done.

Over his shoulder, Picard could see Šmrhová directing her forensic experts. She had everyone out today: looking at the signs of battle, trying to determine the order of events and number of attackers involved. "Report."

"We still think it's just two birds-of-prey," Šmrhová said. "At least that's all that landed. We're getting good prints from inside the camp structures, matching those we found on Gamaral. Possibly twenty or thirty attackers."

"And no evidence of Unsung casualties."

"Correct, but that might not mean anything. They're armed with disruptors. I could see the Unsung vaporizing their dead if they wanted to hide their involvement."

It occurred to Picard that with disruptors involved, the number of Orion dead might be far higher. "So at a minimum the cultists succeeded against odds which at best were four to one." He shook his head. "Anything else?"

"Aye, Captain. The Unsung—or somebody—evidently took some materials from the storehouse. It's been ransacked."

"They're foraging. That could be what this was—a raid to resupply." The violence seemed out of proportion with a mere looting run, but everything the Unsung had done so far was extreme. "Could they have learned of this place from their earlier raid on *Dinskaar*?"

"Possibly. But it's what they took that's strange. They left behind a lot of food, drink, and other necessities—even spare dilithium crystals. But we can see from the inventory manifest that a lot of the hard currency and luxury items are gone."

The concept struck Picard dumb. *What would the Unsung need with money?*

"I doubt we'll be able to figure that storehouse out," she admitted. "There are traces of a lot of different beings having been in the place. It's a mess."

The enslaved workers—or someone else? Picard figured he'd better get out of the way if he wanted that answer. "Thank you, Lieutenant. This is excellent work."

"I knew once we got Qo'noS to filter the candidate signals, we'd be able to track Object Thirteen," Šmrhová said. It had brought *Enterprise* here—although long-range sensor readings were inconclusive as to where the Unsung had gone. "I'm looking forward to catching up with them and trying out Commander La Forge's plan," she said.

"As you were." Picard smiled warily and withdrew.

He'd been unsurprised at his officers' drive. La Forge had been sitting center seat when Unsung agents had infiltrated the *Enterprise* over Gamaral. On the planet below, Šmrhová's security teams had allowed Unsung assassins to slip in from the forest to assassinate their targets. Worf had been unable to stop the murder of Kahless, and he now felt that he had to complete a quest in the clone's name.

Picard understood how his officers felt; he felt the same. Each of them needed redemption. But could he allow it if it jeopardized the seekers?

Picard still had no answers by the time he contacted Admiral Riker with a preliminary report on the raid. En route to H'atoria, his former first officer was about to be too busy with the conference to worry about anything else—and yet Picard knew he *would* worry.

"I've ordered Tuvok to get every ship in the quadrant looking for this Object Thirteen," Riker said. *"Good work, Geordi."*

Seated at an *Enterprise* conference room table, La Forge looked tentative. "Admiral, it's a really hit-and-miss method—we might detect a signal once every few days. And the Klingons' ship sensors don't have the ability to work on the spectrum. We're left with just stationary patrol satellites."

"I can ask General Kersh to get the satellites above H'atoria looking. If she's talking to me, that is." Riker grinned as he scratched his beard. *"The Klingons appear to have security on the surface covered. Lord Korgh assures us the team at the fortress is top-notch."*

Across the table from La Forge, Worf nodded. "The Sentries of Spirits' Forge are warriors of the highest caliber."

Picard could feel he had taken up too much of Riker's time already, but one thing needed an answer. "I know you want to wrap up, Admiral, but did you look at the proposal I forwarded?"

Riker smirked. *"You mean the 'Protocol for Beaming Aboard a Cloaked Ship'?"*

Worf cleared his throat. "Klingons do transport on and off vessels under cloak."

"Yeah, when they know where they are—and that they exist." Riker shook his head. *"I leave this to your discretion, Captain."*

That was the answer Picard expected. "Thank you, Will."

"Riker out."

The screen went black. Picard turned to the trio at the table. "I've stopped counting the number of times I have been approached with a plan I thought too dangerous to be tried. Of course, many of them did eventually have to be tried because of desperate circumstances—so the better question is, 'How many of them worked?'"

No one present wanted to advance a guess.

"I'm not suggesting any of you would jeopardize the lives of fellow officers in an attempt to undo something that happened in the past," Picard said. "You are all far too reasonable for that. But you are also strongly motivated. Geordi,

Aneta—you've both barely slept since the massacre. And Worf—" He paused, studying his first officer. "You have unique obligations to the late Kahless."

La Forge and Šmrhová looked to Worf, curious.

"The clone of Kahless did not fall in battle," Worf said, "so another must perform a great feat in his name before he can gain access to Sto-Vo-Kor."

The chief engineer nodded hesitantly. "I . . . okay."

Picard looked to La Forge. "We all have rituals and obligations that follow the death of a loved one. This is something Worf must attend to—but my concern is that Kahless was such an important figure, it may color his choice of feats."

"When Commander La Forge told me there was a possibility we could locate and beam aboard an Unsung vessel, I knew nothing less would do," Worf said. "They killed Kahless before my eyes. But they have killed others and will continue to kill. By stopping them, we would do more than redeem Kahless."

Watchful all this time, Šmrhová said, "I don't doubt our ability to succeed, Worf. But the Unsung are ruthless—and they have nothing to lose. When we disable the cloak aboard the Phantom Wing vessel we're on, wouldn't the other ships blow it up?"

That startled La Forge. "Would they really kill their own people?"

"Yes," Worf said. "There are twelve birds-of-prey. Unless we beam aboard their would-be leader's ship, he could certainly order it. And they would obey."

One-in-twelve odds. Not good. The captain took a breath. "So what does this mean for your plan?"

La Forge thought for a moment. "We have to be prepared. *Enterprise* might need to defend the ship the two of you are on—taking any incoming fire."

"Things could change very quickly." Šmrhová's eyes widened. "It could get hot."

"The *Enterprise* can take the heat," Picard said. "Remember the Greeks. Salamis was basically a land battle at sea, with marines roving from ship to ship; every vessel in the water might go from friend to foe or vice versa at any moment. Captains were inventing new tactics at every turn." He smiled at his fellow officers. "We won't wait until the battle's joined to figure this one out. Dismissed."

Eighteen

A certain terror overtook Cross whenever he sat in the ready room just aft of *Chu'charq*'s bridge, and he knew what it was. Unlike his lair on deck one where he did most of his important planning, his official office as Kruge came with a big port.

Outside it, he saw the starships multiplying. H'atoria had a recently constructed orbital resupply station, meaning there were always Klingon battle cruisers in transit. The creeping monsters were ominous and threatening, and while Korgh had assured him that the traffic would clear before the conference began, leaving only Kersh's *Gur'rok*, he assumed the battle cruiser wouldn't be going far. Then there were the support vessels Kersh had brought, a flotilla installing new surveillance satellites.

And now the conference participants had started to arrive—including *Titan*. The vessel's size astounded him— and he had heard that *Enterprise* was even larger. Cross had not traveled with the Unsung to Gamaral and hadn't caught a glance of the *Enterprise* during the evacuation from Thane, but *Titan* was plenty large enough for him already. The Federation didn't design its ships to look menacing, but seeing this one sure did a number on his digestive tract.

In his guise as Kruge, Cross did his best to avoid showing alarm—mostly by avoiding looking outside, and by remembering that he had a dozen ships of his own out there, malignant and invisible. Appearing as N'Keera,

Shift showed no fear, standing at the observation port with Zokar playing identify-the-ship.

"That one's Ferengi," Zokar said, pointing. "Are they in this little bargain?"

"Observer status," Shift said. "They want the right to use the free-flight corridor to transport their wares."

"Of course."

Cross found it remarkable that Shift managed to keep track of Korgh's scheme while at the same time remaining up to date on the politics. Not to mention the care and feeding of his ego. He used his Kruge voice. "Are things prepared below, Zokar?"

"They are, my lord." Zokar turned and grinned. "I'm going to enjoy being on the surface when you give the signal."

He'd increasingly relied on Zokar to know what was going on aboard the other eleven ships of the Phantom Wing. The old convict—which is what Cross assumed he was—had found a new life with the Unsung while still nursing a healthy grudge against the Empire. That made him the perfect advisor and surrogate. It also didn't hurt to have someone with shipboard military experience, and while Cross didn't know how much Zokar had, any at all would trump what the Unsung had.

Cross went for his most noble Kruge voice. "You are a true warrior and have served me well, Zokar. I cannot do without you."

"Thank you, my lord."

"This is why I want you in orbit, aboard *Rodak*, coordinating the squadron's tactics when the time comes." He put his hand up to forestall Zokar's objection. "I know you want to be on the surface when the scoundrels arrive. But this act has no value unless we can extract our team and leave. Your work would be as important, if not more."

Zokar looked thwarted. "I understand, my lord. But I wanted to slay Kersh in your name."

"Every warrior below can use a blade. Few can fly a starship as you can."

The bald Klingon frowned. He started to say something before stopping.

Shift noticed his reticence. "What would you have us know?" she said in N'Keera's cooling voice.

Zokar looked down. "I wasn't going to say anything—but it's Valandris. I caught her down in Spirits' Forge looking at one of the old tomes—and someone said they saw her accessing historical files here on *Chu'charq*."

Cross and Shift looked at each other. "What does this mean?" he asked.

Zokar shrugged. "Maybe nothing." Then he got a canny look in his eye. "But she's been acting odd for a while. She brought Worf to Thane against orders—and then she wasn't able to hunt him down when he escaped."

"You question her loyalty?"

"Her devotion. She's young. Young people get ideas."

"Then I will speak with her. Return to your—"

Two arrivals from warp appeared in the space beyond the observation port, one after another. The nearer one was easy to recognize; even Cross knew the Kinshaya favored spherical starships.

The guests attracted Zokar's attention as well. "What's the other one?" Zokar asked, squinting. "Gorn?"

"No, Breen," Shift said mildly, her attention also rapt.

A third newcomer appeared, and this time Zokar had no doubt what he was looking at. "Romulans!" His eyes widened.

"You knew they were part of this," she said. "Every participant will bring one vessel."

"But to send a *D'deridex*-class warbird?" Zokar's body tensed. He looked back at Cross. "Lord Kruge, forget what

I said earlier. It'll be my honor to stay topside." He saluted and excused himself from the ready room.

Alone with Shift and still disguised as Kruge, Cross let his shoulders sag. "A warbird. This is crazier than I expected." From inside his vest, he pulled the handheld device Korgh had given him. "This payday had better be worth it."

His aide stepped over and kissed his cheek. "It's almost over, 'my lord.' I have things to attend to. And you have to go down one last time to give the troops their marching orders."

"One last time." Cross took a deep breath and let it out.

U.S.S. TITAN
ORBITING H'ATORIA

H'atoria at last. Riker looked out at the planet from the observation port with a mixture of resignation and relief. The conference that had been the bane of his existence these last weeks would be over soon, but it also might well end his career as an admiral.

Captain Vale's briefing for the conference had broken up, with her officers heading out to their appointed tasks. Riker and Troi had remained to again go over the list of attendees and the best way to handle them all.

"It's much harder without a partner in the room," she said. "I never would have believed the Klingons would be this antagonistic."

"Kersh is who you'd appoint if you want to blow the conference up," Riker said. "Korgh knew what he was doing."

Troi shook her head. "I'd love to meet this man. I wonder if I could have told he was lying about his identity back when he was Galdor."

"I don't know," Vale said. "Someone who plays a role for fifty years is probably in character pretty deep." She passed Riker a padd. "Here's the final duty roster for Spirits' Forge."

Riker mused over the names. "Kyzak? I thought he was at ops."

Vale looked at Troi, who spoke up. "We believe he could use the chance to see what diplomatic work is like. He's still broadening his horizons."

"Admirable idea, but this is the site support team. The most he'll see are the Sentries. From what I understand, they don't even tell you their names."

"Well, maybe that's all for the best," Vale said, grinning a little.

"Right," Riker said, passing the padd back.

He stood, remembering how glad he was to see his wife again. Facing the conference without Deanna's assistance was something he didn't want to contemplate.

"Just a second, Admiral." Vale checked her padd. "Lieutenant Commander Keru just sent his brief for ground security."

Riker rolled his eyes. "He's persistent. I told him, the Klingons are covering ground security."

Vale nodded, somewhat spellbound as she read. Then she stopped nodding. "I really think you'll want to look at it."

Nineteen

With local space getting crowded, Cross found that transporting down to Spirits' Forge was a relief. Certainly it was better transporting this time, as opposed to his earlier visit, when he'd had *Chu'charq* beam him down from his private quarters to the edge of a blazing furnace to debut his new Kahless impersonation, complete with special effects from *Blackstone*. Lesser practitioners would never have dared such a thing. He was just glad he hadn't fallen into the fire.

In doing so, Cross had defied Korgh's instruction, which was to use his Kruge character to talk the Sentries outside. That his Kahless character had gone over amazingly well had less to do with his own performance, he suspected, and more to do with the gullibility of those he had fooled. Among Kahless's most fervent supporters, the Sentries had been primed to accept him as real—especially when he transported through the fortress's shield using the method Odrok had stolen from the Hunters. In their way, the Sentries had been just like the Unsung: a bunch of sheltered fanatics ready to follow any pretender who was reasonably convincing.

The practitioners of the Circle of Jilaan had been profiting from such naïfs for years. He prayed the galaxy would never run out of them.

The Klingon and the Federation conference prep teams had started to arrive. They were still at the far end of the causeway, giving him enough time for a quick final inspection. On his walk through the redoubt, he found his Number

One Fools doing his bidding to the letter. Dozens of Unsung warriors now wore the gear of the Sentries, with their faces partially hidden by their filtration masks. Others, similarly disguised, remained stationed along the causeway, standing immobile as Kersh's advance team of engineers began their work installing transporter inhibitor towers at the end nearest the landing zone. No one had noticed the Sentries had been replaced.

Then his minions showed him the big surprise they had waiting for the conferees. He'd known about it, having passed along the order from Korgh, but seeing it going into place nearly made him break character with laughter. *Korgh, you're the devil himself.* It took effort, but Cross had kept it together. It wouldn't do for Commander Kruge to get the giggles.

At last he saw Valandris, returning from her shift posing as one of the guardians outside. "Our enemies have started installing transporter inhibitors at the far end. It will take them some time to work their way to the fortress," she said. "My lord Kruge, you will have to depart before they arrive."

A thousand force fields wouldn't keep me here, Cross thought. "You know your assignments. Not a word to the visitors; do not even look on them. This is the behavior they will expect from the Sentries. The diplomats are interlopers on your grounds, and you have been ordered to tolerate them: that is your motivation."

It felt strange to be teaching acting skills to a bunch of fanatics. But if anyone was capable of it, he was.

"They have not questioned our presence at all." Valandris looked to another woman across the room, someone that Cross understood to be the unofficial engineer aboard *Chu'charq*. "Hemtara, do we know if our transporters will be able to defeat the inhibitors they're installing on the causeway?"

Hemtara pursed her lips. "I do not know. Klingon transporter inhibitors may work on the same principles as their force fields—or they may not. It is not something that came up in our studies."

Valandris looked to Cross. "Do *you* know, my lord?"

Cross froze. He had absolutely no idea—and he wasn't surprised that the Unsung didn't know. Even with the remedial lessons they'd gotten from Potok's generation and the resources Korgh had sent, it had been challenging enough to get them up to speed to fly the birds-of-prey within a year's time. They had hit on an area he hadn't been briefed about.

Improvisation, however, was something he understood. *If you don't have the line, at least sound like your character.* "Do you care so much about escaping a fight, Valandris, that you would mewl like a whelp who found the gate closed?" He walked around the room, feeling the eyes of his listeners following him. "You should desire to stay—to give your last breath to kill every traitor on this globe. Ignore trivia about gadgets. If you are worthy, you will find your way back to us."

The Unsung cheered. Valandris joined them, belatedly.

As they went back to their tasks, he found an alcove and called her over.

"Yes, my lord?"

"I am told you have been reading of Kahless," he said, his voice lower. "Do not deny it."

Her eyes widened, but she did not shrink back. "I don't deny it, my lord."

"The *qeS'a'* is not worth your time." Cross was proud of himself for having learned the word in his studies. "It is a tool of the High Council to keep people in line."

"I know. But some of it seems sound. You said we were to be the children the true Kahless deserved."

"Only *after* we have succeeded—then will I decree who the 'true Kahless' really was. Some wisdom ascribed to him is useful. Some has been twisted and must be discarded. Put your faith in me to decide." His eyes narrowed as they focused on her. "Or do you think you can decide better for yourself?"

"No. It's just that our tactics—"

"Are my tactics. I think you have been deciding things. Is that how the Starfleet commander eluded you on Thane?"

"No, my lord!"

"Worf escaped to warn *Enterprise*—and saved the lives of people who intended us harm. People who had staged an event honoring the *petaQpu'* who stole my house. Allies of the Council, who would put you all in chains for another seven generations. Did you free him?"

Valandris stiffened. After a moment, she responded. "I answered my conscience."

"You will answer *me*." Cross reached for his communicator and called for a beam out.

Twenty

Ethan Kyzak had thought it got hot on the prairie back home. The Klingons had chosen to hold a conference in an oven.

Sending him to Spirits' Forge had been the captain's idea. Putting him on the conference's advance team, Vale said, would broaden his horizons—while giving him a taste of interstellar relations. So far, the lieutenant had discovered that venting an active lava tube through a building to create a forge did nothing to make it livable.

Kyzak had also decided that he never wanted to taste Klingon cuisine, ever.

"Y'all really eat it alive?" he asked in the kitchen off to the right of the mess hall. Clumps of *gagh* writhed in an open drum, stirred by one of the Sentries. The Klingon said nothing. Smelling what passed for food in the room, he understood why they left their face wrappings on.

In fact, once his away team and the group sent by Kersh entered, the Sentries had made themselves scarce, taking station outside the building or adding to the numbers posted on the causeway. Food, protection, and a roof—those were their only responsibilities. The rest belonged to Admiral Riker and General Kersh.

Out in the mess hall, Riker somehow looked cool and comfortable. *Maybe it was the frosty reception*, Kyzak thought. He'd been told to expect the Sentries would say nothing, reveal nothing. That was their routine. General Kersh's greeting, if it could be called that, back at the landing site had really surprised him—as had the welcome from the people on her team. The Klingons were definitely still sore at Starfleet.

Kyzak scanned the vats and churns with his tricorder. Everything checked out: nothing poisoned, nothing spoiled. If the guests could stomach the food, they'd live. He took another reading of the atmosphere. He could understand the Sentries wearing filters for long-term exposure to the fumes coming from the furnace room, but the guests should be able to manage without, so long as the event didn't drag on.

Without a word, the Sentry who'd tended the *gagh* finished her stirring and stepped toward Kyzak. She pulled a backpack out from behind the shelving unit he was leaning against. Reaching inside, she drew forth a red mass that smelled worse than anything he'd had the misfortune to notice. Pulling her mask down, she took a stomach-turning bite from it. Kyzak shrank back as the Sentry headed for the rear exit, chomping on her snack of whatever-it-was.

"Lieutenant Kyzak."

Snapped out of his spell, the Skagaran stepped from the kitchen into the mess hall. Three members of *Titan*'s crew were moving an enormous table with an irregular polygonal surface at the behest of the one who had called to him: a being like nothing Kyzak had ever seen.

Almost. People from North Star, his homeworld, *had* seen creatures that resembled Lieutenant Xaatix—only they were centimeters long and to be found crawling along on desert floors. The crustacean-like Xaatix stood a full two and a half meters tall, supported on a tripod of orange legs. Eight stubbier limbs were arranged symmetrically around her heart-shaped frame—and she was so thin that when she turned, he saw her almost disappear in profile.

"Make sure not to let it drag," Xaatix said in an elegant female human voice that emanated from the badge affixed to her chest. "You'll scratch the legs. Or worse, the Klingons' floor."

Seeing his crewmates overmatched by the awkwardly shaped furnishing, Kyzak hurried over to lend a hand.

"Ah, Lieutenant Kyzak," Xaatix said, her carapace color turning a warm maroon. "I'm afraid I don't have the limbs for this work."

"That's all right." Hefting the underside of the table, he asked, "This way?"

"No, around the other way. The Kinshaya insist that their representative face east-southeast."

"Uh . . . okay." Kyzak fought with the heavy table. "Any particular reason?"

"When the conference begins, that location will face Janalwa, their current capital."

"Oh." With the help of the others, Kyzak moved the monstrosity into position and set it down. "Is that it, Lieutenant?"

"It will be once we cut a hole in the table."

"A hole?" Kyzak watched as a crewman ignited a cutting tool. "Whatever for?"

"The Kinshaya consider tables to be culturally insensitive," Xaatix said. She waggled her carapace, causing her upper sets of claws to shake like castanets. "I admit I see their point."

Kyzak stepped away from the table as the cutting began and regarded Xaatix with mild unease. If there was ever a ship to serve on to meet all different kinds of folks, *Titan* was the one—yet he still didn't know how to address everyone. In Xaatix's case, he didn't even know what to look at when talking. The being had no features that could be considered a face, much less any obvious visual receptors.

He'd seen plenty of Lieutenant Xaatix on the way from the beam-in zone to the south, but walking along a solemn guardian-lined path wasn't conducive to conversation. "So you are, uh . . . "

"An Ovirian. And you are a Skagaran."

"Actually, I was wonderin' about what you do."

"Ah! I am *Titan*'s protocol officer."

That was a new one on Kyzak. "I didn't know we had such a thing. Do we, uh, get much call for a protocol officer?"

"The Federation is a multicultural power, so my services are much in demand. I'm attached to a ship when there are major conferences."

Kyzak looked back at the kitchen. "But aren't the Klingons running this show?"

"It is the Sentries' space, and they are the hosts. But we were told that they would not be involved in the meeting room." Xaatix gestured with three limbs toward the table. "The Sentries sleep and eat on the floor. We had to fabricate all of the conference's furnishings."

Kyzak nodded—and then pulled at his collar. The only circulation came from the south, through the anteroom: the front doors, swung wide, would be closed for the main event. "Don't you think it's stuffy in here? We get some hot summers where I'm from, but this beats all."

"The temperature is thirty point eighty-five degrees Celsius, and the humidity is eighty-five percent."

"You did that without a tricorder?"

"An Ovirian trait. In truth, I consider this cool; my planet is close to its star. But I am aware of the biological needs of our attendees." Xaatix swiveled on her tripod legs and began skittering toward the northern doorway. "Let us see what we can do here."

Kyzak followed Xaatix into a large room that was warmer still. In the middle of the wall to the right glowed the forge, a rectangular stone fire pit surrounded on three sides by protective walls that formed a chimney heading out of the fortress. The front of the fourth side was open, revealing the scorching light within.

"That's your culprit," said Kyzak, who had spent time in a smithy or two on North Star. He approached it. "If we can open the flue a bit more, some of the heat will circulate out."

Before he could reach the kiln, the female Sentry who had been standing watchfully by stepped quickly in front of the fire, *bat'leth* in hand. Mouth covered by the cloth filter, she glowered at him.

"Your fire needs adjustin'," he said. "It won't do."

The female Sentry said nothing. She wasn't the same one from the kitchen, Kyzak realized. She was more powerfully built—and her gaze could have burned him as easily as the furnace.

Xaatix stepped behind him. "It is a sacred place, Ethan. Perhaps we can find another way to cool our guests."

Kyzak looked around. "What about that?" He pointed to a wooden screen parked by the far wall and decorated with images of ancient Klingon battles. He looked to the Sentry. "Can we move that in front of the door?"

She dipped her *bat'leth* slightly in the direction of the open door to the mess hall, indicating he could.

"Well done," Xaatix said as Kyzak stepped toward it. The Ovirian's form turned mauve in approval.

Kyzak was pleased to have impressed Xaatix. But he also couldn't help but notice that the Sentry never moved from the fireplace, and her eyes never left him.

Twenty-one

"I'm getting pretty damn tired of that Valandris," Cross said, loosening his collar as he entered the hallway of his deck one sanctum. "It's amazing the hold Kahless has over these people."

Seated on a stool outside the force field to Kahless's holding area, Shift looked back at him in puzzlement. "You mean him?" She gestured to the clone, lying on the deck on his side, his back to them. "As I recall, they threw him into a sewage pit."

"No. The real Kahless—the one from legend, centuries ago." Cross dragged over a chair and reached into the care package beamed over from *Blackstone* on a previous stop. Finding a metal vacuum flask, he opened it and poured himself a cup of industrial-grade coffee. "Valandris didn't know anything about Kahless's teachings before she met Worf—and there wouldn't have been time for him to tell her much. Yet something's gotten into her. I can sense it. A month ago, she only had ears for 'Kruge.'"

"I can answer that, you miserable wretch," Kahless said, rolling over. Cross could see several empty Romulan ale bottles beside him. "The sayings of the Unforgettable are more than words. They are backed with feats, every one." Hairy eyebrows arched in the low light. "Klingons respect his guidance because through battle, he found the inner being, the state that we all aspire to. He obtained that for which we can only grasp."

Cross wiped his mouth and grinned at Shift. "Can you

believe this? It's mumbo-jumbo—but as long as someone who looks like he killed his dinner says it with a growl, they lap it up. It's honey to them."

"Well, Valandris won't be in the fortress much longer," Shift said. "We'll have someone search her cabin and make sure she didn't find any more of Kahless's works."

The clone laughed. "Young fools." He crawled toward a crate and used it to help himself up. "The Unforgettable's words are on every ship in your misbegotten squadron."

Cross looked over at him. "How's that?"

"If the true Kruge was indeed a great warrior, he would have cared about the honor of his crews. All commanders keep some version of the *qeS'a'* in their memory banks. It is good for morale."

"Huh. Well, mixed messages aren't good for *my* morale. Shift, see that the files are deleted on all the ships. Call it . . . a doctrinal purge." He paused and waved off the idea. "No, Klingons wouldn't call it that. They'd say something else." He altered his voice and spoke as Kruge. "*I purged the clone. Now I purge his meaningless prattle.*"

Shift laughed. "You're really getting into this."

Sitting on the crate, Kahless sneered. "Some captains even etch the *qeS'a'* precepts on the underside of all upper bunks, so their warriors wake to the words." He smiled. "Good luck purging that."

Cross sighed. "Forget it. I don't care about Valandris— we only need to ride this beast a while longer. Everything's set up. Kersh and Riker will bring the attendees to the conference. They'll close the doors to Spirits' Forge—and then it'll all be over."

"Nonsense. The Sentries will never let you get near them," Kahless said.

"Near them?" Cross let out a laugh—a big, throaty Kahless laugh. "Thanks to you," he said, adopting the clone's gravelly voice, "the bodies of the Sentries are but ashes in the lava pits of H'atoria."

Kahless stood suddenly and threw something at him. Cross ducked and spilled his coffee, not remembering the force field between them. The bottle Kahless threw bounced off it and shattered on his side of the barrier, spattering Romulan ale everywhere.

"Did you just throw a full one?" Cross asked, wiping coffee from his pants. "You're drunker than I thought."

"Free me, that I can rip the tongue from your mouth!" Kahless snarled, full of fury. "You posed as me?"

"I posed as the Unforgettable. You've made a career of it."

"I never used my likeness to slay honorable warriors!"

"Your 'warriors' didn't even die with weapons in their hands." Cross beat his chest. "If I didn't have the Unsung outside, I bet I could have talked them into climbing into the furnace."

Seemingly under a great burden, Kahless sank down on the crate. "Unarmed Sentries. Unarmed nobles. And now a peace conference. And you speak of this with pride?"

"Ah, I see." Lazing across the chair, Cross templed his fingers and assumed a catlike pose. "'To come to the Peace Rock fresh from a kill of Man—and to boast of it—is a jackal's trick.'"

"What are you yammering about?"

"Not yammering. *Kipling*. Student production—I was Bagheera in *The Second Jungle Book*. I would have done better as the tiger." Seeing Kahless's bewildered expression, he raised his hands. "What? Every word out of your mouth is a quotation. I'm just returning fire."

"Was there a serpent in your play? That—or perhaps a lowly insect—would better suit you!"

"Careful," Shift said.

Kahless raised his fists. "Or what?"

"Or I'll have *Blackstone* beam you into a sun someplace next time we decloak," Cross said.

"You are going to do that anyway when you are done studying me." The clone lowered his fists and shook his head wearily. "You will consider any deed, no matter how dishonorable, as worthy if it suits your little game."

"This is a *big* game," Cross said, closing the vacuum flask and rising. "And of course it's worth it. Our . . . *partner* was right when he said we shouldn't let the Unsung learn too much about Klingon ways. You people waste time thinking about *how* you fight—when you should think about whether you win or not."

Kahless stared at him blankly for a moment. Then he looked to Shift. "Do you agree with this?"

She stood. "I do."

The Klingon stared at her. "I suppose I knew that answer without asking. Then you are both damned." He shook his head. "And me along with you."

Kahless knelt and reached for the broken base of the bottle he had thrown. Finding a little ale still there, he took hold of it and turned his back to them.

The illusionist and his apprentice rarely slept, it seemed. Huddled under the thermal blanket they had given him for warmth in the chilly hold, Kahless could hear them carrying on in their little compartment off the main hallway. They had taken the place as their private nest away from the Unsung on the decks below. They had left him alone with the metal crate and its bottles of Romulan ale to keep him company. Several of the bottles were still inside: intact, inviting, and waiting.

Cross had given him the ale as both a taunt and as a way to keep him talking. In reality, the Betazoid had given Kahless an idea—and hope.

Later scholars of the *qeS'a'* had interpreted that when an honorable death was impossible, escape was a Klingon's only duty. The problem was that since most warriors focused exclusively on avoiding capture in the first place, tales of escapes were rare. The clone had trouble sizing up his situation, thinking up a plan. But Worf and his Starfleet fellows had escaped captivity many times. Perhaps the reason they were less resistant to being captured came not from their different heritages, but the fact that they knew what to do when imprisoned.

Kahless had been at a loss for tactics until the night he had been given the ale. In the pit of despair, he had opened the first bottle—and he had vomited, just from the smell of the liquor. He might have done so again after emptying the bottle—

—had he actually drunk any. Insight struck him instead.

Cross's minions aboard *Blackstone* were monitoring him somehow, Kahless was sure; he could see no sensors anywhere, but he was certain they were there. How else could they project their accursed false images? He had to act in a way they could not see—and then he had to bore them.

So he had feigned drinking. Earlier, he'd found a box of canteens in the storage area; by slipping one of the metal containers under his tunic and hunching in a corner, he'd found he could pour out a third of a bottle while appearing to drink it. Later, the filled canteen would go back into the box.

In this manner, he had convinced Cross, Shift, and anyone watching that he was soused. Then had come the next step: finding a tool. Cross had given it to him in the form of the bottles—and an excuse to break one.

In a deft move worthy of the Betazoid trickster, Kahless had palmed the broken base of the bottle he'd thrown, hiding it in his sleeve. In the hours since, he'd huddled under the thermal blanket he had been given, using the jagged edge to dig at the leather strap around his ankle. The work numbed his fingers; he had to be careful not to sever it too close to the injector, for fear of setting it off and being paralyzed.

Doing something was better than doing nothing. The accursed manacle tore open, and he slipped it off his ankle quickly, fearing the injector might activate. When nothing happened, he carefully maneuvered it from under the blanket to a place where he could covertly examine it.

There was no injector. Just a metal stud, pressed against his skin to simulate one.

Another trick. The remote controller was a lie, a means to keep him quiet. The deceivers probably had no equipment handy for such a circumstance; they had made do with a bond that looked threatening.

Kahless gritted his teeth and tried not to scream in anger. His eyes darted around the hold from crate to crate as he remembered the items he'd seen earlier when he'd been searching for something that would help him. With the H'atorian Conference soon to start, Kahless expected Cross and Shift would again don their respective disguises—and that the *Blackstone* crew would be focused on them, and not being detected by the attendees, rather than him.

Kahless would show them he could not be caged. And he would have a tale of escape that could be remembered in song.

Twenty-two

Kyzak wanted to visit Lieutenant Xaatix's planet some-day. The Ovirian was more nimble than he had imag-ined, her slender form allowing her to whisk quickly back and forth through the facility, ably sidestepping foot traffic from *Titan*'s advance team and the Klingons. Under her orders, the austere mess hall had been completely trans-formed. She was leaving nothing to chance.

"Something is definitely wrong," Xaatix said as she darted inside the kitchen. "The temperature in the meeting room has gone up by a degree and a half."

"Well, you can't blame the kitchen." Kyzak looked around and shrugged. "It's not like there's cook fires or anything."

Xaatix clucked with aggravation. "It's the forge. Noth-ing to be done."

Kyzak agreed. His tricorder readings had found an increase in carbon monoxide—just a trace, nothing to endanger any of the species present. But every time he'd gotten anywhere close to the kiln, one of the Sentries had warned him away.

Seeing the one Sentry in the kitchen leave, Kyzak sidled up to Xaatix. "There's something about the food that ain't right."

"Klingon foodstuffs differ from those you and I are accustomed to," Xaatix replied. "Many things are con-sumed raw or even alive. So long as our guests' digestive systems can handle it, as guests they are expected to eat as their hosts do."

"It ain't that, Lieutenant—though that's taken some getting used to. No, it's the food the Sentries have for themselves. It's not the same."

"Explain."

"Well, I mean it's crawling around, some of it. But they're eating different stuff. They keep it in packs."

"Packs?"

"Yeah. I keep seeing them hiding them away." Looking around to make certain no one else was present, he stepped over to a cabinet and opened the doors. It was stuffed with canvas backpacks. He drew one out.

Xaatix skittered closer. "Open it."

Feeling his stomach wrench, he reached inside and grabbed a jellylike mass. He couldn't tell whether it was the flesh of something or a complete living being. He knew it didn't want to stay in his hand, and the feeling was mutual. He held it up, hoping it was somewhere in the vicinity of Xaatix's visual receptors.

"This is no Klingon dish," she said. "Come with me."

Kyzak shoved the goo back into the bag and flicked his hand in the air to try to dry it. Carrying the pouch, he followed Xaatix as she swept through the meeting area and into the entry hallway. A grim unmasked Klingon stood just inside the double doors open to the front terrace, looking bored.

He noticed Xaatix with annoyance. "What do *you* want?"

"You are Trokaj, General Kersh's security chief?"

"That's right. Are you Starfleeters coming for lessons in protecting people?"

"Sarcasm is unnecessary," Xaatix said, turning an impatient shade of orange. "I have a query about the food served here."

"Would you prefer your meat cooked for you? Or I could

borrow the spoon we use to feed my grandfather who has no teeth."

"This is wasting valuable time," Xaatix said. The Ovirian stepped back a bit, taking the conversation away out of earshot of the Sentries posted outside the front doors. "The Sentries appear to be keeping their own food separate from what's being prepared for the conference."

"What difference does that make? The food they're preparing is safe. Is that what you're wondering about?" Trokaj picked his teeth. "I've tried it."

Kyzak remembered seeing the Klingon doing exactly that several times. "You were testing it? Don't you trust the Sentries' food?"

"Of course I do. I eat because I'm hungry."

"Why would the Sentries not eat the same thing?" Xaatix asked.

Trokaj looked down at the pouch Kyzak was holding open and rolled his eyes. "The Empire is vast. No doubt they eat some foods native to H'atoria." He glanced down hungrily at the stuff in the bag. "Is it any good?"

Kyzak slid his hand into another compartment in the pack. "Look here. Plates, cups—looks to me like a camping kit. Do the Sentries go on maneuvers?"

"The Sentries never leave Spirits' Forge. That's the whole point." Trokaj glanced at the bag. "It is odd."

Kyzak glanced through the crack between the front door and its frame. There were electrical contacts on the jamb and the inside of the door, connected to a small circular device on the wall inside; likely part of a security system. Through the crevice, he could see the two Sentries standing guard at the edge of the veranda. "Maybe we should just ask those guys about it."

"Only the captain of the guard talks to outsiders," Trokaj said. "The captain would be at the arrival area, meeting the visitors."

Xaatix pressed him. "Surely there's someone you know to talk to?"

"I don't know anyone here. Nobody does. I told you, these warriors don't leave. This posting is for life." Trokaj snatched the bag from Kyzak's hands. "Now stop meddling with their things. This is a sacred place." The Klingon reached inside for a red handful, sampled it approvingly, and ambled back inside toward the kitchen, munching as he went.

Kyzak and Xaatix walked back through the meeting area. At the entrance to the stuffy room containing the forge, the Skagaran peeked inside. A Sentry remained standing before the kiln.

"The heat does not concern me," Xaatix said. "I can tolerate temperatures upward of six hundred and twenty-five degrees Celsius without discomfort. But I would rather our attendees not suffer the slightest—"

A bell pealed. The attendees had arrived at the far end of the causeway. At once, the Sentries began to withdraw from the fortress. Kyzak understood that they would take station outside, ceding the facility to their guests for the duration. He edged away as the Sentry guarding the forge exited past him, barely giving him a glance.

Kyzak waited a few moments and slipped into the room. His efforts to close the doors to the kiln were immediately unsuccessful; the doors were permanently bolted open. The Sentries were serious about always wanting to see the fires of their sacred forge.

There's got to be a way to open the flue some more, Kyzak thought, to *air this place out.* He knelt as close as the heat would allow, but craning his neck, he could find no mechanisms.

He hustled out into the meeting room. "Lieutenant," Kyzak asked Xaatix, "how far are you willing to go to make sure your guests stay comfortable?"

"It is my entire purpose. I can't imagine anything I wouldn't do."

"You might think twice once I tell you what it is."

U.S.S. TITAN
ORBITING H'ATORIA

"Please repeat your statement, Captain Picard." Tuvok gave the commander of the *Enterprise* his full attention. "I understood you to say the Unsung were coming *here*."

"Not exactly," Picard replied. On Tuvok's screen, the captain's image crackled and wavered. Aneta Šmrhová was just barely noticeable beside him. *Enterprise* was racing toward H'atoria at maximum warp. *"We fear they might be there already."*

Tuvok blinked. "I have been scanning for Object Thirteen, using the method Commander La Forge devised. The Klingons' surveillance satellites have done the same. We have seen no indication of it."

"You might not, unless you looked for a week or two," Šmrhová replied. *"This information comes from an analysis of data from Klingon listening posts in the region surrounding the Azure Nebula. We have two candidate signals suggesting a trajectory to H'atoria—arriving several days ago."*

That seemed thin to Tuvok—but then he remembered that the Unsung definitely had been in the Azure Nebula, and La Forge's method had tracked them there. "We are scanning for the Phantom Wing with every known protocol. I am not certain what more we can do."

The image broke up for a moment. When it returned,

he heard Picard saying, *"—to take all precautions possible on the ground."*

"Admiral Riker has just shuttled down to H'atoria," he said. "The Sentries have not reported any untoward activity on the planet. While the Unsung have combat gear that hides life signs, a daylight ambush appears unlikely."

"I hope you are correct. We will arrive shortly. Enterprise out."

Tuvok's brow furrowed. He disliked relying solely on the Klingon Sentries, no matter how vaunted their skills or unimpeachable their credentials. Vale had fortified Riker's diplomatic support staff with several officers with security experience, but more needed to be done.

"Computer, please locate Captain Vale."

Twenty-three

At the far end of the land bridge, Valandris stood outside the guardhouse and watched in masked silence as the visitors descended the stairs one by one. Shuttled down or transported from spacecraft high above, each new arrival was greeted at the foot of the stairs by a trio representing the hosting delegations.

The Klingon officer was definitely General Kersh, who looked none too happy to be here; the other two, a male and a female, wore Starfleet uniforms. She had no idea about the dark-haired woman, but the male human was surely the Starfleet admiral: she had seen his image in her briefings and knew his name. Valandris, who was named for a deadly bird of prey on Thane, wondered what kind of an animal a *riker* was.

It was all Valandris could do not to cut down the greeters with her *bat'leth*. But it was not the time Kruge had appointed.

The visitors included members of several species she had never seen. The Ferengi, with ears like the craters of Thane, hadn't impressed her at all. Neither had the Romulan woman, old and officious, being helped down the steps by an aide.

"Ambassador Tocatra," Riker said.

"Greetings, Admiral, General." Tocatra looked at the other Starfleeter. "And this must be Commander Troi. Can you read my mood, empath?"

Troi looked at Riker and then cautiously back at the

Romulan. "You are anticipating an exchange of views," she offered.

"Very diplomatic," Tocatra said, her speech precise and elegant. "You may have one of those views now. If I expire from the fumes on this path, General, my government will expect you to pay for my funeral."

Kersh snorted derisively. Riker waved toward the guardhouse. "We do have breathing filters if you prefer."

"Nonsense. If you can do it, I can." Tocatra and her companion headed off toward the fortress.

Next came the Breen representative, whose appearance *did* impress Valandris. Covered from head to toe in a silver-gray environmental suit, the Breen exuded menace. A glowing green slit of light stood in place of eyeholes, and his faceplate terminated in an angry metal snout. As armor, the Breen's gear was much bulkier than what the Unsung preferred—but Valandris expected it made them formidable warriors.

"Ambassador Vart," Riker said. "Pleased to see you again."

The Breen responded with a series of electronic squawks. Valandris wondered how Riker could tell any two Breen apart, much less understand their gibberish. Their presence sparked confusion—and it appeared to be by design. According to what she had read in one of the more recent updates to *Chu'charq*'s database, the Breen Confederacy comprised multiple different species, all of which sought perfect equality by wearing the same obscuring gear.

Whatever the thing said, Riker acted as if he understood. Without a word to General Kersh, Vart moved along after the Romulans.

She watched Riker whisper something to Troi. Valandris began to perceive the woman was a confidant of long standing. Both Starfleet officers' eyes were fixed on the staircase.

When Valandris saw what was making its way down to them, she was glad of her facial filter—for her mouth fell open.

Kinshaya.

She'd been told what to expect, but the first thing Valandris thought when she saw the three-member Kinshaya entourage was that the creatures were born to be hunted. Walking on four large legs with multicolored wings sprouting from their backs, the Kinshaya were clearly built to flee predators. Yet they were too large-bodied to fly anymore, as she understood it.

Had there been Kinshaya on Thane, Valandris doubted anyone on her world would have wanted to leave. She little wondered that the Empire had gone to war with them many times. The Kinshaya had to be good eating.

"*Aya*, infidels," said the lead creature to the hosts. "You bring shame to the name of Galoya, bringing me amid Klingon devils during the Year of Prayer."

Kersh ground her teeth. Riker quickly spoke up. "Not at all, Envoy Galoya. Your presence, your sacrifice in coming here, will begin a new age for your people, opening many frontiers for travel."

"You are deluded, Admiral-infidel, for this planet is already ours. It was annexed to the Holy Order five cycles ago."

"And immediately after that you all ran away screaming," Kersh said. The Klingon general could take no more. "Mind yourself in this place."

The Kinshaya cocked her head to the air. "I hear the buzz of insects. Maintenance of this world has clearly suffered. The Order must attend to it soon. Or perhaps the war-god Niamlar will simply cleanse the planet altogether of—"

This time, it was Troi who intervened. "Will you walk

with me and tell me about your trip, Galoya?" She looked on the lead Kinshaya with benevolence. "By what title are you known?"

"I am assistant to the vice-deputy director for Janalwa's office of public sanitation, drainage division."

Kersh gawked. "They sent a *sewage engineer*?"

"Those insects again," Galoya said, wings flapping at nothing. Joined by Troi, she led her companions onto the causeway.

Kersh looked at Riker. "Well, you wanted them to send someone." She laughed heartily and walked up the path.

The processional on its way, Riker turned to follow—until he stopped right before Valandris. He looked into her eyes. "You're the captain of the guard?" the bearded face asked.

Valandris did not respond, hoping that would make him leave her alone.

Instead, Riker somehow took her silence to be a response in the affirmative. "I appreciate your hosting us. I know there may be some hard feelings about the Kinshaya being here." He nodded in the direction of the winged envoy. "Their attacking here, right after the Borg devastated H'atoria, was completely without honor. It was abhorrent to the Federation—and to me, personally."

Why tell me? Valandris wondered.

It was as if the admiral had heard the question in Valandris's mind. "I wanted you and the other Sentries to know that in bringing the Kinshaya here, I meant no offense to you, or your great fortress. I believe what we will discuss there will ultimately bring more security to this world than shields or transporter inhibitors ever could. You'll be able to keep station here knowing that enemies who once wanted control of this space have relinquished their claims." His confident gaze melted into a grin. "If I do my job right, that is."

Valandris stared at him. Then she simply gestured with her *bat'leth* toward the fortress.

"Well, thanks for letting me practice my speech." Turning from her, he started walking along the causeway after the others. "*Qapla'.*"

"*Qapla',*" she replied, before she knew she had.

When Valandris finally started to follow, many paces behind, she had arrived at the conclusion that whatever kind of animal a Terran riker was, it was likely known for its calm and shrewdness.

Riker was halfway along the fog-enshrouded path when he saw Troi had stopped to wait for him.

"Ran out of things to say to the Kinshaya?" he asked.

"I was afraid if I kept simply nodding my head I might stumble off the causeway." As Troi began to walk with him, they passed between a pair of motionless Sentries. "The Kinshaya clearly don't respect the Federation—or this process."

"They sent someone. The Kinshaya are the weak link in the Typhon Pact; you can count on either the Romulans or the Breen to be pulling their strings."

"I expect one or the other was behind the political uprising on Janalwa stalling out."

"Likely. But that cuts both ways. If we can make the Romulans or the Breen want the free-flight corridor, then their client—or puppet, or whatever—might come along."

Troi grinned. "I like it when you're positive. I've missed this."

"Well, remember that," Riker said, gesturing to his com badge. "Because a few minutes ago I got word from Vale that the Unsung may already be in the area."

Troi's eyes darted around. "Where, here?"

"Above, below, we don't know." No one was present but

the guests walking up ahead and the Sentries stationed on the causeway; the guard Riker had spoken with was walking about twenty meters behind. "*Enterprise* is on its way. They are working on something."

Her eyes went to him. "Are *we* working on something?"

"You could say that." He gripped her hand. "Like I said, just keep smiling."

Twenty-four

It was time. Cross emerged from his lair. Finding his coffee mug atop a crate, he finished off the cold liquid and strolled over to look in on Kahless.

The Klingon was behind the force field, lying on his side in an apparent stupor, covered by a blanket. Cross pounded the wall beside the force field with the metal cup. "Are we still friends, Big K?"

Kahless passed gas loudly and proceeded to snore.

I'll take that as a yes, Cross thought. The clone would run out of Romulan ale fast at this rate.

He looked all around the deck one hold. Shift was nowhere to be found, evidently having left early to prepare for their big day. He might as well get on with it. "Okay, *Blackstone*, let's have some wardrobe. *Alakazam*."

Tuvok sat at the bridge tactical station and waited. And waited.

He had done all he could. Captain Vale had responded quickly to the news he'd received from *Enterprise*, directing Commander Sarai to contact all the vessels in orbit. Every ship was now running the sensor protocol. Vale had activated Ranul Keru's contingency security plan. It was out of Tuvok's hands.

All that was left to him was his continuing search for Object Thirteen, the cloaked vessel supposedly shadowing the Phantom Wing. He knew it might only be detectable one millisecond out of every billion; it was illogical to expect it to appear now just because he was looking for—

Something changed.

It wasn't the reading *Enterprise* had told him to look for. It was a different kind of energy, in a distinct subspace band. The effect had been pronounced for only a moment—but in that moment, it was noticeable.

Tuvok adjusted the sensors, trying to find the signal again. He detected nothing. But a faint echo, so to speak, came and went, darting in and out. Then it waned and disappeared.

He looked to Vale. "Captain, I may have something."

"What is it, Tuvok?"

"Checking sensors. One moment, please."

PHANTOM WING VESSEL *CHU'CHARQ*
ABOVE H'ATORIA

Disguised as Kruge, Buxtus Cross took his place in *Chu'charq*'s command chair. It was not an honor that he wanted: bridges were the place where one saw everything surrounding the ship. With all the firepower in orbit around the cloaked bird-of-prey, he was almost afraid to look.

But with Valandris on the surface, the crew looked to him. Raneer was an adequate pilot but no tactician, and the others knew it. Cross was here pretending to be a famed Klingon warrior. Of course they wanted the Fallen Lord in command. "Go," he said, and the starship banked and started its descent toward H'atoria, joined by two other Phantom Wing vessels, both cloaked.

Cross felt his stomach flip over. The risks had to be getting to him. He'd been trapped by his own choice of characters—or, rather, Korgh's.

He wondered what Korgh was doing. By now the old operator was probably on Qo'noS, sipping bloodwine in the lounge of the Great Hall, waiting to go to the High Council floor to denounce a range of scapegoats. The Federation for harboring the Unsung. Starfleet for failing to capture them. Chancellor Martok for likewise failing to catch the cultists—and for supporting the Accords. *"The terrorists have continued their vendetta against my house,"* Korgh would say in a few hours. *"Killing my valiant cousin Kersh and bringing death to one of our proudest historic places."* That Admiral Riker had fallen would be relegated to an afterthought; the Empire's feckless "ally" would have deserved no better.

Yes, Cross had a pretty good idea of what Korgh would say. The Betazoid had impersonated politicians of many species before—and the old Klingon codger was definitely putting on a show for the masses. But for all his years pretending to be someone he wasn't, Korgh was just an amateur, as was anyone outside the Circle. He could never be in Cross's league—even if no one since Ardra had tried anything as ambitious as Korgh's Unsung scheme.

On the other hand, Ardra, so far as Cross knew, had never done anything with such a body count. Even if he never pulled off his Kahless plan, the others of the Circle would be talking about Cross's Kruge act for ages. He benefited from the fact that the Circle didn't judge the morality of its practitioners' schemes. Oh, it might once have—long before the days of Jilaan, the last to hold the title of Illusionist Magnus. The Circle's plight had become more desperate since, its opportunities constrained by the advance of the Federation and its busybodies in Starfleet, always out to preserve its precious Prime Directive. The only time his rivals passed judgment was at their occasional convocations, and that was just to rate the quality of the feats.

Cross saw the clouds part in front of *Chu'charq*. A green sea opened up below. Almost imperceptibly, Shift arrived at his side in her N'Keera incarnation. "Where were you?" he asked quietly.

"I had something to take care of," she whispered. "It's a big day."

That it was. The twin peaks of the Spirits' Forge island appeared low on the horizon, pillars of steam rising wherever lava flows reached the ocean. He'd not seen the place from midair before. "Magnify."

After Raneer complied, Cross could make out several transports on the southern island, where the beam-in zone was located—and in places he could see the new transporter suppression towers along the causeway. He wondered what other devices the defenders had brought to the areas the Unsung had not entered. Did the Klingons have antiaircraft guns?

"Five shuttles parked at the southern promontory," Raneer said. "Three Klingon. One Breen. One Starfleet."

"Hold here," Cross commanded as they approached. They were still several kilometers away. "Order *Kradge* and *Bregit* to hold at the same distance."

Hemtara looked to him from the engineer's station. "We can get closer without detection, my lord. A cloak that can evade tachyons will not have trouble with a little fog."

"*Kradge* and *Bregit* may advance. But we will stay here," Cross said, his hands gripping the armrests. The fire would start soon enough. He had no desire to dash into it.

Phantom Wing Vessel *Rodak*
Orbiting H'atoria

Sitting in his bird-of-prey's command chair, Zokar looked out at the vessels gathering over H'atoria and remembered the first time he had flown aboard a ship under cloak. He had been a teenaged trainee on maneuvers, and looking out from his starship, he had felt like a vengeful spirit. He had envisioned himself leading whole squadrons of ghostly attackers, stalking and defeating the Empire's enemies.

Instead, he had been in the wrong place at the wrong time forty years earlier—and all his dreams had died. He did not lead squadrons. Rather, he began three decades of humiliation and misery, alleviated only when he emigrated to Thane and its colony of the discommendated. It was the only place that would welcome him, and he had flourished.

Now he had his invisible squadron. Kruge had appointed him to direct the Unsung forces remaining in space while the operation proceeded below. And unlike his teenaged self, Zokar had something he genuinely felt vengeful about.

There were the Klingons who had discommendated him, of course. But in Zokar's case, unknown to most of his companions or to Kruge, there had been another party worthy of blame. He looked over at the twin-hulled Romulan warbird, hanging in orbit like a poisoned claw: *D'choak*, the transponder reported.

He had been ordered to protect the Unsung forces escaping from the surface from the Klingon and Starfleet forces who would surely pursue them. He had no orders about the Romulans. But what was it that Kruge had said in his broadcast declaration? *"We must punish the Empire. We must punish those foolish enough to ally with it. We must punish any who seek to bargain with it."*

He ruminated over the last part. It was meant to keep anyone from coming to the Empire's aid against the Unsung—but it was also dispensation.

The Romulans had come to H'atoria to bargain with the Empire. And it was Romulans who had killed his brother—and so many others—at Khitomer, forty years earlier. He owed them for that—and more. *Oh, so much more.*

Rubbing the stump of an arm long since gone, Zokar nodded to himself. If the chance came, he would deal a little extra revenge.

SPIRITS' FORGE
H'ATORIA, KLINGON EMPIRE

Once, a precocious friend had talked the young Ethan Kyzak into reaching into a campfire. The experience had given the child a healthy respect for fire and a dislike for anyone who tried to wheedle another person into doing something dangerous.

Thus it was with trepidation that he had suggested that Lieutenant Xaatix climb into the kiln of Spirits' Forge, on the vaguest possibility that someone lithe and heat-tolerant might be able to investigate the fortress's ventilation problem. Kyzak crouched as close on the stone hearth as he could safely get and gave Xaatix a boost. The Ovirian's body curled as she twisted inside the great furnace and grasped the inner wall of the chimney with her suctioning claws.

"Are you okay?" Kyzak asked, not imagining how the answer could be yes.

"This is the most irregular thing I've ever done. I'm a protocol officer."

"I meant, are you all right?"

"I have a secure hold," Xaatix said, her voice echoing.

"The interior walls are metal. Quite hot. It is good that I do not breathe as you do. Or wear clothing."

"I'd noticed, but I didn't know if I should say anything," Kyzak said. It was probably wrong to say it now, but he found it hard to focus on making conversation when helping someone to climb inside an inferno. He hoped against hope the Sentries wouldn't come back inside.

Thrumming drumbeats reverberated and grew smaller. "You're climbing?"

"I've found the problem," Xaatix called down. "There is no damper mechanism. But there is something up here. Something is hanging in the chimney."

"Hanging?" Kyzak's nose wrinkled. "What?"

"Well, it's a kind of a snub-nosed bulky thing, suspended by something. I'd say about two-thirds of a meter across, one meter and a third long." A pause. "There appears to be a marking on it. Klingon."

"What does it say?"

"I don't know this word. Morath. Morath's Fist."

Kyzak's eyes widened. "Did you say *Morath's Fist*?"

"I did. What does that mean?"

"Oh gosh." Responding to the name he remembered from his Klingon ordnance identification class, Kyzak grabbed at his sweat-soaked hair and looked up at the ceiling. *"There's a photon torpedo in the chimney!"*

Twenty-five

"**S**o close," Riker said under his breath.

After scaling the dozens of gradually sloping steps stretching up the hill to the fortress, he had at last gotten to the open doorway. Troi was already inside with Kersh and the other guests, getting situated. It only remained for the admiral to enter with the Breen envoy and the Kinshaya, and then the two Sentries posted outside would close the massive double doors for the duration.

Then Ambassador Vart had gotten a call. Riker assumed that was what had happened; the message must have come in to the envoy via his helmet. The evidence was that Vart had stopped dead, steps from the threshold. The Kinshaya had halted behind the Breen ambassador.

Just a few more meters, Riker thought. *Just so I can say we had the damn meeting!*

Valandris stood at the northern end of the causeway and watched the fortress, which sat higher up the island atop a series of stairs. The dignitaries had finally reached it. The time was nigh.

The plan was simple. The doors would close behind the attendees, triggering the timer rigged to the torpedo. While the disguised Unsung outside the front and rear doors sealed the exits, Valandris would pass along a signal through the forces behind her on the land bridge. Those posted past the halfway point on the causeway would retreat to the southern cape, clear of the transporter inhibitors' effects. The rest would join her on the Unsung's training grounds, under the umbrella of a shield that was proof against everyone else's transporters but theirs.

In the seven minutes it took for the timer to reach zero, all the Unsung would be back aboard the cloaked birds-of-prey hovering nearby. General Kersh and her conspirators would die so dramatically that the Klingon Empire and Federation alike would forever cower in fear of the Unsung.

It was Kruge's plan, and naturally it was brilliant—but it would not have been her plan. It was no hunt; it was purely a trap. She was not sanguine about it, but she wasn't making the decisions.

Then something unexpected occurred. Her keen eyes could tell that something was happening with the diplomats just outside the open doors. The Breen lingered stubbornly on the threshold, and the three Kinshaya had backed away from the doors. Riker was in the entryway, gesticulating as he tried to get the Breen to go inside.

The Breen waved away the Starfleet admiral and stepped over to speak into the lead Kinshaya's ear.

What was going on?

Sweat streaming down his face, Kyzak finally got Commander Troi away from her guests in the meeting area. Troi followed Kyzak to the door of the forge room.

"*Transport out?*" she whispered. "What do you mean? The meeting's about to start."

Kyzak saw past her through to where Admiral Riker beckoned from the anteroom doorway, urgently trying to get Troi's attention. Something was going on outside. "Deanna, I need you," Riker called, before disappearing back through the exit.

"Ethan, I've got to go," Troi said, turning from the Skagaran.

"No, Commander." Kyzak grasped at her arm. It didn't take a Betazoid to sense how alarmed he was—and his eyes said the rest.

She called out over her shoulder, "Just a minute, Admiral!" Troi stepped fully into the room with Kyzak, out of earshot of the puzzled Klingon and Romulan representatives.

"Xaatix has found something in the furnace," he said.

"The furnace?" Troi looked at the blazing fire pit and looked around. "Where *is* Xaatix?"

"She's up the chimney—with the torpedo!"

It was hard for Kyzak to tell which half of the sentence surprised Troi more.

Riker couldn't hear what Breen Ambassador Vart was saying to Galoya—and he knew he probably wouldn't have understood it anyway. Whatever it was, the Kinshaya understood. Galoya's wings flared upward into a defiant vee.

"*So!*" the Kinshaya yelled.

The admiral didn't know what to do with that. "So?"

"So you bring me and my comrades to an abattoir, where the Klingon devils slew and ate my brothers and sisters five years ago?"

This was new. "Envoy, Spirits' Forge is not a—"

"Save your lies, heathen. I saw it as we approached. The chimney still smokes from the carcasses of our lost heroes!"

Riker shook his head. "It's a forge for creating ceremonial weapons that—"

One of Galoya's companions spoke. "I know Klingon ceremonies. They flay the flesh and devour their victims alive."

Riker gritted his teeth into an almost-smile. "One moment, please." He looked over his shoulder and tapped his combadge. "Riker to Troi."

She did not respond—but someone else did, behind him. "What is it, Riker?"

His heart sank into his stomach. *Kersh.*

"It's nothing," Riker said, outstretching his hands in

the doorway. He was having difficulty getting everyone to the table; he wasn't going to let anyone else leave. "Envoy Galoya, there is no danger to you here."

"Danger?" Kersh, now behind Riker's back, called over his shoulder. "You waste breath, Riker, if you expect bravery from a carrion beast. The Kinshaya only attack in the wake of others, just as they did after the Borg strike."

"I've heard enough," Galoya said, turning and trotting down the stairs. Her two companions followed.

Riker glared back at Kersh. "Nice going."

"You mean to say, *Good riddance.*"

Tocatra stood to Kersh's side, grinning. "Problems, Admiral?"

Riker shook his head in disgust and walked onto the terrace outside. Vart was hastening down the steps after the Kinshaya, bound for where the captain of the guard stood mute at the end of the causeway. The admiral heard a low rumble from the south—and mere moments later, the Breen shuttle broke through the haze, heading for the fortress.

Why did they leave their engines powered up? Riker wondered.

The admiral started down the stairs and called after the Breen ambassador. Maybe they could continue if the Breen remained and represented the Kinshaya. But a stream of invective from Vart suggested that the Breen were standing with the Kinshaya—and, in fact, offering them a ride offworld.

Both topography and ceremony prevented there from being a landing pad on the northern cape, but the Breen pilot improvised. Far ahead and below, the shuttle settled awkwardly over a narrow patch of lava-free beach at the distant end of the stairs. A ramp descended from the vehicle.

"Thank you, Ambassador," Galoya said. "You have saved us a trip to the beam-in zone. I couldn't take the stench here another second!"

A few kilometers away aboard *Chu'charq*, Cross was beside himself.

"What is happening?" he said in his Kruge voice. "What's going on down there?"

Raneer increased magnification to the maximum—but only the image of events became clearer, not their meaning. "The Breen shuttle is boarding Breen and Kinshaya passengers," she reported.

"I can see that," he said with disgust. He looked to Shift, who seemed unusually silent. "They were supposed to go inside the building. What's going on?"

"Unclear," Raneer said. "Should we approach?"

Before Cross could answer, Hemtara spoke up. "My lord, there may be a problem with that."

Cross's bushy Kruge eyebrows shot up. "Can we be seen?"

"No. But the steam from those fumaroles could condense on our hull, or precipitate out as rain. We're invisible, not immaterial."

Raneer looked back at him. "Aren't there ways to deal with that, my lord? Something about altering hull temperature or reshaping our cloaking field?"

Cross didn't have the slightest idea. Shift saved him by answering. "Most of the people on the surface are ours. I'm sure our lord would advise that we approach very slowly to unassisted visual range."

"Yes. Do it." Cross sank in his seat. He wondered if the Unsung had anything aboard to treat an ulcer.

"I will tell the admiral," Troi said in the forge room. "And *Titan*." She was gone from Kyzak's side in a heartbeat.

The Skagaran leaned as far into the hearth as he dared and called upward. "Xaatix, how's that torpedo secured?"

"It's suspended on chains," the Ovirian lieutenant said. "Looks like it was lowered from the top of the chimney. Won't the heat set it off?"

"No. They design them so they can be fired into hot nebulae. That casing's duranium and tritanium."

"Ingenious. What do they make chains out of?"

"Neither of those, probably."

"Ah," Xaatix said, as creepily calm as she'd been from the start. "I suppose if the chain gives out, the timer becomes irrelevant."

"*Timer?*" It was the first Kyzak had heard of it. "Um, Xaatix, were you going to mention that sooner?"

"It does not appear to be activated. But before you ask, I am neither aware of how to remove it nor in a position to do so." She went silent for a moment. "Can we deactivate the fortress's shield generator? Get *Titan* to beam the torpedo out of here? Or *us?*"

"The Sentries never showed us where the generator was." Kyzak didn't want to spend the last moments of his life running around looking for something that might be buried in a subbasement somewhere. He knew the shield began its protection several hundred meters above the surface, with a generous opening to the south, in the direction of the causeway.

Thinking of it, Kyzak remembered how he'd arrived on H'atoria—and an idea dawned. He tapped his combadge. "Ensign Bolaji, I need the shuttle over here, right away!"

Valandris watched the Breen shuttle lift off, carrying the Breen and Kinshaya with it. None of the occupants had been targeted by Kruge; she had simply let them board and depart. But she was at a loss as what to do next.

Staring up at the fortress, she saw that Beroc and Bardoc, the hulking twin brothers she'd known on Thane, had left their post at either side of the great doors. As they descended the stairs toward her, she could read the bewilderment in their eyes.

"What do we do?" Beroc asked when he reached the foot of the stone steps. "They're not going inside."

"Should we force them in? Or close the doors?" added Bardoc.

The torpedo timer's countdown was supposed to start at the closing of the doors, yet at the moment the damnable Kersh stood in the doorway, visibly hectoring Riker. Whatever was to have happened here, the conference appeared to have fallen apart.

That changed nothing. Seeing the general—spawn of the vile nobles who had condemned her people—ranting at her Federation lackey in the place where she intended to betray her people to the Romulans outraged Valandris. And there was the old Romulan female beside Kersh, amused with all of them. Her kind won wherever chaos reigned. What duplicities had she devised in her long life?

Valandris decided she was tired of deception. She was going to make sure her enemies knew what she thought in no uncertain terms.

Riker was searching for a swear word in Klingon with which to respond to General Kersh when Troi appeared in the doorway and yanked his arm. "There's a bomb," she said.

"Don't even joke right now."

"No, Admiral, there is," she said. Her eyes were wide. "I just hailed *Titan*. They're standing by to evacuate."

Ambassador Tocatra recoiled. "A bomb? In there?" The gray-haired Romulan moved quickly from the doorway to the edge of the terrace where the stairs down to the causeway began.

Finding the impulse sensible, the others did the same—and as they descended the steps, both Kersh and Riker opened channels on their communications devices.

The admiral was in the middle of a report from Vale when a Klingon voice he hadn't heard before shouted. *"General Kersh!"*

Riker and Kersh looked at each other. The voice came not from their communicators, but from one of the wide intermediate landings below, the one closest to the start of the causeway. The woman he'd thought to be the captain of the guard stood there, flanked by the two Sentries who'd been standing by the doors. With one hand she ripped her mask away and bared her teeth, while with the other she lifted her *bat'leth* high.

"I am Valandris of the Unsung, the people your family condemned at birth. I declare myself to you, General Kersh—and now I will have my revenge!"

Twenty-six

Riker stood his ground, processing the new information. "I take it you're not the captain of the guard."

"I killed him," Valandris said. "We killed them all. You are next." To either side of her, the two young Klingons who'd guarded the entrance discarded their *bat'leths* and drew disruptors from their vests. Behind them, many of the guards who'd been stationed on the causeway approached, similarly armed and ready to support her. Back up the stairs was no escape: Riker could see the Sentries who'd remained on the northern end of the island working their way across the rocky slope on either side of the stairs. They did not look friendly.

The Unsung had replaced all the Sentries.

Kersh looked at them—and then glowered at Valandris. "You slew our honorable guardians in their sleep, no doubt—as befits a discommendated worm."

"They died on their feet. But I have announced our presence now," Valandris said. She pounded her chest with her free hand, as if to declare she thought that was good enough.

Riker glanced at Troi, who was helping Tocatra stand. The aged Romulan's defiance seemed to have abandoned her. "The rest of us are unarmed," the ambassador said to Valandris. "I have done nothing to you. My government will reward you if you free me."

"That's not happening."

"By Kahless, I've had enough!" Kersh yelled. She drew her *d'k tahg*. A ceremonial addition to her uniform, but deadly. She walked down the few remaining steps to the landing. "I owe you for my grandfather—for my whole house!"

"Yes," Valandris said. "You owe us." She stepped forward, gripping the *bat'leth* with both hands, evidently welcoming the engagement. "Beroc, Bardoc, tell the others. Whether she falls or I, finish the rest off. And then the fortress."

Riker spoke up. "Can I say a word first?"

Squaring off, Kersh and Valandris both looked at him. At the same time, they asked in aggravation, "What?"

He touched his combadge. "Aphrodite."

U.S.S. *TITAN*
ORBITING H'ATORIA

The Unsung were below. Sensors showed waves of Klingons approaching where the northern body of the island met the causeway. The admiral and the diplomats were still underneath the fortress's force field; there was no way to transport them up.

And there was the small matter of Lieutenant Kyzak's bomb.

One thing at a time, Vale told herself. While *Titan*'s crew was hundreds of kilometers above the action, Ensign Bolaji was much nearer, lifting off from the southern landing zone in shuttlecraft *Handy*—appropriately named, that was.

And other help was even closer.

"Admiral has given the word," Sariel Rager reported from ops. "Commander Keru's team confirms receipt and is in motion."

"Red alert. Arm phasers," she ordered. "Watch for aerial response." If the Unsung were on the surface, their birds-of-prey had to be close by.

SPIRITS' FORGE
H'ATORIA, KLINGON EMPIRE

It was Ranul Keru's wild card, as they would have said at the poker table. Admiral Riker had approved of the audacious plan immediately upon learning of it earlier, despite the fact that he had agreed that the Klingons alone would handle security on H'atoria.

As the Unsung closed in, Riker's eyes darted past them to the ocean. Dozens of meters from the island's shore, past the zone where the lava flows heated the water, a helmeted head broke the surf. Then another. And another. One of the Unsung gave a cry, and the others looked behind them. On either side of the causeway and surrounding the northern cape, *Titan* security officers in environmental suits rose from the surf like the Aphrodite of Greek myth.

And yet unlike her, as Keru and his crewmates broke the water entirely, carried aloft by antigravs. An hour earlier, *Titan* had transported them underwater to locations beyond the reach of the fortress's shield and the causeway's transporter inhibitors. Beneath the surface, they had watched and waited.

Additionally, Aphrodite had not been armed with phaser rifles. "Drop your weapons," Keru's amplified voice ordered. "Now!"

Vale had told Riker all was ready earlier, but Kersh, who knew nothing of the plan, looked stunned. Kersh's opponent Valandris appeared even more flummoxed. Riker heard her start to say something—but if she had any control over the Unsung forces, it disappeared as they pointed their disruptors outward at their new foes hovering over the sea. Keru's people, ready, began firing.

"Let's go!" Riker yelled. Keeping his head down, he

saw that Troi was helping Ambassador Tocatra back up the long, winding series of steps toward the fortress. The Ferengi envoy was already far ahead. Kersh, apparently realizing melee with Valandris wasn't worth getting shot in the crossfire, chased up the stairs after Riker.

"You weren't allowed to bring security to the island!" Kersh yelled as they reached an intermediate landing a quarter of the way up the steps.

"They're not *on* the island, General," Riker replied.

PHANTOM WING VESSEL *CHU'CHARQ*
ABOVE H'ATORIA

"What the *hell*?"

Aboard *Chu'charq*'s bridge, Raneer looked back at Cross. "Excuse me, Lord Kruge?"

The break in character couldn't be helped. Even after they had moved closer to the action, it had been difficult for Cross to make sense of what was happening on the island. Yes, a problem had broken up the conference before it could start, thwarting plans to bomb the fortress, but the *faux* Sentries should then have massacred Kersh's and Riker's entourages.

Valandris had unmasked, blowing that plan. That had brought their forces out of hiding, turning an ambush into a standoff. Then the Starfleeters had surfaced, and all reason had ended.

"I detect a lift-off of a shuttle from the southern peninsula," Hemtara reported. "It is one of *Titan*'s. The Klingon support ships are powering up."

Standing by Cross's command chair, Shift offered, "None of them can be allowed to reach the fortress. Until Kersh is killed, the mission cannot end."

"Wise counsel from the sage N'Keera," Cross said. "Order *Bregit* and *Kradge* to destroy the shuttles."

"My lord, they will be revealed," Hemtara said.

"Their brothers and sisters fight valiantly below. Carry out my orders, now!"

Cross had thought to suggest the other birds-of-prey fire on the crowd at the northern end of the causeway directly, but with the Unsung from *Chu'charq* down there, he was reluctant to order it. It was better to save confrontations with his dupes for when there wasn't as much enemy hardware in orbit overhead.

U.S.S. TITAN
ORBITING H'ATORIA

"Captain," Tuvok said, "I detect an explosion on the surface."

"The bomb?" Vale asked.

Tuvok looked up from the tactical display. "No, on the southern cape. One of General Kersh's parked shuttles was destroyed. Readings indicate it was struck by a ten-megawatt disruptor burst—equivalent to the yield of a bird-of-prey's secondary cannon. That was the same weapon the Phantom Wing used at Gamaral against the *Enterprise*."

Word came from ops. "Sensors detect no vessels present, Captain."

"They're cloaked. Make sure General Kersh's forces on *Gur'rok* know," Vale said. "Tuvok, the next time you detect disruptors, fire a series of phaser bursts randomly distributed within a hundred meters of the source—so long as it's clear of any friendlies."

"Aye."

To Vale's right, Sarai stiffened. "Captain, I again remind

you of the guidelines provided for the conference by Lord Korgh." The first officer had already balked earlier at Keru's plan, to no avail. "We are not authorized to fire at targets on the planet."

"We're not firing at a target. We're firing at nothing." Vale smirked. "And besides, I think the Khitomer Accords trump Lord Korgh's guidelines."

No matter what the man himself might want to think.

Twenty-seven

For the thirtieth time today, Korgh longed to be at Ketorix, monitoring things from Odrok's secret command center. So much was going on at Spirits' Forge, and while everything up until this morning had gone according to plan, at least according to Cross, he thirsted for knowledge.

Instead, like all the other High Councilors, he stood in the Great Hall's command center and listened to the dispatches coming from the vessels orbiting H'atoria. In a case of marvelous timing, Chancellor Martok was absent, away on some inspection tour; Korgh seized the chance to rail against the Unsung and a timid chancellor who once was respected but was now out of his depth.

And, of course, he spoke against the Accords. The Federation's blunders had once again brought harm inside the Empire. Wasn't it time to look at where the interests of the Empire really lay?

"Someone has destroyed another of our shuttles on the surface," came the audio report from the observer aboard *Gur'rok.* Korgh tut-tutted and prepared to speak, knowing exactly what he planned to say.

He wished he knew how the day would end. It would tell him which version of his speech to give.

SPIRITS' FORGE
H'ATORIA, KLINGON EMPIRE

Breathless as he swiftly ascended the staircases to the fortress, Riker risked a quick look behind him. The carnage at the southern spur could not be missed, even with a firefight going on in the foreground and volcanic fog in between.

A disruptor blast from nowhere resulted in another island-shaking explosion, and a titanic pillar of flame climbed over the southern cape. The fury from Kersh, racing beside him, was almost as hot. "They are trying to destroy ships before they can launch!"

And doing a fine job of it, Riker thought. That made for at least one bird-of-prey in the area. He hoped that was all.

He was about to turn back and resume scaling the stairs when he spied another flash—followed by a blinding sequence of searing bolts from the sky above. One of the shots from orbit struck something, and for a split second Riker thought he saw a cloaked object partially appearing.

"They've hit pay dirt," Riker said. "Wonder if that shot came from my ship or yours?"

"I don't care." Kersh clenched her fist in triumph. "So long as they keep firing!"

Suddenly a ship that was definitely Starfleet's streaked from the fog. Riker and Kersh saw shuttlecraft *Handy* racing out across the ocean, weaving as disruptor bolts came from an invisible attacker. Piloted by Ensign Bolaji, *Handy* rolled over, under, and looped back. Then it streaked toward the southern cape, attracting more fire from the cloaked vessel.

The strange chase attracted the attention of some of the combatants on the ground when *Handy* returned for a long, low pass, cutting across the causeway diagonally. Unsung warriors on the land bridge fired their disruptors upward. A blazing flash of ionized air filled the sky as another series of orbital phaser blasts rained down.

The barrage struck the invisible predator directly, and the unseen vessel slammed into the causeway, causing an eruption of stone and debris. Riker goggled as a Klingon bird-of-prey, jerked into the visible realm by the impact of its left wing, pinwheeled crazily across the ocean before exploding violently a kilometer away.

The conflagration prompted a pause in the melee further down the slope—but it was short-lived, as the Unsung renewed their counterattack with vigor. Riker and Kersh turned and headed up the remaining stairs—only to hear the scream of engines as the belly of *Handy* flashed dangerously close overhead. Rocketing just meters off the ground to pass beneath the fortress's defensive shield, the vessel continued northward.

Riker quickened his pace, hopeful *Handy* was there to evacuate them. When the vessel curled around the fortress and disappeared behind it, he wondered what was going on.

Kersh had a guess. "There is a clearing between the northern exit and the petrified forest. I will get you through the fortress and on board."

"You will?"

"You are my house's guest—no matter how badly this has gone." Kersh's face went dark. "It seems Starfleet is not alone when it comes to failing at security."

From her position behind a boulder, Valandris lowered her disruptor and gaped in horror at the blazing mass out to sea to the east. She found the small combadge inside her sentry uniform. "*Chu'charq*, are you there?"

She waited long seconds for the answer. Then Hemtara answered, "That was *Kradge*."

Who was aboard? she wanted to ask. But phaser fire was in the air, and the list would have been too long to bear. Fully one-twelfth of the community, people she had known all her life, were aboard the *Kradge*.

The flames still reflecting in her eyes, she turned her fire on the Starfleet officers. Riker and Kersh had not deserved her warning. She would chase them to hell.

PHANTOM WING VESSEL *CHU'CHARQ*
ABOVE H'ATORIA

That could have been me, Cross thought as he looked out on the sinking wreckage of *Kradge*.

The Phantom Wing vessels were heavily stocked with ordnance brought from Thane—*too* stocked. Once *Kradge* went in hard, one explosion led to another. He doubted there would be any evidence for the Empire and Federation to discover.

The Unsung on the bridge eyed him intently, sure that their Lord Kruge would order *Chu'charq* into the fray. They expected he would lead them into battle, throwing the ship at the island and blowing away Kersh and anyone who had sought to protect her, heedless of any threat.

And on the *Blackstone*, hovering invisibly five hundred meters off *Chu'charq*'s bow, Gaw and the other truthcrafters would be chewing off their fingernails in hopes he would think of something else.

"We will have our revenge," he finally said. "Open our secure channel to Zokar and the others. Have them make sure whatever ship fired on *Kradge* never does so again."

And then, dear heaven, let them help us escape. I've had my fill of playing Kruge.

U.S.S. Titan
Orbiting H'atoria

"Captain, I have detected something," Tuvok said. "Just above the planet's surface, in the region of the island group. Energy being directed between two points which sensors report are unoccupied." His brow furrowed, and he got a faraway look. *There is something oddly familiar about it.*

"Could it be Object Thirteen?"

"Not enough information."

"Anything cloaked is presumed a hostile," Vale said. They were making up the rules of engagement as they went along, something Tuvok had noticed was to Sarai's distress. "See if you can get a firing solution."

Titan shook. "Disruptor shot to our shields," Tuvok said, "port quarter." Another quake. "Second impact, directly astern." The third blast needed no description: the screen ahead flashed with energy as fire struck the forward shields.

"Looks like the gang's all here," Vale said, gripping her armrests. "Return fire!"

Spirits' Forge
H'atoria, Klingon Empire

Reaching the terrace outside the fortress with Kersh, the admiral found Troi, Tocatra, and the Ferengi envoy waiting. All were unwilling to enter the fortress, considering the reported bomb—but neither could they find anywhere else to go. Riker looked back again. The pursuers were farther back, harried by Keru's forces, but the admiral still worried for his team. The numbers of combatants in the firefight were evenly matched, but now that the surprise was gone, the Unsung had a better position. The *Titan* team was shooting while hovering with antigravs, an awkward affair.

Trokaj, Kersh's security chief, appeared at the door to the fortress, disruptor in hand. He looked winded. "The building is clear, General. The Sentries left before the meeting was to start—and I slew two in the yard behind the fort."

"What about the bomb?" Riker asked. "Our Lieutenant Kyzak told us there was one up the chimney." The admiral didn't even like being this close to the building.

"I met that officer before," Trokaj said. "I thought him insane even then. There was no one even in the hearth room when I looked. And if there was a bomb, why would they not have set it off while you were inside earlier?"

Riker had no answer—and Troi was having no luck raising Kyzak on her combadge. Kersh seemed aggravated by the delay. "Forget that, Trokaj. You have the control mechanism?"

Trokaj produced a small device.

"Use it!"

As the officer worked the controls, Kersh pulled her communicator from her belt. "My turn," she said. "*Gur'rok*, this is General Kersh. The transporter inhibitor towers are deactivated. Strike team, deploy!"

Looking back down toward the causeway, Riker saw the glow of multiple transporter effects. A dozen or more Klingon warriors materialized on the land bridge, outflanking the Unsung. More weapons fire blazed.

"The exercise yard can be used as a landing zone for your shuttle," Trokaj said to Riker. "But the sides of the fortress are vulnerable to attack. We must go through to reach safety."

Riker stared at the Klingon. "The bomb, remember?"

"We simply need to pass through," Kersh said. "Right now there is more danger from behind than within!"

Riker didn't linger to watch. He and the two Klingons stepped across the threshold, took hold of the great doors, and shut them with a slam.

They were lowering the bar into place to seal the entrance when Troi activated her combadge. *"Titan,* we're all right. I repeat, we're all right."

"Understood," Rager replied from ops. *"We've just come under fire ourselves—from cloaked attackers."*

That didn't surprise anyone, sadly. "We read you, *Titan.* We're passing through the fort to the exercise yard. We'll be ready for a pickup there."

Riker's combadge chirped, an incoming message arriving from someone else. "Riker."

"There you are!" he heard Kyzak say, relief obvious in his voice. *"I've been down in the basement—apparently, wherever the shield generator is down here, it's interfered with my combadge."*

Riker rolled his eyes with impatience. "What's your report, Lieutenant? Tell me about the bomb!"

"You don't have to worry about that," Kyzak said. *"Just whatever you do, don't close the doors to the fort!"*

Twenty-eight

Earlier, Xaatix had described the timer's circular design to Kyzak; it had reminded him of the appearance of the security device in the main doorway. Remembering something he had seen in one of his reconnoiters of the basement earlier, he had headed down there, intending to broadcast a warning while searching—only to find that his combadge did not work. But he also found what he was looking for: a foundry grab hook attached via a length of heavy-duty chain to a black oblong coupler. A useful thing to have around a forge—and extremely heavy, when slung over his shoulder.

He had just reentered the furnace room with it when he remembered to try his combadge again. Riker's news had terrified him: the door had been shut. Kyzak looked up the chimney. "Xaatix! What's the timer doing?"

"I was just going to tell you. The timer has just started. If I am reading this properly, we have seven minutes."

Oh, crap. His heart sank, and rose again, as in that instant he heard the arrival of *Handy*, landing inelegantly in the narrow open area outside the back door. He tapped his combadge. "Admiral, the timer's definitely been tripped—evacuate if you can. I've got a plan." With no time to explain what it was, Kyzak signed off and yelled up the chimney. "Stay there, Xaatix!"

"*Stay with the bomb?*"

"Trust me!"

Kyzak turned and ran for the door—catching the arrival in the room of Riker and Troi out of the corner of his eye.

"Lieutenant," Riker yelled. "Where are you going?"

Kyzak couldn't spare a second to respond. He hopped

through the open doorway into the shuttlecraft hovering over the exercise yard. "Bolaji, take me up!"

Rising in the vehicle, he only had time to catch a glimpse of Riker and the others in the back doorway of the fortress, staring at him, stunned. Kyzak had no time to worry about stealing the admiral's ride. If his plan didn't work, he wouldn't live to see a court-martial.

PHANTOM WING VESSEL *CHU'CHARQ*
ABOVE H'ATORIA

"Zokar and the rest of the squadron have engaged the enemy," Hemtara reported. "With the transporter inhibitors down, we can evacuate our forces from the bridge as well as the island."

"Evacuate?" Trying to recover his lordly bearing, Cross turned and gave the Klingon woman what he imagined would be a frightening look when coming from Kruge. "The fortress still stands. Our enemies yet live."

"They have entered the building and closed the doors behind them, my lord. The torpedo's timer has been acrivated. We must move to extract our forces, as planned." Hemtara turned to face him, "That is why there *is* a timer. And with one less ship, bringing our people back will take longer."

Standing by his command chair, Shift nudged him. They were being paid for a job. If it was done, no one needed to twist Cross's arm to get him to leave. He made a dismissive hand gesture, and Shift spoke. "Transport our people up. Order *Bregit* to do the same."

"Priority to the northern cape," Cross added. They swung into action.

As *Chu'charq* banked and approached the island, Cross

let out a deep breath—and hoped no further bolts from the sky would strike. He wasn't just worried about his own ship being struck; a lucky shot to *Blackstone* would kill his illusion.

He fumbled in his tunic pocket for the device Korgh had given him earlier: the key to his reward. *This had better be worth it.*

U.S.S. ENTERPRISE
APPROACHING H'ATORIA

"*Titan*, we are minutes away. Picard out."

Enterprise's bridge bathed in the light from warp speed, Picard looked over to the engineering station. "You have your quarry, Mister La Forge. The Unsung are definitely at H'atoria—and the Phantom Wing is attacking."

The engineer nodded. "Sounds busy over there."

The captain heard the port turbolift open behind him and turned. His first officer stepped from the cab, followed by Lieutenant Šmrhová. "We have them, Number One," Picard said.

"We are ready," Worf said. Like him, Šmrhová was dressed in tactical assault gear and armed with a phaser; but where she had a blackjack strapped to her leg, Worf wore a *mek'leth* strapped to his back. He'd expected that quarters would be too close aboard a bird-of-prey for anything larger. "We have our tracking devices."

La Forge looked to Picard. "I request permission to operate the transporter, Captain."

"Make it so," Picard said. "Good hunting, you two. And be careful."

PHANTOM WING VESSEL *RODAK*
ORBITING H'ATORIA

"Fire!"

Zokar's comrade at the tactical station activated a control—and twin streams of energy lanced out from *Rodak*'s cannons. The disruptor bursts came together at a point slightly removed from the *Titan*'s saucer section. The effect crackled across its shields before dissipating.

"That should get their attention," Zokar said, pounding his armrest with his fist. "And stop them from bombarding our comrades."

The other Phantom Wing vessels were at it as well. He'd been in the same position earlier at Gamaral, firing on *Enterprise*—only then he'd been targeting its transporter systems in support of a boarding action. This was much simpler: there were many more targets. *Titan*, Kersh's *Gur'rok*, and a variety of smaller Klingon support vessels. All were on the receiving end of fire from his invisible brigade, but *Titan* was receiving particular attention, given what it had done to *Kradge*.

True to his expectations, *Titan* suspended its surface blasts and began firing into surrounding space. Probing, searching, chasing: all sensible tactics, but not very effective in fighting off a swarm of attackers.

"It is working," announced the bushy-haired Klingon at the helm station. Harch was young and headstrong, often reminding Zokar of himself. "We should be able to buy Kruge the time he needs," Harch said.

Zokar was satisfied with that—but he had not forgotten who was in orbit. "Report on the other contacts," he said.

"The Breen and the Kinshaya fled like scared children as soon as their shuttle left H'atoria," Harch said. "The Ferengi ship's also fled. The Romulan has moved to a higher orbit. It dispatched a shuttle to the surface a few minutes ago."

"Their ambassador must still be below," Zokar said.

"That's it, then. They've probably thrown together a rescue mission of their own, thinking she was a target."

Zokar smiled. That was all he needed. "Cruising configuration. Plot an intercept course for *D'choak*."

The young warrior at the science station looked back at him. "Zokar, Lord Kruge said nothing about attacking the Romulans."

"They're going to interfere. That's reason enough to stop them." Looking around and seeing concerned faces, he put on his most motivating scowl. "Lord Kruge gave me this duty! Now move!"

The others complied with trepidation. Zokar saw *Rodak* break off from assaulting *Titan*. He smiled. There was plenty of prey to go around today.

Twenty-nine

Kyzak wasn't afraid of heights. If he had been, he might not have come up with this harebrained scheme. He consoled himself with the thought that falling was just *one* of the terrible ways he could die.

Yes, he could tumble from his precarious perch inside the open rear cargo hatch of *Handy* as it hovered above the fortress at the edge of the chimney. He could also be struck by one of the many stray shots from the firefight still raging on all sides of the island. Or the shuttle could be obliterated by a blast from a bird-of-prey; there was at least one more out there, given the way combatants were transporting away. Or the seals on his quickly donned environmental suit could give way, causing him to asphyxiate in the wafts of superheated smoke from below.

No one option seemed worse than another.

The Unsung had rigged two heavy crossbars in an X across the chimney; four black chains descended from them, held taut by the torpedo's weight. There was no seeing them in the smoke, but they appeared relatively cool in his helmet's infrared filter. Had the Unsung used their shield-defeating transporter trick to put the torpedo inside the assembly or had they done it some other way?

It was no time to wonder. His helmet's visor helped him detect Xaatix in the uppermost section of the chimney underneath. He secured the coupler from the implement he'd discovered earlier to a clamp inside the shuttle and tossed the other end to Xaatix.

"Difficult," he heard her say over his combadge. She had to keep her body in position inside the chimney while at the same time lashing the grab hook to the Unsung's brace. He worried her limbs might not be long enough.

But what her appendages lacked in length, the Ovirian made up for in number. *"Okay!"* she called.

Kyzak tested the connecting chain once before turning back to yell to Bolaji. "Pull away!"

Finding a portion of the shore unobstructed by lava flow, a Starfleet security officer rushed onto the island. Valandris sprang from behind a boulder, putting her *bat'leth* to use. The blade sliced through the female officer's gut, killing her instantly. Valandris looked long enough at the corpse to see inside the woman's helmet. She had blue scaly skin.

Another kind of creature killed. It was not enough.

She looked again out at the *Kradge.* Only a piece or two of smoking debris remained afloat. No survivors. There weren't many of the Unsung remaining on the island. When she had found any corpses, she had vaporized them with her disruptor. Dead bodies were of no value in the Unsung's culture, but she would not let the Empire have them.

The good news was that Valandris had seen the doors to the fortress close. Soon, the heart of the island would be ripped apart in an antimatter instant, and she doubted anyone would survive it. She had asked to be transported last, to personally slay whomever else she could.

She heard movement up and over the slope: more Starfleeters advancing inland, or perhaps Klingons charging from the causeway. Disruptor in hand, she quickly scaled the rise—

—and saw through the clearing the Starfleet shuttle awkwardly hovering over the fortress, gingerly lifting the torpedo on its chains from the smoking chimney. Once clear, the shuttle swiveled in the air and dipped. A second later, it rose again, accelerating with the explosive trailing behind it.

Valandris started to swear. She vanished in a transporter glow.

Riker had never seen anything like it. Standing well outside the back doors of the fortress with Kersh and the others, he stared as Bolaji piloted *Handy* low enough to clear the fortress's force field, but high enough for the suspended torpedo to miss the petrified forest on the northern slope. A few seconds later, the shuttlecraft began to accelerate. Soon it was almost to the horizon, where the chain gave way, causing the torpedo to knife into the ocean: an impromptu depth charge.

The observers quickly retreated back inside the fort and waited in the furnace room for the imminent blast. When it came, the whole island shook—and a sudden and pelting rain followed the shockwave.

Veteran of many explosions, the admiral recovered quickly and tapped his combadge. "*Handy*, this is Riker. Status."

"*We're fine, sir.*"

Riker looked first to Troi, who was as exhausted as he felt—and then at the disheveled Ferengi and Romulan envoys. He imagined Tocatra was already making a mental list of the protests she would lodge.

General Kersh and her aide were still on edge—and when a sooty figure twisted her way out of the kiln, both drew their disruptors. Troi and Riker put up their hands to stop them. "She's with us," Troi said.

After shaking hot ashes from her body like a dog drying after a bath, Lieutenant Xaatix faced Riker and spoke. "We have removed the chimney obstruction, Admiral. Your meeting can commence in comfort."

PHANTOM WING VESSEL *CHU'CHARQ*
ABOVE H'ATORIA

Cross stared, stunned, while the bird-of-prey's sensors projected a departure-angle view onto the main screen. The photon torpedo blast had sent an immense geyser ballooning outward, battering the northern cape with waves. Farther south, members of the Starfleet amphibious force could be seen clinging to the shoreline, while Kersh's Klingon warriors fought to keep their footing. One section of the causeway buckled and gave way, slipping into the sea. A sharp-nosed Romulan shuttle was soaring low over the water, looking for a place to land.

And the Starfleet shuttlecraft responsible for the insane feat was settling, undamaged, behind the fortress.

"What are you doing?" came an angry voice from behind. "Didn't you see them?" Cross turned to see Valandris storming onto the bridge. "Did you not see the Federation stealing the bomb?"

"We saw it," Raneer said, looking sheepish.

"Then why didn't you stop them?" Valandris stood before the screen, jabbing at the image. "You could have destroyed the shuttle. You can bombard the fortress now!"

"It was not our lord's wish," Shift said in her most forbidding N'Keera voice. "Our lord decides, Valandris, not you."

Damn right it wasn't my wish, Cross thought. So the fortress and its occupants still existed. *Bregit* had already departed for space with a load of the Unsung—and there wasn't a chance in hell he was sending *Chu'charq* back down when *Titan* was upstairs, taking potshots from orbit at anything on the surface that fired. Forget what Korgh or the crazed cultists wanted. "We will not compromise our location," he said.

Valandris outstretched her arms in indignation. "They destroyed *Kradge*!"

"With one shot. Their weapons are powerful."

She shook her head violently. "No. I saw it—the crew was flying too low, chasing the shuttle. Their orientation was poor." She started to shove Raneer from her seat at the helm. "We can go back and do this."

Cross rose. "Enough!" He traversed the steps to Valandris—and hoped his caution would be seen as savvy and not cowardice. "We have delivered the blow. Kersh's bargain is in shambles." He grabbed her face. "We have lost one of our own. But this is not the last battle, not unless you defy me. I would have no choice but to transfer my flag to another vessel."

"Zokar's *Rodak*," Shift suggested.

"I have *not* defied—" she said, before stopping. Valandris locked her angry eyes with his, and he fought the urge to step back.

No, he had to push, as Kruge would have. "You *have* defied me. On Gamaral, with Worf. On Thane. Do not think I missed what happened below. You gave up the element of surprise—and *that* is why our enemies yet live." Others watched, spellbound, as he stood firm. "I will transfer to *Rodak* unless you submit. Then, when next you defy me, I *will* fire—*on you*."

She gritted her teeth. "There is fighting in orbit. I will take the gunner's station."

"Do that." Cross released Valandris's face.

Chu'charq continued climbing. Cross glanced back at Shift. She appeared concerned. The sooner they were out of the system, the better. *And we sure as hell won't be shooting at anybody on the way out!*

Thirty

His command chair was elevated above all on the *Rodak*'s bridge, but Zokar's anticipation had brought him down to the crew's level. Every moment his bird-of-prey came closer to the Romulan warbird, *D'choak*, Zokar leaned a little more over the helm. Were the warbird much farther away, there was a chance the Klingon might have wound up on the deck.

But it was not far away, and at his command, the bird-of-prey's invisible wings shifted into the attack position. The warbird became a giant on their viewscreen, the ornate pattern on its topside clearly visible.

"Target the generators. Secondary cannons, fire!"

Energy tore outward from *Rodak*'s disruptors and pounded the Romulan's deflector shields. Zokar kept up the bombardment as the bird-of-prey careened even closer—and a bolt got through, tearing into the thin section connecting the upper of the two clamshell hulls to the command section. *A knife to the back of the neck.*

He shook his fist at the now-sparking vessel as *Rodak* swept perilously past. After forty years, he'd finally started to settle accounts. "Hard about for another pass."

"Contact from the surface," Harch said. "It's the ambassador's shuttle."

"Not for long." Zokar headed to his chair and sat back easily. This day was getting better all the time.

U.S.S. TITAN
ORBITING H'ATORIA

"Captain, I recommend getting clear of *Gur'rok*," Aili Lavena said from flight control. "The Phantom Wing ships are running figure eights around us—and increasing the odds we'll shoot at each other."

If only we could get the birds-of-prey to shoot at one another, Vale thought. *Or slam into each other.* It was widely assumed there was some kind of tech aboard the Phantom Wing vessels establishing the positions of their other cloaked ships, but nobody had yet figured out how that information was being transmitted. The captain knew that would be finding the Holy Grail—especially if there was a way to determine those positions across interstellar distances.

For the moment, Vale felt paralyzed. Her crew at Spirits' Forge had reported the Unsung transported away, with no further bird-of-prey attacks—but she was reluctant to move *Titan* from her orbital station. But Lavena's observation was an important one. In the current climate, a Federation and a Klingon vessel accidentally exchanging fire could be extremely damaging.

"Skirt the atmosphere," she said. "We'll heat our mosquitos' hulls a little—and see if they still feel like swarming."

As *Titan* turned hard about and descended, Tuvok reported, "Captain, the Romulans are taking fire."

"So much for staying on the sidelines," Vale said. "Is *D'choak* damaged?"

"Not critically. Fire is now being directed at the Romulan ambassadorial shuttle. *D'choak*'s impulse engines are offline. It cannot get there in time." Tuvok spoke gravely. "Neither can we."

Phantom Wing Vessel *Rodak*
Orbiting H'atoria

It was the most fun Zokar had ever had. Even handicapped by a crew that hadn't set foot aboard a bird-of-prey before a year ago, he'd dealt *D'choak* a fist in the face. Now he was chasing game that was simultaneously bigger and smaller.

Smaller for obvious reasons: the Romulan shuttle was speedy, but relatively defenseless. That he had not destroyed it yet owed to his need to avoid harassing fire from *D'choak*. And it was bigger because the shuttle might hold the ambassador. That was possible, wasn't it? Maybe he'd damaged *D'choak*'s transporters, as he had *Enterprise*'s back at Gamaral. It was almost too much to hope for—but in Kruge's army, hope came easily to him again.

"Keep firing," he said as *Rodak* closed in on the shuttle. "We've almost got—"

"New contact!" Harch yelled—and half a second later, all aboard felt the barrage as a photon torpedo detonated to starboard. This delivery wasn't from *D'choak*, Zokar realized even before Harch made the announcement: "It's the *Enterprise*!"

U.S.S. *Enterprise*
Orbiting H'atoria

"The Unsung vessel has broken off from the Romulan shuttle and is now firing at us, Commander La Forge. Exact coordinates feeding to you."

"Acknowledged. Our program activates the instant it fires again." In transporter room four, La Forge looked over the assault team and made certain they were ready. "We'll try to put you someplace safe. Good luck."

Working alongside Angela Moran, one of *Enterprise*'s transporter chiefs, La Forge watched as the program he had written went into action. Sensors spotting another disruptor blast from nowhere, *Enterprise* randomly probed the area for microfractures in the bird-of-prey's rotating cloaking field. Finding them—and the cloaking generator and its component emitters on the skin of the starship within—the computer overlaid the schematics provided by the House of Kruge as it searched for its interior target site.

It took milliseconds. "We've got it," Moran said. "Transporter lock established on the catwalk in the deck six port deuterium storage area. Energizing."

A second into the process as Worf and Šmrhová stood on the pads as glowing masses of energy, La Forge raised an alarm. "Something's wrong . . ."

An alert came from the bridge. *"Commander, the Romulan warbird just detonated a photon torpedo near the suspected target."*

"I know," La Forge said, hands racing across the controls. "Safety protocols just activated."

Before him, one of the figures on the transporter pad beamed out—while the other solidified into existence. Šmrhová looked about, stunned. "What happened?"

"I'm not sure," Moran replied. "Commander Worf transported—but you didn't."

"What?" the security chief said. "Quick, try it again!"

"Stand by," La Forge said. "We may not get another shot."

PHANTOM WING VESSEL *CHU'CHARQ*
ORBITING H'ATORIA

The void enveloped Cross's spacecraft, but space was hardly empty. He had first seen *Titan* and *Gur'rok* fighting off their invisible enemies—and then he had beheld the mess *Rodak* had gotten itself into.

"*Enterprise* isn't supposed to be here," Shift said.

Clearly, it was here. The sight of it affected his throat the same way seeing *Titan* had. The ambassadorial shuttle, screened by *Enterprise*'s arrival, darted toward the protection of the rapidly firing *D'choak*.

Rodak's position, superimposed by computer onto *Chu'charq*'s main viewscreen, indicated the vessel had come hard about in an attempt to strike back at its attackers. Cross had no intention of prolonging the battle. "Attention all ships," he announced over his scrambled channel. "Our work here is done. Full speed to the rendezvous point!"

Hemtara reported all the surviving ships of the Phantom Wing checking in. All but one. "Direct channel to *Rodak*," Cross ordered. He would put a stop to this.

RODAK
ORBITING H'ATORIA

"*Zokar, this is Kruge! Disengage immediately.*"

The bald Klingon pounded his bony forehead in aggravation. He was so close. Zokar pressed the button to respond. "My lord, we can hold out. *Enterprise* isn't firing."

"*How long will that last? And who told you to assault the Romulans?*"

Zokar froze. Warriors whose attention was not consumed by the battle turned to face him. "My lord Kruge, *you* told me to. Didn't you?"

"*We have lost a starship to rank foolishness already today. You will follow my orders—now!*"

U.S.S. Enterprise
Orbiting H'atoria

Seeing the phantom disruptor shots cease, Picard breathed a sigh of relief. The captain had to find a way to help the distressed Romulan shuttle while at the same time not destroying a ship he was trying to put an away team on. By drawing the bird-of-prey's fire, he had kept the Romulans safe—while the warbird had gotten only a single lick in against the cloaked ship. That still concerned him.

"*Titan* reports it is no longer taking fire," Glinn Dygan said from ops. "The same appears true for the Klingons and Romulans."

"More good news." But what of the away team? "Report, Mister La Forge."

"*Only Commander Worf transported over, Captain. When the Romulan torpedo detonated nearby, something must have happened at the beam-in site to make the safety protocols deem Šmrhová's destination unsafe.*"

The captain's eyes widened. He had worried about that single shot. "Did our systems report Commander Worf as safely transported?"

"*They did—but that only counts for the second he materialized. Now that the bird-of-prey has broken off, the window to send anyone over or to get Worf back has closed.*" La Forge went silent for a moment. "*And I'm not reading anything from his tracking device.*"

Picard had just gotten his first officer back. *To lose him again . . . ?*

Thirty-one

Zokar rubbed his forehead as his bird-of-prey prepared to go to warp. It had sickened him to leave so many targets behind, though the course out had showed him how much damage the squadron had done.

Gur'rok, Kersh's flagship, had predictably been dealt the most serious blow. The *Vor'cha*-class ship's bridge had taken several glancing hits; even though the Unsung had heard Kersh was still alive on H'atoria, they could rest in the knowledge that they'd left a mark she would see.

The *Titan* was in far better shape, and the *Enterprise* was undamaged. He cursed Picard's name for showing up as he had. The only good thing about it was that the vaunted captain had not pressed his advantage. The Starfleet vessel's intervention, he now realized, had been calculated to herd him away from the Romulans, not to disable *Rodak*.

That made no sense to Zokar. He had humiliated Picard at Gamaral. If a so-called legendary captain would give up a chance at a rematch, then legends at Starfleet didn't amount to much. Something wasn't right—

—but there was no time to think about it now. "Kruge has sent over the rendezvous coordinates," Harch said. "We are ready."

"Get us out of here." Zokar would do his second-guessing someplace else.

"Worf, wake up!"

Lying on his side on a cold metal deck, Worf opened his

eyes—and immediately closed them again as searing waves of pain coursed through his body.

"Worf, are you all right?" He felt a small hand jabbing at his shoulder. Forcing his eyes open again, he saw the concerned face of a brown-haired Klingon child. "You fell," the young girl said.

Head pounding, he strained to roll over onto his back. More pain concentrated in his right leg—and he grasped for it. His hand found a bleeding gash. He saw twisted metal all about.

"Hold on." The girl left his sight for a few moments. When she returned, she had a section of cloth, a protective cover from some piece of equipment. Tentatively, she dabbed at the cut with it—and Worf jerked in groaning agony. She hopped back, scared. He clamped his hand hard over the fabric—and in the act, he felt that the wound ran much of the length of his right thigh.

"Remember me?" the girl said, crouching closer. "I'm Sarken. I saw you on Thane."

Worf blinked. He had a head injury, too. Everything was hazy. "Where—where am I?"

"On one of Lord Kruge's birds-of-prey. I live here."

He forced himself to sit upright. It was a large, high-ceilinged rectangular chamber, dominated by an enormous metal drum lying sideways and bolted to the deck. *Deuterium storage, as planned.* But looking up, he saw a large section of catwalk had given way.

"I saw you appear up there," Sarken said, pointing into the low light. "I was playing in the corner and saw you. You showed up on the catwalk right when something hit the ship. That section up there gave way, and you fell."

Worf noticed a huge, scraping dent on the giant deuterium tank where the catwalk had slammed against it on the way down. Sarken pointed to one of the jutting pieces of scrap metal that had been a walkway support. "That part's what cut your leg."

In his pain, Worf remembered the tracking device. It was not clipped to his belt. Bewildered, he tried to move around and search for it—an act that only caused more agony.

"Are you looking for this thing?" Sarken held out the shattered remains of the tracking device. Scraped off his uniform in the fall, it had been smashed by a falling girder.

Tapping his combadge also did nothing. So much for his glorious mission. "Did . . . I arrive alone?"

"I saw another glow up there—but that section of the catwalk was already falling, and it went away." She bit her lip as she noticed the *mek'leth* bound in a sheath on his back. "What's *that* for?"

"Right now, it is helping to keep me upright." Worf scooted around so his back was supported by the bulkhead and sagged against it. At least the field hypo in his pocket was in one piece. He applied it to his leg and did what he could to clean his deep cut. "Sarken, are others nearby?"

"My people live mostly on the higher decks. I came here to hide during the battle. I don't like looking outside. Since my father died, I'm all alone." Her little eyes searched his. "What are you doing here, Worf? I thought you came to Thane to be one of us. Then I heard they were hunting you."

"We had a disagreement. Is this Valandris's ship?"

"I wish it was. She yells a lot, too, but I like her." She pointed upward with her thumb. "This is *Rodak*."

"Who is in charge here? Kruge?"

"No. He's with Valandris. And nobody's really in charge, but old Zokar acts like he is." Her nose crinkled. "Him, I don't like. He's rude, and he smells funny."

Worf looked around. There was no hope of accessing the trunk line for the cloaking device now, with the catwalk gone. Main engineering, he knew, was aft of his location, but while there might be opportunities to sabotage the cloaking device or to signal the *Enterprise* from there, it would most certainly be staffed by the Unsung. There had to be something else nearby he could exploit.

Worf tried to stand—and immediately collapsed onto his hands and knees. "Careful," Sarken said, keeping him from slamming his head into the fuel cylinder. She looked at his head. "That knot looks mean."

It felt it. Worf found any ambitious movements made him dizzy. He needed time to recover, but the chamber wouldn't stay vacant forever. He looked to the girl. "Sarken, they will come here to check the damage soon. But if Zokar finds me, he will want to fight, and I cannot. I need somewhere to rest."

"I know plenty of hiding places. This ship's full of them. It's more fun than the jungle on Thane." She thought for a moment. "There's a closet in the workshop across the hall. Nobody goes there."

Worf nodded. No, the Unsung would likely not be sophisticated enough to need the bird-of-prey's technical workshop and its stores. "I will need your help to move," he said. "What kind of animal is a sarken?"

She brightened, delighted to be asked. "It's a fast little thing. It burrows to outsmart its predators."

"Then, Sarken, I will need to act as your namesake. We cannot let the hunters see me. Is that understood?"

She responded with a gap-toothed smile. He could tell it was the most fun she'd had.

Thirty-two

Once again, Shift had come through for Cross. She'd suggested the perfect hideaway for him to direct the Unsung toward after H'atoria: Chelvatus III, a world on the fringe of the Empire. Species from neighboring powers operated in the world's bazaar with the unspoken permission—and frequent patronage—of the operators of the Klingon mine that was the planet's main concern.

It was yet another place Shift's gangster owners had taken her to in her earlier life, and the location provided a chance to rendezvous with Gaw. Parked outside the settlement, the cloaked *Chu'charq* had beamed "Kruge" and "N'Keera" to the surface for another of their meditative walks. Cross didn't expect that anyone in the bazaar would question an aged, hooded Klingon out and about with his nursemaid, and that was generally correct. But it didn't take a Betazoid to recognize a heightened level of nervousness about *all* unfamiliar Klingons. He wondered if that was in reaction to Spirits' Forge.

Cross and Shift spied Gaw and his associates in a trading pavilion, fencing some of the goods purloined from the Azure Nebula storehouse. The Ferengi's reaction to them, after H'atoria, was predictable.

"That was *insane*," Gaw said. He clasped his hands together and feigned terror. "Please tell me we don't have to go on any more raids, Cross. *Please.*"

"Relax," Cross said, pointing toward a back alley. "We're almost done. Let's get out of here." Outside town, they walked to the secluded area where *Blackstone* was parked under cloak and climbed the invisible boarding ramp, out of sight of anyone.

For the whole year Cross and Shift had been living on rugged Thane, they had always been just a transporter beam away from *Blackstone*'s high-tech refuge. The place was modern, full of the latest equipment—and yet there was something different about it, as if its designers had reached the present by following a different path from the past. There were computer interfaces in its labyrinthine confines, but there was also wrought iron and glass crystal. There was the magnificent imaging chamber off the control center, capable of producing visual replicas more convincing than any holodeck, while the next room held shelves stuffed with ancient books and scrolls. Curtains hung in place of automatic doors—while other doors were hidden from the eye, cleverly placed behind purloined art objects from a dozen worlds.

"I love coming here," Shift said as she walked through the control center. "Everything you do here amazes me."

"That's a good apprentice." Gaw gave the little floating orb knickknack atop his workstation a whirl and smiled at her. "She cares about the people who make the magic—unlike *some* slave-driving practitioners I know."

Eight of the truthcrafters were in the control center. Representing several different species and ranging from young computer prodigies to old hands, they were hard at work making sure that Cross and Shift looked like Kruge and N'Keera. "Take five, everyone," Cross said, canceling the illusion.

Looking like himself again, the Betazoid led Shift and Gaw up a spiral staircase into his loft. Part pleasure palace and part shrine to the past, the room showcased Cross's interest in live theater.

Shift stopped before a paper mounted under transparent aluminum on the wall. "What's this one?"

"It's the front page of the very first edition of what would later become the major newspaper for San Francisco on Earth."

Gaw stared, only barely interested. "What's a newspaper?"

"An information delivery system. Imagine, here's the city where Starfleet is headquartered, and the most important news that day in 1865, in the last days of a major civil war, was that 'the three graces'—Sophie, Irene, and Little Jennie Worrell—were opening *The Grotto Nymph* at Worrell's Olympic." Cross cited from memory: " 'A Nondescript Fantastico Morceau of Absurdity, arranged expressly for this House.' "

Shift read from the ancient type. "Also starring 'Sylva, the fairy queen, with a conventional brevity of skirts.' " She laughed. "What is this?"

He smiled at her. "Armies were annihilating each other half a continent away—yet this announcement took up more than half the front page. That's what I love about humans, Shift. They *get* it. They'll play make-believe while they're killing one another. Or they'll make up grand dramas *about* killing one another. Or they'll use make-believe *to* kill one another."

Gaw sighed and shook his head at Shift. "We cross half the galaxy to get this damn stuff for him."

"A pittance," Cross said. He leaped backward onto his cushy four-poster bed. "*Your* fortune's safe and sound, right here." He patted his vest pocket with his right hand. The pocket went flat. "Whoops!" the illusionist said, acting surprised that the important thing inside was gone. Then he flipped around his left hand and displayed the small device he'd been given by Korgh. "Ah, there it was, all the time."

Gaw groaned. "Stop messing around. You talked to your patron. Was he angry about how Spirits' Forge turned out?"

"Amazingly, no." Cross sat up. Gaw knew the Betazoid had a partner in the Klingon Empire, but by agreement, Korgh's communications with Cross were neither monitored nor recorded by *Blackstone*. "I was ready to be chewed out. But he seemed all right."

"I should hope so," Shift said, looking back from the bookcase she was kneeling before. "How could we have known those other ambassadors would take off before the meeting had a chance to start? It wasn't our fault."

"He didn't care," Cross said. He toggled a tiny switch, activating the device. "Here's the proof." He flipped it to Gaw.

Gaw fumbled the catch and had to go searching on the carpet for it. Bringing the small device close to his face, he donned his pince-nez and peered at the tiny screen. "These are coordinates and times and dates."

"He just sent them. The House of Kruge ships freighters full of latinum to its outposts where hard currency is needed to deal with the neighbors. Their routes are all very hush-hush—but my contact's got connections. That device now contains the routes for the *Ark of G'boj*, carrying—well, more than you can imagine."

Gaw smiled broadly. "I love this kid." He looked to Shift. "Did I tell you I love this kid?"

Shift watched them. "So we grab the *Ark*—and slip away."

"To start the sequel," Cross said, hopping off the bed. "Did you forward my list to the myth team, Gaw?"

"List?" The Ferengi was reluctant to stop looking at the coordinates.

"My *Kahless* list."

"Yeah, yeah, we got it. More background on Kahless the Unforgettable, blah, blah."

"It's important, Gaw. *Really* important. I've gotten the clone to tell me some more about his first appearance. The Clerics of Boreth were confident their cloned Kahless could be convincing on the biological side of things—but he didn't have any answers that weren't in the ancient texts they'd stuffed into his head. So I need backstories developed for all the Kahless legends."

"The myth team." Shift pointed downward. "Those four people down in that little office that smells bad?"

"That's them," Cross said. "If someone asks me about things in the scrolls, *Blackstone* will feed me the answers. But we won't stop there. I'll talk about the side characters. What they looked like, sounded like. What the weather was doing. They won't trip me up the way they exposed the clone."

"Didn't the clone submit to genetic testing?"

"Which the true Kahless would *never* have submitted to—at least, in my interpretation. He'd rather fight than be humiliated like that."

The Orion's brow furrowed. "What if that happens? The clone said it was losing a fight that gave him away."

"The effects team is working on that," Gaw said. "Anyone who tries to lay a hand on him will get a face full of force field, projected by *Blackstone*."

"I'll have to knock a few bumpy heads, but they will kneel down before me." The actor crossed his arms and scowled solemnly. "Beware the wrath of Kahless!"

"And then what?" Shift asked. "Your partner knows about us—about what you can do. This Kahless thing won't be good for him. He could ruin everything."

"Not without ruining things for himself. My dear, he's up to his neck in this with us. If he reveals our sham, we'll reveal his. I don't think he'll find it worthwhile."

Gaw passed the device back to Cross and headed for the staircase. "I'll go light a fire under the myth team. People will be glad to hear payday's coming."

Following Gaw's departure, Shift looked pensively at Cross. "It . . . would be good to know where Korgh's been going with all this—so you know what to expect when your Kahless act begins."

"We'll talk with him one last time before we bring down the lights on the Unsung." Cross waved his hands in excitement. "I can't wait, babe. This is the greatest thing anyone in the Circle has ever tried. It's one thing to fool unsophisticated species—or superstitious dopes like the Ventaxians and the Kinshaya. But it's quite another to do it to one of the premier powers in the galaxy."

She looked back at him. "Someone pranked the Kinshaya?"

"Oh, yeah." He approached the bookcase she was kneeling before. "It's in here somewhere in the *Annals of the Circle*." He thumbed lovingly through one of dozens of ruby-colored books with golden lettering.

"I was wondering what these were," she said.

"Remember when I told you about the convocations—where all the practitioners compare their greatest feats? The best one makes it into the records we all share."

"You get ideas from these?"

"A good practitioner never swipes a trick." He smirked. "At least, not without adding a twist or two."

Shift examined the titles. "It looks like your people have pranked everyone. The Ferengi, the Cardassians—*the Gorn?*"

"Who would dare, right? Who indeed." Cross grinned. "It takes a real operator to go up against someone who could rip your arms off."

Shift pulled out another journal. "Interesting. *The Mystical Manifestations of Jilaan before the Kinshaya, 2293.*"

"I've never read that one—but whatever it is, you could learn a lot from it." He kissed her on the cheek. "Let's get a real meal before we have to get back."

Thirty-three

"Thank you all," Korgh said as he lingered before the gaggle of admirers and well-wishers in the atrium. "Remember what I have said. The valiant warriors of Spirits' Forge deserved much better than to die at the hands of the Unsung criminals. I demand recompense for the damage to the sacred isle—and for the thousands of Selseress who died because of Starfleet's bumbling torpedo disposal."

He had made up the Selseress body count, but no one had called him on it. He closed as he always did lately, crossing his arms in what had become his signature pose of denunciation. "Everything the Federation touches goes wrong. We must remember how to stand on our own before they pull us down."

"*Praxis is past,*" came the chant in response. "*Praxis is past.*" He nodded, smiling. The line had been part of one of his earlier jeremiads and had become quite the catchphrase. In three words, it symbolized an Empire ready to be great once more and solely in charge of its destiny.

Korgh's security personnel extricated him quickly from the facility and escorted him across the street to his apartments. Less than an hour after his speech to the High Council, he was relaxing with a bottle and watching the coverage of his latest oratorical triumph. And it had been a triumph—for while an operational failure, Spirits' Forge had gone far better than Korgh had hoped.

He'd known he wasn't going to be able to prevent the H'atorian Conference; his influence had grown enormously in a short time, but not that much. Since the House of Kruge administered most of the frontier worlds affected, Martok had grudgingly respected his right to select the empire's negotiating representative. Had he genuinely sought the conference's success, Korgh certainly would have chosen one of his sons: Lorath, the eldest, or Tengor or Tragg, both of whom administered factories for the house.

Instead, he'd sent Kersh. And the Unsung, to kill her and ruin the conference. She'd survived, but it was her standing, and not Korgh's, that had suffered. He'd heard the whispers from the other High Councilors: they'd chosen right in honoring his claim to the house.

The attack against the Romulans, while not something he had prescribed, had also worked in his favor. He hadn't given Cross instructions to attack other guests at the event besides Kersh and the Federation's attendees, but they had. The happy result was the series of messages on his padd.

An official notification from Martok that the Romulans had requested the right to join the Klingon and Federation forces hunting the Unsung in imperial territory. A backchannel communication from Tocatra directly to Korgh, asking him to advise the chancellor to agree with the plan, giving the Romulans a chance to save face. Even a plainly worded message from the Breen, who had slipped away with the Kinshaya just in time to miss the chaos: they wanted to attend the task force as observers, fearful of being left out.

A transformation was at hand in galactic politics, and he had created the waves. He was set to change everything— and Korgh owed it to the eccentric Cross and his thralls in the Unsung, who had done everything he had asked of them.

It only remained to settle accounts with Cross, as promised, and to wrap the Unsung operation up. Wrap it up in a way planned long ago, which would not only protect Korgh and his family from exposure, but advance their fortunes still further.

Cross, he knew, was thinking of his own fortune. Korgh was sending one his way. The young Betazoid liked to think he was so smart and mysterious, hiding behind his tricks and his truthcrafters. But Korgh was old, and knew more about the Circle of Jilaan and its ways than Cross could possibly imagine.

If you live long enough, nothing surprises you. Starting with Gamaral, Korgh had been the one to deal the surprises. And he was far from finished.

U.S.S. TITAN
ORBITING H'ATORIA

"I've been saying it's about time we got the band back together," Riker said as he walked from his office into *Titan*'s sector command hub. There was no laughter, but he wasn't expecting any. He approached the large oval table around which several personnel from the *Enterprise* stood across from their opposite numbers on *Titan*'s staff. "Sit down, everyone."

As all complied, Picard smiled. "It's good to see you safe, Admiral."

"This briefing has officially gone on longer than the H'atorian Conference," Riker said, settling in a chair at the head of the table. "I want to thank the *Enterprise* for saving the Romulan ambassador. My commendations to *Titan* for bailing us out down below." He looked to the Trill security chief. "I'm sorry for the lives lost on your team, Ranul, but they made a difference."

After an acknowledgment of the heroics of Xaatix and Kyzak, Riker went over the status of the investigation on H'atoria. Work to recover the remains of the destroyed bird-of-prey had been hampered by lack of cooperation. The High Council was furious at the loss of the honorable Sentries, and Korgh was fanning the flames, even accusing Starfleet of causing Selseress casualties when none were in the area. "The only thing our investigations can confirm," Keru said, "is that the downed vessel was part of the Phantom Wing. It matches the material and engineering specs that Korgh released."

Less was known about the fate of the Sentries. No bodies had been found, but there was evidence of a massacre in the petrified forest north of the fortress, suggesting the corpses had been incinerated. How the Unsung knew when and where to attack at all was another question.

"Will, you said Lord Korgh decided only a short time ago to hold the event at Spirits' Forge," Picard said. "Could there be a mole in his operation?"

"It's entirely possible. I was in his factory less than an hour when those two copycats came after us. Maybe there's someone higher up."

Lastly, there was no indication of the course the Phantom Wing took from H'atoria. La Forge sounded hopeful that Worf had survived beaming aboard the Phantom Wing ship; transporter logs indicated a successful transporter lock. But no signals from his tracking device had been detected.

"I wish I had gone across too," Šmrhová said. "I would have taken my chances."

"The computer didn't like what it saw," La Forge said. "I'm not sure we should use this tactic again." The engineer's tone was bleak. Riker knew that both La Forge and Šmrhová blamed themselves for Worf's original kidnapping by the Unsung. Worf had volunteered for this mission, but it hadn't made dealing with the results any easier.

Riker moved on to a topic where La Forge could respond in the affirmative. "You said you got a reading on Object Thirteen?"

La Forge nodded. "It came from one of Kersh's satellites—they didn't notice it at the time but spotted it in the records after the attack." He touched a control on his padd, and the location appeared on one of the holographic displays above the table.

"It was detected in H'atoria's atmosphere," Tuvok said. He stared at the image intently.

"Yes, once they knew the Unsung had been on the planet, they recalibrated their sensors and had another look." The commander increased the magnification, and the small sphere that was H'atoria ballooned into a broad arc, with the island appearing in relief. "The contact was one point seven kilometers from the fortress and four hundred meters off the ground."

Riker tried his best to remember what he'd seen in the conflagration. "Does it match the locations of the ship *Titan* hit? Or any of the places where we saw vessels firing?"

"No, it's off to the side. I'd say they were watching the action." La Forge had never felt Object Thirteen was a bird-of-prey; that was why its presence evoked such interest.

Tuvok stood. "Admiral, I would like permission to be excused to perform an analysis. This new information may connect with a line of inquiry I have been following."

Riker gave his consent. Tuvok never did anything without a good reason—and the admiral wanted every possible lead followed. He said as the Vulcan departed, "I was just speaking with Admiral Akaar and Kellesar zh'Tarash."

A low murmur came from the table. "The president," Picard said. "Has this ascended to that level?"

"The Federation has been at peace with the Klingon Empire since Kirk visited Khitomer. The Accords have expanded, making it possible to keep the peace. With significant exceptions, the two parties have taken the same approach to those who would threaten us. If we want space to be about exploration and not warfare, we have to come together—not be divided by internal politics. Theirs," he said, "or ours."

Dalit Sarai straightened at that remark. Everyone present knew she'd been a supporter of the disgraced former Federation president. Riker continued, "The president is concerned. I'd thought the conference would help to strengthen the Accords—but it hasn't. The Unsung are disturbing the peace—that's obvious—but if we fail to catch them, reactionary forces inside the Klingon Empire could do the Accords irreparable harm."

"We?" Picard repeated. "Not we *and* the Klingons?"

"*We*," Riker said. "Starfleet is working with them. But Lord Korgh has made it a test of *our* honor. One hour ago, according to Admiral Akaar, Chancellor Martok gave permission for Typhon Pact forces to join the hunt in the Empire's frontier regions. The Romulans, perhaps more."

Vale shook her head. "Sharing the same space. I guess we got our free-flight corridor."

"Only we never envisioned it would be ships of war crossing," Riker pointed out. "Chancellor Martok agreed because Tocatra and *D'choak* were attacked. It's a matter of honor. Now he's got to answer to people like Korgh, who would be happy to see the Accords nullified."

Picard frowned. "We don't meddle in Klingon politics— we made that clear during their civil war. And while we should welcome the fact that the Typhon Pact wants to help," he said, shaking his head, "I don't see how this ends well."

Riker stood and paced in front of the ports that lined his command center. "Ambassador Spock wasn't wrong to let the exiles go. We weren't at fault at Gamaral. Or Thane. Or here," he said, gesturing out the port to H'atoria. "But many people of the Empire are now convinced that we were. If we want to preserve the Accords, *we* have to find the Unsung. And fast."

Thirty-four

They were on their way, at last, to the treasure. Aboard *Blackstone*, Cross and his team had calculated the best place at which to intercept *Ark of G'boj*. He returned, as Kruge, to the Unsung and delivered the coordinates as part of their next mission.

After the events at H'atoria, they had been ridiculously easy to convince. Kersh's conference might have failed, he'd said, but her treachery continued. Cross told the Unsung that the Romulans had given her a bribe, carried aboard *Ark of G'boj*. An Unsung sympathizer on Chelvatus III had provided "Kruge" with the *Ark*'s itinerary, he said. The *Kradge* could be avenged, and Kersh bloodied, in one simple strike.

Cross figured bringing the Unsung with him would prevent any double cross by Korgh—and the new mission had solved another problem. He'd considered transferring the troublesome Valandris to another vessel: Cross couldn't be the one to leave *Chu'charq*, not with Kahless aboard. But Valandris had accepted the *Ark* mission with zeal, and for a moment he saw the devoted woman he had once known. That was fine. He would only have to deal with her a short while longer.

On the other hand, *Chu'charq* would be losing a different passenger soon—one that no Klingon knew was present. Kahless had been reaching the end of his usefulness even before the H'atorian operation; since then, he'd spent most of his time drunk or asleep. Just before the squadron went to warp, while *Chu'charq*'s shields were down,

Blackstone would initiate a site-to-site transport, delivering the clone to an icy end in space. The role would belong to Cross, once and for all.

Appearing again as himself, Cross ascended the steps to his deck one sanctum and quickly peeked in on his compartment. Shift was napping, the edition of the *Annals* open and on her chest. He thought she looked lovely asleep.

By contrast, the sleeper at the other end of the hall never looked good, but at least Kahless wasn't snoring this time. Cross had been on Chelvatus for the better part of a day and hadn't seen him since his breakfast feeding; Kahless had refused enough food lately that they'd given up on more than one meal a day. Through the force field, Cross saw the food still on the plate beside the blanket-covered mass. More bottles—they had to be the last—lay empty nearby.

So much for a last meal, Cross thought. It was better to do it now. Shift had seen a lot of killings in her life, and he figured to spare her the last moments of their houseguest.

Still, he could never pass up good material—and Cross desired to hear any last words the clone of Kahless thought suitable. He called out, to no response.

Again: no movement. Shift appeared barefoot in the doorway behind him, yawning. "What's wrong?"

"The clone's playing games—or he's dead." He picked up a mug and pounded it against the wall. "Kahless! Wake up!" Getting no response, he looked to Shift. "Give me the thing."

Shift located the control mechanism they'd crafted and passed it to Cross. "Get up or I'll have that manacle give you a shot that'll really put you out."

Still nothing.

Shift retreated to their room and emerged with a disruptor. "Okay, I'm dropping the force field," Cross said. She slipped past him. "I've seen this drama before. If this is a trick, it's your last."

Shift poked the body with her toe—and then in a quick move swiped the blanket upward. Below, amid overturned empty bottles, were three large sacks of dry pellets, fuel for one of the devices on the lower decks.

Immediately on her guard, the Orion searched the storeroom. Crates climbed to the overhead, where pipes crisscrossed beneath vents. When placing the clone inside, neither Cross nor Shift could imagine the fat Klingon making it up there. Shoving containers aside, Shift overturned an open box, spilling the canteens. One popped open, losing its contents.

She sniffed. "Romulan ale."

Befuddled, Cross stepped into the area. One empty bottle was partially wrapped in the ankle binding. Cross picked it up and saw that the manacle had been severed in half. Pulling it off the bottle, he saw Klingon letters scratched into the label by a shard of glass. Cross recognized the saying instantly.

Death before chains.

U.S.S. ENTERPRISE
ORBITING H'ATORIA

Enterprise, which had remained in Klingon space following the H'atorian attack, was now part of Admiral Riker's larger task force, comprising all Starfleet vessels in or near Klingon space; for the better part of a day, it remained in rendezvous with *Titan* for the captains to work out their next steps.

His postmeeting shift ended, La Forge had returned to stellar cartography, the place that he spent almost every off-hour, searching for the Unsung. So did Aneta Šmrhová, who had spent so much time there she had taken to sleeping on the deck.

Responsibly, La Forge had demanded that she get some rest in her quarters, lest he sic Doctor Crusher on her. Then he had promptly brought in a cot for himself. He figured he might as well: if he was going to waste time on sleep, the engineer felt it might as well be looking at the artificial star field before he closed his eyes.

With no one else in the room, he collapsed on the cot and—

Light caught his eyes. He bolted upright to see a figure materializing on the catwalk beneath the holographic stars. "Tuvok?"

The Vulcan crossed the platform and stepped down into the darkness. "When I found out where you were, I asked Captain Vale to transport me directly here." He stepped over to an interface. "There is something you must see."

H'atoria expanded again, just as it had in the meeting aboard *Titan*. La Forge stood. "The Object Thirteen contact."

"Correct. As I stated in my report, I noticed an anomalous reading while in orbit over the planet. One that I saw again—*here*." Tuvok touched a control, and the flashing point overhead now had a streaming line projecting from it.

Tired artificial eyes opened wide. "That marries right up with Object Thirteen." La Forge looked more closely. "It's projecting something. A signal of some kind."

"A high-intensity signal, meant for a vessel we were also not able to see—coming from a type of ship you encountered nineteen years ago. Projecting a signal that I encountered *ninety-three* years ago . . ."

INTERLUDE

THE HAWK'S RUSE

2293

"Witchcraft to the ignorant . . . simple science to the learned."

—*Leigh Brackett*

Thirty-five

U.S.S. EXCELSIOR
STARBASE 24

"Commander Rand, I appreciate your suggesting me for this duty."

The blond-haired woman in the red uniform smiled gently at Tuvok. "Here's a suggestion, Ensign," Janice Rand said. "Don't thank me too soon."

The young Vulcan raised an eyebrow. "I expressed gratitude at the culturally appropriate time."

"Ensign, not every 'very important person' who boards a starship is an easy assignment," she said. "Every so often you get a Dohlman of Elas."

"I am unfamiliar with the reference."

"One of Captain Sulu's cautionary stories from the old *Enterprise* days. I think I'm glad I missed that one. Your guest today is someone I think it would be good for you to meet. But let's just say that the previous times he was aboard *Excelsior*, things were a little . . . *rocky*."

"Rocky." Tuvok contemplated. "Should you not have assigned Lieutenant Valtane as escort? Geology is one of his specialties."

She chuckled. "Good luck, Ensign."

Tuvok walked the length of the hallway toward the transporter room. He had joined *Excelsior*'s crew as a junior science officer near the end of the ship's three-year mission exploring planetary bodies in the Beta Quadrant. His timing was less than fortunate. The quadrant was home to both the Klingon Empire and the Romulan Star Empire, traditional adversaries of the Federation. Ever since the Kudao

Massacre, it had become a hostile place for scientific pursuits. More than once, Captain Sulu and his ship had been redirected to aid in some matter of state or mission of mercy relating to the testy situation.

Now *Excelsior* was tasked to head for Yongolor, homeworld of the Kinshaya, sworn and ancient enemies of the Klingons, after a brief stop at Starbase 24 to pick up a diplomat. Tuvok, already unclear on how much pure science he could pursue in a possible war zone, was equally vague on why he was chosen. But Commander Rand had taken on Tuvok's development as a personal project and had seemed to think he needed to broaden his horizons. While it was hard to gainsay such an experienced officer, Tuvok had been, as yet, unable to see the potential benefit.

He entered the transporter room. "The starbase is ready," the transporter chief said.

Tuvok ordered, "Energize." On the transporter pad, a young man with short brown hair, a high forehead, and copious spreads of freckles going down each side of his face materialized. He wore the modest gray attire of a Federation diplomat—and when he locked eyes on the ensign, he affected a mischievous grin.

"Well, hello," he said in a voice that slightly grated. "What have we here?"

"Captain Sulu sends his regards. I am Ensign Tuvok. Welcome to *Excelsior*."

"Curzon Dax of Trill, at your service." He stepped off the pad and studied Tuvok up and down. "Vulcan, are we?"

"We are not. I am. According to your file—"

"My file! Good heavens." He whispered into Tuvok's ear. "Tell me, did you find anything . . . *entertaining* in there?"

"Entertaining?"

"Juicy. I have lived an interesting life."

Tuvok maneuvered himself away. "I am a science officer, Ambassador—it is not my duty to know your personal affairs. But it is consistent with the responsibilities of a Starfleet officer to know the public record of whom we are hosting."

Dax only seemed to grow more amused. "I stand in awe, sir, of your elaborately constructed sentences. It's a shame to waste such carefully considered words in the service of science." His smile grew more impetuous. "Will you favor me with a contraction during my stay? Or perhaps a gerund with a clipped *g*?"

Tuvok stared.

"Well, we'll see about that later." Dax offered his hand. "I am overjoyed to meet you, Ensign. Absolutely overjoyed." He shook the puzzled Vulcan's hand vigorously. "Tell me, did they tell you about the first time I was aboard *Excelsior*?"

"I read the report. You were to attend peace talks with the Empire, but they were disrupted by terrorism."

"We wound up chasing a crazed albino Klingon across the stars. I only hope our adventure together will be half as interesting." He slapped Tuvok on the back. "No, why wish for half? *Twice* as interesting! Where do we begin?"

"I am here to escort you to your quarters. Then I will return to my duties analyzing data already collected about gaseous anomalies."

"Your days sound riveting. Tell me, is the officer's club in the same place?"

"I am unaware of the past configuration of this vessel."

"Discovery is half the fun, Tuvok." Curzon Dax marched to the exit. "Come along! They can send my luggage to wherever luggage is sent."

Tuvok followed, having realized why Captain Sulu sent somebody else.

TRADING POST KURABAK
CHELVATUS III

"I can only give you five hundred *kurabakas* for this," said the merchant.

"Five hundred?" Korgh snorted. "This *d'k tahg* is a valued relic of my family. You of course know of the great Commander Kruge?"

"Scourge of the Klingon frontier? Of course."

"I was his protégé. In fact, his heir. This weapon was given me by Kruge in honor of our relationship."

The orange-skinned creature's eyestalks extended, giving it a better look at the blade. "There is no emblem, no inscription."

"Would I lie about this?"

An eyestalk cocked toward the Klingon. "Would a scion of a great house peddle weapons in a market on a neutral world?" He passed the knife back to Korgh. "Five hundred, no more."

Korgh glared at the merchant. Then he grabbed the eyestalk with one hand and put the blade to work with the other. The merchant screamed in agony as viscous goo spurted onto the Klingon's hands. It stank.

Armed with the blade, he looked around the trading post to see what attention he'd attracted. Some—but he had a moment. Finding the merchant curled up on the floor in pain, Korgh rifled through the thing's many cloth pouches. "I will take five hundred *kurabakas* for my time."

"Take it! Take it all!"

"No. I am no thief." Korgh pocketed the money and made his way to the exit, aware of all the eyes on him. He didn't care. One of the eyes was on the floor. In his mood, he would happily add to the total.

Both his stomachs grumbled loudly as he stepped onto the street. Seven years had passed since Spock had stolen his chance for revenge on James T. Kirk, and Korgh's world had completely fallen apart.

He had soldiered on for several years, looking to recruit crew for the Phantom Wing; his efforts had been completely without success. The nobles who had taken control of the House of Kruge through their ridiculous and offensive *may'qochvan* bargain had cornered the market on hired muscle in the regions where the family was active, forcing him to look ever farther afield. The sheer number of hirelings he required further compounded Korgh's problem. His best chance to surprise his enemies involved attacking with the entire squadron at once; employing ships piecemeal jeopardized that. But he could not staff a dozen birds-of-prey without selling off one of the ships—and he had steadfastly refused to do so. The Phantom Wing was part of Kruge's dream, the only legacy Korgh had from him. He would keep it whole.

The delays had eroded both the patience and the numbers of the cadre of engineers who'd been loyal to him. "The Twenty" were now the Ten. Korgh had killed three back on Gamaral; since then, one a year had fallen. To different reasons, yes, but always because of their own stupidity. One had been electrocuted in a mishap, trying to install Odrok's enhancements on one of the Phantom Wing vessels. Two more had been killed in foreign ports of call as the weaklings had failed miserably at defending themselves.

But the four most recent had died because they had threatened to leave the group. Now he was so shorthanded he could no longer staff *Chu'charq* as his personal vessel. His only recourse had been to repeat Odrok's original relay of the Phantom Wing from Gamaral: one ship at a time. They had brought all twelve ships to a hiding place in an abandoned mine on an unpopulated Klingon world. Along with the few workers he was left with—the truest of the true believers—Odrok had remained there to continue modifying the ships while Korgh struck out on his own.

Four months of travel had brought him nothing but ruin. He had found no allies, no riches, and on several worlds, his frustrated outbursts had brought him the wrong kind of attention. He grew paranoid. What if the nobles really had known about him and his claim after all? Could all the people who failed to help him have been paid to thwart him? He saw potential assassins around every corner.

Chelvatus III, close enough to the Klingon frontier that it would almost certainly be part of the Empire someday, was no haven. He was being followed, he was sure. There was no police force here; he could not imagine the bleeding merchant had any muscle. Darting into an alley between hovels, he drew his *d'k tahg* and turned, ready to pounce on those following him.

Someone else pounced instead. *"Get him!"* A net fell from one of the rooftops, covering Korgh.

He ripped at the cordage, desperate to remove the thing. He could hear motion on the roof above. This was it: the nobles had finally come for him. "Come down and face me, cowards!"

Finding the edge of the net, he pulled it free and turned toward the way he'd arrived from. Two humanoids stood there, holding phasers. "Stun him!"

Korgh saw a flash of auburn and fell to the pavement, his last conscious thought being that his enemies had finally gotten him.

Thirty-six

TEMPLE OF THE GODS
YONGOLOR

Hikaru Sulu's experience with Trills had told him they were nothing if not changeable. Sulu had met Curzon Dax when he was an aide to Ambassador Sarek. The Trill had been impatient, blunt, arrogant, sometimes frivolous—all the things a successful diplomat should not be. On the other hand, when the captain heard that Curzon had embarked on an adventure to aid the Klingons he was negotiating with, Sulu realized his character had significant depth.

The Curzon who'd met him in *Excelsior*'s transporter room as they entered Kinshaya space had evolved. Experiences as envoy had made Dax overfull of the joys of life, turning his aggressive instincts toward relishing whatever situation he was in. One brief subspace conversation with him, before his arrival, had nearly been enough to exhaust Sulu. He felt for whatever poor ensign had been assigned to serve as his escort; scuttlebutt was that Dax had done all his mission prep in the club.

"Long night?" he asked Dax as they walked the grand halls of the Kinshaya Temple of the Gods.

"And a long day. And another night. You should have been there, Captain." The Trill smiled broadly at him. "I taught your barkeep some delightful new concoctions."

"I'm sure you've got quite an arsenal."

Flanked by their security detail, the two looked up in wonder at the immense structure around them. Duranium-reinforced marbled columns rose nearly twenty meters to a ceiling far above. Sulu was sure he was not the first to wonder how the Kinshaya, whose forward limbs served half the time as another set of legs, had ever been able to build the place.

"We are supposed to be impressed," Dax said.

"Mission accomplished. I guess our goal is to see that they put even more industry into architecture rather than weapons."

"Leave that to me." Since the Kudao events, Dax had been charged with looking for ways to defuse tensions with the Klingon Empire. His theory was that conflicts anywhere near the Federation's border just served to concentrate Klingon hardware in the region, creating instability.

The Kinshaya were poorly understood by the Federation, but their ultrareligious culture was known to be a xenophobic morass. They loved to poke the Klingon bear and were doing so again, potentially upsetting hopes that the Empire would direct its expansion toward deep space.

A tasseled Kinshaya with regal blue fur clopped down the hall toward them. Her wings flared, showing their golden colors. Dax and Sulu introduced themselves.

She responded in a high-pitched voice somewhere between a purr and a chant. "Federation heathens, welcome. Have you come to repent?"

Sulu and Dax looked at each other. The Trill gave him a wink and a smile. "We come for an audience with the most great Pontifex Maxima, whose wisdom is known throughout the stars. She who is called Urawak. Have you seen this magnificent blossom?"

Pontifex Urawak shuddered. "Flattery from a sure heretic. But you come at a time of wonders which even you cannot deny."

"You refer to the Year of Prayer, just begun," Dax said. He looked to Sulu. "At the end of every thirty-year cycle, the Kinshaya cloister for a year to pray for the return of their gods."

"I see." Sulu was happy to see Dax really had brushed up.

"If you would *truly* see, follow me," the Pontifex said. "Prophecy has been answered!"

The security officers were asked to surrender their weapons; Sulu protested, but Dax waved it off as expected. Afterward Urawak brought them through a wide arch into the large dome.

Sulu gawked. There, across a fiery chasm on an immense circular dais, rested a dragon. That was the only word Sulu could think of to describe it: a silver serpent, ten meters tall, resting on folded Kinshaya-like legs. Its wings, tucked behind, looked large and functional. Its eyes burned red as steam escaped from its forked proboscis. Its whole body shimmered with an otherworldly glow.

The chamber evoked hell in some religions, perhaps in the Kinshaya one also. Pillars of flame leaped randomly from the gap surrounding the giant's roost. Kinshaya of many colors knelt around the outside of the ring, chanting.

The Pontifex advanced into the chamber and made the Kinshaya equivalent of a curtsy. "Great Niamlar, behold the unbelievers."

The creature's enormous head lifted from its position of repose, and Niamlar spoke in a voice that sounded like the whistling wind. "*You come to disturb my faithful.*"

Sulu looked at Dax, who gamely stepped forward. "We do not . . . Great Niamlar, is it?"

"Of course it is." Urawak glared at the visitors. "Niamlar, one of the Thirty-One, gives us the bountiful blessings of her house."

"I see. And what is her house?" Dax asked.

"*War,*" Niamlar said, and the fiery plumes fluttered against her breath.

With all the Kinshaya paying attention to the creature, Sulu surreptitiously removed his tricorder from a pocket and silently activated it. He was pretty sure he couldn't look at any readings of the creature without offending his hosts, but he hoped to at least record part of the event. Niamlar's mighty frame went into motion. *"I am Server and Protector,"* she intoned as she circled the platform. *"Shield and lance of the Kinshaya, guardian against the great demons."*

Sulu knew this part. "Demons. You mean . . . ?"

"Yes."

On the floor of the platform, an aperture opened. A post arose from the trapdoor, with someone chained to it. It was a Klingon, Sulu saw—wide-eyed and stunned.

The monster circled back and regarded the prisoner as someone whose arrival was expected. *"I have spirited from the frontier a great general among the infernal ones. He will see how Niamlar protects her people."*

Chants from the Kinshaya rose, all demanding death. Niamlar's great jaws opened.

The captain whispered in the envoy's ear, "Curzon, we have to stop this."

"Agreed." Dax shrugged. "Any suggestions?"

U.S.S. Excelsior
ORBITING YONGOLOR

Tuvok had seldom started a watch on no sleep—and yet, he found the science station a welcome refuge. No matter where he had gone aboard *Excelsior* since the day of the ambassador's arrival, Dax had found him—and always when the ambassador was on his way to the club to "relax." The Vulcan had always attempted to beg off, his duties to escort Dax having long been since discharged. But the Trill was a force of nature.

Not a bad thing in a diplomat, Tuvok observed, and perhaps that was the lesson Commander Rand hoped he would learn. If so, he had learned it, and that was enough. He longed to study anything else, but there was not much of interest around Yongolor. He adjusted the controls, searching for anything remarkable. Perhaps the star's magnetic field held some secrets that would advance Starfleet's knowledge of—

The reading from one of his sensors spiked high. It returned to normal an instant later.

Curious. Tuvok adjusted the system's sensitivity and restarted the test. Perhaps there was something here of note after all.

Thirty-seven

Korgh had awakened in the dark, shackled to the post. In his drugged haze, he'd heard the rumblings above, heard the chants. Assuming the Kruge family nobles had found some way to humiliate him, he'd readied himself to give them a piece of his mind.

Then the trapdoor above him opened, and he had been elevated into a bright room with a colossal monster breathing in his face.

"Back, fiend!" he yelled, futilely pulling against his chains. Wrenching from side to side, he saw flames, chanting Kinshaya—were there humans? He had never heard of the existence of anything so large, so foul. The drooling creature backed away for several moments. "Free me to fight," he yelled, "or leave me be!"

Fire raged in the creature's eyes—and then it appeared in its maw, opening wide. Korgh saw the flames envelop him, felt the heat like a dry wind. He closed his eyes and screamed—

—only to materialize a second later along with the post and chains in some sort of an atrium. The place was all white, with another high ceiling; it was as if he had gone from an infernal temple to an antiseptic surgical theater.

"One baked Klingon, coming up," said a bipedal creature of a sort Korgh had never seen. He was all nose, it seemed, with a breathing apparatus of some kind stuck in his mouth. "Take him down, folks."

Under the watch of several guards armed with disruptors, two technicians wearing headsets unchained Korgh from the post. The links dropped to the deck, and he moved to strike one of the techs—only to fall.

"Easy there," the blue-skinned creature who'd greeted him said. "We tranked you up pretty good."

"Who are you? What is this?"

"I'm a truthcrafter. This is a job. You're a Klingon, and you're a prop." The speaker listened to his headset and gestured to the guards. "Get him off the transporter pad. We're about to bring the lady back from the planet."

"This is a starship?" Bewildered, Korgh allowed himself to be moved to the side of the cavernous chamber. A glow filled the room, forcing him to avert his eyes. When he looked again, the monster was there, leering at him from its platform.

Korgh tensed, ready to wrest free and run, but he stopped when the abomination spoke words he never expected: "Good job, everyone."

Another flash, and in place of the creature stood a tall, slender female with pale skin and long, braided white hair. An egg-like knot sat in the middle of her forehead, flanked by two cranial ridges that extended from her skull almost like a pair of horns. She wore a gown of flowing burgundy—but as she walked from the pad, the garment appeared to change colors in the light.

"Any trouble from the Starfleet visitors?" her aide asked.

"None. If the *Excelsior*'s sensors could see us, we'd know by now." She noticed Korgh. "Ah! We meet again."

He eyed her with suspicion. "You are that . . . that *thing*?"

She snickered. "In a way. I am Napean by race, a practitioner by trade. This wonderful ship is the *Zamloch*. And I," she said, long fingers on her neck, "am called Jilaan."

"And I am Korgh—Lord of the House of Kruge. You will release me!"

Jilaan looked at the guards and then back at the green

man who was apparently her aide. "Oh, Lallabus," she said in her singsong voice. "Your people kidnapped a lord?"

Lallabus scratched his bald head. "I guess we screwed up."

"Maybe not," she said, walking around the restrained Korgh. "Some of those Klingon houses control a lot of assets. Maybe they'll give us something to get him back."

"Our emitter needs service badly," Lallabus offered.

Korgh growled. "What is this babble about?"

Jilaan smiled at him primly. "We were about to send you home, Lord Korgh. But now I think we'll keep you."

U.S.S. *EXCELSIOR*
ORBITING YONGOLOR

"It just vanished." Putting the napkin on his plate, Sulu snapped his fingers. "Gone, just like that. And a second later, the platform Niamlar was on disappeared, along with the fountains of fire."

"All gone?" Commander Rand looked across the mess table at him in amazement. "No transporter effect?"

"It sure didn't look like one," Dax said. "The thing was enormous."

Sulu tapped his finger on the table, explaining, "I've transported whales. But I agree. My tricorder said the thing was there. It even read heat from the flames—though it didn't feel nearly as warm in there as it probably should have. Odd."

"Poor Klingon," Dax said. "This Niamlar thing breathed fire, and he vanished in a puff of smoke. There was nothing left of him."

"Nothing we could do," the captain said. "Niamlar then called for all Kinshaya to tithe to the temple. She said once she was satisfied with the offerings, she would bring back another Klingon—a much more important one—and then ask for a devotional act."

"A crusade, I'm sure," Dax said. "The total war we were hoping to avoid."

Sulu nodded. "And when Niamlar disappeared, the Pontifex said we must have offended her and ordered us out."

Dax emptied his wineglass and glanced around the room. He could see Tuvok lingering at another table, his meal finished. The Trill gave a little wave, but Tuvok seemed not to notice it.

"What does this do to our mission?" Rand asked.

"The Kinshaya are convinced a god has commanded them to carry out a holy war," Sulu said. "It's not up to us to find out whether or not this god is real."

"Real?" Rand winced. "You don't mean you believe what you saw?"

"Some beings really do have powers that would make them seem godlike," Sulu said. "Remind me to tell you about Trelane—or the thing we found beyond the Great Barrier. We need to consider all the possibilities. There may actually exist a being called Niamlar, and it might be the same being at the center of Kinshaya mythology. On the other hand, it could be a pretender. The Excalbians wanted us to think Abe Lincoln and Kahless had come back to life."

"If it's the Kinshaya's own scheme," Rand said, "they won't welcome our interference."

"Let's say we learned someone else was playing them," the ambassador said, "someone from offworld, for personal gain?"

"Then we'd bag them." Sulu rose and excused himself.

Rand stood. Seeing Tuvok, she nudged Dax. "There's a familiar face." She called the Vulcan over. He approached, dutifully, if reluctantly. "I was just leaving, Ensign," Rand said. "Perhaps you could keep the ambassador company while he finishes."

"Certainly, Commander." He sat in her chair—and immediately seemed to Dax to be the most uncomfortable dinner companion he'd ever had.

"Did you hear our story, Ensign?"

"It would be wrong to eavesdrop on a private conversation."

Dax twirled the ends of his fork on his plate. "Don't make me tell a joke about ears, Tuvok. I've been trying to behave myself." He set the fork down, put his elbows on the table, and rested his chin on his templed fingers. "I believe you have heard quite a bit. You're a science officer, so you've studied the captain's tricorder readings. You know what I think, Ensign?"

"I do not."

"I think you have a theory. A theory that you would love to share."

Tuvok stiffened. "I have provided my theory to my immediate superior officer. It is his responsibility to decide whether it merits further consideration."

"Aha. So your superior has the ears that don't hear everything. I have seen it many times. So why don't you just tell *me* your theory?" He looked at Tuvok and grinned. "I *know* you're dying to . . ."

Thirty-eight

The lights in the thrumming chamber blinded Korgh. He had gathered from those who had placed him inside that it was some kind of imaging device, studying him and all his movements. Two minutes inside had made him hate it; two hours had pushed him to the brink. He put his hands before his face. "Turn these damn lights off!"

The cylindrical compartment rotated—and he saw a dark and blurry figure standing outside the opening, arms outstretched. She cried, "'Go back and tell the king that at that hour I will smother the whole world in the dead blackness of midnight!'"

As the guards pulled him from the chamber, Korgh rubbed his eyes and tried to focus on the speaker. It was Jilaan in yet another dress, this one a cascade of black frills. "What are you babbling about, woman?"

The woman smiled. "*A Connecticut Yankee in King Arthur's Court*," she said. "A Terran story of time travel, long before it was possible. The speaker was using his knowledge of an eclipse to fool primitives."

"'Release me or I will kill your kin and drink their blood.' The Klingon opera *The Death of K'pash*," Korgh said, angrily eyeing the guards.

"Amusing." She swept into an aisle between dozens of technicians hard at work at various interfaces. Korgh had gathered that Jilaan and her crew were tricksters, using their equipment to fool the Kinshaya.

Jilaan hovered above one of her workers and studied the

readouts from his screen. "Mmm. That would have gone faster, Lord Korgh, had you followed our directions."

They had asked him to perform a variety of actions, from assuming various poses to doing calisthenics. He had ignored them. "I am not your puppet to command."

"But you will be, in a sense. It is why my people borrowed you—"

"Borrowed!"

"—we have never had a good Klingon model to work from. It's hard to get close to your people." She looked back at him and smiled. "You're a testy species, but likable."

She walked to a doorway and beckoned, and the guards led him into another room. There, he saw a life-sized doppelgänger of himself standing in a squared-off area and looking bored. "Morath's bones!"

"Ooh, good line," Jilaan said. She turned to Lallabus, who stood nearby. "Make a note of that one."

"Yes, master."

Korgh stepped toward his double. No one stopped him as he reached out to touch it. It was a strange feeling—and a stranger sight still—as his hand passed through the other Klingon's shoulder with only partial resistance. "What is this?"

"Oh, holograms and force fields," Jilaan said, "and more I shouldn't talk about."

"It does not react."

"There needs to be an actor inhabiting the character. We didn't have time to model you before you were needed for my scene down on Yongolor—that's why we beamed you straight onto our set. But you did a fine job."

"I don't believe any of this. You play gods?"

"And more."

"I suppose simpleminded dolts like Kinshaya deserve no better. You could never do this to Klingons," Korgh said. "We killed our gods. We fear no demons."

"You seemed afraid of Niamlar," Jilaan said. "And we don't just do gods. Wherever there is a great figure who commands respect, we can move masses."

"To what end?"

"To say we did it. Stories. A lot like your songs, I should think."

"Foolishness."

An aide brought her a message. "Well, well," Jilaan said, reading it. "It looks like we have another actor in our midst, after all." She smirked at him. "We've checked into your story, 'my lord.' Your House of Kruge does exist, and there are quite a lot of people who claim to be the head of it. But nowhere did we find anyone by your name in connection with it."

Korgh groaned in frustration. "Of course not, you old fool. I have yet to claim my legacy. But the house is mine."

"A lot of good it's done you," Lallabus interjected, his words whistling through his breathing apparatus. "You had barely enough on you for a week's food."

Korgh glared at the alien, who he had since learned belonged to a race called the Benzites. "Vex me again, ugly, and I will shove that mouthpiece down your throat."

"Touchy." Lallabus toggled a control on an interface, and the faux Korgh disappeared. "It looks like they've added some detail to our character for the next scene, Master Jilaan."

"Excellent. If you're ready, give us a show." Jilaan folded up the message—and it seemed to disappear in her hands. She looked at Korgh. "Lallabus is my apprentice."

Lallabus stepped into the corner where the false Korgh had been. He clapped his fingers together—and an instant later was transformed into a Klingon male. He looked different from Korgh; his hair and beard were fuller, and his cranial ridges were softer. When he spoke, his voice sounded not like the Benzite, but rather a booming Klingon orator. *"I am Kahless, and I have returned!"*

The transformed Lallabus continued, striking a heroic pose. *"The fight tempers a warrior and makes him stronger."*

Korgh laughed out loud. "What is this, a joke?"

"What is wrong?" Lallabus-Kahless said. "Didn't I say it right?"

"There is nothing right here," Korgh said. "It is the hunt, not the fight—and you should not be saying it. These are our words."

"Understood," Jilaan said. "We took the dialogue from a Federation text on Kahless's life."

Korgh laughed. "What would *they* know?"

"Point taken. But how does he *look*?"

"Terrible. He barely resembles a Klingon." He started walking toward the false Kahless; Jilaan nodded to the guards to let him advance. Korgh grabbed at the fake Klingon's arm. It felt real, more substantial than the Korgh model from earlier. "You have also made him look an undernourished weakling."

Jilaan nodded. "I told you, we haven't had a good model. That's a mix of imagery we've obtained and materials from historic records. We're planning to use some of your physiognomy to inform the model."

"The problem only starts there," Korgh said. "He does not sound like Kahless at all."

"But Kahless lived more than a thousand years ago," said Lallabus in his modified voice.

"And all Klingons know not just his words, but the circumstances in which he said them. We know what he must have sounded like." Korgh looked back at Jilaan. "You will never fool a single Klingon with this—this *thing*."

"Oh, we don't intend to," Jilaan said. "It is to fool the Kinshaya during our last scene in the temple. So we can rob the offertory."

Korgh stared. "You mean this is all for money?"

"And the story." Jilaan raised her hands, self-effacing. "We've got repairs to make—and a treasure vault could come in handy." She gestured, and a technician touched a control to dispel the unconvincing Kahless illusion. "We've got a lot of work to do in a short time, Korgh. These gentlemen will accompany you to your cell. You can rest easy until we have time to drop you—"

Korgh spun and punched Lallabus squarely in the face. The Benzite slammed against the wall and fell, choking on part of his own breathing apparatus. "*That* is for presuming to impersonate Kahless," Korgh said as the guards rushed to restrain him.

Jilaan hurried to her fallen apprentice's side, joined by a medic. After a few minutes, she rose and glared at Korgh. "Hotheaded fool! You broke his proboscis—and the unit lacerated his tongue badly. He won't be able to speak for a week!"

"A shame," Korgh said, flanked by the guards. "If you decide you need someone who actually knows something about Kahless to appear in your final scene—for a share of the fortune—I will be in my cell."

U.S.S. Excelsior
ORBITING YONGOLOR

While Ambassador Dax found President Ra-ghoratreii less objectionable than most Federation politicians, his timing left something to be desired. The hail for Dax had arrived at the same time he had convinced young Tuvok to open up. Dax had hurried to take the call—whereupon he had learned that Starfleet Intelligence had detected a mobilization of the Kinshaya battle fleet. It came as no surprise to Dax. It was hard to argue peace in someone's house when a god of war was staying in the guest room.

Tuvok had surprised Dax later that evening by contacting him, asking to continue their conversation now that he'd had the chance to gather his research. The ensign presented it to Dax in his guest quarters.

The Trill read the final line of the report. "You believe there is a vessel—"

"Not necessarily a vessel."

"—*something* under cloak—"

"Not necessarily under cloak."

"—*something* our sensors detected in orbit of Yongolor," Dax said. "And you believe it is projecting some kind of signal that nobody's ever seen before, down to the Temple of the Gods to produce an illusion."

"Yes, ambassador, that is my theory," Tuvok replied.

"Holographic technology?" Dax shook his head. "This looked real. Something that convincing is years off. Maybe decades."

"I have no facts for speculating about the method. I can only claim to have detected a possible means of projecting a signal."

"What is the motive?" Dax frowned. "Why would someone try to start a war?"

"The goal may be something we do not understand," Tuvok said. "It appears to be a common truth that sentient life-forms seek advantage through imitation. Many use mimicry for protection, profiting from their resemblance to dangerous predators—or beings that are poisonous or otherwise unpalatable."

Dax grinned. "Avoiding a jealous husband by dressing as the local tax collector, eh?"

"I do not take your meaning." Tuvok went on, "But there are also examples of creatures using mimicry aggressively. The gurda worm of Risa twists itself into the shape of a coiled stoneflower, so as to tempt insects into its maw.

And the zone-tailed hawk on Earth so resembles a turkey vulture that it flocks with them, in order to surprise animals that think the vultures harmless."

"Those crazy hawks."

"Most of these creatures lack higher brain functions. Have they somehow reasoned the relationship between two other beings and used that to advantage? Or has evolution simply favored the hawks that most resemble vultures and which flock with them?"

"Are these the questions that keep you up nights, Tuvok?"

"I sleep adequately."

Dax gestured toward the door. "Lead me to the club, and while I look to see what's available, you can tell me more about zone-tailed gurdy worms."

Tuvok gathered up his evidence. "If the report is correct that war is approaching, I must go to my superior. If the signal I detected is indeed generating the illusions in the temple, perhaps the science and engineering divisions can find a means of interdiction."

Dax followed him into the corridor. "Are you sure you don't want me to take this to Captain Sulu?"

"No, Ambassador," Tuvok said. "There is a process in place. Either my arguments are logical, or they are not. I trust in the mechanisms Starfleet has developed." He turned and went on his way.

I gave up on bureaucracies lifetimes ago, Dax mused. *But he's young.* The Trill headed for the turbolift, intent on making sure that whoever needed a nudge would get one. Chain of command might be the Prime Directive for Starfleet officers, but Dax had a few rules of his own.

Thirty-nine

"*Niamlar, save us! Save your faithful followers!*"

The Kinshaya petitioners wailed, and for good reason: Kahless lived again. Or, rather, that was who the Kinshaya thought was in the Temple of the Gods—thanks to the quick work Jilaan's truthcrafters had done. Korgh appeared as Kahless, *bat'leth* held high, threatening the beast Niamlar from a dais on her own platform.

"Silence, vermin—or I will feast on your hearts!" His voice boomed. Korgh had to admit he liked the sound they'd created for him—along with everything else.

Korgh had figured out that while Jilaan's party wasn't the only group of truthcrafters, *Zamloch* was the largest vessel in their peculiar trade. It was able to project larger characters and settings—and, importantly, it could haul away more loot. After Jilaan agreed to his terms, Korgh had assisted her programmers in designing the authentic-looking *bat'leth* he now appeared to hold, as well as the robe of white hides he seemed to wear.

After the ship's sensors had confirmed the arrival of an impressive amount of wealth into the temple, Jilaan had reappeared to them as Niamlar. She had been in the middle of a prepared speech when Korgh had transported down. Whereas the truthcrafters' tricks had made his earlier departure appear as the result of consumption by fire, this time they had disguised their transporter effect to make it seem as if coalescing smoke had given birth to "Kahless." He and Jilaan had then launched into their repartee.

"I stand for all Klingons, Niamlar! You may be large, but my sinews hold the power of my entire race!"

"Klingon wretch! You foul this holy place with your presence." Niamlar's colossal form circled the platform, giving her enemy a wide berth. *"Pontifex, I will battle this devil—but I require a show of your devotion."*

"Command us!" said Urawak. The other Kinshaya picked up on it. "Command us!"

"Every Kinshaya in the Order must go to the streets. Raise statues to my wonder, create monuments to my name. Your faith will give me the power to dispel this horror."

"At once!"

"Return tomorrow when the sun is high above the temple. But hear me, O devoted ones. Should any Kinshaya step inside before, that one's lack of faith will cost all."

A stampede followed, with Kinshaya racing for the exit in full religious fervor.

Korgh waited for the noise to abate. He gazed upon the great serpent-thing, now not fearsome in the least. "Did they truly believe you?"

"They did. Napeans are empathic, my young friend. I know."

"What now?"

"We wait until Zamloch *gives the word. Once there are no life signs in the temple, we will beam down our team to tag and transport the treasury."*

Korgh looked at the *bat'leth* in his hands. So real, and yet nonexistent. The technology, as near as he could tell, was the product of a multispecies effort and the possession of no single state. Obtaining cloaking equipment had been vitally important for the Empire, and yet the ability to make things disappear paled before the power to make something look like anything—or someone look like anyone. It might be more valuable than any treasure in the temple, if he could learn it.

Jilaan's monstrous incarnation spoke again. *"I just received a call in my earpiece from* Zamloch. *The building is empty, but for us. We may now—"*

Korgh spotted a glow out of the corner of his eye. Transporter beams deposited four figures in the temple. It was the Starfleet party he had quickly glimpsed earlier: a captain, two security officers, and someone dressed as a civilian.

"I am Captain Hikaru Sulu, of *U.S.S. Excelsior,*" called the dark-haired human.

The name startled Korgh. He had heard it after the trial: Sulu was part of the renegade group that had confronted Commander Kruge on the Genesis Planet. He'd known *Excelsior* was in orbit; he'd seen it from *Zamloch* and been amused at the Starfleeters' obliviousness. The thought that Starfleet had rewarded another of Kirk's co-conspirators with a command left a putrid taste in his mouth. But even if he could trust the illusory weapon in his hands, a crevasse separated him from the visitors.

Jilaan seemed to roll with the interruption. *"You trespass in this holiest of places, Federation trash. Begone, while you still breathe."*

"We're breathing fine, thanks," said the civilian. "Just a little smoky in here." He flashed an awkward smile. "Oh, sorry. Ambassador Curzon Dax, at your service. Our sensors said everyone had left the building—except you two. We thought there might be a problem."

Jilaan's creature form stalked the perimeter of the platform. *"What did your mortal sensors say about us?"*

Sulu spoke up. "That he's a Klingon—and you're a very large being, generating warmth."

"The fires burn within. Would you taste them?"

"That's not necessary. We have several theories we could share about how you might be generating life signs—and heat—but we're not supposed to be here right now," Sulu pointed out. "You're not, either, which makes it appropriate for us to act."

"Act?" Korgh asked. "Act how?" He raised his *bat'leth*. "I welcome a fight!"

"Don't bother," the captain said. "Instead, in a few moments, *Excelsior* is going to begin bombarding the ship you have in orbit with every kind of particle we can imagine—and there are quite a few of those. Whatever it is you're using to project your presence here, we're pretty sure we can disrupt it."

"Do your worst!" Korgh yelled.

"Umm . . ."

Korgh looked back at Jilaan. "What?"

"This Excelsior. *I have never seen its like before."*

"First ship of its class," Dax said. "And a fine dining room."

"So it is new. What does it matter?" Korgh asked Jilaan.

The creature was silent. "I think," Dax said, "your large friend wants to say she doesn't know how our bombardment will affect your presence here. And whether it would hurt you or not, I suspect we could do it at a most inconvenient time. Say, the next time you appear here to the Kinshaya."

"Hah!" Korgh said. "We are leaving as soon as we—" He stopped.

"And if you're thinking about sending anyone here for this," Sulu said, gesturing around to the riches, "I can get more security forces here in a hurry. A *lot* more. We're trespassing already. Forty more officers won't make a difference."

Jilaan's giant body tensed, as if preparing to strike. But Korgh knew very well there was no chance of that happening. There was just an old woman manipulating some malleable force fields, along with some quickly agitating microfields to generate the illusion of body heat.

"This round to you, Captain Sulu," Jilaan said. The platform glowed around Korgh, resolving back into the nothingness it really was—and they were beamed away.

Zamloch
Orbiting Yongolor

Korgh looked like his old self when he appeared on the ship's transporter pad. He also wore his old expression: disgust.

"Where are you going?" he asked as Jilaan stepped off the pad. "We could still transport up some of the riches. Get something from all this!"

"I'm more concerned with what we might lose," Jilaan said. She looked back, and he saw a gentle sadness on her face. "The Federation's expansion has made our Circle's lot difficult, Korgh. With all the Starfleet busybodies running around, we've been forced to spend and spend to continue improving our technology—all the while, focusing only on simple cultures that the Prime Directive doesn't allow Starfleet to interfere with." She sighed. "It has become tiresome—and not at all fun. I had hoped with the Kinshaya we might have a chance once again against an advanced civilization."

"You chose well," Korgh said. "There is no more foolish race traveling the stars."

He caught a trace of a smile from her. Then it faded. "Perhaps someone else can try the Kinshaya again one day. But we must go—while we still can."

Forty

Curzon Dax found Tuvok waiting in the transporter room to see him off to his next assignment. The Trill grinned. "Forget science, Ensign—you should try security. You figured it out. 'Niamlar' went away and hasn't come back."

"Were the Kinshaya appreciative?"

"They kicked us off their planet." Dax laughed and raised his palms upward. "The Pontifex publicly blamed *us* for the apparition leaving."

"She did not accept a scientific explanation?"

"The appearance of even a false god advanced her personal cause."

"Then my discovery solved nothing," Tuvok countered.

Dax studied the science officer. "Hey, friend, are you all right? Something's been bugging you, I can tell."

"I am still trying to decide whether Starfleet is the best use of my skills," Tuvok replied. "It was not my idea to enter the Academy."

"You sound like a man with a dilemma."

"It would only be a problem if it harmed the performance of my duties. It has not."

"Listen, Tuvok, I may not look it, but I've got a lot of experience," Dax said. "I can tell you it does no good to sit around waiting for the right path to appear."

"You think I should make a change? Ask the captain for a transfer?"

"Oh, you should definitely make a change," Dax said, stepping onto the transporter pad. "But don't change ships.

Change your *approach*. I happen to think your captain is all right. Give him a chance. Make sure he sees you. Polish the apple a little bit." Dax put up his hand preemptively. "And don't ask me what cleaning citrus has to do with anything. I've been around a long time, and I've seen a lot. Give me my expressions."

"I would never have asked that question," Tuvok said. "But I must point out that the apple is part of the rose family."

Dax chuckled. "You're wonderful, Ensign. Don't ever change."

"I thought you *were* advising change."

"Exactly." Dax smiled. "Energize."

ZAMLOCH
DEEP SPACE

Anxious to make sure *Excelsior* wasn't following them, Jilaan and her truthcrafters had charted a roundabout course away from Yongolor toward parts unknown. While disappointed about the lost loot, Korgh understood their concern. Every technological leap made by Starfleet or another power represented an existential threat to her operation.

He had no idea how old Jilaan was, but it was clear she had spent half her life trying to better her rivals and the other half trying to stay ahead of the people who could smoke her out. Her quest differed from his, and while Korgh still did not understand what she took from it, he respected the drive she and her people displayed.

After promising not to harm anyone else—and a forced apology to Lallabus—he had been allowed to stay aboard as a laborer. Raiding loot from their marks took muscle and an ability to work fast, and he was nothing if not a good organizer. Korgh had even participated as a character in a few of Jilaan's illusions, usually those set in places where her puny apprentice was fearful to go. He had learned much about acting and dissemblance; talents he considered distastefully Romulan or human, but nonetheless of possible use some day.

His real motive had been to learn about the truthcrafters' technology in order to appropriate it—but it was completely beyond him. He had not built the starships on Gamaral; he had managed those who did. He longed to have Odrok or one of her coworkers around. But the Klingon moon Praxis had exploded in the interim, throwing the political situation into flux; like most ships, *Zamloch* had steered clear of the Empire.

It proved an infernal, maddening year to be away from Klingon space. Chancellor Gorkon's daughter—*how was she in charge of anything?*—made peace with the Federation at Khitomer, with none other than Kirk and Spock involved. Kruge would have been mortified. Korgh could delay his revenge no longer.

When the *Zamloch* approached Klingon space, he prepared to take his leave, carrying a bag holding what he'd earned. It wasn't enough to hire crews; Praxis had sent inflation in the Empire soaring. But it would be enough to keep Odrok and her Phantom Wing engineers supplied for years if necessary.

When the time came to depart, Jilaan called him into her study—a bizarre section of the ship where someone had fooled with the artificial gravity to make furniture sit on overheads and bulkheads. She spoke to him from a colossal high-backed chair. "When anyone leaves our company, Korgh, it is final. The Circle's secrets must be protected. You may seek us out, but you will never find us."

"I will simply wait until you need a Klingon prop again—and allow myself to be kidnapped."

As if floating on air, her chair rotated so he could see her wan smile. "I will miss you," she said, appearing older than he'd remembered. She was wearing flowing white. He had never seen her in the same clothing twice. "I realize you and your kind are bred for war, but I hope you found our travels of interest."

"I did," Korgh allowed, "though I do not understand some things. Back on Yongolor, you never intended to send the Kinshaya to war with the Empire, did you?"

"No, we were just there to take what we needed—and to see all the tributes they made to Niamlar." Her minions had brought back images of hundreds of monuments from all over the Holy Order's territory. "Those will be good fodder for *The Annals*."

"Those who worship you would kill for you, if you told them to."

"I try not to do that. It's a matter of personal preference. Certainly there are practitioners who've sent people to their deaths—even prompted mass suicides. It's a cheap thrill, and there's no art to it. It defeats the purpose."

"Which is?"

"To fool a society so absolutely that you become embedded in their civilization's mythology. That's when a feat goes immortal. I've done it on a dozen worlds in my career—it's why I'm Illusionist Magnus. I wouldn't have accomplished much, though, if I made a habit of wiping out everyone who saw my performance." Jilaan sighed. "Ah, times have changed, Korgh. Gone are the days when we did grand things for the sake of transforming reality. It is all about survival now. It's a pity."

Hearing her regretful tone, a notion dawned on him. "What if I were to invite you and your people to assist me in taking control of my house?"

"Duping Klingons?" Her eyes widened as she considered the idea. "No one in the Circle's ever tried, so far as I know." She paused. "But what's in it for me? And don't tell me you're going to lavish wealth on us after the fact. We don't work on spec."

Korgh frowned. He knew he had only one asset hidden away. He had no choice but to offer it. "What . . . what if I could trade you a Klingon vessel with our latest cloaking technology?"

"You have such a vessel?"

"I do. And I could arrange for ongoing technical assistance for your cloaking device—which you and I both know requires constant updating to stay ahead of Starfleet." He didn't pause long to wonder if Odrok would agree or approve. She worked for him. "I could have a bird-of-prey here within days."

Jilaan was impressed. "You *are* full of surprises. Why didn't you offer that at the start?"

"I did not trust you."

She laughed. "That's a good reason." After thinking for a moment, she shook her head. "My answer is still no. It doesn't sound like a problem conducive to one of our ploys. I remember what we found out about the House of Kruge. You have a lot of different rivals, and it seems like they're already entrenched. I'm not going to be able to fool them one by one."

Korgh agreed that could be a problem. "But what if I could get them all in one place?"

"What if you could? You're trying to get these people to part with the things dearest to them—wealth, power, title. That means they won't be easy marks. It's no good tricking them for an hour. The set-up's going to have to be a very long game."

"How long?"

"As long as it takes. And that's too long for my crew. It's

the same problem as before—we don't know much about Klingons. There's any number of places where I could trip up, be given away." Jilaan studied him. "Now, if *you* could do that groundwork yourself—"

"Me?"

"You're a Klingon—and the interested party. Nobody better to get close to these rivals of yours and soften them up. Didn't you say that they were not aware of your existence?"

"Yes—no. I don't know. I would probably have to change my face and name—no Klingon would do these things." Korgh grimaced. "And I loathe the so-called nobles. I could never stand to be around them, holding my tongue, pretending to be another."

"Your loss, my dear. But I think a day will come when you might well decide any sacrifice is worth it."

Korgh straightened. "May I never live so long." He took his bag and left.

ACT THREE

THE HUNTER'S TRAP

2386

"Some days you get the bear. Some days the bear gets you."
                                        —*William Riker*

Forty-one

Worf was sick and hurt. And he was convalescing in an ODN access room not much larger than a storage locker.

Since his botched beam-in to the *Rodak*, the commander had holed up in the tiny room off a workshop area, just across the hall from where he had arrived. His surmise had been correct: the Unsung never bothered with the room or its closet. It was at the end of a corridor, on the way to nothing. Occasionally, warriors entered the room farther up the hall, but that was it.

Worf knew the basic *B'rel*-class design and had studied the schematics of the Phantom Wing vessels well. Well enough to realize that on this deck, he only had one option: a support room far aft had systems he might be able to use to sabotage *Rodak*'s cloak, or otherwise give away the ship's position to anyone watching. The problem was that to reach the room, he needed to traverse main engineering—normally one of the busier areas aboard.

But *Rodak* was no normal ship, nor the Unsung a regular crew. Its engineers had nothing like a duty schedule, Sarken had said. Sometimes, those present gathered at the far end of the cavernous room for lessons on running a starship. At other times, when the vessel was not in flight, the false Kruge occasionally ordered the crews of all the Phantom Wing ships to the meeting rooms to hear his remotely delivered addresses.

The opportunity to reach his destination was there. But

while Worf's plan was sound, his body was not. He had discovered that the first night, sleeping hunched over on the cold deck of the closet. A fever overtook him, clouding his mind and causing his bones to ache. The morning after he arrived, he was almost too woozy to stand.

Sarken had brought him food and water, and he continued to treat his leg, assuming he had an infection. Nothing had helped. He worried that the transporter had erred in reconstituting him. It had certainly failed to predict the compromised state of the catwalk.

Twice the fever subsided enough for him to venture into the main area of the workshop. He had grown momentarily excited upon discovering a padd, but he soon realized it was detached from any kind of subspace network. Its sole contents seemed to be instructional text and schematics, as well as audio recordings of a Klingon woman giving lessons in starship operations.

Worf had absconded with it back to his hiding space and studied it when he felt well enough. He listened to the narrator's voice playing softly on the device. Her elocution suggested a woman of education, perhaps even of Mempa Institute caliber, and two other things were clear. She knew everything about the Phantom Wing vessels, and she knew she was teaching exiles whose interaction with technology had been sparse.

In his best hour, Worf discovered the padd had been initialized more than a year before—and that he was the first to access its files. Sarken had told him there were dozens of them aboard, one at every duty station. Whoever had provided the Phantom Wing to the Unsung wanted to be certain they understood what they were doing.

The quandary occupied his thoughts as he tried to sleep. Starfleet's working theory had been that General Potok, the founder of the exile colony on Thane, had sent an ally to return with one of the ships of the Phantom Wing. That individual, or some associate, was possibly behind the Kruge doppelgänger. But the existence of the padds combined with previous facts—including the inside information the Unsung had used for the Gamaral attack and the communications satellites that once led to Thane—suggested something else. Whoever was responsible for weaponizing the discommendated exiles had three things in plentiful supply: resources, technical know-how, and time.

That suggested a hostile government—but that only sent Worf's feverish mind into a swift spiral of suspicion. He was amid another maddening catnap when the secret knock he shared with his helper sounded outside the door.

The door opened and Sarken entered carrying a new bucket and a satchel over her shoulder. The first he had no need to ask about: the nearest head was on deck five. The pack, which she opened as she knelt, contained dried rations, a canteen, and a rag. She moistened the cloth and put it against his forehead.

"Where are we?" Worf asked.

"Still in that black spot with no stars. We're just sitting here."

Worf understood. He'd gathered from her reports that the Unsung were on another mission. Perhaps they were hiding in a void, preparing. Or maybe they were lying in wait.

"I heard your name today," Sarken said as she mopped more sweat from his face. "They told me you attacked everyone on Thane after they executed the clone. The one they called Kahless."

Worf sighed wearily. He knew this was coming. He looked up at her. "Did you say anything?"

"No." She wrung the cloth into the bucket. "But why did you do it, Worf?"

"Because the clone was a person, and that person was my friend."

"Oh."

Worf struggled to sit up straighter. His answer seemed to satisfy her—but only to a point.

"Why did my people want to kill your friend?"

"They were told to by the man who leads you."

"Lord Kruge?"

"That is what he calls himself, yes." Worf felt too horrible to go into the topic of impersonation. "He saw Kahless as a threat."

"Why?"

"Because of the ideals he stands for. Honor. Loyalty to family and friends. If your people had known Kahless, they would never have harmed him—or anyone else."

He took the open canteen she offered and drank thirstily. It aggrieved him that the malady he suffered from, whatever it was, represented maybe a minute's work for *Enterprise*'s medical staff to cure. Meanwhile, medical equipment was the one thing *Rodak* didn't seem to have. Whoever had provisioned it hadn't thought much about prolonging the lives of its occupants.

Sarken passed him some of the accursed protein crackers—all his stomach could tolerate. "Do you have children, Worf?"

"I do," Worf answered between bites. "His name is Alexander. He is an adult now. An ambassador."

"What's an ambassador?"

"A sort of messenger between friends. I do not see him as much as I would like."

"Most parents on Thane don't spend much time with their kids. Everyone kind of raises us together."

That made sense to Worf. Discommendation was tied to lineage, so the family would not have been at the center of exile life. "My parents died when I was young," Worf said.

"Were there wild animals? That's how my mother died."

"No. There was war. People called Romulans attacked the planet I was living on. My parents died. I was raised by the people who rescued me."

"I was sad when my mother died," she said, rocking back and forth as she sat beside him. "But my father started talking to me more after that. He was the one who told me about you, and how you made the other Klingons not hate you anymore. They let you be one of them again."

Worf's eyes narrowed. Perhaps the man could be an ally in the sense that Valandris was—someone who understood who Worf was and was reluctant to harm him. "What is your father's name?"

"Tharas." Sarken pursed her lips. "He died too—back when we were leaving Thane."

Worf stopped chewing—and felt his throat contract. Earlier, in his own escape from Thane, he had killed Tharas in honorable combat.

Appetite gone, he swallowed and passed back the remaining food. Eyeing her, he chose his words carefully. "Sarken, did they tell you *how* Tharas died?"

"Valandris called me from *Chu'charq* after we left Thane. She just said he didn't come back. He was still out in the jungle when the camp blew up."

Then Valandris kept the facts of his death secret, Worf thought. What did that mean? Had she wanted to spare the girl's feelings? Or had she not wanted to spoil the reputation Worf had?

Sniffling, Sarken wiped her face. "We were just starting to spend more time together too. He was teaching me how to hunt. But then Lord Kruge came, and he started spending all his time helping him." She frowned. "I hate the Unsung, Worf. I want my home back."

"You can make a home in another place," Worf said, "as

I did. And as Alexander did. You simply need the chance—
and the right people."

"I guess." She packed her satchel and stood. "I'll see
you tomorrow. I think they're about to do whatever they're
going to do. Don't go out into the hall."

There is no danger of that happening, Worf thought. But
their conversation had given him something else to worry
about.

Forty-two

Where the hell is Kahless?

Cross thought it for the hundredth time while he hobbled onto the bird-of-prey's bridge as the elderly Commander Kruge. He approached the engineer's station.

"Hemtara," he said. "Scan this vessel for life signs."

"Again? The previous three scans had no unusual results," she said. "I do not understand, my lord. Is someone aboard who should not be?"

This time, Cross had prepared an answer for the question. "Chelvatus III was home to many Klingons loyal to the Empire. If someone sensed our vessel's presence while we were there, they could have put an operative aboard then."

"I do not see how. We were cloaked the entire—"

"Do it!" he barked. "And do not include the bridge in your scan." The truthcrafters' projected facsimiles of Kruge and N'Keera were designed to fool biometric sensors, but there was no reason to take chances. "Do as I say, or I will forget your loyalty."

"Right away, my lord." Hemtara set to work.

Cross saw that Shift was watching him. Disguised as N'Keera, she sat by his command chair with a book on her knees. No words were necessary between them; she knew the problem as well as he did. Days had passed, and they still had no idea where Kahless had gone—and they only had the roughest idea of how he had escaped.

Gaw's truthcrafters aboard *Blackstone* had been taking turns monitoring the storage room aboard *Chu'charq*;

after watching days of apparent drinking by the clone, their attention had been waning for a while. But the breaking point had arrived when the squadron put in at Chevatus III. Many of the *Blackstone* staffers had either been out selling the goods taken from the Orions or had been working on Cross's future project. In focusing on how to make Cross look like the original Kahless, they had let the current one go.

The only evidence from *Blackstone*'s sensors had been Kahless, carrying a bundle of some kind under his arm as he stepped to the back of the storeroom, past the limits of their static surveillance. Suspecting that the clone had clambered up the pillar of crates, Shift had nimbly scaled the tower to inspect. In the overhead, she'd found a ventilation shaft that sloped downward, following the shape of the dorsal blister atop the port wing. There it reached a junction that curved toward the main body of the bird-of-prey. Afraid of becoming trapped in the darkness, Shift had returned. If the clone had gone that way, he could be anywhere aboard *Chu'charq*.

Yet the life sign scans had said he wasn't.

That left Chelvatus III. When Shift had returned, Jilaan's *Annals* book in hand, from *Blackstone*, Kahless had not stirred; that meant he might already have been gone by then. If the clone had found his way off *Chu'charq* somehow, could he have sought refuge among the Klingons of the outpost? There had been no disturbance in the village before *Chu'charq* left and certainly no word had come from the Empire that Kahless yet lived.

Hemtara looked back from her interface. "The same results, my lord. There are fifty-one Klingons aboard beyond the confines of the bridge. Our original passengers, plus warriors deployed at Spirits' Forge who could not return to *Kradge*."

Cross sighed in exasperation. Shift slipped over to him and whispered into his ear.

"There is something I must tell you," she said, clutching the book from his *Blackstone* library in her hands. "You will never believe this."

"So wait," Cross said. He and Shift, looking like themselves again, sat together in their deck one hideaway. "You're telling me that Jilaan's Kinshaya caper nearly a century ago involved *Korgh*?"

"Jilaan's account doesn't call him by name," the Orion replied. She opened the book and set it on his lap. "But the Klingon in the story fits him perfectly. He's twenty-seven, he says his house was stolen from him—and he speaks of having a secret squadron of ships at his disposal."

"And he worked with her for the better part of a *year*?"

"As near as I can figure the dates. Jilaan describes in the afterword that they parted just before one of your convocations. I guess that's when the details of her operation were recorded here."

Cross paged through the book. It was stunning news. "You were right. I don't believe it."

"Don't you see? It makes sense now. We've thought Korgh was canny for a Klingon, but the level of deception he's been involved with is way beyond the Romulan Tal Shiar."

Cross rolled his eyes at her playfully. "You met a lot of Romulan spymasters in your previous life?"

"Of course not." Shift gave him the little glare she always did when he brought up her slave-girl past. "But think about what he's done. Korgh spent fifty years pretending to be someone he wasn't so he could get close to his old house and build it up. Then he attacks it with his puppets."

"He wipes out the people who screwed him and gets control of the house."

"But that's not the end. Korgh continues to have the Unsung attack his own house with an operation against H'atoria—and up next, the *Ark of G'boj*. The strikes throw off suspicion and create sympathy for him—and because the targets were his, he was able to show us how to walk in virtually unopposed."

"I wouldn't have gone along otherwise. As it was, H'atoria was too dangerous for my tastes."

"This scheme is beyond a teeth-gnashing Klingon, as you call them—but not an apprentice of the Circle." Shift smiled with excitement and poked the book with her finger. "And while he wasn't an official adept, he was learning from Jilaan herself."

It boggled Cross's mind. "I knew we'd drawn from all kinds—but *Klingons*? And this was in the *Annals*?"

She gestured to the book in his lap. "I'm surprised you never read it."

"You know me. I probably started and got pulled into watching a recording of a five-hundred-year-old Andorian stage play instead." He stared at the book and chuckled. "So Jilaan had the idea of impersonating Kahless first. Great minds think alike." He flipped to the end. "Korgh must not have stayed with her long enough to become a full practitioner—I'd have heard about that."

"Korgh's never said he knows how we create our illusions. What would it mean if he does?"

"He's got leverage. Secrets are sacred to magicians," Cross said. "Our methods are our power. It gives him some insurance against us blackmailing him, I'd guess."

"So even if we do find Kahless," Shift said, "Korgh could sniff out our plan and blackmail *you*."

Cross nodded. "It depends on how much she told him about the Circle. If he spills his guts about how many teams there are and what we can do, it could make Ardra's capture look like nothing."

"I've been meaning to ask how the Circle survived that."

"Everyone was terrified. Practitioners were afraid to impersonate anyone for fear of their truthcrafters getting pinched. But Starfleet must have decided Ardra's act was a one-off. During the Dominion War, Changelings became the big threat. Our kind of impersonation fell off the sensors."

Shift nodded. She checked the time. "*Ark of G'boj* is about to arrive from warp. It's payday."

"It's about time." He stood and straightened his collar. "And don't worry about getting caught. Starfleet's still fast asleep. I bet Picard's forgotten Ardra even existed."

Forty-three

"**Y**ou're going all the way to the bottom," the ensign said as the turbolift doors closed in front of La Forge and Tuvok. "Can't say she gets a lot of visitors."

"She?" La Forge asked.

"Doctor Aggadak." The ensign shook her head. "I can't even begin to explain. You'll find out."

Tuvok had already found out quite a bit. Realizing that the emanations he had detected over H'atoria were similar to what he'd encountered at Yongolor while serving aboard *Excelsior*, the Vulcan had reviewed the data banks and discovered a similar episode in 2367. On Ventax II, a female con artist had posed as Ardra, the devil from that world's mythology. Her efforts had been assisted by a kind of fakery technology never seen before—projected, it turned out, by a companion ship.

Houdini, as Ardra's crew called their vessel, had been the key that unlocked the Ventaxian mystery. Then-Lieutenant Commander La Forge had pierced its cloaking device. Boarding the ship at Picard's instruction, the *Enterprise*'s chief engineer had defeated the pretender's illusions by projecting his own. The woman calling herself Ardra—who, Tuvok learned, had twenty-three aliases in that sector alone—had been arrested along with her accomplices.

Her assistants were long gone, having served their time. "Ardra," who remained in custody at Thionoga Detention Center after several escape attempts, had steadfastly refused to assist Starfleet in understanding how her amazing illusion technology worked.

However, the *Houdini* still existed. After some bureaucratic fencing, Tuvok located it at a research-and-development depot associated with Starbase 24. Located between Khitomer and Gamma Hromi, Starbase 24 had long been a cutting-edge deep-space research center, despite its proximity to the Klingon frontier. Tuvok had visited the original station aboard *Excelsior* ninety-three years before. A new station had replaced the old one, destroyed during the Borg Invasion, but the R&D depot had survived.

While Admiral Riker had called it a stroke of luck that *Houdini* was so near their position, Tuvok thought it had more to do with the fact that Ventax was far from suitable research facilities. Regardless, the admiral had immediately detached him to *Enterprise*, which made the trip to Starbase 24 quickly.

The turbolift doors opened. La Forge and Tuvok left the ensign behind and stepped into the massive bay. Dozens of ships were mothballed here, waiting. Vessels were triple- and quadruple-parked, with little room even to walk between them.

"I have to hand it to you," La Forge said as they wended their way through the metal maze. "I never would have connected Ardra's ship to Object Thirteen."

"We both had half the necessary information," Tuvok said. "You had detected *Houdini* at Ventax II. The object you began tracking at Thane was similar enough to attract your attention, yet different enough that it did not jog your memory." He stepped around a landing strut and turned a corner. "For my part, I detected a projection at H'atoria similar to that which I had seen at Yongolor—but it was not until I connected it to Object Thirteen that I realized it had been at Thane."

That had made the difference for Tuvok—because of what the still-missing Worf had discovered on Thane: another imposter. A holographic charlatan pretending to be Commander Kruge, commanding the Unsung.

Chancellor Martok had insisted that Starfleet limit knowledge of the existence of the false Kruge to those who absolutely needed to know. A logical move, given the number of disaffected individuals who had been inspired to violence by the Unsung. Kruge was a hero to many, and his name might empower them. With Ardra's whereabouts already known, no one knew who might be impersonating Kruge. But Tuvok and La Forge hoped *Houdini* might hold answers as to *how* he was being impersonated.

"There she is," La Forge said. He hadn't seen the ship in nearly two decades. *Houdini* was about the size of the command portion of a *B'rel*-class bird-of-prey: forty meters long with warp nacelles on either side and a curious-looking lance jutting forward from atop a center strut. "She crewed twenty when I boarded her. Three decks, including Ardra's penthouse up top."

"Penthouse?"

"I'm not going up there again." La Forge shuddered. "The way Ardra had it decorated, it was something out of a Risa pleasure den."

"You experienced discomfort."

"And she wasn't even in the place." La Forge stepped toward the vessel and knocked on the hull. "Well, at least it's here. I was a little afraid that Ardra had gotten loose again."

Tuvok's eyebrow arched. The worry seemed odd, almost paranoid. "Is this possible?"

"They were a clever bunch. They used *Houdini*'s cloaking device to hide the *Enterprise* from us."

"The entire vessel?"

"Believe it. And when 'Ardra' got loose the year after we

caught her, she found *Houdini* where it was first impounded and went back to her old tricks. But we crossed paths with her on Shanzibar, and soon they were both locked away again."

Walking about *Houdini*, Tuvok was perplexed. "When would you estimate this vessel's construction?"

"This century."

"I concur." Tuvok ran his fingers along the hull, examining the material. "It cannot be the vessel I encountered in Kinshaya space."

"That's good, then, isn't it? That would mean there's more than one."

"Correct." On the port side, Tuvok found a closed hatch elevated a meter off the deck and went to work on the access panel. "We can test our theory by seeing if its projection equipment creates the same emissions we saw at—"

The hatch opened before Tuvok was done working the controls. A large hairy head appeared in the aperture and snarled, causing La Forge to take a step back. "What are you doing messing with my ship?" the tusk-faced woman demanded in a braying voice.

"It is not your ship," Tuvok said. "It is the property of Starfleet."

"What do you think I am, a squatter?" Reaching in the folds of her jacket, the Nausicaan woman produced a Starfleet combadge. "I work here."

"Are you Doctor Aggadak?" Tuvok asked.

"Don't let it surprise you." She cycled the hatch further, causing a small stepladder to descend to the deck. "Not every Nausicaan is as dumb as a bag of rocks."

While Tuvok did not think that, he was nonetheless surprised to see her. Nausicaa was located near Federation space, but its natives were generally too pugnacious to take part in the cooperative ventures of Starfleet.

The hydraulics for the steps unexpectedly started cycling shut again, prompting Aggadak to pound the interior controls with her fist. *Perhaps still aggressive*, Tuvok thought.

Aggadak stepped down and put her considerable weight on the steps, forcing them back to the deck. This time, they stayed down—and the woman rose to her full two-and-a-half-meter height. "The ship's temperamental. But I love her anyway."

"I am Commander Tuvok of *Titan*. This is—"

"Geordi La Forge!" Looking closely at him for the first time, Aggadak outstretched her hands. La Forge took two steps backward, this time, fearing a bear hug. "I didn't recognize you without the VISOR."

"You have met?" Tuvok asked.

"I know him by reputation," Aggadak said. "And I could recite his report from Ventax by heart. He brought my baby here." She patted the side of *Houdini*, causing an access panel to pop open. She slammed it back shut. Then she pointed at the panel and growled, like a parent scolding a petulant child. "*Don't.*"

La Forge looked at Tuvok and then back at the Nausicaan. "What's your duty here?"

"Administrator for closed-case evidence."

Tuvok understood at last. "These ships relate to crimes that have been adjudicated. But the ships cannot be returned because no ownership can be established."

"Or they are considered too dangerous to be given back," La Forge said.

"Some of them are just stuck." Aggadak looked around and waved her mighty hand dismissively. "Not *Houdini*. She's mine."

Tuvok's eyes narrowed. "Your project."

"*Mine.*" Aggadak glared at him. "Do you want to play word games, or do you want to see inside?" She stepped back onto the stairs. "Come on. You're our first guests in fifteen years." She looked back. "Make sure your boots are clean!"

Phantom Wing Vessel *Rodak*
Lankal Expanse, Klingon Empire

Worf's fever had returned with a vengeance.

Hours earlier, Worf had thought it was breaking. The burning in his throat had subsided, and his spirits had even been enlivened by a discovery in the tutorial recordings: a way existed to alert Starfleet not only of *Rodak*'s location, but of all the ships of the Phantom Wing.

The birds-of-prey contained a stealth positioning system, covertly informing one another of their locations. The system was designed to send the information locally, but it could be made to transmit across interstellar distances. *Enterprise* wouldn't know where to look for the signals, but he believed he could create a signal that Lieutenant Šmrhová couldn't miss.

And best of all, the device was accessible from port engineering support, exactly where he'd intended on heading.

Not wanting to wait for Sarken's help, he had gone to the hallway door to see if the path was clear—and had promptly lost his balance. Dizzy and shivering, he crawled back to his hiding place. A warrior, so close to success—defeated by something he could not see.

He lay in anguish, the events of Gamaral and Thane flooding his addled mind. He was on the edge of delirium when Sarken appeared over him. He couldn't tell if she was real or not.

"Sarken, is that you?"

"What is it, Worf?" Her face came and went in his mind, and he felt her hand touch his. "Is it bad?"

He moaned. She spoke about something having arrived, but in his clouded state he couldn't tell whether she was referring to herself or to *Rodak*. He could only remember the thing that had been stuck in his mind that he needed to say.

"I did not . . . tell you all, earlier." He gripped her hand hard. "*I* killed Tharas."

"What?"

"Your . . . father. I killed him."

The girl shook her head. "You're sick, Worf. You don't know what you're—"

"No," Worf said, sitting partially up and looking, wide-eyed, directly into the young face. "I killed him. In the jungle . . . before the explosion."

Sarken was astonished. "Why?"

"He was hunting me. I *had* to." His head pounded, and he released Sarken's hand. "It was . . . honorable."

"*Honorable?* What does that mean?"

"How . . . I did it. I called out to him . . . it was not an ambush."

Sarken recoiled. "But you killed him. My father!"

"I am sorry." Worf lay back down, exhausted. "I tell the truth . . . it is the thing to do."

The girl bolted upright. He saw three of her in the doorway, every face looking down at him with horror. In his haze, he knew he had done the right thing—but something else told him it was the completely wrong time.

"Please," he said. "Do not . . . say anything about me . . ."

The last thing he saw before he fell back into his stupor was that she was already gone.

Forty-four

"We're getting a lot of looks," said the head of Riker's security detail.

"I'm used to it." Flanked by his protectors, the admiral paid little mind to the unhappy Klingons on the gravel path and headed into the bazaar. *Titan* had uncovered that the Unsung's birds-of-prey had recently been on the outskirts of the settlement. Riker was damned if he was going to let a little Klingon resentment keep him from learning more.

After Tuvok had departed with the *Enterprise*, the orbital satellites surveying Klingon space had discovered a possible signal from Object Thirteen. Eager to stop the Unsung and locate Commander Worf, *Titan* had taken on the pursuit. They had gotten a taste of what *Enterprise* had been doing: tracking, eliminating false leads, and following sensor ghosts. Finally, the trail led to the frontier world of Chelvatus III.

A Klingon outpost with a transient population of traders and refugees, the planet had given *Titan* the chilliest of welcomes. The warriors on Chelvatus III, understandably infuriated at the desecration of Spirits' Forge, had turned their ire on Starfleet in the wake of increasing demagoguery from Lord Korgh and his growing list of allies on the High Council. *Titan* had destroyed a Phantom Wing ship at H'atoria, but just as in the aftermath of the Borg Invasion, only an empty fortress was left.

That the structure stood at all was thanks to Kyzak's and

Xaatix's heroics, but that didn't matter. The Federation had allowed the Unsung to take root in the Briar Patch, and Starfleet had failed to stop their violent acts. The result had been hostility at every turn, and while no one had dared to threaten a Starfleet officer, Vale had doubled the admiral's security detail when he insisted on going down to the planet.

"Sir." Riker saw a hulking Orion security officer beckoning to him from the entrance to the trading pavilion. "I think I've got something."

Riker approached. "What is it, Dennisar?"

"The Unsung were here." Chief Petty Officer Dennisar had escaped a life surrounded by criminal activity to join Starfleet. His understanding of that seedy underworld had come in handy.

"Some of these goods were from Fortar's storehouse," he said as the two stood before a busy merchant's table. He picked up a yellowish brick and showed Riker a tiny symbol imprinted on it. "That's his syndicate's stamp. It's an auditing aid for the warehouse—it shows Fortar's already taken his piece of the action."

Riker turned the brick over in his hand. *Enterprise* had identified Fortar as the victim in the Unsung strike in the Azure Nebula. "Could the dealer have gotten this long ago?"

"No, sir, no!" The Bolian who ran the stall stepped over. "These goods are fresh. Just traded to me last week." He ran his hands lovingly over the bricks. "Pure *gorbakka* root extract, ground and ready to season your stew. If it was more than a month old, it would be coming apart in your hands. Fresh, I say."

"How did you get it?"

The Bolian studied the officers' uniforms. "I . . . do not recall."

Riker rolled his eyes. Dennisar sighed and looked at the merchant. "Would you rather be bribed or threatened?"

"That depends. Bribed or threatened how?"

"I've got some gold-pressed latinum just for the occasion. Or we can discuss how the previous owner of these goods wound up dead a short while ago."

"I see. And what gives you jurisdiction?"

Riker stepped in closer and said, "I have a *Luna*-class starship overhead with a crew of three hundred fifty. I'm pretty sure a very curious Starfleet vessel and crew can be bad for business."

"Hmmm." The Bolian put his finger to his lips. "*Bribe*."

While Dennisar fished for the payment, the merchant rounded the table and spoke covertly to them. "A group of traders came in a few days ago. Nobody knows who they were—but they had all manner of goods from Fortar's stores. And they weren't Orions."

Riker nodded. "They were Klingons."

"Oh, no. There was a Ferengi, a couple of humans, a Cardassian—all different sorts. They didn't look like pirates at all. They looked more like—I don't know, technical types."

Riker and Dennisar looked at each other. "No Klingons?"

The Bolian thought. "There was a Klingon couple who came in later—they met the Ferengi and left. An old man and a young woman."

"An old man?"

"I never heard a name, but I could never forget that face. He wore a cowl—but he was so scarred. He'd clearly been burned long ago. But Klingons are a hardy lot."

Riker's eyes widened. The Bolian had just described the aged character claiming to be Kruge whom Worf had met on Thane. He'd worked with a female Klingon too. Could the Ferengi and the others have been his accomplices?

Dennisar passed the Bolian his payment. The merchant quickly pocketed it. "Are you looking to find who killed Fortar?" he asked.

Riker nodded.

"I met him once when he visited here, years ago. He had a little daughter then—I can only imagine the life that girl had. I hope she was spared." With that, the Bolian stepped back behind his wares and returned to work.

Riker took Dennisar aside. "You've got more of that latinum?"

The Orion nodded. "We keep it for moments just like this, sir."

"You're going shopping. I want your squad to buy every single thing in this pavilion with a stamp from Fortar's warehouse."

Dennisar looked around. "That could be a lot."

"It's all been handled. But we know for a fact that whoever was working with the Unsung handled it. We'll analyze the goods for DNA to see if we can find anyone we have a record of."

Dennisar looked around and chewed his lip. "Yes, sir. We'll, ah, *encourage* the merchants to give us biometric samples so we can rule them out."

"I'll have Commander Troi beam down. Maybe she can help you broker cooperation. The locals are on edge about us as it is."

The chief told Riker, "The attacks on Leotis and Fortar—they've never seemed right to me, sir."

"How do you mean?"

"We know the Unsung attacked Leotis to get the itinerary for the Gamaral event. But you'd have to know something about Leotis's operation to know he had it—much less knowing how to find *Dinskaar*." Dennisar's brow furrowed. "How in the hell did a bunch of Klingon exiles from the Briar Patch stumble across Fortar's hideaway? Neither we nor the Klingons have ever been able to find it."

"And they did it while on the run." Riker scratched his beard. "You've got something there, Chief. Carry on."

Phantom Wing Vessel *Rodak*
Lankal Expanse, Klingon Empire

Worf fell, and the fall seemed to last forever.

As he tumbled, the emptiness below resolved at last into the brownness of muck and mire. He landed face first in the foul-smelling filth.

Blinded by the mud, he struggled to get to his hands and knees. Reaching out, his fingers found something metal and taut. A chain. He pulled against it to help himself upright and wiped at his eyes.

"Kahless . . . I am sorry I have failed you."

"Why do you say this?"

Startled, Worf looked to see the source of the words. The chain he held bound Kahless, in harness and yoke just as he had been in the sewage pit on Thane. "Kahless," Worf said, "I have come for you." But seeing Kahless bound again in this place took the life out of him, and above all there was no light. Worf sagged against the restraint. "I have come for you—but I have failed. I cannot help you to Sto-Vo-Kor."

Kahless looked on him and laughed. "That, Worf, is because I am supposed to come for you . . ."

Worf opened his eyes to blinding light. "Kahless? Is that you?"

"Kahless?" A laugh, male and guttural.

Worf vaguely saw two blurry figures. One, large, held the light. The other he knew. "Sarken," he said, seeing the girl before him.

She pointed. "I told you he was here, Zokar."

Worf blinked, his feverish mind only beginning to understand. The Klingon with the light was bald and one-armed, and older than Worf; he vaguely remembered seeing him across the exiles' camp in Thane. "A stowaway," Zokar said. "Has he been aboard since we left the compound?"

"No, I saw him beam in. It was when we were in that big battle."

"Hmm." The adult passed the light to the girl and knelt. Frisking Worf, he pulled off his combadge. Then Zokar noticed the *mek'leth* sitting nearby. "I like this," he said, taking it. "A long time since I have seen a good Klingon blade."

Worf looked up at the girl. "Sarken, I asked you not to tell."

Sarken's face twisted with hurt. "You killed my father. This is what I am supposed to do."

"Supposed to do?" Rising after his completed search of Worf's body, Zokar donned the *mek'leth* and its holder and looked back at her, amused. "Has he been talking to you, girl?"

"He said family was important. If he's right, then I had to say something." She watched Zokar's face. "Right?"

Zokar looked puzzled for a moment—and then he laughed again. "A few words with you, Worf, and she's picking up Klingon morality!" Then he leaned close to the little girl and rasped into her ear, "He's not telling you the bad parts."

"What bad parts?"

"The parts that make it okay for him to kill your father and feel proud of it," Zokar said. "Or the part where Kling-ons can turn their backs on you for something you didn't do." His answer seemed to confuse her.

Worf tried to get up, but his muscles gave out. Zokar looked back down at him. "He is sick?"

"He got cut when he beamed in," she said. "But he's had aches and a fever and wants water all the time."

Zokar took the light back from her and examined Worf's leg. Then he knelt over and shined it in the commander's face. "Worf, my friend, you have *tharkak'ra*."

Worf looked at him blankly.

"A virus from Thane. Children are carriers. Adults get it once and get over it. I have seen it a dozen times."

"But . . . Kahless and I were several days on Thane . . ."

"Not around children. We carry many in close quarters. The ventilation systems are likely crawling with it."

Zokar started to rise. Feeling a sudden burst of energy, Worf reached out and clutched at the warrior's collar. Zokar shoved him away, as one brushing off dust. "What were you to do, Worf, fight us all singlehandedly? Like you attempted during the muster on Thane?"

"He brought some things," Sarken said. "He was going to use them to call his friends."

"Ah." Zokar loomed over Worf. "You can forget about that. Cause me the least trouble, and I will kill you. And I would have words with you first."

Worf shook his head in delirium. "Words? With me?"

Zokar rose and looked at Sarken. "Watch him. I will go to the transporter room and beam him to medical bay overflow two. No one will see him in there—and it will do for a prison while I need him." He stared down at Worf. "The son of Mogh and I will tell stories of great battles."

Forty-five

In the illusion projection control center aboard *Houdini*, La Forge and Tuvok watched—and listened—as Aggadak tromped back through the room. Since they'd boarded an hour earlier, she had been on a tear trying to get the systems activated. In that time, she had ranted about her job, Starfleet food, the station's bedding, and, most of all, about the lack of respect she was getting from her superiors.

As she vanished into another corridor again, La Forge stepped over to Tuvok and smirked. "Definitely detecting a low pH level here."

Tuvok caught the allusion. "Her attitude is indeed caustic."

"Doctor," as it turned out, was a term of respect attached to the Nausicaan by the staff. Aggadak was fascinated by the technologies of non-Federation starships; the fact that no one at the facility shared her unbridled enthusiasm for *Houdini* and its mysteries had not stopped her from lavishing interest on it.

Reentering the room, Aggadak forced her immense form beneath a control station. La Forge could hear electrical sparking. "Why Starfleet, Doctor?" he asked.

Her voice came from below. "Have you met other Nausicaans, Commander?"

"I have."

"Then that answers that." Aggadak slid out from beneath the console and pointed to her forehead. "The males in our society only use their heads when they need something dense enough to punch a hole in a wall."

La Forge grinned. "And the females?"

"Have to live with the males, and have the moods to prove it. Most do not share my pleasant manner." She stood and tapped a control on the interface—and when nothing happened, she beat it repeatedly with both fists. *Houdini* responded, with the room lighting up. Screens flickered as computer systems came alive.

"You were saying," La Forge said, "that I had how *Houdini* works all wrong?"

"That's right. At Ventax II, you concluded that Ardra's illusions were a combination of force-field projection, holography, and transporter effects."

"Yes, they were monitoring Captain Picard via his combadge, and she was using an eye implant to control her activities." La Forge gestured around. "*Houdini*'s computers were managing the whole thing. It appeared that the middle topside nacelle was for transmitting the holo-projections."

"That's what the engineering team that looked at it before it was impounded figured. That was only partly right." Aggadak walked to a bulkhead and slammed her fist against it. "Damn, it's reset itself again." She looked to Tuvok. "Can you whistle?"

"Excuse me?"

"Can either of you whistle? I don't have the lips for it."

La Forge blew air.

"Not like that," Aggadak said. "The 'Snake Charmer Song.'"

"The what?"

"Come on. You're human. You *must* know it. 'There's a place in France, where the ladies do a dance . . .'"

La Forge looked at her blankly. "I must've missed class that day."

"I have it here," the Vulcan responded, looking at his padd. "An Earth song, 'The Streets of Cairo, or the Poor

Little Country Maid.' Introduced at the World's Colum-
bian Exposition in Chicago in 1893, where it accompanied
a dancer known as 'Little Egypt.'" Tuvok pursed his lips
and raised an eyebrow. "There are apparently many ribald
alternate lyrics."

"Never mind that," Aggadak said. "The tune, the tune."

Tuvok touched a control on the device, and a bamboo
flute played a warbling tune.

Aggadak waved her hands. "No, no. What's wrong with
you? Whistle."

Tuvok looked at La Forge. "We fail to see why we—"

"*Whistle!*"

La Forge began whistling, and Tuvok joined in as best
he could. With the last note, a blue light appeared along
a seam in the bulkhead—and what had appeared to be a
curve in the surface opened. Beyond was a conical chamber ringed with strobing lights. It could have been a small
transporter room—except that none of the equipment
inside looked familiar to Tuvok. A sonorous hum filled the
room.

"That tune cycles the door," Aggadak said. "You can't
believe how I searched for it—once I knew that room was
there." She stepped inside and began throwing switches.
"Harry Houdini—the Terran illusionist this vessel is
named for—was a young performer at the Chicago expo.
He played what they called an Indian fakir."

"It was a 'midway show,'" Tuvok read from his tricorder.
"Apparently some kind of festival area."

"And 'Little Egypt' danced beneath the Ferris wheel at
the far end—to *that* tune." The Nausicaan looked inside the
chamber with pride. "Commander La Forge and the other
investigators thought this part of the ship was an auxiliary
warp core. I realized it was something else—and then it was
a matter of finding the pass key in the ship's records."

La Forge looked around in wonder. "How long did that take?"

"Eight years. I was bored."

Tuvok studied the interfaces in the illusion projection control room. The screens by each terminal were awash with information. "Are the projection systems operative?"

"Hah!" Aggadak pushed past Tuvok and toggled a control. "Watch this."

At Aggadak's command, the lights in the chamber glowed brighter. Tuvok looked around, expecting something. Instead, he saw La Forge staring at him, his mouth open.

"Commander—you look like the devil."

Tuvok put his hands before him. They were a deep red. His clothing, too, appeared different to him: a crimson cloak. Aggadak knocked over two chairs trying to fetch him a mirror.

"Fascinating," Tuvok said, and the voice was not his, but rather that of some infernal being. Seeing his reflection, he reached up and felt the curved horns extruding from the top of his forehead. "These additions have no weight that I can feel—and yet there does seem to be substance. Miniature holo-force-field projections?"

"Correct," Aggadak replied. She set down the mirror.

La Forge moved from interface to interface, leaning down and getting a better look. "The detail's uncanny. This was one of Ardra's characters." He looked at Tuvok. "Say something again."

"What did you have in mind?"

"Aggadak, am I seeing this right?" La Forge pointed to the side of Tuvok's mouth. "The devil image's movements are a little out of sync with his words when he speaks."

"I knew you were bright." The Nausicaan pointed to the cylindrical chamber. "The actor has to be digitally mapped in there before a projection can be accurately transferred. And I think it must help to have some skill at acting. There are many characters programmed in the system—even one for your Deanna Troi."

"Impressive," Tuvok said, feeling the sleeves of his garment. The crimson cloak was there, and yet not there. "The image is immaterial except when it needs to interact with a real surface."

"You've got it!" Aggadak clapped. "The secret to *Houdini* isn't just that it can project its images from afar—through shields, through bulkheads, from orbit if it has to. What makes it work is its sensor package."

La Forge nodded. "It would have to have sophisticated sensors so it could read the environment the actor's in. And it would have to sense the actor's movements, in order to instantly map the holographic model around them." He looked back at the chamber. "They were doing this twenty years ago."

"Longer," Aggadak said. "The ship's relatively new, but I've found systems aboard that date back a hundred years or more, just based on interfaces I've discovered. It's just— *different.* I would call it an offshoot strain of holographic science."

La Forge studied the chamber and marveled. "I wish I'd had more time at Ventax." He looked back at Aggadak. "You've been working here how long?"

"I first opened the chamber ten years ago. I filed a report, but the Invasion . . . well, I'm not getting the resources I need."

"What resources *have* you been getting?" La Forge asked.

"Um . . . let me think." She raised a finger and began doing arithmetic in the air. "Ah, yes. In the past standard year, *none.*"

"None?"

"That's right. This facility is where the flotsam of the sector collects, Commander, nothing more. My supervisor believes 'research' should only benefit the fleet."

Tuvok activated his tricorder. It was in his uniform's pocket, but to the observers—and to himself—it appeared that he had found it in the folds of his devil's cloak. He fine-tuned the settings.

La Forge watched the devil with a tricorder and chuckled. "This is too weird. Can you turn that off, Aggadak?"

"I think he looks all right." She shrugged and walked back to the control station.

"Look at this reading, Commander," Tuvok said. "The same emissions we saw coming from Object Thirteen on H'atoria."

La Forge took the tricorder. "The same, all right—and hugely amplified." To the side, Aggadak touched a control on an interface—and Tuvok returned to normal. "Emissions gone," La Forge said. He looked back to the chamber—and then smiled at Tuvok.

Tuvok took his tricorder back with satisfaction. "Q.E.D."

"What does that mean?" Aggadak asked. "Some Vulcan thing?"

"He means," La Forge said, "that we've come to the right place. And we hope you can tell us in a few hours everything you've figured out about this ship in ten years."

Forty-six

This time Valandris had no compunctions about the Unsung's manner of attack. The lumbering Klingon behemoth *Ark of G'boj* appeared from warp with its shields already up; it seemed a ship delivering precious goods spent every moment on high alert. As Kruge had foretold, the vessel sported a prominent transmitter array: it had to be taken out immediately. The Lankal Expanse was a majestic-sounding name for a large region of absolutely nothing, but this deep inside the Empire there was no telling how many battle cruisers were an emergency hail away. Two birds-of-prey appointed to the task blew the assembly to bits.

There had been no tactical choice but to fire without warning—but this time, strategy called for several of the vessels to decloak. Still reeling from the destruction of their transmitter array, the *Ark of G'boj* would have seen the *Rodak* decloaking dead ahead, weapons energized. Simultaneously, five other Phantom Wing vessels appeared aft and to the sides of the transport. The cargo transport wasn't built for high-speed evasion; Kruge's plan removed the option entirely.

The next move went to Valandris, beaming aboard the transport's engineering section with a team from *Chu'charq*. With swift and deadly accuracy, her forces eradicated any-one who might have the capacity to scuttle the transport—and that meant everybody. Within minutes, the teams transported forward by other birds-of-prey reported that they, too, had eliminated all opposition.

Stepping over bodies to reach the bridge, Valandris recognized Weltern, one of Thane's most skilled hunters and the ostensible leader of the team from *Latorkh*. Pregnant and not far from her due date, Weltern had been unable to impersonate any of the Sentries of Spirits' Forge. By acclimation, she had been given the much-desired assignment of taking the transport's bridge.

"It looks like you got the better fight," Valandris said, surveying the dead. "The engineers we saw weren't much."

"I'd rather have faced the Sentries." She patted her stomach. "Could be my last fight for a while."

Valandris checked the control screens. No alarm had been sent. *Ark of G'boj* had suffered no internal damage from the strikes on the transmitter, and its warp drive was undamaged.

She activated her communicator. "*Chu'charq*. Lord Kruge, we have the traitor's ship." Remembering what she had seen in the hold, she gave a satisfied chuckle. "It carries all that he was expecting and more."

The man himself answered. "*Sweep the ship for tracking devices that might attract the Empire here. I will inspect the ship in my own time.*"

PHANTOM WING VESSEL *CHU'CHARQ*
LANKAL EXPANSE, KLINGON EMPIRE

It had been all Cross could do not to start dancing as he left the bridge—but it would have been very strange for Kruge. Instead, he solemnly stepped back into the ready room behind the bridge and sealed the door behind him. Shift was there, appearing as herself and watching the sensor feeds coming in from the *Ark of G'boj*'s hold.

Her eyes goggled. "I've never seen so much gold-pressed latinum in my life."

"Considering the places you've seen, that means something." Cross snapped his fingers and dispelled *Blackstone*'s Kruge projection. "You'll be able to buy and sell anyone who ever bought and sold you."

Shift gave him a chilly look, but it didn't last. There was too much joy to be had. Gaw was speaking in his ear, having intercepted the feed. It sounded like a party was going on in *Blackstone*, which sat cloaked not far from the treasure ship. *"I've got people over here licking the windows."*

"Hang on, hang on," Cross said. "There's a couple of steps left."

Valandris had confirmed what Korgh had told them about *Ark of G'boj*. The booty aboard the transport would never fit on a dozen *Blackstones*; it had to be taken somewhere for unloading. However, the vessel's systems were hardwired to only accept the next preprogrammed destination.

A keycode was required. Gaw transmitted the planned signal indicating the need to confab. Minutes later, Cross's secure portable computer activated with a *Blackstone*-relayed comm signal from Korgh.

The digitally masked image on the small screen was barely identifiable as a Klingon. Cross held the communicator in front of one of the screens depicting *Ark of G'boj*'s treasure-stuffed hold. "I've got to hand it to you, 'my lord'—you sure know how to spread the wealth!"

Korgh growled in exasperation. *"You are aboard the bird-of-prey? I thought you would call from the transport."*

Cross smirked. "Yeah, I thought it would be wise to have the Unsung give the ship a once-over. We're nearing the end of our little partnership. I don't want any surprises."

"The feeling is mutual. Search away. You will find that the vessel holds what I said it did."

"It's money well spent. I've done everything you asked. I've played the Unsung like a baby grand piano."

"A what?"

"Never mind. All we need from you now is the code to unlock the *Ark*'s navigation systems so we can send it on its way."

"Stand by."

Cross's computer received a code. He glanced at it. "Okay, we're going to check that system too. Just in case your little code triggers rabid *targs* to pop out of trapdoors."

"You have become paranoid, Cross."

"I have half the Klingon Empire chasing me—not to mention Starfleet, which could easily have shot me down at H'atoria. My paranoia is quite healthy." Cross straightened. "Okay, that takes care of *Ark of G'boj*. We're down to the last act: disposing of the Unsung. Have you decided where you want me to send them?"

"Ghora Janto."

"Ghora Janto," Cross repeated, making a note. "Nice to have a name for their happy hunting ground."

"What does that mean?"

"I heard it in *Peter Pan*—the Earth story. It's the place where you're going turn the Unsung into unpeople."

"I will be happy to be done with your bizarre quotations."

Cross chuckled. "Oh, you love a good line. You know more about acting than you're letting on, Korgh. I know you worked with Jilaan."

"Who?"

"On Yongolor, nearly a century ago. Are we going to waste time?"

Korgh went silent for several moments. *"What gave you this idea?"* he finally asked.

"Jilaan described your adventure to one of the Circle's convocations—and it got entered into the records. She didn't use your real name, don't worry—but the details match up. It was you."

"That was . . . a long time ago."

Cross looked to Shift excitedly. "He *did* know her!" He turned back to the screen. "I envy you, Korgh. She was gone before I could meet her."

"*She was a skilled person who knew her trade, if it can be called that. And she was by no means as undisciplined as you are.*"

"Well, if knowing what practitioners can do led you to seek me out, then it worked for both of us. And," Cross said pointedly, "it means you know how important it is for the Circle to keep its secrets."

"*I have no interest in undermining your childish little stunts. If you send the Unsung to Ghora Janto, nothing more need pass between us.*" Korgh paused. "*Is that all?*"

Shift nudged Cross. *Ask him*, she mouthed.

"Korgh, I know you haven't wanted to discuss the long game—and it's no business of ours. But we're dying to know where all this has been going. You've already won back your house. What's the rest been about?"

"*You should be able to guess,*" Korgh said. "*You've been playing at being Kruge long enough to know his views. He desired primacy for the Klingons—and he detested the Federation.*"

"So this has all been about throwing out the Accords? You want war?"

"*I already have the war that I want—with the Unsung. And I have engineered the exact response I wanted. The example of the Unsung has inspired other discommendated fools to act in a similar manner. A diaspora of despair threatening all places that have taken them in, Klingon or otherwise.*"

"Ooh, I like 'diaspora of despair,'" Cross said. "And we've heard broadcasts with some of the stories. It's flattering, being imitated."

"*It takes only a few imitators to create a backlash. Spirits' Forge has amplified it. All governments are now on alert. A* coalition has formed to hunt the Unsung, with the Typhon Pact assisting the Klingon Empire. The Federation hunts the exiles, too—but it is distrusted by all for having unleashed the problem in the first place."

Cross laughed. "I'm sure *you* had something to do with that."

"*I gave you the flint to start the fire—and I fanned the flames.*"

Shift looked as if she were slowly piecing together the implications. She spoke cautiously. "You . . . intend the Empire to join the Typhon Pact?"

"*The apprentice speaks,*" Korgh said, irritation in his voice. "*Cross, must I be bothered with this person?*"

"She asked what I was about to," Cross said. "What's the answer?"

"*Pacts and accords are unimportant. What matters is that the Klingon Empire wins any conflict it is in—and that the Empire is at the forefront of whatever 'side' it is on. Klingons lead.*"

Shift's eyes narrowed. "I . . . always heard that the Typhon Pact powers were all equal within the group. If you join with them, they will never—" She paused and started again, sounding less confident. "From what I've heard, there are no senior and junior members. Are there?"

Korgh laughed. "*The Kinshaya are animals to be hunted—and the Gorn are a third-class power if there ever was one. The Tzenkethi and Tholians hardly matter to Beta Quadrant politics. And if the Romulans were what they were before Shinzon, they wouldn't have needed a Pact in the first place.*"

"But what of the Breen?"

"*What of them? Any culture where you cannot tell between the members is one where individual feats do not matter. The Breen are born lackeys, woman, nothing more.*"

"Well, color me impressed," Cross said, smiling. "It sounds as if you've shuffled the deck—and given the Klingon Empire the best hand."

"I don't know what you mean—but I have no more time for this. We will not speak again, Cross. If you try to contact or otherwise extort me in any way, you will not live to regret your error. Good-bye."

Cross chuckled. "And I thought *I* was under stress. He's ready to pop." He looked to Shift, who appeared lost in thought. "What's wrong?"

"I'm . . . just wondering about your Kahless plan. Can we wrap this up without finding the clone?"

Cross shrugged. "Didn't you hear? We may not have to find him. If the emperor is still aboard, Korgh will do the dirty work for us."

Forty-seven

Korgh stared out across the shipyard, the shifting light casting shadows into his darkened office. He had returned from Qo'noS to Ketorix that morning to consult with Odrok and make his final preparations. He had placed the final call to Cross—and now the instrument of his ultimate success had arrived.

It was time. "Lorath, the Unsung are headed for Ghora Janto."

"Ghora Janto? Father, are you sure?"

"I am." Korgh turned to see his son the general looking back at him from the doorway. As soon as he'd learned the Unsung had arrived at the Lankal Expanse, Korgh had called for the clandestine meeting; Lorath, ever dutiful, had raced to Ketorix aboard the *V'raak*. He gestured for his son to take the seat in the center of the office. "The Ghora Janto refueling station. If you lay a trap for them there, you can destroy the whole accursed squadron."

"How do you know?" Pausing, Lorath rephrased the question. "And how would *you* know?"

"Indeed, no other could." Korgh stepped toward his desk. "You remember I found the schematics for the Phantom Wing in Commander Kruge's old files. I turned them over immediately to Chancellor Martok."

"Of course," Lorath said. "It was right to do."

It was right for Korgh's plans; he would not have done it otherwise. Releasing the files had been a calculated act, getting out ahead of the *Enterprise*'s discovery of the hidden hangar on Gamaral. His next act would similarly craft events his way. "I have recently discovered another file," Korgh said, "relating to a subsystem not mentioned in the original plans." He picked up a padd and walked it to his son. "Read this."

Lorath did. He shook his head. "This is amazing." He looked up. "A way to find the Phantom Wing—from anywhere! This was there all along?"

"Yes." Korgh wandered the room. "All those years ago, Kruge's designers devised a stealth positioning system unique to the Phantom Wing vessels. While cloaked, each bird-of-prey broadcasts a microburst detailing its location to the others every ten seconds. Every transmission is on a different subspace frequency and it is otherwise indistinguishable from cosmic background noise."

"Unless you know the algorithm telling you where to listen. Each ship has it—and you have it?"

"It is in your hand." Korgh walked back to the window and pointed to the night sky. "I applied it to the house's network of satellites. They say the path leads to the refueling outpost at Ghora Janto."

"A natural move. It is remote and lightly defended—and they are sure to need fuel sometime." Lorath curled a fist in excitement and rose. "I must tell the Defense Force immediately."

"No!" Korgh crossed the room and grabbed for his son's arm. "This information must be for you alone, Lorath. Trust no one else."

"Why? Our military—"

"Could be infiltrated with Unsung sympathizers. If they were here in our factory, they could be anywhere. We will only have this opportunity to strike the Unsung once."

Lorath frowned. Korgh knew his eldest son had never been one to buck authority or to strike out on his own. This was why he was laying greatness in the general's path now. Lorath simply had to seize it.

"What of our allies?" he asked.

"Allies? What allies?"

"The Federation."

"Ah. I thought you meant the others helping in the search." Korgh shrugged. "I suppose if the Romulans and the Breen arrive in time to assist, that would be good—after Spirits' Forge, they may think it their right. But only after you have engaged the Unsung with your forces. The right of revenge belongs to us."

Korgh watched as Lorath stared at the padd. At last, he heard a hint of aspiration in his son's voice. "To be the one who finds them . . ."

"You must spare no one," Korgh said, stepping in so his face was centimeters from his son's. "The Federation will want to capture the Unsung, not kill them. This is exactly why I do not wish them involved. If Potok's rebels had been executed after Gamaral a century ago, none of this would have ever happened. Even a single cultist left alive could become a hero to the discommendated. We would never have peace."

Lorath nodded. "Father, you are wise."

"You will know what to do. And if, by chance, they get the upper hand—contact me."

"What can you do?"

Korgh responded with a cagey smile. "I will keep studying. I have a feeling I may discover more in those files." Korgh clapped his hand on Lorath's shoulder and led him out into the hallway.

They walked in silence through the darkened atrium past the statue of Kruge. In the long corridor beyond, the two prepared to part. "I am sorry you missed young Bredak's launch," Korgh said. "Your boy looked strong and proud."

"He is proud of his grandfather," Lorath said, "and appreciative."

"You have heard from him?"

"He and *Jarin* are on the assignment you asked me to give him, patrolling near Gasko. There is little there for him to do, but he remains hopeful for action." The general studied his father. "Did you want Bredak to join my forces at Ghora Janto?"

"No. He should become a hero in his own time, in his own way. It is wrong to engineer greatness." Korgh smiled. "Remember, tell no one of the Phantom Wing's stealth positioning system until you are ready to strike. Then apply it as needed."

"I will, my lord father."

"*Qapla'.*"

He stood outside the doorway to J'borr's office and watched as Lorath receded into the darkness. To his left, the door opened wide. Odrok appeared, looking haggard from stress and overwork. "You still have not told him the truth," she said.

"He has the truth I want him to have." Korgh looked back down the hall. "My sons and their children will have the life I would have had, if I hadn't been forced to spend a century clawing after my name and house. My life is in eclipse. Theirs will rise. And the deception, the things I have done—they will be mine alone."

"Not only yours," Odrok replied. "I have sacrificed, as you have."

"The end is in sight. Are you sure he will be able to use the algorithm to find the Phantom Wing?"

"I've been using it all along to keep track of where they are—the same way Cross's support ship does." She gestured into the office that served as her secret command center; he saw the symbol indicating the Unsung squadron on the display. "The exiles know they have the system, but they assume it's only for local use. They have no idea about the range."

Or the other surprise you've installed, Korgh thought. It was a last-ditch option, something he hoped he would not need to employ. If Lorath did his duty, there would be no need for it. He could not allow the Unsung to continue to exist. That would increase the likelihood his complicity would be discovered.

And then there was Cross. Korgh studied Odrok's display screen. If Cross acted according to plan, he would have boarded the *Ark of G'boj* as Kruge and declared the latinum to be filthy blood money sent to a traitor. He then would have entered the code, saying he was sending the treasure to the heart of a black hole. Of course, he would be sending it someplace else, for his cohorts to loot at their leisure. "Is the tracking hardware still operational?"

"Yes. I told you they would never inspect the bases the stacks of latinum bricks were sitting on; too heavy to move. I will know their destination soon."

"Excellent. I am going to hail my grandson aboard *Jarin*," Korgh said. "Ignore what I said to Lorath; his son *will* have glory of his own. I will see to it."

Odrok stared, her eyes tired. "Everyone will be rewarded," she said limply.

Korgh forestalled the usual theatrics. "Go to bed, Odrok. It will all be over shortly. Then we can discuss the future."

Forty-eight

"So the old man, Lord Kruge, looks at us and says, 'With this act, I send the riches of the wicked into oblivion.' And then he turns around and pushes the button, and tells us we all have to beam off *Ark of G'boj* before it launches."

Leaning against a metal counter in the sickbay, Zokar laughed with incredulity. "So five minutes ago I watched from the bridge as enough latinum to buy a star system warped off to a black hole! Can you believe it, Worf?"

Worf didn't know what to believe anymore, but at least he was feeling better. The Unsung might not have had much use for medical technology, but Zokar seemed to know how to use a hypospray. He had speeded the breaking of Worf's fever—though only after manacling Worf to the table first. Since then, Worf had lain in solitude, his existence apparently unknown to anyone else, save for Sarken, whom he had not seen since her betrayal.

Zokar's behavior was unlike that of any of the other discommendated he'd met. Starting with the bottle in his hand: bloodwine, found in some recent raid. Zokar had brought the bottle aboard hidden in a canvas bag—opening it here, with Worf.

"Morath's bones, I have missed this," Zokar said after taking a drink. "The others don't know what they're missing." He eyed Worf. "We were cloaked. How did you beam aboard?"

"How did *you* beam through *Enterprise*'s shields?"

Zokar laughed. "Fair enough. Keep your secret. I will not try to pry it from you."

"Why am I here?" Worf asked. "You saw your Fallen Lord. Why didn't you tell Kruge I was here?"

"I told you, I wanted to talk to you first. This is the first chance I have had." Zokar set down the bottle and wiped his mouth.

"I saw you on Thane," Worf said. "You did not speak with me."

"I didn't need to," Zokar replied. "I already knew all about Worf, son of Mogh, the Starfleet officer. I was the one who told the exiles about you."

Worf's eyebrow arched. "Then you are not native to Thane."

Zokar laughed. "No. I was born where you once lived— on Khitomer." He watched Worf's expression and laughed again, even more heartily. "If that surprises you, wait until you hear this. *We were* both *discommended over Khitomer too.*"

Worf's eyes went wide. Forty years earlier, his parents had died when the Romulans attacked Khitomer; twenty years after that, the venal Duras family had falsely accused Worf's father of betraying the colony to the Romulans. Worf had volunteered to accept discommendation to prevent a civil war, a conflict that soon became unavoidable. Half a lifetime ago for Worf; he preferred not to think about it.

But his encounter with the Unsung had dredged it all up, and now Zokar was picking at the wound. "How could *you* have been discommended over Khitomer?" Worf asked. "I have never heard of you."

"You wouldn't have," Zokar said, bottle again in hand. "I was charged forty years ago. You were still a runt, and I was a raw recruit. I wanted to prove my worth in battle, to serve aboard a ship like this." He gestured around him. "The chance never came. I kept getting foolish, mundane jobs—piloting supplies back and forth to the colony."

Zokar paced from the counter and stared into the corner of the room. "The day the Romulans attacked, I was piloting a shipload of munitions to Khitomer. Every weapon, every explosive you could ever need for defense. In fact, I was *overloaded*—which I discovered when I dropped out of warp short of the system. Warp drive, impulse—everything was shot."

Worf's eyes narrowed.

Zokar pivoted. "Imagine it, Worf. There I was, sitting in space, hearing the cries of our people as the Romulan curs slaughtered them. I had an arsenal, but no way to get it to them. No one answered my hails." He winced. "It was agony."

Worf knew too well. He had only survived the Khitomer massacre buried in a pile of rubble. He watched Zokar finish the bottle. "Someone came for me," Worf said. "And you?"

"Eventually. No one believed my story." His face reddened. "I was accused of sabotaging my own systems."

"They thought you a coward?"

"They said I'd stopped my transport short of Khitomer when I heard there was a battle. Some even said I was in league with the Romulans. Can you imagine?" He crushed the bottle in his hand, sending shards onto the deck—and lacerating his hand. Blood coursed from it. "I'd never even *met* a damned Romulan!"

Worf understood how it could have happened. Feelings still ran high over Khitomer many years later.

"My gut ached, Worf. My own brother had been killed. People I had known all my life. When the Council wouldn't let me join the war to avenge them, I begged to be permitted *Mauk-to'Vor*, so I could join them in death." He looked at his dripping hand. "They wouldn't have it. My blade was taken. Their knives were drawn. I lost my soul."

Worf knew the feeling.

Zokar kicked at the glass on the deck. "The Empire scraped me off its boot, like filth. And like filth is how I lived for the next thirty years." He stared directly at Worf. "It was during that time that I learned you had lost your name over Khitomer, and that you had regained it. But there was nothing out there that could bring my name back."

"How did you find Thane?"

"I'd spent years working just for scraps. I cut metal at a graving yard. Hot, filthy work." He gestured to his stump. "I lost my left hand in the factory long before Thane took the rest of my arm. Losing my hand finished me as a laborer— and should have ended me altogether, but someone at the plant knew I was discommendated. I didn't merit speaking to, but he spoke to me. He said there was a place in the Klagh D'kel Brakt where people like me lived, together."

Worf's attention was piqued. "Someone directed you to Thane? Who?"

"I never asked names. I was just glad for a way out. A tramp freighter took me. The pilots were hirelings—they didn't even speak Klingon. They beamed me down and left without ever setting foot on the planet."

"How were you received?"

"Routinely. They'd had newcomers before, arriving the same way. They showed me how to survive on Thane—and I was mostly successful." He raised his stump of an arm and grinned. "When I didn't die after the first season, it looked like it could be a good thing. I could live just as everyone else did—and of course the hunting was good. I thought I might even find a mate."

Zokar's hopeful expression gave way to a scowl. "But I didn't realize that Potok had been so hard on everyone. The elders took every opportunity to remind us that we were nothing, lower than vermin. Soon, I missed the Empire. At least there Klingons ignored me. The exiles beat themselves up, constantly. I wasn't exactly tempting to women hoping their great-grandchildren would escape from their forebears' shame. Under Potok's rules, I was part of Generation Zero."

"You were poison."

"Hearing of Kruge set me free, Worf. He set me free."

Worf shook his head. "Zokar, you of all people must know the truth. Kruge has been dead for a century. This story of his survival is a fable, a lie. I do not know how he has accomplished it, but you are being tricked."

Zokar slammed his bloody fist on the counter, rattling medical instruments. "I don't care if he's a Changeling, Worf. He is saying the right things. Things people like me have never heard." He shook his head. "These descendants of the exiles—Harch, Valandris, even little Sarken—were judged before they drew breath. They had no dreams, because Potok never allowed them any." He thumped his chest. "But I existed as a Klingon before discommendation. I had dreams. I never got my chance, because of the words of the high and mighty. That is over now. Now I fight!"

"Whoever this 'Kruge' sends you to fight." Worf strained at his bond. "There is no honor in battling the wrong enemy."

"Kahless's honor, the Empire's honor!" Zokar grabbed Worf's neck and leaned low over his prone captive. "What do I care about that? I didn't come from a house like you. I didn't have Starfleet to crawl to when I was condemned—and I didn't have the chancellor's ear to help me get my name back!"

"You have a chance now," Worf said, feeling Zokar's

breath. "Forget the charlatan. Convince the others to stop this madness, and I swear I will accompany you all to Qo'noS, for you to tell your story!"

"Why?" Zokar released Worf with a shove. "So they can discommendate us for seventy generations this time?"

"So the children of your squadron might live. They might have a better chance before—"

"Oh, no." Zokar shook his head vigorously. "We will go to Qo'noS, Worf, but only under Kruge's flag. I owe the Empire for how I was treated—and the Romulans, for what they did." Anger seethed in the elder Klingon's eyes. "If I kill enough people, eventually I will get to someone who deserves it."

Worf held his gaze for a long moment. "You are lost, Zokar."

"And you are in prison. Again."

A moment's silence—broken by the chirp of Zokar's communicator. *"Zokar, it's Harch. Where are you?"*

"Dealing with a problem. What is it?"

"Lord Kruge wants your advice on a local landing site. He wants to stage a muster of all his most loyal."

"On my way." Zokar deactivated the device and headed for the door.

Worf called out. "Do you go to tell 'Kruge' I am here?"

"I wasn't going to, but now I might." He looked back and glared. "We are brothers, of a sort—brothers in Khitomer blood and the blame surrounding it. I had thought to keep you safe a while longer because of it. But after this talk, I am close to forgetting what we have in common."

"That should be easy to do, for we are nothing alike. If you do not believe in honor, whether a man is your brother or not cannot possibly matter."

Zokar left and sealed the door.

Forty-nine

The muster was hastily called, and yet it seemed to Valandris that Lord Kruge had been planning the event all along. The man was like that, acting on sudden inspirations yet leading them to places he seemed to know all about. Perhaps this was what it was like to grow old, Valandris thought. The people of Thane lived short lives in a small area. To reach past a century traveling the stars, one might naturally develop encyclopedic knowledge.

Kruge had certainly chosen a good setting for their gathering. The box canyon on Omicron Lankal's frigid surface was easily the warmest place on the planet. Volcanic vents supplied the depression with gas jets; the first arrivals had lit them, transforming them into spectacular pillars of heat and light. The result was a natural amphitheater in the ice, open to the cold starry sky above.

As Valandris descended one of the snowy pathways into the arena from *Chu'charq*'s landing site, she marveled at both the setting and the turnout. The area could accommodate everyone: all the warriors who had fought and desired to keep fighting for Kruge. Only children and invalids had remained aboard the eight vessels that had landed, and the three birds-of-prey on orbital patrol had transported down their warriors, leaving only skeleton crews.

"This place is amazing," she said, watching her own breath crystalize in the air. "Lord Kruge found it here, already formed?"

Ahead of her on the path, Zokar looked back and

sneered. "You people. This was an old deuterium mine—I dug that path over there myself, thirty years ago. Lord Kruge asked me for a good local site for his muster."

"Never missing a chance to make yourself look good," she replied.

He smiled at her. "I haven't even gotten started. I've got something on *Rodak* that'll make me his number one general."

"Is that right?"

"You'll see. I caught something the great hunter Valandris could not." Zokar's companions laughed and converged around him as they reached the floor of the depression.

Valandris worked her way through the crowd and saw the rostrum her advance team had crafted from empty cargo containers. It would be enough to allow Kruge to address his most loyal warriors—a group to which she'd always thought she belonged. Looking at the stage—and then at all the other excited attendees—she wondered how much she deserved to attend. Valandris had been on her best behavior since Spirits' Forge; there were no more writings of Kahless to be read. She had shown her loyalty at the treasure ship, executing Kruge's orders—and the guards—without question.

She was surrounded by almost everyone she had ever met. How could she possibly feel alone?

RODAK
OMICRON LANKAL

With every passing hour, Worf felt his strength returning. He didn't know if it was the hypospray or if the virus had run its course—but it was of cold comfort. He could tell from the sounds of the ship that it had landed somewhere; his time was running out. Again and again, he had tested the bonds that held him to the table. He had been tied down with leather straps cut from uniforms. It had been a long time since he'd heard anyone outside. When someone worked the door, he assumed it was Zokar or someone sent by the exile. He was wrong.

"Sarken." He turned his head and looked at the little girl. She had her satchel over her shoulder, as usual. "Why are you here?"

"Everyone is gone," she said. "Kruge is holding a muster outside. There's nobody on this deck at all."

"Did Zokar go too?"

"Yes. He said he was going to tell Kruge you were here." She looked away, and Worf's heart sank. "He was acting funny—and his breath smelled. Worse than normal, I mean."

"That would be the bloodwine." Worf nodded in the direction of the glass fragments on the deck. "Watch your step."

Sarken looked up at him with eyes wide. "Worf, did you know who my dad was when you—"

"When I killed him?" Worf took a deep breath. "Yes. I had met Tharas. He had been my guide in the camp." He looked at her. "But I did not know he was your father."

"Would you have killed him if you *had* known?"

Worf was silent for a moment. "Tharas had come to kill me. I had no choice." He looked at her. "But if I had known you—and the kind of person you are—then, yes, I might have looked for another way."

She smiled weakly. "That's what I wanted to hear." She opened her satchel and produced a *d'k tahg*. Worf's eyes widened as she brought it closer to him. He flinched. "What's wrong?" she asked.

"I feared you wanted revenge."

"Oh, no," she said, starting to work on his bonds with the dagger. "Besides, if you caught *tharkak'ra*, you most likely got it from me. You've suffered enough."

She cut through the strap holding his right hand to the table. He took the weapon and went to work on his other bonds. "No one else is on the deck. How long will they be gone?"

"I don't know. But you'd better hurry."

OMICRON LANKAL
KLINGON EMPIRE

A transporter glow heralded the arrival of Kruge and N'Keera. The high priestess wore a fur wrap to protect her small frame from the cold, but Kruge looked no different.

No, Valandris thought from the front row. He looked radiant and magnetic, just as he had when she'd first seen him on Thane. It was as if someone else had undertaken the exertions of the past weeks, as if there were a default Kruge state that he could magically transform into at will. It was a foolish thought—but it seemed to fit. He was their lord Kruge.

And when he spoke in this place, his words boomed across the canyon, echoing off the walls. "You have done well!"

Cheers erupted, raucous and prolonged. N'Keera stood solemn throughout it, her hands together out of sight inside the sleeves of her garment. Kruge reveled, raising his hands to the stars and taking in the adulation.

"You have done well. But you have not done enough. For while we have grievously harmed the people who wronged you, they will try again—*at a place called Ghora Janto.*"

He asked them to repeat the name, and the Unsung said it as one.

"When we destroyed the bribe Kersh received from the Romulans, it angered many people she made promises to. The so-called lord of her house is her puppet, a mere house-keeper elevated to stand in as her spokesman. The Defense Force has discharged her. Her position in the Empire is finished—but she still has time to hand over the worlds my house holds to the enemy. Kersh will meet them at Ghora Janto, where she intends to surrender the house's battle cruisers and begin life as the owner of an estate on Romu-lus." He looked to the audience with a canny smile. "You will see that she never gets to lovely Beraldak Bay."

The Unsung erupted with more cheers.

"When we do this, your revenge—and mine—will be complete. We will take the territory that was rightfully mine and use it to build a new Klingon Empire, free from the influences of—"

"*Never!*" Kruge's eyes went wide as N'Keera whipped a *d'k tahg* from her voluminous sleeve and plunged it into his chest. The audience gasped as one. Blood coming from his mouth instead of vapor, he clutched at the handle of the blade—as N'Keera drew a disruptor from elsewhere in her robes. "You are old, your followers scum. I serve Kersh. You will never kill her—nor anyone else!" She fired the weapon point-blank. Kruge disappeared with a screech.

Many other screams followed as the crowd surged for-ward, Valandris at the forefront. But before a single weapon could be drawn on N'Keera, she closed her cloak around her and vanished in a transporter effect.

"No!" Valandris yelled. "No! What have you done?"

BLACKSTONE
ORBITING OMICRON LANKAL

Shift materialized in *Blackstone*'s transporter room, still in her N'Keera persona. "We've got them," Gaw yelled. "Get out of the system fast and go to warp!"

Cross, crumpled on the deck in the pose he'd held when the fake disruptor had fired, took Shift's hand. As she helped him up, he pulled the trick *d'k tahg* from his chest. The point had slid back into the handle when she struck him. Cross put his arm around Shift and pulled her closer to him. He kissed her cheek. She seemed overwhelmed by the praise.

"You did great, babe. I'm just glad you remembered to use the safety switch on the dagger!" He handed it back to her. "A souvenir of your first triumph."

Truthcrafters surrounded them, rewarding the death scene with a standing ovation. "You are the best," Gaw said. "Both of you!"

Cross basked in the cheering and applause. He snapped his fingers to dispel the illusions. "Good-bye, crazy Klingons—and good-bye, Kruge. I'm glad I'll never have to do that growl again!"

Fifty

"*Kruge! Kruge! They have killed our Lord Kruge!*"

Valandris ignored the clamor as she ran through the halls. Throughout the bird-of-prey, her fellow exiles were either wailing in sorrow or screaming. This, she knew, was when Klingons sang their songs. Potok had never taught them any. There was only sadness and rage, expressed randomly and creating a cacophony of sound.

Many of the other witnesses to the murder had transported directly back to their ships. Valandris had remained on Omicron Lankal's surface long enough to lead her trackers on a reconnoiter of the area; N'Keera must have transported to another location. It took the hunters little time to find a network of ice caverns once used as housing for the Klingon miners, but it had been twenty years since anyone had set foot inside. The lord's trusted assistant was nowhere to be seen.

Trusted. N'Keera had been that, Valandris knew: Kruge's expression was unmistakable. He had no idea the blow was coming. A foul, vile act. N'Keera had yelled, yes, but the tip of the blade was already heading for the old man's heart. Was *this* honorable Klingon combat? How was this any different from the Unsung striking while in disguise? Valandris had given Riker and Kersh warning at Spirits' Forge, but now she wondered why she had bothered. Kersh and her agent had shown Kruge the same respect the Unsung had shown the so-called nobles on Gamaral.

But the Unsung were dealing justice to vermin. N'Keera

had killed all that was good in her people's world. The bastion of bravery, the man who had given them respect and hope. He was as close to a god as they had. Mythology held that the Klingons had killed their gods. The Empire had killed the Unsung's before their eyes.

Raneer appeared in the hall as Valandris ran. The young pilot looked distraught. "Zokar's powering up *Rodak*. What should we do?"

"Get us running," Valandris said, not stopping. "Tell the ships in orbit to wait!" They all wanted to make for Ghora Janto and revenge, she knew; so did she, with every fiber of her being. But first, if there was a chance N'Keera had returned to *Chu'charq*, the villain needed to be dealt with.

Valandris scaled the ladder to the deck one port storage area that had been the Fallen Lord's private haven. No one had questioned his claiming of the space; it was far from the noise and bustle of the ship, a place to meditate. Reaching the main corridor, she saw Hemtara looking pale.

"He had been asking for life sign scans," the woman said. "I did not understand why. But he must have suspected . . ." She trailed off, clearly shaken.

"You've checked again?"

"No one who isn't supposed to be aboard." Hemtara gestured into a side chamber. "I think that's where they stayed." Valandris looked past to see a small room with a rectangular impression in the dust. A mat had been there.

"And then there's this." The engineer led her to the end of the hall, where a stool sat beside the entrance to a storage compartment. Hemtara pointed to projectors in the door frame. "Someone installed a force field here. I don't know why."

That was odd. But Valandris's attention turned to the storage section itself, and its mountain of containers. Several other members of the Unsung were rifling through the crates' contents. A blanket sat balled up on the deck beside broken glass.

Valandris picked up the blanket and sniffed. It was a Klingon's odor, that of a male. But she had never been close enough to Kruge to notice if the scent was his. Hemtara walked to the open crates. "When we left Thane in a hurry, people packed things anywhere they could." She drew out several pairs of gloves. "It's mostly surplus gear. Canteens, clothing. No weapons."

The only weapons that mattered were the ones N'Keera had used—and the weapons the Unsung would use in response. Kruge had given them the Phantom Wing, and they would use it to make Kersh's allies pay. She reached for her communicator. "Raneer, take us to orbit. We're going to Ghora Janto."

PHANTOM WING VESSEL *RODAK*
OMICRON LANKAL

"Lift off! Lift off!"

Harch looked back at Zokar, both of them just returned from the surface. "We still have people left on the ground!"

"Let Valandris pick up the laggards—we have to get to Ghora Janto before that turncoat warns Kersh that we're coming!" He pointed behind and to his right. "Start jamming subspace frequencies."

The breathless youth at the engineering station looked back at him in confusion. "We were never taught how to—"

"Move!" Zokar leaped from his command chair. He dashed over and shoved the kid out of the way. "There," he said, after a few moments work on the interface. "Do I have to do everything?"

He looked back out at the icy surface visible on the main viewer. How had it happened? N'Keera had always been a loyal retainer, so far as he could tell—and according to Kruge, her family had cared for him for a century.

Her departure was as mysterious as Worf's arrival had been. Zokar couldn't imagine they were associated. Worf might try to thwart the Unsung to protect the chancellor and the Federation, but he would never engage in outright treachery.

But Worf wouldn't be going anywhere, and right now, the Unsung needed a leader. Feeling the ship powering up around him, Zokar returned to his command chair. He had a target—and vengeance to deliver.

BLACKSTONE
EN ROUTE TO CRAGG'S CLOUD

"Our cleanup crew beamed into and out of your lair on *Chu'charq* with no problem," Gaw said. "They cleaned out anything incriminating."

"Good work." Looking back from the conn station, Cross smiled. "I've just laid in our course. It's where I sent *Ark of G'boj* to—the perfect place. A nebula outside Klingon space."

"Thank the stars!" Gaw looked at Shift. "We can loot that thing for years. I think you signed on with the right bunch."

Cross stepped over to another bridge position. "Any reaction from our crazed cultists back there?"

"Vessels on the surface powering up," a technician responded. "Orbital vehicles scanning, but they haven't pierced our cloak."

"Are they moving?"

"Yes. But not toward us."

Shift looked at the technician's screen. "In the direction of Ghora Janto?" She looked at Cross. "They're really going. You sold it!"

"'So Rosencrantz and Guildenstern go to't,'" Cross said. "And maybe the clone of Kahless goes too." He grinned at her. "Ready to celebrate your first successful performance?"

She continued staring for a moment, and then looked up at him. "Sure, I'll see you upstairs in a few minutes. There's something I want to take care of first."

PHANTOM WING VESSEL *RODAK*
EN ROUTE TO GHORA JANTO

Something has happened, Worf thought. The forces aboard *Rodak* were grappling with an emergency—and he suspected it had nothing to do with him.

Sarken had been right earlier about almost everyone leaving the ship. Worf had seen no one on the way from *Rodak*'s infirmary to the ladder, nor during his descent down it. That had been interminable and painful; Zokar had not treated his leg. He had needed Sarken to help him along through the abandoned engineering section to reach port engineering support.

The door had just closed behind him when the commotion started. Multiple voices could be heard in engineering cursing, and shouting Kruge's name. Sarken had panicked, fearing that Zokar's forces had returned to discover him missing. But as Worf strained to tilt the massive plate upward, that theory was challenged. *Rodak*'s thrusters ignited, and the whole bird-of-prey jerked upward. It was not a planned evacuation, he could tell.

Had *Enterprise* arrived? If so, then his chance had too. "Sarken, I must enter the insides of the ship," Worf said. "Will Zokar harm you if he suspects you released me?"

"Nobody else knew you were aboard," she said, eyes wide. "I'm afraid, Worf."

"Then you are my responsibility. Lock the door—he already suspects I will hide in the maintenance areas." She complied. At his direction, she grabbed a small handheld light from a worktable. Worf heaved at the access plate to make room for her to slip into the darkness. Seconds later, he joined her, still wondering why the engineers outside kept yelling Lord Kruge's name.

Fifty-one

Riker walked quickly into sickbay. "I came as soon as I could. Are you okay?"

"Just a little shaken up," Troi said. She sat atop an exam table as Doctor Onnta, *Titan's* assistant medical chief, treated the bruise on her forehead. "Things got strange at the bazaar."

Several other medics were at work treating security personnel from the Chelvatus III away team. Dennisar had a ripped tunic and an eye socket that had gone from green to an angry yellow. "You should see the other guy, Admiral, sir."

"Glad you're in such high spirits." Riker stepped toward his security officer. "What happened?"

"We'd just gotten done interviewing merchants and were on our way out when we saw an old Klingon outside—a beggar. They were beating him, sir."

"Who was?"

"Other Klingons," Dennisar said. "At first. Then others in the crowd got into it, throwing rocks. We, uh, moved to protect him."

"I should hope so," Riker said. "But where were the security personnel from the Klingon outpost?"

"I couldn't say for sure, Admiral, but I think there might have been security among the assailants." Dennisar shook his head. "It was hard to tell, because once we got into it, the stones started coming at *us*."

Troi hopped down off the table. "They were accusing

the old man of having been discommendated. They wanted him to leave the settlement."

"*Was* he discommendated?"

"I don't know. I could sense that some people thought so. They were afraid. But I also sensed that others there just didn't like him."

That squared with reports Riker had been hearing. Violent backlashes against discommendated Klingons had multiplied since H'atoria, far outnumbering the number of Unsung-inspired acts. Incidents had been reported not just in the Empire, but also in the neighboring regions. "What happened to the beggar?"

"The head of the outpost finally showed up and arrested him," Dennisar said. "Then he ordered us to leave the planet. I told him he didn't have that authority, that the High Council had granted us access. But I figured we'd better get out of the way."

"*Bridge to Admiral Riker,*" called Keru. "*Sir, there is a priority-one message for you from Ambassador Rozhenko.*"

Riker stepped out to the CMO's office. When he returned minutes later, Troi could tell he was frustrated and furious. "That was fast," he said. "The chancellor has asked us to withdraw."

Dennisar looked guilty. "Sorry, Admiral."

"Never apologize for doing the right thing, Chief. Any IDs on the goods sold at bazaar?"

"So far, no. But we'll keep checking."

Seeing that Deanna was ready to leave, the admiral made his way to the exit. He waited until they were alone in the corridor to embrace her. "Not my favorite day," she said.

"The feeling is mutual." Riker released her and they began to walk to the turbolift. "While you were down there, I was speaking with Chancellor Martok for half an hour. The Typhon Pact—minus the Kinshaya—are taking full advantage of the crisis. They might have more ships in the search now than Starfleet does."

"I can't believe Korgh would keep silent about that, given the xenophobia he's been expressing."

"Silence would be a blessing. No, he's been supportive of the help because it gives him one more chance to undermine the Accords."

She looked at him with concern. "How much danger are they in?"

"Martok hopes he can prevent the Empire from abrogating them. But it's the 'thousand cuts' that concern me."

As the lift arrived, Riker's combadge chirped. *"Ssura to Admiral Riker. We've been hailed on a secure channel from I.K.S. V'raak. General Lorath wants to speak with you most urgently."*

The admiral rolled his eyes. "If this is about Chelvatus III, you can tell him we've already heard from Martok. We're pulling out."

"I don't think that's it, Admiral. The general sounded . . . odd," said Riker's aide.

Riker looked at his wife and shrugged. "Tell him I'll be right there." As they stepped onto the lift, he ordered, "Operations center."

"Lorath," Troi said. "Lord Korgh's son?"

"And he's leading the hunt for the Unsung." When the Klingon Defense Force had put Lorath in charge of its investigation of the Gamaral massacre, it was not yet public knowledge his father was the heir to the House of Kruge. Even Lorath had not known, so far as Riker knew. According to all reports the admiral had received, the revelation had made Lorath redouble his efforts to bring the Unsung to heel. Gamaral was now an attack on *his* house, and so far, he had been cooperative with Starfleet.

Riker hoped that wasn't about to change. "Join me? I may need your impressions. And the moral support."

Minutes later, they entered his office. On-screen, Riker saw a face that he'd first seen in the Great Hall on Qo'noS, the day Korgh's true identity had been revealed.

"Greetings, General. To what do I owe—"

"Are you alone?"

The admiral gestured to his side. "This is my counselor, Commander Deanna Troi."

"Must she be here?"

Riker and Troi exchanged glances. "Why don't you tell me what this is about?"

Lorath's face froze, and for a moment, Riker wondered if there was a problem with the transmission. "General?"

"I am told you attended the launch of my son's ship," Lorath said. *"I appreciate the gesture."*

"It was an honor." Riker assumed a comment about the attack that had followed would be next.

"Honor is in short supply these days. I believe you are a man of honor . . . the Federation has fought valiantly alongside the Empire." Lorath looked away. *"I am not supposed to share this information—but I would have such a friend at my side during the battle."*

Riker's forehead crinkled. "What battle?"

"I have learned that the Unsung are headed for Ghora Janto." Lorath faced them again, and his edginess seemed to melt as the words poured out of him. *"I cannot share how I know this, Admiral. I have not even filed a report with the Defense Force. But I am in the process of moving all the ships under my command there now."*

"Have you told—"

"The Typhon Pact? No." For a moment it looked as if the general was about to spit. *"As I said, this information is extremely sensitive. You belong in this fight."*

Riker thought for a moment. "We are not far from Ghora Janto. I can also summon the *Enterprise*."

"*They rescued my father from Gamaral. They are welcome. But no word to Starfleet Command.*"

Riker looked at Troi and then back at the screen. "I answer to Starfleet, General. I can't send ships into combat without informing them." He paused. "But I can limit my contact to Admiral Akaar. I will avoid mentioning this conversation."

A pause. "*That will do.*"

"The Unsung have one of our officers prisoner aboard one of their ships, General. If at all possible, we should try to disable rather than destroy."

"*After what they have done, you understand I cannot promise this. But do what you will.* Qapla'." The transmission concluded.

Riker scratched his beard. "Stranger and stranger. His father has only scorn for the Federation. How does he know this—and why would he come to *me*?"

"Just from body language and tone," Troi said, "I sensed no duplicity. Only an earnest desire to include a brother-in-arms."

"Earnest," Riker said. *Not a word I would have associated with a son of Korgh.* He stood and called out to his aide. "Ssura, contact Captain Vale. Tell her, with my compliments, that I need her crew's assistance, working the angles. If this is a stunt to make us look bad, I want no part of it. But if this is real, we might be the only hope Worf has."

Fifty-two

"Okay, Tuvok," La Forge said. Trying to keep his balance atop *Houdini*'s hull, he braced himself against the large spire-like emitter with one hand and took another reading with the tricorder in his other hand. "I think we're ready."

On the deck, Tuvok walked into the space they had created by relocating other parked ships. Facing *Houdini*'s forward ports, he spoke into his combadge. "Ready, Doctor Aggadak."

A flash of light—and in place of Tuvok stood a giant Gorn, nearly double his mass. The creature waved to either side, where a group of engineers from the *Enterprise* wheeled over the portable sensor arrays comprising dozens of slate-colored panels. "*Whaaat is the reeeeading?*" the Tuvok-Gorn hissed.

Lieutenant Corrine Clipet checked the array data on her padd. She walked over to Tuvok and showed it to him. "Aggadak's theory checks out."

"*I concurrr,*" Tuvok said. He raised his hand—and turned back into himself. He waited for Aggadak to exit the *Houdini*. "Our work would be more efficient if the transformed subject did not have such a pronounced vocal effect."

Aggadak shrugged off the suggestion. "That's the biggest creature in the database—and you get more of a reading from bigger illusions."

"Agreed. The illusion we apparently interdicted on Yongolor years ago was immense." Tuvok passed the padd to the Nausicaan. "You were correct. *Houdini*'s emitter is indeed opening a pocket subspace continuum."

"An ad-hoc dimension," Clipet said, "strictly for the purposes of channeling information to and from the illusion site."

Aggadak laughed loudly, slapping the Vulcan on the back. Tuvok endured it. "I told you," she said. "There was no way such a high-powered transmission could go through normal subspace without someone sensing it."

"Indeed, I barely noticed the effect a century ago. And the technology appears to have advanced since then."

La Forge approached from the foot of the ladder they'd placed beside *Houdini*. "We know what it's doing, but without completely dismantling the ship, I couldn't tell you why."

Aggadak snarled at him. "You are *not* taking apart my ship!"

Clipet was about to say something, but Tuvok's raised eyebrow silenced her. "Drastic steps may not be necessary. Does what we have learned give us a method for both detecting and interdicting these signals?"

"I think so," La Forge said. "If the system can sense its own illusions, it ought to be able to do the same for data coming from another ship. That should be no problem for *Enterprise*'s computer to replicate."

"Excellent," Tuvok replied. "In the vicinity, a protocol suggested by *Houdini*'s systems could help us locate the vessel following the Unsung."

Aggadak looked back on the starship with maternal pride. "Dunsel, they said. I knew there was more to this ship than—"

La Forge's and Tuvok's combadges activated at the same time. "La Forge here."

"Enterprise *has been called to rejoin* Titan," Captain Picard said.

La Forge and Tuvok looked at each other. "What has happened, Captain?" Tuvok asked.

"*The Unsung have been located. They are racing for Ghora Janto, presumably to attack. General Lorath intends to stop them.* Titan *is already on her way.*"

La Forge frowned. "That doesn't make sense, Captain. The data you just sent us on Object Thirteen suggest it left the Lankal Expanse in the direction of Morska. Ghora Janto's nowhere near that."

"*The admiral would not share the source of his intelligence. But we were looking for Object Thirteen as a means of locating the Phantom Wing, after all. It appears it has been found.*"

Tuvok interjected, "Object Thirteen may be more than that, Captain. If our theory is correct, the ship generated the fake Kruge. If it has split off from the Phantom Wing, it may be advisable to follow both parties."

"*I have my orders. Stand by to beam up.*"

"Captain," La Forge said, "there is another way. There's *Houdini*."

"Ardra's *ship?*" Picard's distaste in saying the name was audible.

"The ship's already set up to detect the emissions created in illusion generation. Tracking the flaw in Object Thirteen's cloak just gets us in the neighborhood. But if we take the *Houdini* there, we can pinpoint where they are."

"It's hasn't been out of the bay in years," Aggadak said, looking alarmed. "I don't have the authority to remove it. They don't even invite me to staff meetings."

Picard said, "*I may have some pull with the administrators. Your plan is approved, Commanders—and I have a certain security chief here who would be eager to join you. Good hunting.*"

Phantom Wing Vessel *Rodak*
Ghora Janto

Ignoring the pain in his leg, Worf clambered over an aggregation of pipes. The bird-of-prey had no Jefferies tubes in the Starfleet sense: only a network of crawlspaces and crannies wending around the guts of the vessel.

Sarken was built for this kind of travel. She had been instrumental in helping him keep to the right path. "Shine the light over here," he called out, and she skittered along a crossbeam like a Cardassian vole.

His search had taken far too long and had been aggravated by the fact that *Rodak* was at high warp. The whine from the straining engines reverberated in these spaces, making it difficult to concentrate, let alone communicate. Worf didn't think anyone was looking for him, but he had no idea how long that would last.

"These are the correct ODN lines," Worf said. They matched what had been detailed in the plans he'd studied. "We are nearly there."

The goal was up ahead: a small crawlspace beneath a jutting metal protrusion. Arriving at the spot, Worf took the light from Sarken and lay on his back. Scooting underneath, he was just able to clear the obstruction. Fumbling with the light, he brought it upward and took a look.

A minute passed. "Worf?" Sarken called out from the space beyond his feet. "Worf? It's scary out here."

"Do not fear."

"What's wrong? Is it not what you expected?"

"You could say that. Stay there—I am coming back," Worf said, beginning to reverse his direction. "And then I will need you to be brave. There is something very important you must do."

Fifty-three

*K*orgh walked through the forests of Cygnet IV. He had never been to the planet before, but somehow he knew the name—just as he knew the name of its sole resident. It was the sylvan home that the emperor had retired to. The clone of Kahless had lived here before Korgh got him away with the invitation to visit Gamaral.

Gamaral, where the emperor had been kidnapped at Korgh's orders. Kidnapped and taken to Thane, where the clone had been executed, again at Korgh's behest. There should be no one on Cygnet IV at all.

And yet Korgh could see a figure up ahead, carrying a bat'leth and lurking after something. Korgh approached quietly, careful not to disturb hunter or prey. The stalker pounced. An animal roared—and fell, the blade having found a neck. It was over in seconds.

As the hunter severed the creature's head, Korgh stepped forward. His breath caught in his throat. It was Kahless wielding the weapon. "How is it that you are alive, clone?"

The hunter did not respond. Circling the majestic warrior, Korgh put his hand over his mouth in wonder. His eyes grew wide. "Are you the clone? Or—are you the true Kahless?"

Still no response. The hunter draped the now-headless carcass over his shoulders and rose. He walked away, his back to Korgh, never having noticed the old man once.

"Kahless! Why will you not hear me?"

"Kahless!" Korgh awoke sweating and wondering where he was. In the dark, it took him several seconds to get his bearings. Days earlier, he had moved from the humbler *gin'tak*'s quarters that he had resided in for fifty years to the lord's suite. It was deservedly his, but he had still not gotten accustomed to it. Perhaps that explained the bad dreams.

He was not given to placing stock in dreams. That was for the simple-minded and the superstitious, those who deserved to be ruled. Never for him—he had made visions into reality. Korgh had created a nightmare for the Empire in the Unsung and had profited from it. Now, with their puppeteer departed, Korgh would dispel the nightmare— and all credit would go to his eldest son.

He lit a burner and checked the time. A message had arrived from Lorath. The general was lying in wait a short warp jump from Ghora Janto with a hastily assembled battle group. *V'raak* was supported by two other *Vor'cha*-class attack vessels, more than enough to eliminate the Unsung—especially given the modifications Lorath had quietly ordered made to their targeting systems. Attuned to the Phantom Wing's stealth positioning system, the war-ships' disruptors and photon torpedoes would eliminate all evidence and make Lorath a hero in the same swath.

Donning a robe, Korgh rose and left the residence, step-ping into the atrium. Past Kruge's statue, he could see down the hall that the door to J'borr's office was open. He walked toward the light, confident Odrok was inside, monitoring the impending battle.

Instead, he found the room unoccupied. The screens showed the positions of the ships she'd been tracking; the Phantom Wing was almost to Ghora Janto. Standing in the doorway, he heard voices from one of Odrok's computers. It was the audio feed from *V'raak*, piped in from the Klingon Defense Force's network. The voices were excited, expect-ant. The game was on the hoof.

He looked back and forth down the long corridor. Even though Odrok and Korgh were the only two beings on this floor of the building, he considered her absence a breach of operational security. *All our secrets, and the door wide open!*

"Curse you, old woman." He entered the office and closed the door. He had worked too long to miss the last act.

Houdini
Deep Space

Houdini raced through interstellar space, and seldom had a stranger ship been operated by Starfleet. It was now an official/unofficial part of the Unsung investigative task force. It had only navigational shields and no weapons. The ship's illusion generation and sensor package required immense power, so there wasn't any power available to protect or arm the ship.

Before departing for Ghora Janto, *Enterprise* had detached Šmrhová and five security officers as well as six additional engineers to fully crew the vessel. Clipet had also remained. Picard had cleared *Houdini*'s departure with Starbase 24, but he had needed to report the name of the commandeering captain.

"You've got seniority within the task force," Commander La Forge had said.

"I have never wanted to command," Commander Tuvok said. "Your knowledge of this vessel both precedes and supersedes mine. And there is someone else who is better suited to be first officer."

A simultaneous look at their Nausicaan lieutenant followed. They reported Commander La Forge as *Houdini*'s commander with Aggadak, over Tuvok, as its first officer. She seemed to appreciate her temporary field promotion, and it also reflected reality. Aggadak knew more about the vessel than anyone else.

Houdini dropped in and out of warp as it followed the projected path of Object Thirteen. *Houdini*'s propulsion systems, long idle, had required some coaxing. Tuvok had taken the time to study the vessel—and to reflect on its history.

"I have been looking more into this Harry Houdini," Tuvok said as he dropped in a seat, his uniform covered in lubricant from the systems he'd been working on. "While he is known as an entertainer, he also debunked people who claimed to be mystics, particularly when they did so for personal gain."

"Then this mission is following in his footsteps," La Forge said, poring over a display. "I think we're getting close. Do you see where the highest probability path leads to?"

"Cragg's Cloud." Tuvok studied the data. "A classic absorption nebula—nearly opaque. Carbon monoxide, nitrogen, ammonia."

"You wouldn't even need a cloak to hide in there."

"Small, with no planets. In an unclaimed region partially surrounded by Klingon space." Tuvok nodded. "It is a logical destination for someone evading pursuit."

La Forge saw Aggadak approaching. "I think we have our next stop, Number One."

"I heard," she said. She crossed her arms. "If this cloud damages my baby's finish, I'm holding you both responsible."

BLACKSTONE
CRAGG'S CLOUD

"That's the most beautiful thing I've ever seen," Gaw said as he looked out the forward port. "To the extent anyone can see anything here."

Cross agreed. The unmanned *Ark of G'boj* had slowed to a stop right where it was supposed to, deep inside Cragg's Cloud. That location, however, made the massive freighter no more than a hazy smear outside *Blackstone*'s front port, even though it was less than a kilometer away.

"I had our pet Klingons go over the thing already," he said. "But to be safe, give it a life-sign scan."

"Our regular sensors are pretty much useless in this guck," the Ferengi said. "We're going to have to decloak and turn the projector on it, full power—model the interior as if we were going to generate an illusion. It'll take a while, but if something's moving, we'll know it."

Cross's attention was on something else moving down the spiral staircase from the loft. Shift descended as lithely as one walking on air. Dressed in a gray jumpsuit with a black jacket and boots, she had put her hair up into a tight bun. It was exactly what she'd looked like the day he met her—right down to the gym bag she carried holding all her belongings.

"Hey, you're not running away, are you?" Cross grinned. "This is the best part."

"You said we'd go over to get the first taste." She jerked the bag upward, indicating it was light. "I want to bring a couple of bars of latinum over to sleep with."

"Smart woman," Gaw said. His eyes darted to Cross. "Too smart to be with you."

Cross chuckled. "It'll be just a few minutes—we're scanning for Klingon stowaways. Take a seat."

With all the truthcrafters on deck, she looked in vain for a chair. When he indicated his lap was available, she smiled primly and approached. Cross smiled back.

Life doesn't get any better than this.

Fifty-four

"I think we've got something," La Forge said as *Houdini* cruised into the darkness of Cragg's Cloud.

"I have a ship identification on the nearer contact," Tuvok said, examining records on a screen. "It is a Klingon high-security cargo hauler—of the sort the large houses use to transfer valuables. According to an alert issued by the Klingon Defense Force, one such ship has just gone missing: the *Ark of G'boj*."

The discovery of the *Ark* would have disappointed La Forge were it not for the second contact beyond—the vessel whose emanations had led them to the nebula.

"I can just barely see an outline," Šmrhová said, her eyes on the long-range sensors. "Hello, Object Thirteen. You look a lot like us."

Tuvok raised an eyebrow. "It is not cloaked?"

"Probably not expecting anyone," the *Enterprise*'s security chief offered. "They're directing their image-projection energy toward the Klingon ship. Good thing for us. I don't know that we would have found it in here otherwise."

The Vulcan nodded. "They could be projecting an illusion—or simply using their sensor package to monitor the drifting vessel. We must assume that *Ark of G'boj* is under hostile control—perhaps even that of the Unsung." Tuvok looked forward to Aggadak and the *Enterprise* crew at the controls. "It would be helpful to engage the cloaking device before we approach."

"It doesn't work perfectly," La Forge and the Nausicaan said almost in unison.

"In this morass, perfection is not necessary. We only need to get close. But I am concerned that under the Treaty of Algeron, our use of the device, even aboard this ship, might be seen as a violation."

"I'll take responsibility," La Forge said. "I have a feeling the Federation will back us up on this one."

"Very well." Tuvok turned, and ordered, "Security team, stand by in the transporter room."

Houdini hummed, indicating the cloaking device had powered up. La Forge kept his eyes on two vessels ahead. "Whoops—Object Thirteen just shut off its projections and cloaked."

"In reaction to us?" Aggadak asked.

"I doubt it—but I can't say for sure."

Tuvok made a quick decision. "Keep scanning as we approach and remain on alert." He headed for the transporter room.

BLACKSTONE
CRAGG'S CLOUD

Gaw had been right about the scan of *Ark of G'boj* taking a while. Cross and Shift had taken seats in the transporter room—and while they waited, he'd shown her on his padd the locations of the Phantom Wing vessels.

Blackstone's systems had long had, via Korgh's engineer, the ability to track the birds-of-prey's movement through their stealth positioning systems; he'd loaded the key algorithm onto his padd. The inventory of the treasure ship might take days, and he wanted to know the instant the Unsung met their doom.

Gaw entered. "Looks good," he said. "There might be a few rodents running around the ship—if the Klingons forgot to eat them. Otherwise you can count to your heart's content."

The Bynars, 1110 and 1111—no one aboard *Blackstone* seemed to be able to name them in anything but numerical order—entered the transporter room with their equipment, ready to go to work. Cross put the padd in his vest pocket and stood and stretched. He patted the Ferengi on the shoulder and followed Shift and the Bynars onto the transporter pads.

Turning, he pointed back at Gaw. "Make sure the myth team wraps up its work today. I still want to get started on Project Kahless."

"The last bit ran longer than a year, and you're ready for the next one? You're incorrigible." Gaw waved. "You kids have fun now. Don't let any piles of latinum bricks fall on you."

Phantom Wing Vessel *Rodak*
Ghora Janto

Ghora Janto had two stars and no planets—and yet Zokar thought something about the system spoke to the Klingon imagination. Long before civilization arose in the Empire, a rogue white dwarf passed too close to a blue main-sequence star. Locking onto one another in gravitic battle, every planet in both systems was torn to shreds.

Debris from the cosmic altercation continued to course around and between the combatants, switching direction frequently as the forces on them shifted. It had made mapping almost impossible—thus creating one of the Empire's more secure refueling locations. Either you knew on which of the billions of chunks of rock to find the station, or you looked for it forever.

Once again, Zokar's experience had come in handy. The first bird-of-prey to arrive had paused outside the debris field, cloaked and confused. He had redirected their attention to a lone ship, vectoring into the system. It would lead them right to the meeting Kruge had spoken of, and Kersh.

"Steady," he said as *Rodak* cruised forward through the mineral miasma. The widespread distribution of debris made it highly unlikely the invaders could collide with anything large, but striking small particles worried him. Could plowing ahead too fast compromise their cloak? He didn't have enough experience with this cloaking system to know. But the others followed his lead.

"Five additional Unsung vessels have arrived," Harch said. "Nine out of eleven."

"A quorum. And there's the quarry." Zokar studied the growing image onscreen. One of the larger asteroids exhibited signs of habitation, with towers and domes on its misshapen surface. Several ships were tethered to the low-gravity body. "The depot is beneath the surface. If Kersh is meeting anyone, it's in there."

"Where's *Gur'rok*?" Harch asked. "I thought that was her flagship."

"You heard Kruge. She is on the run, making a secret deal. We will see her ships soon enough—after we kill her." His hand gripped the armrest. "Arm photon torpedos."

Harch looked back. "Valandris isn't here yet."

"Too bad for the laggard. This revenge cannot wait." Zokar was about to give a command when he noticed Harch's expression. It had gone from concern to surprise. He looked back to see four Unsung warriors entering the bridge, two on either side of their prisoners: Worf and Sarken.

"Hold position, Harch." Zokar laughed and stood. "What, did you two go for a walk?"

"We found them in engineering," said one of the guards holding on to Worf's arm. "You knew he was here, Zokar?"

"He's a stowaway. I was about to tell Lord Kruge about it when he was killed."

Worf raised an eyebrow. "Kruge was killed?"

"Now you care? You thought him a fraud." Zokar approached the prisoners and glared down at Sarken. She looked terrified. "Did you free him, stripling? It's good we are busy, or I would lock you in a torpedo tube."

"Do not blame her," Worf said.

"Right." Zokar punched Worf hard in the stomach. "This was your idea."

Worf shrugged it off with gritted teeth. "Zokar, this girl may have saved your lives. I surrendered because of what she found."

The word hit Zokar like a club. *"Surrendered?"*

Worf spoke with urgency. "Your stealth positioning system—the thing that tells you where other ships in the Phantom Wing are—is accessible from deck six. I had intended to adjust the setting to broadcast your location to Starfleet."

"Ah, your plan. So you failed."

"No."

Zokar's eyebrow tilted. "You succeeded?"

"No. I discovered the system was *already* set to broadcast your locations to someone far away."

"Who set it?"

"Whoever supplied you with the Phantom Wing."

Zokar looked around the bridge. The other Unsung were as puzzled as he was. "Why would they do that?"

"To track you, I am certain. But also to trigger the thing Sarken identified by crawling into a space I could not reach.

The system is connected to a detonator and a photon torpedo warhead. Whoever is tracking your vessels also has the means to destroy them by remote control—and I cannot imagine it is unique to *Rodak*."

Zokar goggled. "Do you mean there is a *bomb* on board every ship?"

Worf stared at the older Klingon. "You thought the Unsung lived free, Zokar. In truth, you only exist while someone else allows you to."

Fifty-five

"**M**adness!" Zokar said. "Utter madness. There is no warhead. You waste my time."

"He tells the truth," Sarken said. "I saw it."

"You do not even know what a warhead looks like."

"I live on a bird-of-prey—and before that my hut was next to the armory. I know."

Worf gave the little girl a reassuring look. "Send someone. But tell them not to try to deactivate it. I doubt anyone here has the skills."

"Then what good is knowing about it?" Zokar asked. "Son of Mogh, you speak in circles."

"Valandris has just emerged from warp," the woman at the comm station said. "We are all here."

"Fine. No more of this." Zokar pointed to the guards. "Take the girl back to the hold. As for Worf—"

Before he could give his command, an alarm sounded on the bridge. "Three battle cruisers have just appeared in sensor range," the woman at the navigation station said. "The lead vessel is identified as *V'raak*. Kersh's ship is not with them."

Zokar walked over to see for himself. "This makes no sense. Kruge told us she would come here."

"Yes, Zokar. Why would he lie?" Worf asked. As he did so, the Unsung holding him tensed. Others growled.

"Careful, son of Mogh," Zokar said. "You are among true believers."

"What will it take to make you understand? Battle cruisers arrive just as the whole squadron is in the system." Worf strained against his captors. "There is a deception at work—"

"Incoming!" Harch had scarcely finished the word when a photon torpedo exploded near *Rodak*. The bird-of-prey pitched sideways, throwing prisoners and captors alike to the deck.

Zokar clambered back to his command chair. "Who is firing?"

Harch looked back. "That was *V'raak*. The other two are firing as well—at our other birds-of-prey!"

"But we are cloaked!"

A second blast struck the starboard shields, sending debris from the asteroid field slamming into the ship. A console exploded, sending sparks raining across the deck. Worf grabbed Sarken, yanking her clear of the spray.

"Evasive action," Zokar ordered. The ship rolled. "Start our attack run on the depot."

"It is too late for that," Worf yelled. As if to punctuate his words, the proximity alarm sounded again.

"A Romulan warbird is decloaking before the depot," Harch said. "No, two!"

Zokar's eyes bulged as he saw the enormous vessels before the large asteroid. "Are they targeting us, too?"

"Definitely blocking us, and—"

Another alarm. The navigator reported, "We have Breen ships arriving, directly aft."

Worf scrambled forward and grabbed at the bald Klingon's shoulder. "You are betrayed, Zokar!"

PHANTOM WING VESSEL *CHU'CHARQ* GHORA JANTO

"Something is wrong," Valandris said. Her investigation of Kruge's death had made *Chu'charq* the last bird-of-prey to leave Omicron Lankal. Arriving last gave her a wider perspective on the developing situation. A battle raged: a peculiar-looking one-sided affair, with the three Klingon battle cruisers firing—and striking—unseen targets in the asteroid field.

The Romulan warbirds and the Breen battle cruisers were doing something else entirely. "They're firing torpedoes into the debris field," Raneer said, "using it to bombard everything in sight."

"And not in sight," Valandris said from the command chair. "I don't think the Romulans and the Breen can see us—they're just responding to the Empire vessels' shots and trying to limit our field of movement." But the Klingon battle cruisers definitely had found a way to target them.

"Heavy damages being reported from—" At her station, Hemtara stopped in midsentence. "Valandris, *Kaanz* has been destroyed."

A Phantom Wing vessel. "Get us in there. Start firing back!"

Chu'charq wheeled and accelerated, careening toward the fight. Another alarm sounded. "Now what?"

"It's *Titan*," someone said. "And *Enterprise*."

Hemtara called out. "Starfleet is here!"

Valandris had sensed an apocalyptic feeling in the squadron ever since Kruge's murder. *I think the moment has arrived.*

House of Kruge Industrial Compound
Ketorix Prime, Klingon Empire

Korgh rocked back and forth on the chair in Odrok's command center, almost too excited to sit. The audio feed from *V'raak* detailed a magnificent battle. One shipful of his puppets had already met their end, with the kill going to Lorath. And there would be more. Ten more.

He didn't understand how the Romulans and Breen had gotten there so quickly, but that didn't matter. Their participation would give him more ammunition against the Federation. The arrival of *Titan* and *Enterprise* had been unwelcome, but the important thing was that they were last, and had no idea how to target the cloaked ships. Lorath did. The accolades would be his.

Not once did he worry about Odrok's absence. She would regret missing this, for sure.

U.S.S. *TITAN*
GHORA JANTO

Vale heard the turbolift open. "The Romulans and Breen are already here, Admiral."

"How did *that* happen?" Riker walked onto the bridge and stared at the conflagration in wonder. *Titan* had held position at the edge of the system, waiting for *Enterprise*'s arrival and for Lorath's vessels to make the first move. Once the Klingon battle cruisers entered the debris field and started firing, that was Starfleet's cue to close in. But how had the Breen and Romulan party crashers found a fight that was only minutes old?

"We are tracking the shots the Klingon battle cruisers are firing," Keru said, "and creating contacts in our targeting database."

"It'd be a lot easier if they'd tell us how they're doing this," Vale said. She looked over to Riker, now watching on her right. He shrugged. "Bring us toward the nearest contact, conn."

"Aye, Captain."

Riker stood behind Kyzak, serving at ops after his unusual adventure on H'atoria. "Send our modeling to

Enterprise. Have them disable anyone trying to escape on this vector."

The challenge facing the Starfleet vessels could not have been more daunting. They were entering a firefight with ships they could not see, but they were also concerned about Worf, who might be aboard any one of them. If any disabled Phantom Wing vessel decloaked, *Titan* and *Enterprise* had to get to it in time to transport survivors off the ship.

"Security teams, stand by in the transporter rooms for possible evacuees," Vale ordered.

She didn't see the look her first officer gave her, but Riker did. Sarai had never liked the idea of going into battle with one hand tied behind their backs. In the earlier briefing, she'd stopped just short of implying that Riker's judgment was compromised by his personal concern for Worf. Riker didn't care. He knew finding survivors among the Unsung was absolutely necessary to unraveling the mysteries surrounding them.

And if they netted Worf in the process, all the better.

On the main viewscreen, he saw disruptor fire lancing from nowhere at one of the Klingon battle cruisers. Fire came in from all directions at the source. A bird-of-prey rippled itself into view—and then tore apart.

"When they fire back, everybody lights them up," Sarai said from Vale's side. "This won't take long."

PHANTOM WING VESSEL *RODAK*
GHORA JANTO

"There goes *Garada*!"

At the sight of another destroyed bird-of-prey, Worf felt jubilant, restored—and then he looked down at Sarken, clinging to his leg and wailing. Each call of a destroyed ship hit the bridge like a sledgehammer. Every ship had one-twelfth of the Unsung community aboard. Everyone he had seen on Thane.

Some Unsung had slain on the false Kruge's command, but some hadn't. There was no time to waste, he thought. Lifting Sarken into his arms, he moved in front of Zokar. The older Klingon seemed frozen, paralyzed with rage and frustration. Every attempt to strike at the Klingons—or his preferred enemy, the Romulans—had resulted in *Rodak* being beaten back, with damage to its systems.

"Do you see, Zokar? There is your answer. We know who has access to the stealth positioning system. *They do!*"

Zokar gripped his armrest with his hand—and then looked up at Worf, his normally stern face fraught. "What am I to do?"

"If you drop your cloak, you will disengage the device."

"Fool! If we drop our cloaks, they will destroy us!"

"They are doing that anyway," Worf said. "But while the stealth positioning system is activated, they can find you. And you will be in danger from whoever set those bombs!"

It was clear Zokar had forgotten all about the warhead hidden inside his hull. He looked to Harch, his closest advisor. Receiving no counsel, he growled. "Today is a good day to die!"

PHANTOM WING VESSEL *CHU'CHARQ*
GHORA JANTO

"Drop your cloaks," Zokar said in an announcement to the squadron. *"I have no time to explain."*

"I was about to do it anyway," Valandris said. *Chu'charq* needed all power to its shields and engines to stave off the assault.

"Are you insane?" Raneer asked, looking back in horror. "They will see us!"

"And nothing at all will be different." Valandris's jaw stiffened. "Give me close approaches on the attacking ships. I want them to see me wave. Hemtara, tell the whole squadron to do the same."

The woman looked back at her, stunned. "Suicide?"

"As soon as we decloak, we'll take fire from everyone. But I am betting the different factions only have permission to attack *us*. They will think twice before shooting closely at one another!"

Fifty-six

"Steady," Picard said. "Be prepared to move in."

He was unaccustomed to playing the vulture, but that was the *Enterprise*'s role. The Romulans and Breen had been the sheepdogs, keeping the Unsung from leaving the field while the Klingon battle cruisers thinned the herd. *Enterprise* was herding, too, but Picard's focus was on beaming out survivors before they were annihilated. As yet, he hadn't been given the chance—but when several birds-of-prey decloaked, Picard figured it was time.

Then the calculus changed.

"Seven birds-of-prey decloaked," Dygan announced from ops. "With two destroyed plus the one at H'atoria, that leaves two unaccounted—"

"Aspect change on the nearest target," Šmrhová announced. "Birds-of-prey converging on the battle cruiser nearest us."

"Attack pattern gamma four," Picard said. "Target only the vessels more than two kilometers from the Klingon cruiser. Phasers only, fire to disable."

The captain's eyes narrowed—and then widened as fire ballooned from the battle cruiser's bridge. He wasn't watching suicide runs. The Unsung knew what they were doing.

"Hail the cruiser," Picard ordered. They might be bringing a different sort of survivor aboard entirely.

HOUSE OF KRUGE INDUSTRIAL COMPOUND
KETORIX PRIME, KLINGON EMPIRE

Something had gone wrong. The Unsung had not turned
the tide, but the voices Korgh was hearing on the Defense
Force feed were no longer as joyous. They should have been
ecstatic, because several of the Phantom Wing ships had
unexpectedly dropped their cloaks.

But those birds-of-prey quickly moved to close quarters,
risking annihilation in exchange for a chance to stay tem-
porarily out of harm's way. Worse, they were using their
proximity to exact damage. Like buzzing insects, several
had converged on one of Lorath's companion cruisers. They
had delivered a devastating blow, striking at its bridge; no
reports had come from it since.

Korgh still did not doubt victory, but he began to worry
that Unsung survivors might be captured—and while he
did not fear that, it was a complication he preferred to
avoid. It was one he had prepared for. He shuffled around
the documents on Odrok's desk. There was a program in her
computer systems for such an eventuality; it just required
the activation code.

He was searching the mess under the desk when a hail
arrived, nearly scaring the old man out of his wits. It was
on the private channel he'd established with *V'raak*'s ready
room. "What is it, Lorath?"

*"I must speak quickly, Father. Something is wrong. Our
targeting is tied into the Phantom Wing's stealth positioning
system. But now that most are decloaked, we are no longer
receiving data from them."*

"Then switch to manual targeting."

He heard shouting in the background. *"Doing so now, but
it will take a minute to reset the systems and expel the old code."*

"I—I had not thought of that." He couldn't imagine why the squadron was decloaking. Such behavior made no sense.

"You said to call if things went wrong. We have the upper hand, but one of my ships is out of action—and the Unsung are tenacious. If you have found something else that will help us, you had better tell me."

"Ah!" The request delighted Korgh. Lorath's forces had done enough damage to qualify him as the hero of the engagement; now was the time to detonate the bombs Odrok and her minions had installed aboard the ships, eliminating all evidence. It would be the mass suicide everyone expected from the Unsung.

But the code was nowhere to be found.

"Fight on, my son," Korgh called out as he stood. "I will be right back."

He swore loudly as he left the office. *Where is Odrok?*

PHANTOM WING VESSEL *RODAK*
GHORA JANTO

"Hit them again!" Zokar shouted. "Show them who we are!"

Worf looked at the main viewer to see another battle cruiser being pummeled at close range. Two of his guards were gone, dealing with an aft hull breach; the other two had remained inside the doorway to the bridge, mesmerized by the fight outside. A bone-shattering impact to *Rodak* sent a girder falling, crushing the warrior beside the engineering station. Worf rushed to aid her, and the guards hurried to assist—to no avail. She was dead. Neither guard stopped him as Worf clambered over the girder to the engineering station.

"We are taking heavy damage," Worf called out as he

read the displays. "You must surrender—or begin transporting people off the ship."

"And miss this?" Zokar laughed. "Never!"

HOUSE OF KRUGE INDUSTRIAL COMPOUND
KETORIX PRIME, KLINGON EMPIRE

"Odrok! Odrok, you fool, where are you?"

Korgh passed through the kitchen into the larder. There he saw the older woman seated at the small table, her cheek pressed against the surface. A bottle sat overturned nearby. She snored—and drooled.

In a rage, he rushed forward and seized her shoulders, pushing her up. She gurgled and woke. "Wha—?"

"Old sot! Imbecile!" He forcibly turned the chair around, and she sagged from it. He grabbed her chin and brought her eyes up to meet his. "Where is the code to destroy the Phantom Wing?"

Woozy, she struggled to focus on him. She started laughing. "Funny. Thought you said *destroy* . . ."

"My son is in danger! The code!"

Odrok fumbled for a pocket in her robe. On the third try she drew forth a card. "You must use the program on—"

Korgh did not hear the rest. He ran as fast as his old legs could take him.

PHANTOM WING VESSEL *CHU'CHARQ*
GHORA JANTO

"Score another," Raneer said as a photon torpedo struck home. "It'll be two cruisers out of action soon."

Valandris wished she felt as confident. Her tactic had

worked, but at great cost. For a short but welcome time, the battle cruisers had seemed unable to target the Phantom Wing; the only fire had come from the Romulan, Breen, and Starfleet ships, and the latter were thankfully holding their weapons in reserve.

But then the battle cruisers had opened up again. While *Chu'charq* had been mostly spared, the other decloaked birds-of-prey now displayed serious damage. Only *T'khaz* and *Bregit*, which had not heeded Zokar's suggestion to decloak, thinking him a madman, were completely intact. Whatever trick the Empire was using to hit the cloaked ships was no longer working.

"Be prepared to cloak again if things get bad," she said. "And get the transporters ready, Hemtara. If you spot the chance to save some refugees from the other ships, take it."

HOUSE OF KRUGE INDUSTRIAL COMPOUND
KETORIX PRIME, KLINGON EMPIRE

Breathless, Korgh stumbled into J'borr's office. With the panicked voices on the military feed in his ears, he found the appropriate program. The squadron he had helped build, which had occupied his thoughts for a century, had to die so that his son would live—and as a hero. He entered the code and hit the execute command.

His eyes shot over to the map display, where a twinkling light indicated Phantom Wing vessels were at Ghora Janto. It blinked again—and went out.

PHANTOM WING VESSEL *RODAK*
GHORA JANTO

"Look!" Sarken yelled.

Across the stellar battlefield, a cloaked object burst violently into view, exploding. Sarken clung to the side of Worf's engineering station, her fear having given way to a wild-eyed fascination at the battle.

"That was *Bregit*," Harch said. "But I didn't see anything hit her."

Rodak swerved past its battle cruiser target—and Zokar pointed. "Look there. The same just happened to *T'khaz*? Nothing was anywhere near her!" He gaped. "Did they fly into something?"

Worf strongly suspected a different reason. "It is the bombs. Those were the only two ships still under cloak. Someone triggered them."

Zokar looked back. "I do not believe it."

"I do not care what you believe. If you engage the cloaking device again, you will suffer the same—"

A blast hit *Rodak* hard. The station Worf was at exploded, forcing him to cover the screaming Sarken with his body. Metal clanged all about, and smoke clouded the bridge.

Looking up, he could see *Rodak* was not only still functioning—but, amazingly, continuing its attack run. Zokar, who had failed to arrive in time to fight the Romulans at Khitomer forty years before, sat in his command chair, his face charred by some projectile, directing the assault.

In the din, Worf heard the warrior at the comm station shout. "Valandris hails. She wants to know if we need to be evacuated."

"She can to go to Gre'thor," Zokar said. "I am not finished."

"Tell her yes!" Worf yelled.

Zokar turned toward him and leered. "Running, Worf? Would Kahless approve?"

"He would have condemned your seeking this fight in the first place. And he would not carry children to their deaths in order to settle a vendetta!"

Zokar froze for an instant. Then he snarled and returned his attention to the fight. Worf saw the warrior at the comm station speaking, but could not hear her words to know whom she obeyed.

U.S.S. TITAN
GHORA JANTO

"What happened?" Vale asked in wonder. The two cloaked birds-of-prey had simultaneously exploded for no apparent reason.

"Antimatter explosions in both cases," said Melora Pazlar from the science station. "Reading traces of magnetic borotenite emanating from the zero point."

"Torpedoes? But nothing hit them," Riker said. "Did their own munitions go off?"

"No way to know, sir."

"We're not getting a chance to pluck off survivors," Vale said. "We're going to have to catch someone before they go critical." Her eyes locked on a single bird-of-prey, heavily damaged, tangling with *V'raak*. "Maybe that one there— the reckless one. Chase contact number four."

Titan moved, following the running battle through a debris field that was quickly becoming more man-made than natural. Riker held on to a console and gritted his teeth. *Worf, if you're over there, we're doing our best.*

Fifty-seven

It had not worked.

Korgh knew he had detonated the bombs aboard two of the birds-of-prey; the confirmation signals had come back, and the audio from the Defense Force feed confirmed it. It also told him that seven vessels remained, decloaked— and all dealing damage to his son's task force.

Lorath was no longer on the private channel; he was back on the bridge. Korgh could hear the general's voice as he commanded the ship's defense. A bit of good news came over the comm: a Romulan had picked off and destroyed another Phantom Wing vessel. But *V'raak* could not count on anyone for deliverance—and Korgh's own attempt had evidently failed.

Korgh reentered the code again and again, wondering what had happened. In fury, he punched the display.

"What is happening?"

He looked to see Odrok leaning against the doorframe, looking in. She looked pale. "You! What is wrong with you? I found you passed out in the larder."

"I have nowhere to sleep here." She rubbed her temples. "You won't give me a place."

"The battle is on at Ghora Janto. Lorath is in trouble— and the bombs on the Phantom Wing ships will not respond to the code!"

Odrok stepped inside and focused on the map screen. "They must not be cloaked. The stealth positioning systems only work when they are."

"What do you mean?"

"That's what the stealth positioning system does. It tells cloaked ships where other cloaked ships are. And it also tells us." She rubbed her nose with the back of her hand. "The system is what triggers the bombs. If a Phantom Wing bird-of-prey decloaks, we have no way of getting a signal to its SPS."

"That's foolish! Why would you design it in that way?"

"You said to assume they would always be cloaked once they were on the run." She looked back at him. "If you wanted a more robust system, you should have killed fewer of my coworkers over the years. I am your only devoted engineer left."

"Devoted? Devoted drunk!" Korgh turned his attention back to the battle. "Would the bombs detonate if they cloaked again?"

"Yes, so long as they have not been discovered and disconnected."

That was it, Korgh thought. He had to raise Lorath again—tell him to order all the other ships present to disengage at all costs. The Unsung would either flee or regroup, cloaking in either case. That would be the end of it.

PHANTOM WING VESSEL *CHU'CHARQ*
GHORA JANTO

"That was *Latorkh* the Romulans just destroyed," Raneer said.

Valandris's breath cut short, remembering the friends she had aboard. "Weltern?"

"We transported her off," Hemtara said. "Our people are working overtime back there."

"They'll have more to do." As *Chu'charq* weaved through

the melee, Valandris could see two other vessels were in dire straits—including one that was still attacking the lead Klingon battle cruiser even though it was on fire. Zokar had lost all sense, it had seemed: heedless even of the approach of *Titan*. "Tell the remaining ships to recover people from *Gleft* while they still can. We're going for *Rodak*."

Raneer looked back. "Not your favorite person."

"He's not the only one aboard," Valandris said. "Go!"

U.S.S. TITAN
GHORA JANTO

"What was *that*?" An intact bird-of-prey had just buzzed low over the hull, Vale saw, racing toward its ailing Unsung compatriot. That ship, ablaze, was tangled up again with *V'raak*; she worried it might not survive long enough for *Titan* to recover anyone alive.

"We've got life signs on the damaged bird-of-prey," Pazlar said. "All Klingon, no surprise. But shields are somehow still up."

"Can we disable the shields without destroying them?" Riker asked.

"We'll have to try," Vale said.

PHANTOM WING VESSEL RODAK
GHORA JANTO

The ship was coming apart—and inside, people were disappearing, beamed away. While guiding the wayward vessel, Harch vanished, transported through *Rodak*'s remaining shields. Zokar screamed Valandris's name in anger and rushed to take the helm himself.

Worf called out from just inside the doorway of the slowly depopulating bridge. "Zokar, you must stop the attack!"

"Go to blazes, Worf! I die, as I should have!"

There was no reaching the man. Worf had waited long enough. Taking Sarken's hand in his, he exited the bridge. A small transporter room lay beyond—and escape pods past that. One had saved him in his escape from Thane. Either would do—

—but another shock struck *Rodak* first, piercing the skin just ahead of the bird-of-prey's neck. Something in the forward weapons cabinet responded by exploding.

"*Help!*" Sarken screamed as explosive decompression began. Wedging his body against a support column, Worf put the girl in a bear hug and fought against the raging air currents. He clawed with his free hand, desperately seeking a hold.

PHANTOM WING VESSEL *CHU'CHARQ*
GHORA JANTO

As Valandris's ship raced toward the blazing wreck of *Rodak*—now venting to space—it seemed to accelerate away from her and toward the lead battle cruiser's bridge. *What is that maniac doing?*

"Transporter lock, deck five forward," Hemtara yelled. "One adult, one child."

"That's probably Zokar," Valandris yelled. "Bring him straight to the bridge." Time was almost gone. "Get them out of there!"

House of Kruge Industrial Compound
Ketorix Prime, Klingon Empire

There had been no time for Lorath to find a private place to speak to Korgh this time. *"My lord, our forward shields are failing! What is it?"*

Odrok had her hand over her mouth as Korgh spoke. "My son, you must order your forces there—"

Cacophony responded across the private connection, echoing over the still-active Defense Force feed. *"Collision alert! All hands—"*

Static came from both audio sources. Standing, Korgh froze, his eyes wide. "Lorath, answer me! *Lorath!*"

Odrok took her hand off her mouth. "What have you done? *What have you done?*"

U.S.S. Titan
Ghora Janto

The renegade bird-of-prey slammed through the damaged shields directly into the battle cruiser's bridge, igniting an inferno forward on the larger ship. The assailant shredded in the act, its component pieces dashing against *V'raak*'s superstructure.

Riker stood slackjawed at what he had seen. He quashed the impulse to give a command; Vale was on top of it. "Transport teams, switch recovery efforts to *V'raak*."

"Other birds-of-prey are breaking off," Keru announced.

"Let *Enterprise* have them," Riker said, swallowing hard. "We're needed here."

Phantom Wing Vessel *Chu'charq*
Ghora Janto

The last year of Valandris's life had been one surprise after another. But nothing prepared her for seeing Worf materializing on the deck in front of her feet, his body protecting Sarken's. Both adult and child panted, having gone from a depressurizing cabin to *Chu'charq*'s bridge.

"Disengage, disengage," she said to Raneer. "*Worf?*"

He looked up at her, still winded. "You cannot . . . cloak. There are bombs aboard."

"Bombs!"

"They will detonate if you cloak. If you must escape, go to warp. But do not cloak."

Valandris blinked. Was that what had happened to *Bregit* and *T'khaz*? It was too incredible to believe. "What happened to Zokar?"

"I did not see." Rising, Worf looked out at the plumes of debris surrounding *V'raak*. "Oh," he said. He turned Sarken so she could not see.

Valandris stood and looked at Hemtara. "Is Zokar aboard?"

Hemtara checked. "Not here, not aboard any of the other ships." She had a sad expression. "We are four now."

Valandris could barely process the scope of the tragedies. Two-thirds of their force, wiped out—and possibly as much of their community. And while she did not understand Worf's hand in it, she could tell from the reactions of the others aboard that they suspected his role in it. How else could he have been aboard *Rodak*, after having attacked the muster on Thane? Might he even have had a role in the murder of Kruge?

"*Enterprise* is giving chase," Raneer said. "Do we—I don't know, trade him if they'll let us get away?"

Valandris found her disruptor and pointed it at him. "The Unsung do not bargain—and we do not need anyone to let us escape. Find your first clear lane and go to warp."

"What heading?"

"I don't know. But whatever you decide, tell the others."

House of Kruge Industrial Compound
Ketorix Prime, Klingon Empire

Four birds-of-prey had escaped. *Titan* had taken its fill of refugees from the three stricken Klingon battle cruisers; *Enterprise* had been summoned back to take the rest. Riker and *Titan* had then followed the Unsung's suspected escape route into warp, as had Romulan and Breen pursuers. The hunt was on again.

Korgh was on the floor of the office, howling his son's name and screaming for vengeance as report after report came in across the Klingon Defense Force feed. Odrok, frightened, slipped into the hallway. Korgh had been undone. His machinations had killed his son. He could not imagine a more terrible sequence of events happening in a hundred years.

But his nightmare was not over.

Fifty-eight

"I don't know who this G'boj guy was," Cross said as he walked between the towers of gold-pressed latinum bricks. "But I like how he furnishes a ship."

In their years of running scams, Cross and his companions had looted the treasures of many different species. Most had protected their riches in vaults with thick walls or in chambers buried deep underground. The more sophisticated types had multilayered defenses, requiring the Bynars to do more than play accountant. But the Klingons hadn't locked up anything aboard *Ark of G'boj*. The safety of the cargo depended entirely on the ferocity of the defenders aboard and the fact that no one knew where the ship would be at any one time.

Their loss, thought Cross as he reached the back of the hold. He'd lost count of the number of stacks of bricks he'd passed; the Bynars would know. He considered it highly unlikely that the bricks were pure in content, as they were simply scrip the Klingons kept for dealing with outsiders. But with this much of the stuff, it shouldn't matter.

"Wow," Shift said, bag slung over her shoulder. "What happened here?"

Cross and his henchmen approached the pile of bricks she was standing nearest. Like the other stacks, it sat upon a base anchored to the deck. But where the other bases were made of the same thick duranium, this one was composed of plasteel. The result was that the mountain of latinum rode lower, sagging toward one side.

"Gaw wasn't joking," she said. "Watch for falling treasure."

"How do you run out of duranium when you've got this much latinum?" Cross said. He looked to the Bynars. "Is the stack sound? We don't want it tipping over on someone."

Eleven-Eleven whipped out a tricorder and waved it across the base of the pile. "It is secure," she said in a squeaky voice, "but something is odd. I read an extremely low frequency subspace transmission, sourced from the base."

Shift and Cross looked at each other. "A homing signal?"

"The Unsung didn't notice anything," Cross said. His brow furrowed. They might not have gotten away as cleanly as they'd hoped. "Let's go to the bridge. We can get a team over to shut the thing down and then move the ship again if we need to."

They moved forward. Shift was distracted, he noticed; he could well understand. Excepting extreme situations such as Spirits' Forge, he had an easier time dealing with pressure while he was in character. During the aftermath, when he had to be himself, he felt relatively defenseless. But he and the *Blackstone* crew were good enough at what they did that most of their marks never knew they'd been hit; the rest never pursued them for long. He had no doubt they'd slip away this time.

The quartet rounded the corner and entered *Ark of G'boj*'s bridge. The gloom of the nebula lay beyond the forward port; only the ship's control stations offered illumination.

"Do not move," said a voice from behind.

Cross's heart jumped. He turned to see six people in Starfleet uniforms standing at the rear of the bridge, three on either side of the door they'd entered through. All had phasers trained on Cross and his companions. "Put your hands in the air," said the dark-skinned Vulcan who had spoken before. "Commander Tuvok of the Federation *Starship Titan*."

"What a relief," Cross said. "I thought you were Klingons."

"And you would fear Klingons because this is a Klingon cargo vessel, reported missing." Tuvok stepped forward from the shadows and gestured to a human woman to his left. "This is Lieutenant Šmrhová from *Starship Enterprise*. You are under arrest on suspicion of piracy."

"On whose authority?" Shift asked. "We're in neutral space."

"The United Federation of Planets, in concert with the Klingon Empire under the Khitomer Accords. And I suspect that piracy is not all that you are involved in."

Cross eyed him. "What do you mean?"

"We're aware of the vessel cloaked off our bow." Šmrhová gestured to the dark space ahead. "We believe that vessel is associated with the terrorist actions of the Unsung."

"Huh?" The Betazoid's mind raced through all the characters he'd ever played—and found one. "Folks, I'm a journalist. I've been embedded with a group of pirates." He nodded to Shift. "She's my secret source. The Bynars are my vid team. We knew the gang had hidden this ship here and came to get some images. I've got my scoop, Commander, so the ship's all yours. Enjoy." He put his hands down and started to reach for his communicator. Safety was just a transporter beam away.

"Hands back up." Tuvok stepped forward and took Cross's communicator. Šmrhová's security detail closed in on Shift and the Bynars. "Your story is unlikely. I regret not finding the Phantom Wing, but you will explain—"

"*Attention!*" blared the bridge comm. "*Persons aboard* Ark of G'boj, *this is Captain Bredak of the* I.K.S. Jarin."

Cross and Shift looked at each other, while Lieutenant

Šmrhová hurried over to the ship's controls. "Commander, sensors indicate a bird-of-prey approaching through the nebula."

A bird-of-prey? Cross swallowed, not knowing which would be worse: a ship of the Klingon Defense Force or one operated by the Unsung.

"We have been informed you have a companion vessel cloaked alongside. You will order it to decloak, or we will destroy the ship and all inside."

Tuvok left Cross under guard and stepped to the comm system. "Captain Bredak, this is Commander Tuvok of the Federation *Starship Titan*. We have recaptured *Ark of G'boj*. We welcome your aid."

"A lie. I was told by a very important source there might be tricksters aboard. If you are from Starfleet, where is your vessel?"

"It is nearby, cloaked."

A laugh. *"Starfleet has no cloaked vessels! Haven't you heard of the Treaty of Algeron?"* A pause. *"Ready torpedoes!"*

Tuvok responded, "A moment, Captain, and we can—"

An explosion blossomed outside, lighting the eternal nebular night. The nearby blast shook *Ark of G'boj*, sending all aboard off their feet. Cross's communicator slipped from Tuvok's hand and clattered across the heaving deck, landing near where the Betazoid had fallen.

He snatched it and pressed the control. "*Blackstone, Blackstone,* come in! Gaw, get us out of—" Before he could finish, another searing flash, far closer, sent the bridge yawing sideways. This time, *he* lost the communicator.

In scrambling to find it, he chanced to glimpse out the forward port. *Blackstone* was partially visible, as nebular particles, supercharged by the torpedo, coursed over its form. Flushed out, the vessel, seemingly intact, turned quickly away from *Ark of G'boj*. Beyond it, the outline of the *Jarin* could be seen as well, soaring with its wings in attack position.

Cross looked over at Shift, huddled behind a control station, her eyes wide. She had found something in her bag—a communicator of some kind? It didn't look like his. He didn't care, as long as she was hailing *Blackstone*. *Gaw, don't you dare run away without getting me off this ship!*

HOUDINI
CRAGG'S CLOUD

"Deactivate the cloak," La Forge ordered. "Hail *Jarin* and show them we're here!"

"And have them shoot at us too?" Aggadak splayed her big hands across her command interface. "Not this ship. No way!"

Information was coming in so quickly La Forge couldn't respond. *Houdini* had no tactical station; the commander was piecing together information from various bridge displays with the help of Lieutenant Clipet. La Forge wasn't sure Aggadak's advice was wrong.

He'd never heard of *Jarin* before, and while that wasn't unusual given the size of the Klingon fleet, *Houdini* was chasing an impersonator who'd been directing birds-of-prey. The bulk of the Phantom Wing might very well be at Ghora Janto. What if a single bird-of-prey had been left behind?

"Our Klingon captain's pretty green," Clipet said. "He's firing randomly into space, trying to flush Object Thirteen out."

Green—or a fraudster? The bird-of-prey hadn't fired on *Ark of G'boj*, but neither had Tuvok called to be transported off the ship. "Someone try to establish contact with—"

The interface nearest him beeped. The nebula was fighting their sensors, but something else had appeared on his scopes. "Wait," La Forge said. "There's another contact approaching."

Aggadak looked back at him. "Is it coming after us?

La Forge had no idea. But he expected he was about to find out.

Fifty-nine

Tuvok struggled to regain his bearings. The *Jarin* was circling madly, firing its disruptors, then its torpedoes. Every so often a blast would jar the cloaked Object Thirteen—*Blackstone*, the Betazoid had called it—partially back into view. But it survived to keep running, thanks to its cloak, the surrounding nebula, and the clumsy approach of *Jarin*'s crew.

On board *Ark of G'boj*, the Bynars had decided as a pair to bolt off the bridge, resulting in a scrum with the security team. Tuvok found the Betazoid would-be journalist and his Orion companion forward, crouching behind a console. The woman had opened her shoulder bag, but if there was a disruptor inside, she wasn't wielding it. Backed up by Šmrhová, Tuvok raised his phaser and approached them.

"Your friends are under fire," Tuvok said. "They will not come back for you."

The Betazoid stood and looked through the port at the firefight. The Orion woman rose and stood next to him. "Wait, wait," her companion said, facing Tuvok. The smooth-talking voice of the self-proclaimed journalist had become nervous and pitchy. "You're still after the Unsung, right?"

The Orion looked at him, startled. "What are you doing, Cross?"

"Shut up, Shift." Cross reached into his vest and drew forth a padd. "I can give you the Unsung, Commander Tuvok."

"How?"

"You give me immunity—and I'll give you this." He held the padd before him. "It's connected to the system we used to track the Phantom Wing. It'll tell you where every ship is, even cloaked. I can delete the file with a single command— or you can help us out and put a stop to all of it."

Tuvok could see Lieutenant Šmrhová shaking her head in disbelief. "Mister Cross," he said, "the Klingon Empire has authority in this matter. We may perhaps discuss—"

The woman, Shift, was looking outside the port, where *Jarin* was continuing its bombardment of *Blackstone*. Only something new was lighting the nebula: a full spread of photon torpedos, slicing the clouds. Not coming from *Jarin*—but from some unseen vessel in the cloud *toward* the bird-of-prey.

"Down!" Tuvok yelled.

Explosion after explosion ripped the bird-of-prey to pieces. The nebular material amplified the successive shockwaves rocking the *Ark of G'boj*, sending everyone reeling again.

Tuvok's combadge chirped. *"Commander, be advised,"* La Forge said. *"An unidentified ship is in the cloud!"*

"We are quite aware of that, Commander." Rising, Tuvok saw that whoever it was had not fired at *Blackstone*, which soared away, partially visible. He looked over at the couple. They had braced themselves against the console, but now the Betazoid's expression was one of sheer panic.

"Enough with the shooting!" Cross proffered the padd again. "So what is it? I'll give you the Unsung! I even know whose idea it all was! Do we have a deal?"

Tuvok never had the chance to answer. Shift grabbed the back of Cross's shoulder and used her other hand to draw a *d'k tahg* from inside her bag. She plunged the blade into the astonished Betazoid's heart. *"You* shut up."

The Vulcan was just as amazed. Tuvok lifted his phaser, set to stun. Shift grabbed the padd from the slumping Betazoid's hand and called out, "Now!" Tuvok's phaser blast pierced only air as a transporter beam carried her away.

Inside *Ark of G'boj*, all went silent. Tuvok and Šmrhová hurried to Cross's side. Gurgling, his eyes wide, Cross pawed helplessly at the handle of the dagger protruding from his chest as the Vulcan futilely tried to apply first aid. The Orion's act had come as a complete surprise to Cross.

"It looks like a trick dagger," Šmrhová said.

"She didn't . . . set the safety . . ." Cross said, before coughing blood.

Tuvok opened the Betazoid's vest to access the wound. A small packet fell from an inside pocket. Šmrhová picked it up. "Playing cards."

Tuvok adjusted settings on his tricorder. It was no use. *Houdini* had no medical facilities, and the wound was too severe. With a lurch, Cross grabbed Tuvok's arm and locked eyes with the commander. It seemed as if he had something important to say. "What is it, Cross?"

"Feels like . . . I should have come up with . . . a better line for this scene . . ."

BLACKSTONE
CRAGG'S CLOUD

"I don't know who saved us, but they're my new best friend," Gaw said. Dripping sweat, the Ferengi leaned forward in his chair and tried to regulate his breathing. The bird-of-prey had *Blackstone*'s number: it would have destroyed the vessel, if not for the guardian angel firing from the darkness.

After darting into a denser section of Cragg's Cloud long enough to reestablish their failing cloak, they had returned to do a quick scan of *Ark of G'boj* with the illusion generator's sensors. "Sweep's established," announced Bezzal, the Cardassian who helped run sensors on the bridge.

Revived, Gaw sprang from the seat. "What are you waiting for? Get a transporter lock on them."

"I can't find Shift," Bezzal said. "The Bynars have just been beamed out by someone."

"What about Cross?"

"He's dead." The Cardassian pointed to the screen. "I just watched his life signs go."

Gaw stared, not registering what he was seeing. "That's not right." The Ferengi staggered backward to his chair and fell into it, nearly missing the seat. The words caught in his throat. "C-can we beam him back?"

The Cardassian shook his head. "They just beamed him out."

Gaw looked at the deck—and then around at the other truthcrafters. He felt as if the temperature in the room had plummeted. "Do we try to find Shift and the Bynars?" Bezzal asked.

"Find them where?" He shook his head. "We don't know who else is out there. Let's find a place to hole up. We can't all get pinched."

HOUDINI
CRAGG'S CLOUD

"I caught the other ship using its projector to do a sensor sweep of *Ark of G'boj* a few minutes ago," La Forge said as Tuvok stepped down off the transporter pad. "Object Thirteen must still be functional."

"It is called *Blackstone*," Tuvok said. "It is the name of another Earth magician." He glanced at the bagged corpse—and then produced the box of playing cards Šmrhová had recovered. Tuvok placed them on a counter. "You may find these interesting."

Carefully, La Forge examined the faded box. "Century of Progress, 1933."

"The Chicago World's Fair, forty years after Houdini's debut in the exposition there. Commander Worf described finding this packet in the hut of the fake Kruge on Thane."

La Forge cautiously opened the fragile pack and spread the cards across the counter. One caught his eye. "The ace of clubs," he said, drawing the dingy card from the deck. Unlike the rest, it was soiled and had gummy residue on its back. "This is the card Worf used to signal us from the Unsung compound!"

"This is the proof. The individual named Cross had knowledge of the Kruge impersonation, or conducted it himself."

La Forge put his hand over his chin and thought. "Was he their Ardra?"

"Insufficient information. But the arrival of whoever destroyed *Jarin* appears to have come as a complete surprise to this person Cross. As did his partner's betrayal of him. She could have transported either to *Blackstone*, or to its savior."

"*Blackstone* was running for dear life after *Jarin* was destroyed," La Forge said. "I doubt they had time to transport her away."

"There is another participant," Tuvok pointed out. "Cross indicated the entire plot was set in motion by someone else. Perhaps that person is behind the beam-out and the unknown ship."

Or it could be someone else entirely, La Forge thought. They'd come so far—and had more questions than answers. And still no Unsung.

Aggadak entered. "I've been speaking to your Bynars, but they won't talk—at least not to me. If they're like Ardra's techs, they won't give away their secrets."

"Yet Cross seemed willing to tell all," Tuvok said, "before this Shift person killed him."

"To protect their secrets?" La Forge asked.

"Ardra's people never physically harmed anybody," Aggadak said. "Maybe this bunch is different."

"We must inform Chancellor Martok," Tuvok said. "that we have found the *Ark of G'boj*, intact, and report the destruction of *Jarin*, under Captain . . ."

"Tuvok, what is it?" La Forge asked.

"Captain Bredak. I just realized I have heard that name before. These events have taken on an even greater importance."

HOUSE OF KRUGE INDUSTRIAL COMPOUND KETORIX PRIME, KLINGON EMPIRE

Unable to stay in J'borr's old office, Korgh closed up the command center and staggered into the darkened hallway. Through the windows, he could see the fires burning in the Ketorix foundries—but nothing had parted the clouds hanging over his heart.

At the far end of the hall, someone pounded on the front door.

"Go away," he yelled. He was expecting no one at this hour.

"It is General Kersh," came the response from beyond.

Korgh felt revulsion at hearing his hated rival's name—and then realized why she had come. Forcing one foot before another, he went to the door and opened it. Out in the darkness, the woman looked grave.

"You come to tell me of my son's death," Korgh said. "I have already heard."

Kersh nodded respectfully. "Lorath and his crew fought bravely. He brought honor to our house."

Korgh thought, "*Yes*. Yes he did." More than it deserved.

She looked at him cautiously. "That is not the only reason I came."

"I will not discuss the politics of the house now with you." He started to close the door. "Not when—"

She blocked the door with her hand. "We have received word from Starfleet of an incident in a nebula known as Cragg's Cloud. Our missing transport, *Ark of G'boj*, has been found."

Korgh received the news mildly. He had forgotten all about it. "Who discovered it?"

"Lorath's son, Captain Bredak. He and the *Jarin* found it."

"And?"

"The *Jarin* was destroyed by a mystery attacker in the nebula. All hands were lost."

Korgh looked at her, his eyes unseeing. He sputtered. "W-what?"

"Starfleet was not able to identify the attacker. We have sent forces to investigate," Kersh said. "They told us Bredak died honorably, in the service of his duty."

Korgh fell to his knees, clutching his head with both hands. "No," he said, his voice small. "No. No."

She pushed the door all the way open and helped him inside. She stood there for long moments while he wailed.

At last, she reached for her dagger—a ceremonial *mevak*.

"This is a grievous loss," she said, "a blow to your honor, here at your time of triumph. Do you wish *Mauk-to'Vor*, Korgh? Do you want me to kill you?"

His eyes widened—and his broken heart hardened.

"No, spawn of J'borr." He looked up at her, eyes red. "You will never have that pleasure—and you will never inherit." He stood and pointed out the door. "Now get out of my house."

ENTR'ACTE

DEATH'S DOOR

2386

"You are Klingons. You need no one but yourselves. I will go now . . . to Sto-Vo-Kor. But I promise one day I will return. Look for me there, on that point of light."

—Kahless the Unforgettable

Sixty

A hundred years before, Korgh had been stranded for weeks as the only sentient being on Gamaral. He had not felt as alone then as he had during the day that just ended.

Yes, he had interacted with many. He had communicated with his allies back on Qo'noS, making sure they spoke for him during his time of mourning. The Unsung were still at large. Starfleet had stood with the Empire in battle and both had failed. He would extract more concessions.

Just not personally. Not now.

He had studied the secret report Chancellor Martok had sent him: the preliminary report from Starfleet about what had happened at Cragg's Cloud. Cross had died at the hands of his henchwoman; one deceiver killed by another. Where had she gone? Cross's support ship had vanished. Where had they gone? He knew from his time with Jilaan that blackmail wasn't the Circle's style; it was too low, not theatrical enough. Did these tricksters feel the same way?

And most importantly, who had destroyed *Jarin*? The report said nothing about that at all.

He had spoken with Martok, who had mouthed half-hearted words of remorse. The chancellor would not publicize the events: bringing up the existence of someone pretending to be Kruge was folly for both of them. It would be bad publicity for Korgh's house—and Martok definitely didn't want it circulated that the Unsung thought they were following a leader of legend. Anything that justified their actions might create even more copycats. Or worse, it would remind Klingons that they once had leaders far more strident about the Empire's interests than he.

Korgh would remind them of that, in his own words and in his own time.

Finally, he had gone to the factory floor where *Jarin* had been laid down. There, in the same place where he had launched the bird-of-prey not long before, he gathered with his two remaining sons and a host of factory workers in singing the songs of the glory of his house. It was no sad memorial to Lorath and Bredak; that was not the Klingon way. But none present could avoid thinking of the father and son improbably killed many light-years apart at nearly the same moment.

Korgh had stood there, all eyes on him, trying to sing while knowing that he had sent them to their fates. And for the first time since his scheme began, his voice failed him. Those watching found it a moving demonstration of grief. He didn't care.

Alone at last, he crossed the threshold into the family headquarters, lit by the evening shadows. Only sleep could save him, he knew—that and a healthy amount of blood-wine.

He was wondering whether Odrok had drunk it all when he noticed a light coming from an open door along the big corridor. *Not again*, he thought, his step quickening. But this time when he arrived at J'borr's office, he saw Odrok inside. "You," he said.

She did not respond. She was gathering her personal items, he saw, and placing them in her housekeeper's cart.

"There were songs," Korgh said, sidling into the room and leaning against the doorjamb. "It was glorious and deserved."

"I am sure." She looked up at him. Her eyes were bleary, but she seemed sober. "Lorath and Bredak were honorable warriors. They did not deserve this."

"Where are you going?"

She gestured to the screens in the office, all deactivated. "We can no longer track the Unsung. Cross is dead. There is nothing more for me to do."

"I still need your help. Some of the birds-of-prey are at large. So are Cross's confederates."

"I am sure you will think of something." She went back to her collecting, ignoring him.

After a dreadful day, Korgh felt his ire rising. "You are giving up now?"

"You have your house. You do not need old Odrok."

"Old Odrok." He snorted. "And you thought to be my mate."

"Only recently, only when I thought the house was something worth winning." She glared back at him. "I wanted the House of Kruge. You have made this the House of Korgh."

"What do you mean? There is no difference—"

"You are as blind as you are vain." She looked at him, unbelieving. "I have never loved you." She took a deep breath. "I loved *Kruge*."

Korgh gawked. "*Kruge!*"

"Kruge. He recruited me from the Science Institute of Mempa V himself. He told me I was brilliant, special above all others. He said he was not ready to take a spouse, but I was willing to wait. He told me I could serve his cause as a spy—and so I did. I hoped . . ." She trailed off.

"He was your better," Korgh said, mind reeling. "He was from a grand line, a great house. You were nobody."

"Until I met him, yes. But then, you were nobody until you met Kruge, as well."

"Stop being ridiculous. I was his heir—"

"So you say. I seem to recall we had to hire a Betazoid to fake a vid."

Korgh pounded the wall with his fist. "Insolence! You really think he cared about you?" Odrok looked at him, eyes wide with fright. "Kruge did love a spy. But she was not you. Her name was Valkris."

"*Valkris!*" He watched her face as her mouth formed the word. It hung open.

"You knew her?"

"I-I remember the name."

"Another agent of his. I do not know how many he had." He walked the room, waving his hand dismissively. "I learned of her accidentally, when I was Kruge's aide. I think she helped him on the Genesis scheme. She disappeared around the same time Kruge died." He turned his eyes back on Odrok. "But I overheard them speaking. And if Kruge loved any woman, it was she."

Odrok held his gaze for a moment—and then seemed to wilt. He had wounded her.

She reached for the cart. "I am going home."

"What home?"

"That hovel, on Qo'noS. It is the only place for one such as me."

Korgh looked at the cart and advanced toward it. "What are you taking?"

She sagged with exhaustion. "Personal things. From too much time working here." She slouched toward the door. "Forget it. Keep it all."

He followed her into the hall, pausing only to seal the door behind him. She looked small in the corridor, shambling toward the exit. He called out. "Odrok—the things you have known, have seen. I would hate if . . ."

She spoke without looking back. "Do not fear me. I sacrificed all the years of my life not just to a man, but to his cause. The Empire is better off without the Federation. But you will not hear the name Odrok again, nor see her face."

Sixty-one

Admiral Akaar spoke evenly. But Riker could tell the stern Capellan was very unhappy with him. *"Admiral Riker, the president has been in near-constant conference with leaders of nonaligned Beta Quadrant worlds. You can imagine what they've been talking about."*

"Yes, sir." Half of them feared the Unsung would turn up on their doorsteps. The other half suspected the Klingon Empire would use the crisis as an excuse to annex their worlds. And they were all afraid the Federation's strained relations with the Klingon Empire meant it wouldn't be able to act as a moderating influence. "We've cut the Unsung's numbers by two-thirds, sir."

"It hasn't helped. People think they'll be desperate, lashing out against everyone." Onscreen, Akaar sat up even straighter, nearly putting the top of his head out of the frame. *"I'll tell you whom the battle* has *helped: the Romulans and the Breen."*

The vessels from the two Typhon Pact powers had joined *Titan* and the surviving Klingon ships in chasing the surviving Unsung birds-of-prey. "We still don't know how the Romulans and Breen beat us to Ghora Janto," Riker said. "General Lorath made it sound as if we were the only ones he contacted."

"We'll never know."

Riker had developed a whole list of questions for the late general. How had he known where the Unsung were traveling? How was it that his battle cruisers had been able to target the birds-of-prey while cloaked? *V'raak* had been obliterated, and the other two battle cruisers' bridges had both taken direct hits. The survivors had provided no answers. "*Enterprise* is at Ghora Janto," Riker said. "I'm hoping they can find some more information in the wreckage."

"It would be good to know anything. The internal situation in the Empire is starting to unravel."

Riker understood. Discommendation was extremely rare. There weren't neighborhoods of the dishonored, ready to revolt. That was what had made the Unsung, a concentrated group, so unusual. But the judgment of discommendation touched many generations, amplifying their numbers to the point where many Klingons suspected their neighbors.

And suspicion bred hatred. Riker described for Akaar what Troi had seen on Chelvatus III. "The backlash is way out of proportion. This thing has given some Klingons an excuse to attack people they didn't like anyway."

"You need to know," Akaar said, *"the Federation is suspending its expansion of the consulate on Qo'noS. The construction site is too much of a flashpoint. And there's more. The loss of his son and grandson has generated even more support for Korgh. While he mourns, his new allies in the High Council blast us at every turn."*

"Didn't our recovery of *Ark of G'boj* count for anything?"

"It did: more ammunition. According to Ambassador Rozhenko, Qolkat, a member of Korgh's cabal, advanced the view today that Starfleet destroyed the Jarin."

Riker's jaw dropped. "*What?* We didn't even have an armed ship in the area."

"And that, in these perilous times, is too much for many Klingons to believe. Yes, our people were just there looking for

Blackstone, *but we can't tell anyone about the Kruge imper-sonator, so anything involving* Blackstone *is still classified information. Even if we could, all we've got is a dead Betazoid who escaped custody nineteen years ago."*

"And even then, it wouldn't help," Riker said. While her race suggested how the Unsung had moved through the Orion underworld, little else was known about Cross's murderous associate. By contrast, genetic analysis had quickly confirmed Buxtus Cross's identity. But that had come with bad news: he had once been a Starfleet officer. Korgh had already railed at Spock and the Federation for looking the other way when the exiles settled in the Briar Patch. Conspiracy theorists would have a field day with Cross.

"Starfleet needs to find the Unsung. But that requires access to the Empire. Ambassador Rozhenko believes Korgh's next move will be against Starfleet's freedom to travel. Korgh is asking for a public hearing where we list every honorable thing the Klingons and we have done together since the Accords' inception. It's a ploy, a way to keep you and Titan *out of the search."*

"Me, sir?"

"Chancellor Martok gets to choose the Empire's representative; chances are he'll pick himself. The councillors who demanded this get to pick the other speaker. It's a way of putting someone who's disappointed them on the spot."

Riker swallowed. He didn't like being thought of in that way. "Sir, I don't want to pull *Titan* from the chase."

"And you shouldn't. I just wanted to warn you now—you're probably going back to Qo'noS."

The admiral took a deep breath. The last weeks had exhausted him, but the alliance had to be protected at all costs. "Very well. Captain Vale will keep *Titan* on the Unsung chase. I'm planning on dispatching *Enterprise* to rendezvous with *Houdini*, to see if it can help flush out

Blackstone. If Cross was telling the truth about their having a way to track the Phantom Wing, maybe we can get them to cooperate."

"Agreed, Admiral. Let everyone know—if anyone has any real magical powers, now would be the time to put them to work."

Sixty-two

Picard woke to the first good news he'd heard in days. *Enterprise*'s sensors had found a section of the superstructure of a destroyed bird-of-prey. Ejected from the blast, it contained a couple of compartments that might have remained pressurized. Beverly had already been called to sickbay, raising his hopes that some survivors had been found.

Instead, Picard found sickbay empty of patients. He'd been about to go to the bridge when Crusher emerged from an isolation ward, wearing a sterile protective suit.

"Did we find anyone?"

He had done nothing to hide his hopes from her—but her expression after she removed the helmet was not encouraging. "Come with me. It's safe."

Picard could hear the hum of a full-body medical scanner as he entered the ward behind her. "We didn't find any remains in the wreckage," Crusher said. "Everything was battered and half-melted. But there was a blast-proof chest—and we found this inside."

He looked through the coursing beams of the scanner at the object on the table. It was a *mek'leth*—and the inscription was just visible near the grip: *To Worf, son of Mogh, on the honorable defeat of Unarrh.*

"It is Worf's blade, given him by Emperor Kahless, years ago."

"The scan confirms it. Trace DNA as well as fingerprints."

Picard remembered Worf had been carrying the *mek'leth*. "How recent is what you've found?"

"Somewhat." Doctor Crusher pointed to the readout. "Someone else has handled the blade more recently."

"A Klingon?"

"Yes. We'll send the data to the Empire. We think the cabin with the locker came from the third or fourth decks."

Picard turned away from the table. Worf—or at least his blade—had survived the transporter trip to a cloaked bird-of-prey. It was also probable that vessel was the one that had rammed *Jarin*. The captain knew Worf never would have abandoned the blade. "Do you think he was killed for this?"

"There was no fresh blood on it, and given where we found it, I think it's more likely someone took it. At best it means he was a prisoner." She looked at him. "No escape pods had left any of the birds-of-prey. Would the Unsung have transported off a prisoner?"

"I'll hope for the best." Picard quickly squeezed his wife's hand before stepping back, returning to his professional demeanor. "I've received orders. We're to wrap up our investigation and rendezvous at Cragg's Cloud with Commanders Tuvok and La Forge."

A tear visible in her eye, Crusher shook her head. "Why did Worf insist on going over there?"

"He had seen Kahless executed. The emperor could not enter Sto-Vo-Kor without an act of intercession—a heroic venture. This was what Worf chose."

They stood together for several moments, comforting each other in silence as they stared down at the blade.

Then a thought occurred to the doctor. "If Worf was killed when the bird-of-prey was destroyed, is that dying in combat?"

"I'm not sure. I don't think so. A Klingon would want to die with a weapon in hand." Picard gestured downward. "His is here."

"Then that would mean someone would have to undertake a quest to get Worf into the afterlife."

Picard took one more look at the blade. "We'd better get started on it."

BLACKSTONE
ATOGRA SYSTEM, KLINGON SPACE

Gaw thought that as hiding places went, a comet's tail left a lot to be desired. But beggars couldn't be choosers. They were still in Klingon space, and the damage to *Blackstone*'s cloaking device and other systems had to be repaired before they could be on their way.

But on their way to *what*? He didn't know. None of them did.

Blackstone's team was without a practitioner for the first time since his meeting Cross aboard *Clarence Darrow* nineteen years earlier. The division of labor in the Circle of Jilaan was absolute. Centuries earlier, the human illusionist Howard Thurston had been able to hire other magicians for his workshop to design his tricks. Truthcrafter technology, by contrast, was so advanced only lifers who specialized in it could figure it out. Picard's crew had only been able to use already-programmed characters against Ardra. Anything more ambitious would have been beyond them. Cross had never learned how the truthcrafters did anything because he'd never needed to know. That was what Gaw was for.

The problem was that the division cut both ways. Fully

inhabiting a truthcrafter character required acting talents most technicians didn't have. It required someone special: an empath, such as Cross—or a prodigy, as Shift was becoming. Gaw saw no options. He couldn't promote from within, and he didn't think the *Blackstone*'s crew was up to another prison break. That left disbanding or merging into another outfit, neither of which appealed to him.

He was on the bridge studying his files on other Circle crews when the question suddenly became moot. "Contact approaching," Bezzal said from the helm. "Coming fast."

The once-somber room became busy with activity. "Can we cloak?" Gaw asked.

"We can't even run. We've got too many systems offline."

Gaw saw a massive warship enter the comet's effluent. It didn't look like a Klingon or Federation vessel. "What kind of ship is that?"

"Breen," the Cardassian said. A squawking hail erupted from the comm system—an angry stream of gibberish. "Damn universal translator is no help with these people."

"Does anybody speak that?" Gaw asked. No answer from those on *Blackstone*'s bridge—and outside, a disruptor warning shot sliced the space right outside the port. "Okay, I understood that. They want us to—"

A transporter effect appeared on the bridge. A lone Breen warrior materialized, holding a disruptor. The snout-nosed helmet and padded uniform gave no indication of the wearer's species or gender. The warrior faced Gaw and let loose with another stream of gobbledygook.

"All right, all right! We surrender." The Ferengi raised his hands. "What's this about?"

The Breen warrior squawked again—and placed the pistol in a holster. Gloved hands went to the helmet and unlatched it. Gaw stepped back, gobsmacked, when he saw the green-skinned face inside. "*Shift!*"

All aboard the bridge cheered. Gaw rushed forward to embrace her. "Thank the stars you're safe, dearie!"

She wasn't smiling. *Broken up about Cross,* Gaw figured. He stepped back to get a good look at her gear. "You disguised yourself as a Breen?"

"No," she said, her voice cool and calm. "I disguised myself as Cross's apprentice—as a con artist." She held the helmet forth proudly in her gloved hands. "I *am* a Breen. And you—and this ship—are now under our control."

Sixty-three

"This is a joke, right?" Gaw said, reeling. "You can't be a Breen. Tell me this is a joke!"

"Not unless you consider the guns trained upon this ship a laughing matter." Shift smiled.

"Hey, we surrender," Gaw said. "We didn't do anything to the Breen." Suddenly uncomfortable, he looked to the other techs and whispered, "We haven't done anything to them, have we?"

"Not this decade," came a nervous response from someone on the bridge. But now more Breen warriors materialized, all armed. Immediately, they began apprehending the truthcrafters.

"Don't worry, Gaw," she said as she watched the dumbfounded Ferengi being shackled. "They're not going to hurt you. They—*we*—need you, and what you know how to do. That was why I joined you in the first place—to steal your fakery know-how." She walked from the bridge into the control center and watched as more troops arrived. It had taken so long—and yet it had worked.

Theft was an easy thing for one born into a world of crime. But theft for a reason was something relatively new for Shift. It had come after years of abuse had pushed her past the breaking point. Sick of being chattel, the young Orion woman had fled the people who had made her life miserable. She'd expected a fight to the death to keep her freedom—a fight she was likely to lose.

Instead, she'd found something else: a new life, new respect. The Breen were the ultimate egalitarian nation. One's class at birth didn't matter. One's species didn't matter. And her beauty, which had been such a mixed blessing, would be hidden away behind her suit. No one would abuse her again. And when she finally chose to use her appearance again, it was her decision, in service of the Breen as an agent for the Intelligence Directorate.

The Breen had been interested in the workings of the Circle of Jilaan. The truthcrafters' brand of artifice came from a technology that neither the Breen nor their rivals understood; that made it invaluable. Once Shift had found Cross and introduced herself, it had been an easy get. Cross was a ridiculous being. He was a gifted actor and mimic, but otherwise eccentric and myopic. Certainly he'd been blind to her, seeing only her physical attributes as she inveigled herself into his confidence to learn his methods.

In time, she'd realized Cross was not the key: the truthcrafters, the illusionists behind the scenes, held the real power. With their skills making everything possible, all that was required was a reasonably talented actor to complete the illusions. And what was a spy, if not an actor?

The moment of the truthcrafters' capture—*this* moment—would have come a year earlier, had she not learned of the "big score" *Blackstone*'s crew was working on. Realizing the Kruge scam was a deception ordered and financed by a powerful figure within the Klingon Empire, she had reported it back to the directorate. Thot Roje, her case officer high in Breen intelligence, had ordered her to remain in character, reporting back whenever she could.

Once she and Cross moved into the hut in the Unsung compound in the Briar Patch, her chances for contact dwindled. She didn't dare use Odrok's secret chain of repeater stations to get a message out of the nebula. After *Chu'charq* departed Thane for good, she finally checked in using her secret communicator. Foolishly, Cross had never asked why she kept disappearing.

Thot Roje had guided her every play. As long as Korgh

was using the Unsung to undermine the Klingon alliance with the Federation, the Breen let the plot play out. Her warning had prompted them to withdraw Ambassador Vart from Spirits' Forge in advance of the Unsung strike. The Breen had won the appreciation of the Kinshaya by hustling their representatives away before the shooting started. After her "death of Kruge" scene, Shift had told the Breen to rush for Ghora Janto, to be able to take credit for stopping the Unsung. The Breen had invited their Romulan allies to join them, earning diplomatic capital.

Korgh and Cross had played the Klingon Empire—and then they had tried to play each other. At every turn, she had been there, working the angles for the Breen. When Cross lied to Korgh about killing Kahless, she learned all she could about the Betazoid's plot to impersonate the emperor. They had information on Korgh, but that paled before the prospect of controlling a fake Kahless. It still sounded like a good plan to her.

Of course, Korgh had betrayed Cross as well, planting a homing device aboard *Ark of G'boj* in order that *Jarin* would destroy his coconspirators. Shift had called the Breen to Cragg's Cloud to prevent that.

The only wrinkle had been the unexpected arrival of Starfleet. She still didn't know from where they had transported to the Klingon treasure ship or how they had uncovered the scheme. Cross, predictably, had tried to bargain by revealing the location of the Unsung. That information she intended for Breen hands, not Starfleet's. She had killed him. He was unnecessary. The real power was in the truthcrafters and their amazing starship.

Shift had enjoyed killing him. She had been forced to pretend to like some real scum in her time. Had she not been acting in service of a higher cause, she could never have tolerated Cross for an instant.

She'd learned from her Breen rescuers that more than half of the Phantom Wing had been destroyed at Ghora Janto; she'd also discovered that the mechanism on Cross's padd for tracking the Unsung no longer worked. It didn't matter. Korgh and Cross and their crazy Klingon minions had already wrought significant damage to the Khitomer Accords.

In Korgh's scheme, Thot Roje had seen something she hadn't: a chance to completely upend the Accords—putting the Breen on top of the Typhon Pact. "Lord" Korgh would continue to rise in the Empire, not knowing what the Breen had on him. In *Blackstone*, the Breen had an unmatched tool for mischief. A tool she had spent a year learning how to use. By using her body in service of the Breen, she had made her mind an asset of immeasurably greater importance.

Breen warriors shoved Gaw into the control room, where his companions were under guard. "What is all this? What are you doing with us?"

Shift lifted her helmet in preparation of putting it back on. "It's not what we're doing with you, Gaw. It's what *you're* going to do for *us* . . ."

PHANTOM WING VESSEL *CHU'CHARQ* DEEP SPACE

The Unsung had delivered Worf to the same prison cell he had awakened in after his abduction from Gamaral: converted personnel quarters protected by a force field. At least this time they had not drugged him.

The first time he was taken by the Unsung, most had looked upon him reverently; Worf was the discommendated Klingon who had won back his name. This time his walk to the cell had taken him through corridors crowded with Unsung: the noncombatants from the community, refugees from other birds-of-prey. A ship designed for three dozen now carried twice that, at least. His cell was taking up valuable accommodations.

The respectful looks had vanished. The Unsung seemed shaken, lost, angry, and afraid in equal parts. Before ordering him imprisoned, Valandris had described the assassination of the false Kruge, as well as the mad dash to Ghora Janto and what was almost certainly a trap. Without Kruge's guiding voice, they did not know what to believe—but they did remember that their Fallen Lord, now truly fallen, had once ordered Worf's death.

Now he could only wait to see what they would do.

Movement caught his eye. He rolled over and saw Sarken standing outside the force field. She seemed mesmerized by it. Her fingers traced millimeters above its surface, causing excited particles to glow vibrant red. "I like this," she said.

"You will find many interesting things in the galaxy." Worf sat up and faced her. "I do not think you have come to free me."

"No." She fretted. "But I told Valandris about how you appeared on *Rodak*, and how you and I found the bomb."

"Did she find one on this ship?"

"Oh, I showed everyone where it was," she said with pride. Sarken had shed her fear of the starship's innards. "They found them in the same place on the other three ships. Why would someone want to do that to us, Worf?"

"I do not know," he said, stretching the truth only a little. The child had confronted enough without learning her people were expendable puppets in someone else's game. "Did they try to disarm the torpedoes?"

"They figured out how, thanks to one of those things you found."

"A tutorial padd?"

"I guess. It didn't say anything about the bomb, but they learned enough from it to remove the bad part and reset the other thing so it stopped telling everyone where we were."

Worf figured that might happen. *Then we are again cloaked, and no one can find us.* He was reluctant to involve the girl in another escape plot. "Have they said what they intend to do with me?"

"They said I won't be able to see." She put her hand before the force field, her fingers splayed outward. "I am sorry."

He reached out and put his hand across from hers, just skimming the surface of the energy field. "I think you have acted honorably, Sarken. Your father would have been proud."

She held the position for a moment—and then looked behind her. "They are coming for you."

Sixty-four

Valandris had hidden what remained of the squadron to the best of her ability. Her knowledge of the region was minimal; Kruge had made all their decisions. But she'd been one of the warriors who took part in moving the birds-of-prey to Thane. On that journey, they had stopped over on Cabeus, a deserted Class-M planet.

She had found it again on her charts not far from their avenue of escape. The Empire and its accomplices had swarmed the sector, searching for the Unsung. She hoped that Cabeus, devoid of anything but a breathable atmosphere, would escape the hunters' notice long enough for the exiles to decide what to do.

The mood of the discommendated was black. They had been given a promise, a purpose. And then they had been abandoned, leaderless and without direction. Valandris was a talented hunter, and Weltern commanded respect. But of the Unsung, only Zokar had ever presumed to consider himself first among the Unsung. Kruge and his murderous aide-de-camp had made all the decisions. Now no one was left.

Confident that *Chu'charq* and its three companion vessels were safely cloaked on the surface, she proceeded to the deck five mess hall. Most of the lights were out along the companionway; the ship had been running on low power to conserve energy for the cloaking device. Hearing the raucous voices from outside the darkened room, she could tell they were already under way.

Before Kruge came to Thane, the exiles had no system of justice beyond Potok, and the endless helpings of shame he and the elders distributed. The Klingons in the Empire literally turned their backs on discommendated individuals, refusing to speak to them. On Thane, everyone faced the accused, leveling excoriation. It was one practice Kruge had adapted rather than supplanted, adding public and physical humiliation. It was what was done to the late clone of Kahless, yoked down in the sewage pit.

There was no pit aboard *Chu'charq*, but a yoke had been created. It ringed the neck of Worf as he stood atop a hexagonal table whose legs had been removed. The ceilings in the mess hall were low, but there was no chance that Worf would strike his head—not when the yoke was attached to chains, ropes, ODN cables, and whatever else *Chu'charq*'s occupants could find. The other ends were in the hands of dozens of jeering Unsung, all pulling him downward. Many had come over from the other ships for the occasion—and all were yanking on the cords from their positions on the deck.

Worf, a marionette whose controllers were all around him, fought to remain standing.

"To your knees! To your knees!"

"Never!" Worf clutched at the bonds, trying to keep from choking.

Valandris entered, and the crowd parted. "You are late," Harch said to her, yanking on a cable with evil glee. "You have missed getting a chain."

Weltern offered her chain to Valandris. "Take mine."

"No," she said. "What has come before?"

The woman responded. "We told him his crimes. He sought to stop Kruge on Thane—attacked the muster."

"He killed Tharas!" said another.

"He came aboard *Rodak* by stealth," Harch said, "intending to expose us to discovery. He was trying to finish what N'Keera started!"

Worf strained at his bonds. "You are wrong! I was trying to stop you, yes—because you were being led by a false ruler. The real Commander Kruge died a century ago!"

"Liar!" several shouted. A renewed tug-of-war broke out, causing Worf to stagger and gag.

"Hold," Valandris said. She looked up at him with a mixture of sympathy and indifference. He had told her of Kahless and honor that had sounded good—yet it all rang hollow after Kruge's death and their betrayal. "Worf, you saved Sarken, and warned us of the bombs—but you are not one of us and never will be. There is a divide between us that can never be crossed."

"*D-discommendation*," Worf said, struggling to speak.

"You have something we can never have. Either we are trash—or your honor is." She scowled. "We are not shells. Your existence serves only to taunt us."

She felt the words and believed them—but seeing their effect unnerved her. The yanking intensified. Worf would soon fall to his knees and then to the deck—whereupon she was certain they would strangle him.

"*K-K-Kahless*," Worf said, the word barely audible.

"What?" Valandris touched the arms of the others nearest her, stilling them. She shushed the group. "What did you say?"

"Kahless." He coughed hard before looking at her wearily. "If you sought someone who returned from the dead, you wanted Kahless."

"We killed your clone!" Harch yelled.

"Kahless the Unforgettable." Worf tried to straighten, gripping the taut chains to steady himself. "The original Kahless. He will return to bring Klingons to a place of honor."

"You cannot still believe that," Valandris said. "You are the only honorable person here—and *this* is happening.

Where is your Kahless now?" She took the chain Weltern had offered. "Worf, words will not protect us. They are not magic!"

"You . . . are wrong," Worf said, his voice ragged. "There *is* magic in the words, in which all Klingons believe: *batlh, qajunpaQ, vIt*—honor, courage, truth. Or the words with which we call for Kahless to return from the dead: *torva luq do Sel!*"

Something clanked above.

Valandris looked around. "What was that?"

Another odd sound. Worf looked up at the overhead, just above him. He squinted, half-dazed—and the group went silent.

"What do you see?" Valandris asked him.

"A point of light."

Looking up, she saw it too—a pinprick in the overhead, at the juncture of four bordering metal plates. Most of the bird-of-prey's access panels were on the deck, but some were above. Worf looked at it, unbelieving—and said his words again, adding an ancient name: "qeylIS, *torva luq do Sel!*"

An ebony boot slammed downward, smashing the panel open. As one, the astonished warriors slackened their holds on Worf's bonds and watched the figure plummeting from above onto the tabletop. He landed between two of the chains holding Worf. He wrested the chain from Valandris's hands.

He looked like the clone they'd kidnapped on Gamaral and enslaved on Thane. Only he was slimmer and dressed all in black, the garb the Unsung wore on their missions that required stealth. Such gear, she knew, had been stored in the deck one cargo bay, the place where Kruge had kept his mysterious prison—and its sensor-dampening properties were proof against life-sign scans. Had he been alive and between decks all this time?

Worf was not expecting him. He stared, amazed and speechless, as the new arrival began wresting the leashes away one by one.

The Klingon's words boomed through the hall. "I am Kahless, clone of the Unforgettable—and I have returned!" He smiled at Worf. Then he looked around at the Unsung, his eyes wide and full of purpose. "I have returned—*and I will judge who here is worthy!*"

STAR TREK®

PREY

CONCLUDES IN

BOOK 3:

THE HALL OF HEROES

ACKNOWLEDGMENTS

The crafting of illusions has always had a major role in the *Star Trek* universe, and I was delighted to get the chance to work it into my larger story about the alliance between the Federation and the Klingon Empire. I thank my Pocket Books editor, Margaret Clark, both for the opportunity and for her patience. I further appreciate the helpful suggestions of John Van Citters of CBS, as well as the contributions of Ed Schlesinger, Scott Pearson, and the Pocket Books crew.

Inspiration again came from a variety of sources, most significantly the fourth season *Star Trek: The Next Generation* episode "Devil's Due." (Teleplay by Philip LaZebnik. Story by Philip LaZebnik and William Douglas Lansford.) As it was originally a story for *Star Trek Phase II* later adapted for *TNG*, I enjoyed the chance to show the illusionists at work in both eras.

And in addition to the works cited in the last volume, I greatly depended on Rick Sternbach and Ben Robinson's *Klingon Bird-of-Prey Owners' Workshop Manual* from Gallery Books. Readers interested in the settings aboard the Phantom Wing will find them all in its pages. Locations are based on *Star Trek: Star Charts* and *Star Trek: Stellar Cartography*.

Thanks go again to Trek mavens James Mishler, Brent Frankenhoff, Michael Singleton, and Robert Peden for their feedback and assistance, as well as to Meredith Miller, proofreader and Number One on my bridge.

Two down, one to go. *Engage!*

ABOUT THE AUTHOR

John Jackson Miller is the *New York Times* bestselling author of the novels *Star Trek: The Next Generation: Take-down*; *Star Wars: A New Dawn*; *Star Wars: Kenobi*; *Star Wars: Knight Errant*; *Star Wars: Lost Tribe of the Sith—The Collected Stories*; and fifteen *Star Wars* graphic novels, as well as *Overdraft: The Orion Offensive*. He has also written the eNovella *Star Trek: Titan: Absent Enemies*. A comics industry historian and analyst, he has written for franchises including *Halo*, *Conan*, *Iron Man*, *Indiana Jones*, *Mass Effect*, *Planet of the Apes*, and *The Simpsons*. He lives in Wisconsin with his wife, two children, and far too many comic books.